NEVER MISS

Jill and Delores Plumage, Kristen Potts, Loye Ryan, Eric Shirt, Phillip Shortman, Angie Simons, Michelle Singer, Paul Skyhawk, Woodrow Star, the Stiffarm family, Lydell Suppah, Ray Tate and family, Julie Taylor, Ted Teather, Stephanie Thornley, Bob Tom, Jason Umtuch, Kathy Van Raden, Dale Walker, Patrick Weasel Head, Denice Wickert, Butch Wolfleg, Monica Yellow Owl, Eleanor Yellow Robe, and too many others whose names escape me.

It's been a good ride—thanks to you all.

About the Author

Originally from Fort Belknap, Montana, John Spence now lives in Beaverton, Oregon near his kids, Erik and Joy, and their families. He shares a small house near the city library with his roommate Angie, two dogs and two chickens.

He credits his recovery from alcoholism and 38 years of sobriety to the healing and wellness movement in Indian Country. At age 79 John still rides his horse Koda whenever old rugby and rodeo injuries allow it.

Amber Jones photo collection (2015)

CPSIA information can be obtained
at www.ICGtesting.com
Printed in the USA
BVHW081404120521
607050BV00008B/1665

NEVER MISS

MELISSA KOSLIN

Revell

a division of Baker Publishing Group
Grand Rapids, Michigan

Published by Revell
a division of Baker Publishing Group
PO Box 6287, Grand Rapids, MI 49516-6287
www.revellbooks.com

Printed in the United States of America

Library of Congress Cataloging-in-Publication Data
Names: Koslin, Melissa, 1979- author.
Title: Never miss / Melissa Koslin.
Description: Grand Rapids, Michigan : Revell, a division of Baker Publishing
    Group, [2021]
Identifiers: LCCN 2020042210 | ISBN 9780800740030 (casebound) | ISBN
    9780800738396 (paperback)
Subjects: GSAFD: Romantic suspense fiction. | Christian fiction.
Classification: LCC PS3611.O749175 N48 2021 | DDC 813/.6--dc23
LC record available at https://lccn.loc.gov/2020042210

21 22 23 24 25 26 27   7 6 5 4 3 2 1

In honor of Uncle Robert Vaile Artman
and Aunt Aurel Jeane May.

ONE

"SARAH JEANE ROGERS," she muttered. "Elizabeth Jeane Jones." Which ID to use this time? "Eenie meenie minie moe . . ." She held up the license in her right hand. "Sarah Jeane Rogers it is."

She took the license with the name Mary Jeane Smith out of her wallet and replaced it with a license with the name Sarah Jeane Rogers. She finished cleaning out her wallet and put Mary Jeane Smith away in the safe, closed the door, and checked that it was securely locked.

She walked out of the shadowed storage space, empty except for the small but heavy safe bolted to the concrete floor. The space was a little bigger than her last storage unit, but it'd been the smallest available and she didn't want to go searching all over LA in this heat and traffic for a better deal. She'd enjoyed Montana much more, but she knew better than to stick around anywhere too long. And they wouldn't likely spend much time looking for her in a place like this—crowded and hot, two of her least favorite things.

She pulled the overhead storage unit door closed with a clatter and locked it.

Inside the car, Mac had his paws up on the window and was watching her. She made a shooing motion, and he scooted back

7

over to the passenger seat, still watching her as she unlocked the car with her spare key and got in.

"What?" she said. "I left the car running. You were fine."

He sat down on his seat and curled his fluffy tail around himself.

She tossed her drill on the back seat floor next to the case for her McMillan TAC-50 rifle, took a drink from the water bottle in the console, opened the apartment guide she'd picked up, and started scanning for studio apartments.

Mac got up on his hind legs and pawed the passenger window.

"You want to hear and smell what's going on? All right, just a few inches." She pressed the button to lower the passenger window. She kept waiting for that button to stop working too, like most of the buttons in this old Chevy Blazer. Mac stretched his long body to stuff his nose out the window. She smiled as he sashayed his tail contentedly.

People were gathering at the end of the block of blue roll-up doors. She'd seen a poster in the office about abandoned storage unit auctions today. She decided to stay a little longer until she figured out which apartments she would look at and allow Mac to enjoy watching the people.

She caught a glimpse in her rearview mirror just as Mac's tail stopped and his fur went up. There was a man walking up from behind the car. The man walked around the passenger side of the car, surely headed toward the auction.

A low growl sounded from Mac's throat.

The man stopped and looked at Mac, less in a shocked way but more like he was intellectually curious. "Is that a dog or a cat?"

"He's a Maine coon. He won't hurt you." *Unless you do something stupid.*

"A what?"

"It's a kind of cat."

He looked from Mac to her, made eye contact.

She started to think he was going to say something, do something. She felt his focused attention on her like the weight of a piano. Then his expression cooled, kind of detached, and he walked away.

She turned back to her apartment guide, not sure what to make of him. Mac purred, and she stroked his fluffy orange fur.

Then she looked out the windshield at the man, now standing at the back of a small crowd. He stood straight with his arms crossed and interacted with no one. There was something there, something a little different about him somehow, but she couldn't quite put her finger on it. Or was it just that he stayed back away from the other people that made him stand out to her? He was pretty standard-looking—tall, dark hair, jeans and T-shirt. Well, *standard* wasn't the right word . . . Around here, the lack of man bun made him seem unique. She laughed and went back to her apartment guide.

She started making calls to a few of the apartments to ask some key questions, the ones she didn't like to ask in person because people looked at her like she was a crazy paranoid.

Then the group of people moved down the row of storage units, closer to her. Mac changed to paws on the dash so he could look out the windshield at the people.

"Just a few more minutes, buddy." She dialed the next number. She wasn't having much luck so far finding a place that met her requirements.

A man wearing work pants and a T-shirt with the name of the storage facility on it cut the lock on the unit where the crowd was gathered. He lifted, and the roll-up door rumbled up on its track. An older man, surely the auctioneer, started giving statistics about the unit while all the people craned to get a look inside. Once everyone had taken a look, the auction started.

The man from before remained behind the rest of the crowd. He made a bid a hundred dollars higher than what the auctioneer called for, and several people turned and glared at him. He adjusted his rectangular glasses, re-crossed his arms, and remained focused straight ahead.

She realized she'd stopped apartment hunting and was just watching him. She didn't like to admit to herself when she found a man attractive, but that wasn't what really had her attention. She narrowed her eyes. *He knows something—he knows there's something of value in that unit that the others don't see.* Or was he just stupid?

No . . . he definitely wasn't stupid.

She crossed her arms and studied him.

A few seconds later, the auctioneer announced that the man had won the auction. The crowd started to disperse, except the man who'd won. He walked up to the auctioneer, surely to finish the transaction.

A glint from across the way caught her eye.

She turned back to the man. The auctioneer shifted around to the other side of him and drew him a couple of feet over.

She put her Blazer in gear, in reverse, and eased on the gas, wondering if the man had any idea he was about to die.

"CASH ONLY."

"Of course," Lyndon said. As if he didn't know the auction had to be paid in cash.

The beat-up Blazer that he'd walked past earlier started backing up. He'd wondered why she'd sat there for so long.

The auctioneer—Walter—thumbed through his papers. "And there is the matter of the auction fee."

"Yes, of course." Lyndon had his hand on his cash in his pocket. "How much is the total?" He already knew the answer, of course, but thought it might be rude not to wait for Walter to calculate the simple figure.

The Blazer drove forward now, slowly around them, rather close to the line of storage units on the opposite side of the drive lane.

"And you'll need to have the unit emptied within forty-eight hours," Walter said.

Lyndon did his best to keep annoyance out of his tone. "What was the total?"

The door to the Blazer opened, and the young woman with the odd cat got out and opened the back door as well. Then she jogged toward him, and her long dark braid bounced on her shoulder. "Hey, can I ask you something?"

Lyndon watched her approach—though he knew he shouldn't—even while Walter talked to him. She looked like she had Native American blood in her veins. He saw it mostly in her eyes—large and dark, framed with long lashes.

"You bought that unit, right? Can I buy something from there off you?"

Walter rested a hand on her arm and attempted to guide her to the side. "We're almost done here. Then you can talk business all you like."

But she didn't move. Rather, she appeared to brace herself, which seemed at odds with her casual tone.

Walter gave up on her and put his arm around Lyndon's shoulders to guide him away. While Lyndon didn't particularly care for being touched, he moved with Walter. He was curious to know what she wanted, curious about her in general if he was being honest with himself, but he would not let himself feel this kind of intense interest.

The woman pushed him to the side.

Before he could get angry, he heard something hit the wall behind him. He looked over and saw a . . . Was that a bullet hole in the block?

The woman had taken his hand and was already dragging him toward her vehicle. He followed.

"Get in," she ordered.

He obeyed, and almost tripped on the long case that was on her back seat floor. She jumped in the driver's seat and tore down the narrow drive lane.

"What's going on?" he asked.

"Someone just tried to kill you. A sniper on the building opposite."

"What?" He paused to allow his thoughts to catch up to reality. "No, they had to have been aiming at something else."

"You mean the auctioneer who was nudging you into position? Don't think so." She turned out of the storage facility and merged with traffic, driving at the same speed as the other cars. Her voice didn't waver, her hands didn't shake, she didn't even appear to be sweating. And that odd cat lay on the front seat, curled up as if nothing out of the ordinary had just happened.

"Who in the world are you?" he asked.

"No one important." She made another turn.

"How did you know what was going to happen?"

She said nothing.

"Okay," he said. "Then let's go with, who are you and why did you do that?"

Again nothing.

"Are you going to tell me anything?"

"I don't know anything to tell you. Other than you really got on someone's bad side. You need to figure out what you did and remedy the situation."

"I haven't done anything that could possibly warrant being shot at." Unless . . . his theory had some merit. But no one else even knew about it.

"I don't know what to tell you other than figure it out." She stopped the car.

"You're not even going to tell me who you are?"

"This is where you exit the car."

He didn't move.

She shifted and took something out of her waistband, and she turned and aimed a semiautomatic handgun at him. "Out."

He hesitated for a second, confused, a feeling to which he was not at all accustomed. Then he looked more closely at the gun—a Glock 19. "There's no magazine in that gun."

"You wanna bet I don't have a bullet in the chamber?"

He lifted his chin. "You won't pull the trigger anyway."

She raised an eyebrow, and as he looked into her dark eyes, he considered changing his opinion about her killer instincts. Her eyes were deep, but not in a romantic way—more like she'd seen terrible things no one should have seen, carried memories she longed to forget.

He focused on a calm voice, and it came out almost gentle, which he hadn't heard in his own voice in years. "Please tell me who you are and how you knew that was going to happen."

Some of the cold in her eyes faded, and she lowered the gun. "Please just go. Trust me—it's for your own good."

"What do you mean 'for my own good'? Someone just shot at me, and you put yourself in the way of the bullet."

"They weren't going to shoot until they had a good line of sight."

"How do you know that?"

"Because that's how it's done. You lie in wait until you have a clean shot. If not, it gets messy real fast."

He felt his expression twist in frustration. "Who are you?"

She sighed, and he heard years of wariness in that quiet exhale, more years than her smooth skin seemed to hint at. All the cold finally melted out of her eyes, and he saw kindness looking back at him.

He could do nothing but stare back at her, at those dark eyes that now looked like the night sky, vast and beautiful, and so far away.

Her voice came out in a murmur. "Please."

He felt a strange instinct to stay. "You just put yourself in the middle of this. Whatever this is. Maybe we shouldn't separate."

"I'm sorry I can't explain, but no."

"I don't want you being hurt because of me."

"Trust me, you're better off alone."

"I'm worried about you, not—"

Her voice was still soft. "Please trust me."

He hesitated, still staring back at her.

Then he opened the car door and stepped out. He'd barely shut the door when she punched the gas and left him standing there. He watched her car disappear around a corner, irrationally unable to look away.

LYNDON CLIMBED THE STAIRS TO HIS APARTMENT. His heart had stopped pounding, but his mind continued to race, which made his head feel like it was splitting in half with pain. He couldn't quite believe that she was right—that someone wanted him dead. And instead of focusing on the immediate issue, his mind kept turning back to her . . .

Lyndon rubbed his hands over his face. *I'm losing my mind.*

His neighbor's door opened, and a middle-aged man with a dark mustache stepped into the hall. "You're home early," Mr. Porchesky said to Lyndon with a smirk.

Lyndon felt his patience running thin. He continued walking.

"When are you going to get a real job?" Mr. Porchesky muttered.

"When my endeavors stop providing the income I need."

"*Endeavors*," Porchesky scoffed.

Lyndon suspected his neighbors thought he did something illegal. He'd never bothered telling any of them that he had three PhDs plus a master's in cybersecurity.

"Good afternoon." Lyndon unlocked his apartment door, walked inside, and locked the door.

He looked around, making sure he didn't see something different from what he'd left this morning, but everything was the same as always—his desk and other makeshift work surfaces took up most of the living room, with one little corner reserved for his business of reselling items of value from abandoned storage units, the one armchair in the corner, and bookshelves covering every other wall. Everything appeared to be in the same order in which he'd left it.

And yet something felt very different.

He headed to the kitchen and filled a glass with water. That just made him think of the water bottle in her console, which made him think of the way she'd turned and aimed a gun at him.

Then he thought about how she'd looked at him in the end, the kindness.

He sighed.

He was accustomed to being able to see angles others could not, but just now he couldn't see any of the angles—neither that shooter firing at him from atop a building nor the woman who'd first saved his life and then threatened it. Though he felt certain she wouldn't have actually fired at him. Why save his life just to take it herself?

When did my thoughts turn to such things?

His morning had started off so normally. He'd gotten up at his usual time of five a.m., and he'd worked on his research for several hours. He was waiting to hear back from Dr. Grant about his thoughts on his most recent email, so he'd been focusing on the one wild theory he'd developed. He wasn't one for wild theories, but this one was feeling more and more logical as he continued digging.

No one else even knew about this theory.

Something didn't fit. Maybe someone had mistaken him for someone else? Or perhaps the shooter was some lunatic. But if he was one of those shooters who stole headlines from time to time, he'd have shot up the crowd at the auction rather than wait for everyone to leave.

And the woman . . .

She'd said the auctioneer had been positioning him. As he thought back through the event, he had to admit that seemed accurate.

That was a place he could start—the auctioneer.

He walked over to his computer and sat down. He researched Walter's name and the name of his auction company.

After about an hour, Lyndon clicked on his desk lamp and set his glasses down with a clatter. He'd found nothing of great interest. Walter had what appeared to be a perfectly average family—a daughter and two grandchildren in Garden Grove. His business brought in decent money, but nothing terribly noteworthy. Lyndon found nothing that might possibly explain his behavior today. Perhaps he was nothing but a pawn? Being blackmailed? Based on the research, that seemed like the most rational explanation.

Another idea came into his mind like the slide of a gun snapping a bullet into place. She'd said to figure it out. If there was one thing he was good at, it was figuring things out. But he had nowhere to start—other than with her. He'd noticed several things during the brief time he'd been able to observe her, some things that seemed to nudge him in her direction, no matter how much he felt the need to fight against it. He put in his earbuds, blasted "Iron Man" by Black Sabbath, typed the first search—her license plate number—into the computer, and began piecing together her mystery. Or rather, discovering exactly how deep her mystery went.

TWO

"MS. ROGERS WAS IT?" the leasing agent asked.

"That's what it says on my license." She purposefully made her grin a little off.

The leasing agent's smile went tight, and she turned back to the apartment brochure. "You're looking for a studio you said."

"I don't know if I actually said it."

The agent looked up. "But that is what you're looking for?"

"That's the floor plan I saw in the apartment guide."

Any tighter and the agent's smile was going to snap. "Okay, well, would you like to see the unit we have available?"

"Can I bring my cat?"

"Your cat?"

"I need to make sure he likes it."

"Uh . . ."

"I can have a cat here, right?"

"Yes, we're pet friendly. I've just never had someone bring their cat on a tour."

"How do the cats know if they'll like the apartment?" She twisted her expression in confusion until her face felt like a washcloth being rung out.

"I suppose your cat will be fine to come along." The leasing agent took a key from a drawer and led the way out of the rental office.

The building was one over from the rental office, close to the main exit and also a small wooded area. On the way toward the building, she opened the door of the Blazer and let Mac hop down. He followed her up the sidewalk.

The agent stopped and looked back. "You don't need to carry it, or . . . have it on a leash or something?"

"He's perfectly capable of walking." She continued forward, and so did Mac.

The agent kept going.

The tour went the same as all the other apartment tours she'd been on—she spent maybe two minutes looking at the place, checking certain aspects of security, and made the agent as uncomfortable as possible.

Mac accompanied her as she signed the lease with the name Sarah Jeane Rogers. At least her middle name was real, if nothing else about her was. That was why she kept using it. Without that one link to her past and Mac to keep her company, she felt she might completely lose herself.

She took immediate possession of the apartment and lugged her duffle bag into the little place. Mac walked in behind her, and she closed and locked the door. The apartment had no furniture, so she sat on the floor, took a book out of her duffle, and allowed Mac time to investigate their new home. He was always more at ease if he had time to sniff every corner and crawl into every nook. Though she was starving, she waited patiently for him to be done.

A while later Mac sauntered out of the bathroom and sat down in front of her.

"Meet with your approval?" she asked.

His meow almost sounded like a bark.

"Good." She got to her feet. "Because I'm starving." She'd slept in her car the night before and hadn't eaten, maybe too on edge after her reckless behavior yesterday. But she'd done the right thing by stopping that man from being killed, right? She sighed—she could never really know. What if he deserved to die? She knew nothing about him.

But he seemed kind. For some reason, the man kept popping into her head, and she continued to push him back out.

She headed for the door. "Come on, buddy."

He meowed. Barked. Whatever.

A knock on the door made her stop. It was like all those times waiting for the target to appear, for the perfect shot, listening to every blade of grass, each snap of a flag in the wind, her own almost-silent breath. Mac stopped next to her and watched the door. His hearing was even better than hers—she watched him listen, waiting for his reaction.

He slowly crouched toward the door. He, apparently, didn't think it was the leasing agent back to welcome them one more time. It was someone unknown. She assumed that as well—she'd done quite well at making the agent uncomfortable, assuring she'd never darken this door again if she could help it.

Silently, she walked up to the door and looked out the peephole.

There was a man standing at her door. He had blond hair pulled up into a man bun—she rolled her eyes—and he wore a big smile. "Hi," he said through the door. "Just thought I'd stop by and meet my new neighbor."

She walked silently away from the door.

Mac stayed by the door and looked at her expectantly.

She shook her head.

He sat down.

She plopped back down on the floor to wait for the man to leave. She'd learned not so long ago to stay hidden and anonymous as much as possible. No friendships, and certainly no romantic relationships. Memories of James still gnawed at her. She wasn't sure if it was from anger at the betrayal, frustration with herself for not realizing he wasn't who he said he was, or maybe it was still . . . pain.

She sighed.

Mac walked over and climbed into her lap; he always seemed to know exactly what she needed. She pulled him closer into a hug, and he rubbed the top of his head against her cheek. He was big enough that it almost felt like hugging a person. "Thanks, buddy," she murmured against his fur.

A minute later, Mac's ears perked. She looked up. "Is he gone?"

He hopped down and walked over to the door, fluffy tail up in the air.

"Good." She pushed herself up to standing and forced the pain deep down inside. "I'm dying of hunger." She headed out the door with Mac trotting along beside her. Like always, she pretended the pain wasn't there, hadn't ever been there. If she didn't pretend, she'd never survive.

And if her training had taught her anything other than how to kill, it was how to survive.

LYNDON THANKED THE UBER DRIVER and then stepped out of the car. While he walked, he kept track of everything around him peripherally. The shooter yesterday had obviously been a sniper, and a very good one. Lyndon was typically an astute observer, but he hadn't seen him. Or maybe it'd been a *her*. Not much would surprise him at this point.

He'd spent all night looking into every angle he could think of, all the time waiting for the police to come knock on his door and question him about the shooting. But no one came, which again told him how skilled the shooter had been to be that stealthy. Lyndon couldn't even remember hearing the shot, only the sound of the bullet hitting the concrete wall behind him.

So, how had that woman figured out what was about to happen?

He walked down the row of storage units. It could prove to be unwise of him to come back here, but he needed to get his car.

And hopefully no one would expect him to come back, at least not so quickly after the incident.

He heard a sound and stopped, until he realized it was the breeze rattling the roll-up doors.

He continued forward.

At the corner, his truck came into sight, the old familiar 1964 Chevy K10. The dark blueish-green paint was worn from years of serving his grandfather well. It had more miles than Lyndon liked to admit, but it was the only thing he had left from his grandfather, the last of his family.

He took a good look to make sure no one had tampered with anything. Then he put the key in the ignition, and the engine rumbled to life. He put it in gear and drove out of the storage facility.

Now he had to decide what to do next. He had an idea of how to find the woman from yesterday, but he wasn't sure that was the wisest course. He'd found enough about her to know he should be cautious, or rather it was all the things he *couldn't* uncover about her that warned him to be cautious. Or maybe it was that ridiculous instinct he'd felt to stay with her. *No, it isn't anything more than a bit of physical attraction. That's all.* And he certainly wouldn't let himself act on that.

He resigned himself to what he should do. Focusing on the elements of the equation that were the most unique was typically the best way to start, and she was certainly the most unique thing he'd found in a long time.

SHE WALKED IN WITH HER REMINGTON 798 rifle in its soft case slung over her shoulder. She kept this quality but common hunting rifle because her McMillan TAC-50 wasn't legal in California, nor did she want to draw attention by walking in with a tactical weapon. She handed the man at the counter the ID she was currently using and opened the rifle case to allow him to inspect the weapon. Then she paid for range time, bullets, and some of her favorite HALO Thompson targets and headed for the door to the range.

"Hey," the man at the counter said. "You can't have pets in here." Apparently, he had just noticed Mac at her feet. "He's my support animal."

He hesitated. "I'm sorry, I need to see—"

"According to California law, you cannot require proof of service animal registration." Though they also weren't required to allow emotional support animals, only service animals, nor were cats considered any kind of support or service animal, only dogs, none of which she was going to mention. She held eye contact and waited for a response.

He glanced from her to Mac several times and finally said, "All right, I guess."

She continued walking, and Mac followed. From what she read online about this place, they were a bit relaxed about things, so she figured she'd get away with bringing Mac. He didn't like to be left alone wherever they were staying at the moment, and it was too hot to leave him in the car.

Out at the range, she walked down to the last spot, which was thankfully not already taken. Mac curled up under the counter along the wall behind her. If the loud sounds bothered him, he always found a way to cover his ears, either with his paws or by crawling into her gun case. She took her Remington 798 out of its case, set the case on the ground so Mac could climb in if he wanted, and loaded the gun. Now to find her first target . . .

She looked around at the other people, all men. She'd met her fair share of talented female marksmen, but the craft was still dominated by men for some reason. Well, at least that made her goals a bit easier to reach. She adopted her patented innocent expression, the same one that had served her well for many years— basically just slightly raised brows, softness to her eyes, and maybe a bit of tilt to her head.

A middle-aged man with receding gray hair approached with a smile. "Need some help with that?"

"How do I set up a target?"

He took her target out of her hand and operated the panel at the side of her station to recall the arm holding a piece of cardboard. He stapled the target to the cardboard, and then he asked, "How far? Ten yards to start?"

"All right."

He pressed a button, and the target zoomed out ten yards.

"Thanks." She pressed her lips together and picked up her rifle.

"Ever shot that before?" he asked.

"My dad showed me one time." Which was actually true. A very, very long time ago. She made a show of figuring out how to brace it against her shoulder. Thankfully, this guy was a gentleman and didn't try getting handsy under the guise of showing her how to hold it.

"Just take your time and squeeze the trigger when you're ready," he said.

She nodded and aimed the weapon, purposefully too low, and pulled the trigger.

"Not bad," the man said. "You took the recoil real well." He gave her some basic instruction, and she pretended to listen.

"Thanks," she said. "I think I just need to practice now."

He smiled. "You'll do fine." He walked back over to his station a few down from hers.

She spent some time "practicing," all the while gauging the men around her. About ten minutes later, the nice middle-aged man left.

She noticed the man at the next station glance at her with a slight smirk. She wouldn't have caught it if that hadn't been exactly what she'd been looking for.

She smiled over at him. "I think I'm getting better."

"Sure you are." He struggled against another smirk.

"I think I might even be better than you."

He looked at her with raised eyebrows.

"What do you think?" she said. "Want to place a little wager?"

He snorted and turned back to his Winchester Model 70.

"Afraid of a girl beating you?"

He looked at her with his brows raised and pulled together in kind of an *Are you stupid?* expression.

"Well . . . ," she baited.

"All right. Ten bucks."

"Ten bucks? If we're going to do it, let's make it worth it. Hundred bucks."

He hesitated and glanced down at her slender figure. She purposefully wore loose shirts, both to hide the strength of her frame and to conceal the Glock tucked in her waistband. "All right," he said. "Let's do it. I hope you know what you're getting into."

He took several twenties out of his wallet and set them on the counter. She set down a hundred-dollar bill.

She smiled. "You first. Fifteen yards."

He smirked and then turned back to his rifle. He set the target at fifteen yards, aimed, and fired. He pulled the target in to show he'd struck the second circle around the bull's-eye.

"Pretty good." She moved her target to fifteen yards, aimed, controlled her breath, and squeezed the trigger. Then she pulled in the target.

He gaped at the hole perfectly through the bull's-eye. "Beginner's luck."

"Double or nothing?"

"You're on."

They both laid down more money. A minute later, he again gaped at her target, and she picked up the money.

"Again?" she asked.

"I'm out." He packed up his stuff and left.

She glanced around in search of her next target. Eventually, a man in sleek black slacks and hair so perfectly shiny and styled it almost didn't look real took an interest in her. He had a fat wallet and a lot of attitude—her favorite kind of opponent. They spent some time playing her game.

After taking her next shot—another perfect bull's-eye—she set the butt of her rifle down on the low counter in front of her and looked over at the man with perfect hair.

He picked up his rifle and took aim, pausing several seconds, as if his aim would get better if he just waited long enough.

And as she scanned the rest of the people around her, as she did routinely, she noticed the bay on the other side of Perfect Hair had a different occupant. He stood with good form, strong shoulders and back and rippled forearms, and aimed his Glock 17 at the target twenty yards away. She started planning a covert exit even as she watched him fire several shots—a tight cluster on his target. She stood shocked for about half a second before forcing her mind back on track. *Sneak past him?* But she had to put her weapon away properly before she could leave her bay. One of the range masters would stop her if she didn't.

She turned to pick up her case off the floor. Luckily, Mac wasn't lying in it. He just sat there, with his fluffy tail curled around himself, looking at her. *Thanks for the warning,* she mentally muttered.

"What a lovely coincidence," said a flat voice.

She stopped, halfway bent over toward her case. Before looking, she knew who it was. She'd already memorized his voice, apparently.

She turned to see the man from yesterday.

He straightened his glasses and smiled at her, though it didn't reach his eyes.

THREE

SHE TOOK THE LARGE STACK OF CASH on the counter and stuffed it into her jeans pocket. "Thanks," she said to the man with perfect hair.

"You all right?" Perfect Hair asked her.

She bent down toward her case again, and the man from yesterday leaned closer to her and spoke under his breath. "Really want to make a scene?"

She stood straight and stared at him for about two seconds, just long enough to wonder how much he knew, how he could possibly know anything, if he was a plant like James.

Then she turned to Perfect Hair and smiled. "An old friend taking me by surprise is all. Sorry I have to cut our fun short."

Perfect Hair laughed. "Boyfriend didn't know you hustle guys at the range." He laughed again. "I had better stop while I'm way behind, anyway. Maybe I'll see you around again, when I'm not under the weather and my aim is where it usually is."

She wanted to roll her eyes. Why did men so often find the need to make excuses for why a chick beat them? But that arrogance worked to her advantage.

Perfect Hair slipped his rifle into its case and walked away.

She glared at the man from yesterday. "Back. Off."

"What's your name?" he asked.

She crossed her arms.

"I couldn't find your name," he said. "I even hacked the storage facility's security feed from yesterday and completed an image search online, and nothing came up."

"Of course not." No one had her real picture—all her licenses were fake, a picture of someone who looked a lot like her, close enough to fool most people, but not close enough to flag facial recognition software.

"Interesting," he said.

"I'm not something to be studied by some college geek. You can run along now, Skippy."

He leaned closer and spoke more quietly. "Everyone's picture is online somewhere. Everyone."

"Apparently, you're not as smart as you think you are."

"I know you're not nearly as aggressive as you try to seem. Let me just clarify now that aggressiveness won't make me back off."

As he'd proven yesterday when she'd aimed a gun at him and he'd barely reacted. She took a deep breath and sighed. Her voice turned calm, not warm necessarily, but normal. "What're you doing out in public? You need to be more careful."

He glanced behind him, surely to make sure no one could hear them. "I haven't a clue why someone would want me dead. I—"

"Wait, how did you find me?" There was no way he'd just happened across her.

"You keep rifles on the floor of your back seat, and you carry a handgun in your waistband."

"That doesn't explain how you tracked me to this particular place at this particular time."

"I saw the apartment guide in your car and noticed the studio apartments were circled, so I thought about searching all the nearby apartment complexes that offer studios and are pet friendly— assuming that ball of fur is actually a cat, as you claim—but there are quite a few of those. Then I thought, you were frustrated yesterday, so I assumed you'd want to blow off some steam, and given that you have what appears to be a rather specialized rifle, I thought a gun range might be where you would want to do that. There aren't that many gun ranges in LA. I know most of them very well. I drove through a couple of parking lots until I saw your old Blazer and license plate."

She'd hoped—assumed—he'd been too distracted or upset to pay attention to much of anything. She kept the McMillan TAC-50 case covered in towels and such to camouflage it, and he'd maybe had a few seconds to see her license plate before she'd driven off. How, with all the insanity that happened to him in a matter of minutes, did he notice all these things?

"What do you want from me?" she asked.

"What's your name?" He held himself straight and squarely facing her, but it didn't feel like some attempt to use his height to be dominant, no crossing his arms or blocking her path; it was more about focusing his full attention on the person in front of him, a study of the person. Being studied made her uncomfortable.

"That's what you want? My name?"

"I came here to ask you how you knew the shooter was there and if you saw anything else out of the ordinary. Obviously, you're extremely observant, and I need any information I can get." He shrugged, but it didn't feel casual, more like he was trying to look casual so he could make her feel at ease and better study her. "But then I spent all night trying to figure out who you are. It's starting to drive me a bit nuts, to be quite honest."

"Not used to being stumped?"

"No," he said simply. His features were stronger than she'd noticed before, more angular, which the rectangular shape of his glasses seemed to emphasize.

The corner of her mouth twitched, but she controlled it. "I saw him because I happened to catch a slight glint of the sun, and no, I didn't see anything else out of the ordinary." Then she added, "Who in the heck are you?"

"Lyndon Vaile."

"Are you going to expand on that?"

His voice was quiet, almost soft. "What's your name?"

"Kadance." She said it without thinking. Her real name. She hadn't said it aloud in years.

Mac jumped up on the counter, sat down, and looked at her. *I don't know what to tell you, buddy. It just popped out.*

"I don't think I've ever heard that name before." He paused. "I like it."

She liked how he actually thought about it before saying he liked it, not some obligatory thing.

He kept looking at her. "You're nicer than you let people see."

"Why would you think that?"

"You saved a perfect stranger's life by walking into the line of fire."

"I told you he wouldn't have taken a shot without a clear line of sight."

"You couldn't have known that, not for certain. What if he'd simply taken the collateral damage and shot through you? Some rifles are high-powered enough for that."

She'd thought of that as well, even as she'd walked up to him at the storage place, knowing full well there was a sniper perched behind her.

"Why'd you do it?" he asked.

She picked up her rifle, ready to put it back in the case. "All that matters is it worked, and you need to figure out what's going on and get someplace safe."

"It's an important question," he said. "I don't think you did it solely out of goodness. Not that you're not a good person, but you're in the habit of protecting yourself, not taking risks like that."

"Why does any of that matter in relation to your current circumstances?"

"I need to understand the entire situation before I can formulate a workable hypothesis."

She lifted her chin. "You're a scientist."

"Yes."

"You definitely sound like one." Then she muttered, "Slave to logic." Maybe if she helped him form a hypothesis, he would go away. "Okay, we know you buy storage units and we know you're a scientist. I'm going to guess your work in storage units isn't terribly dangerous."

"Several of the regular bidders don't harbor pleasant places in their hearts for me, but no, there is no danger in my work."

"What about your work as a scientist?"

"It's just research."

"What kind of research?"

"Medical."

She waited for more of an answer, but he didn't give it. *He's hiding something—or maybe not hiding but protecting information.* "Look, here's my advice, and it's really good advice. Leave town, disappear. Find somewhere else to live, and just remove yourself from this situation."

He looked at her for a long moment. "That's what you're doing—you're removing yourself from some situation. You're running."

She motioned to Mac to tell him to get down so she could use the counter to slip her rifle into its case.

"So, why did you do that yesterday?" he asked.

Mac jumped down, and she set her case across the counter.

He touched her arm lightly with his hand. Instead of throwing him off like she'd normally do, she stopped and looked up at him. His touch seemed to jolt through her. But that was likely because she hadn't been touched by anyone in so long.

"Why?" he murmured.

"Because there's enough death in the world. I wanted to stop it just once if I could."

His gentle hand stayed on her arm. "Death you've caused?"

She was quiet. It dragged on for several seconds. And she kept looking at him, at the calmness in his eyes—no judgment, no fear, no anger.

Finally, she murmured, "Yes."

A few seconds passed, and he nodded. "I understand."

She hesitated, and then stepped back and looked away. He didn't understand—he couldn't possibly. He wouldn't be standing here now, speaking so calmly, if he had any idea.

Mac rubbed against her leg, bringing her back to herself. She faced Lyndon. "That's my advice," she said. "Disappear. Even if you don't want to disappear forever, getting out of the line of fire will allow you to figure out what's going on, and hopefully, put a stop to it."

He took a breath and dropped his hand away from her arm. "It's a rational argument."

"So, you'll leave?"

"First, I have to go back to my apartment for my research."

"I really don't think you should."

"I can't leave it. It could potentially help save lives someday. I need to preserve it."

"This is your life we're talking about."

"It's the lives of a lot of people if . . ." He smiled a little, though it still didn't reach his eyes—she wondered if it *ever* did. "I think you're right that I should leave, and I should do it quickly." He shifted back a step.

"Did you really mean that?" she asked.

He stopped. "Mean what?"

"That you would put your life at risk to save others."

"Yes." There was a heaviness to that word, more to this determination of his. Something in his past?

Her eyebrows pulled together.

He moved a step closer. "It's no different from what you did yesterday."

She just looked at him. At the angles of his face, the dark stubble that he hadn't bothered shaving today, the green and gray of his eyes. The lack of fear, of judgment. How he seemed to see some good in her.

She sighed. "All right. I'm coming with you."

His brow furrowed, though she wasn't sure if it was from confusion or concern.

"I already saved you once—I won't let you get killed now."

FOUR

SHE FOLLOWED HIM, her in her Blazer and him in his old truck.

She started to turn the wheel to take the next side street and ditch him, but then she straightened it and kept following. She did that several times before finally parking next to him at a small apartment complex.

"Stay here," she said to Mac. "I'll be right back." She lowered his window several inches and turned off the ignition. He stood up on the passenger seat and meowed at her. She usually left the car running and locked it with her spare key, unless she wanted to make sure he had a way out if she didn't come back—he'd apparently caught on.

"I'm not the target this time." She petted his head and rubbed a thumb down his nose like he liked.

She looked out her windows and scanned the area. What she hated was that she didn't know anything about whoever was targeting him. Would they try a sniper again? Would they pay some random gang members? Or something else entirely? She couldn't even extrapolate possibilities based on what might work best on Lyndon—she didn't know him either. Thankfully, she'd loaded the Glock in her waistband before leaving the gun range parking lot.

They both exited their cars. "Get inside," she ordered.

He walked quickly for the door, and she followed him inside. The building was nothing special, a generic walk-up. *No one is after him for money, that's for sure.* Up the stairs and down the hall, she saw nothing interesting. Then one of the doors opened. She rested her hand on her Glock in the back of her waistband.

"Hello, Mr. Porchesky," Lyndon said with a flat voice.

Mr. Porchesky barely glanced at Lyndon and stared at Kadance.

"Hello," she said to him and followed Lyndon to the next door.

Lyndon unlocked the door, and she followed him inside and locked the door.

They both stared at the mess. The books from the multiple bookshelves were all over the floor. Wires were strewn across the desk, where they had apparently been connected to a computer. She could see the clean square where it had been in the thin layer of dust on the desk.

"I was just here a little while ago," he said.

"Then it's a good thing you left when you did." She pointed at a spot next to the door, away from the window. "Stay there for a minute." Thankfully, the blinds were already closed.

"What're you doing?" he asked.

"Checking the apartment."

He walked over to the desk along the wall. He was away from the door and the window, so she didn't complain. She expected him to freak out—about the destruction of his home, the invasion of privacy, the loss of his work. Though he was certainly tense, he didn't yell or curse. His hands didn't even shake. She was impressed. But then, maybe it wasn't bravery so much as lack of emotion.

She took a quick look around the living room. She found nothing concerning there, other than a chaotic mess. Same for the kitchen and bathroom. She heard him in the living room, sounded like going through the books. Then she went into his bedroom. The bed was unmade, and his clothes were strewn all over the floor. She felt a twinge of guilt in her stomach going through his personal space like this. The room held that subtle scent unique to each person. She would've expected his to be different, maybe that harsh smell of a hospital or maybe nothing at all. But it was clean, like a breeze through clotheslines of freshly laundered linens, comfortable.

"I need to pack a bag." He was standing in the doorway holding a book.

She tossed a backpack that was on the floor in the corner at him. "Make it quick."

"Did you find anything?"

"No."

"What were you expecting to find?" He stuffed some undergarments into the bag.

"I'm not expecting anything. I'm just paying attention."

Though his expression was still almost emotionless, the corner of his mouth twitched as he stuffed jeans and a few T-shirts in the bag.

"What's that smirk for?"

"You accuse me of being a slave to logic, but you have a scientific mind as well."

"My mind keeps me from getting killed. That's about it." She walked back out to the living room.

He followed a few seconds later.

"Did they take all your research?" she asked.

He grabbed his desk chair and pulled it over to the other side of the room. He climbed up on the chair and used a tiny screwdriver on his keychain to unscrew the air vent cover. Then he reached his arm into the hole. She heard as he shifted wiring and soft ductwork out of the way. He drew out a small black thumb drive, got down off the chair, and stuffed the drive into his pocket.

"That's all your research?" she asked.

"I back it up every day."

"If you didn't know you were in danger, why do you keep a hidden drive?"

"Backup in case of computer failure."

"That doesn't explain why you hid it."

"We should leave." He turned for the door.

She filed her questions away for later and focused on watching him even more closely. Maybe it was time to leave him to his own devices. She'd helped him get his research and convinced him to leave town—that was enough, wasn't it? None of this was her concern. She didn't owe him anything. She didn't even know him and had no reason to trust him.

They walked out of the building toward their cars, and she scanned the area. The road was only two narrow lanes but busy and loud.

Across the street, there was a parked truck with a man inside just sitting there.

She glanced around and then looked back to the man. He was watching them, both hands in his lap, out of sight. She saw a break in traffic coming.

She shoved Lyndon between their two cars.

The taillight of his truck blew out.

"What was that?" he asked.

"Black truck across the street, gun with a silencer."

Lyndon looked up at Mac watching him from the passenger window of her car. He reached up through the window, unlocked the car door, opened it, and dove inside. Mac jumped to the back seat.

"Get in," Lyndon said to Kadance. He climbed over the gear shift into the driver's seat.

She got in and closed the passenger door. He held out his hand for the key. She saw no other options and handed him her key. He started the engine and backed out of the parking space.

"Keep your head down," she said.

He slouched down in the seat the best he could.

The tires peeled as he pulled out of the lot.

She turned and looked out the back window, while peripherally making sure Mac was down on the seat out of the line of fire. "Black F150. He's following us." *I need to be driving. I should've insisted.*

He made several quick turns down various side streets.

Okay, maybe he can handle this. He certainly knew the area extremely well. He took several obscure streets and even alleys, all while avoiding congestion and driving very fast. But the truck managed to stay right behind him.

They drove past the garage entrance for a group of high-rise buildings, someplace called Barrington Plaza. Then he flew into traffic on a main road. She glimpsed a street sign at an intersection—Wilshire Boulevard.

He cut off a Toyota and turned right onto Federal Avenue, but then he immediately U-turned around the median.

She looked behind them. The truck's tires started to lose grip of the road, but then it recovered. "He's still with us."

Mac was clutching the seat with his claws.

She turned back around. She watched Lyndon for any indication of losing focus or flipping out. His gaze stayed focused on the road.

He turned down another side street, and then another.

Eventually, he turned onto a freeway.

"Are you crazy?" she asked.

"Just wait."

"Traffic is slowing down ahead. You need to exit."

"Not yet."

"What're you doing?"

He ignored her and blew by an exit.

Kadance started formulating ways to take control of the car. If she punched him hard enough to knock him out, could she get control before they crashed? Hold her gun on him again? But that hadn't worked the first time.

Traffic in the right lane slowed to a crawl. He blew by—even though traffic ahead in their lane was all red brake lights.

Then he cut the wheel at a solid white line just before the median started and squeezed between cars on an exit.

The F150 flew by and barely missed slamming into a Porsche.

The car behind them blared their horn for a good twenty seconds.

Kadance took a breath.

"You all right?" Lyndon asked.

"I'm not scared. I'm angry!"

"Why?"

She couldn't get her words to form coherently.

"Because you had to let someone else be in control?" he asked. He didn't smirk or sound arrogant, just curious.

For some reason, his tone calmed her down. She looked out the passenger window.

He turned at the next road. "Any idea where we should go next?"

She hesitated.

Then she looked over at him, at his anodyne expression. She started giving him directions. She didn't know LA very well yet, but she always made sure she could at least find her way on the major roads and freeways.

After ten minutes or so, he asked, "Where are we going?"

"My apartment."

FIVE

KADANCE UNLOCKED her apartment door and walked inside.

Lyndon followed her inside and then closed and locked the door. "Why did you decide to bring me here?"

She picked up Mac and cradled him to her chest. He'd been all tough saunter from the car to the door, but she knew he was freaked out from that crazy car ride. He nuzzled into her and took a deep breath. She turned away from Lyndon and whispered against Mac's fur. "I'm sorry, buddy. You're safe now."

Lyndon was quiet while she comforted Mac. She didn't much care if he thought she was an idiot for being so concerned about a cat. She rested her cheek against the top of his head, and finally Mac started purring.

"Is he all right?" Lyndon asked.

She turned and looked at him, ready with her walls up to defend against stupid jokes about how she wasn't as tough as she liked to think.

But he didn't make any jokes. He was looking at Mac with concern. "I'm sorry that all scared him. I didn't even think about it."

"He's fine." He'd been through a lot worse, and he still liked to be with her. Sometimes she felt selfish for not giving him to some quiet family in the country, but he'd made it clear over the years that he wanted to be with her. Simply because he liked her. She'd never had that before.

Lyndon looked around at the complete lack of furniture or anything else. "This is your apartment?"

"I just moved in."

"Your stuff is with the moving company still?"

"That's my stuff." She nodded toward her duffle on the floor.

He raised his eyebrows. Then he looked from the old duffle to her. "Must be kind of freeing."

She shrugged. Then she turned and walked around the small room that encompassed the living, bedroom, and kitchen areas. She paused by the window and opened the blinds so Mac could look outside.

"Can I ask why you brought me here?" he said.

She didn't answer.

"Do you have any idea who that was in the black truck?" he asked.

"I assume he was hired by whomever wants you dead."

He paused. "I'm not sure they were aiming at me."

She looked over her shoulder at him with an incredulous expression.

"The path of the bullet was closer to you than to me," he said.

She turned back to the window. She'd noticed that but assumed the guy wasn't that great of a shot. "Your admirer needs to hire more skilled thugs."

She felt in his silence that he wasn't sure it was so simple. He was a scientist—not willing to accept the most obvious answer if he hadn't fully explored all other options, even if it was by far the most plausible. She let him have his doubts. She didn't have the freedom for such exercises.

Finally, he spoke again. "Thank you for your trust."

"My what?"

"You must trust me a little, or else you wouldn't have brought me here."

40

She opened her mouth to point out that she wasn't exactly tied down to this place. But then a calm voice came out of her mouth. "You're welcome."

He didn't really smile—more like looked at her with a friendly expression.

Mac looked up at her and meowed.

She set him down on the floor, walked over to her duffle, took out a big ziplock bag of cat food, and set it on the floor open for him. She took a small plastic bowl out of the bag, filled it with water, and set it next to the open bag. He crunched at the food.

"How'd you know that's what he wanted?"

"He likes to eat. Can't you tell?"

"He's a big boy, but he looks like mostly muscle." Then he took a breath and sat down on the floor with his back leaned against the wall.

"Now that you have a minute to think," Kadance said, "where do you plan on going?"

"Thanks for giving me that minute to think." When he looked at her with that open honesty, it freaked her out a little. "I really appreciate your help. Not many people would have done what you've done."

She sat down across from him, her back against the kitchen cabinets. Mac was between them crunching away.

"So," he said, "are you going to tell me anything about who you are?"

"Not much to know."

"That's not usually the case when most of a person's history has been scrubbed. Who did that? The government?"

"I can't talk about it."

"The options are likely either you were involved with something high-level in the government—probably classified operations of some kind given your skillset—or you have a nefarious past and managed to get it scrubbed yourself."

She met his gaze for several seconds, ignoring how the color shifted in the light, sometimes more gray and sometimes more green. He didn't look at her with the intense gaze of an interrogator. His curiosity didn't seem to come from some drive to find something scandalous but from intellectual curiosity, as if he simply liked to decipher puzzles.

"Why aren't you more freaked out?" she said—almost demanded.

"I'm concerned. Certainly." He adjusted his glasses.

"But you're sitting there all calm. That's not normal."

"So are you."

"We've covered that my past is a bit different from yours."

"We haven't really covered anything about you." His manner remained frustratingly placid.

"You're a scientist with your head buried in research most of the time. You should be more freaked out."

"How do you know I'm buried in research most of the time?"

"You had a desk where a couch should be and bookshelves where a TV should be."

The corner of his mouth twitched, though he didn't actually smile.

She could almost hear his thoughts and answered them. "I don't have a scientific mind. I have the good sense to be observant." Then she noticed his arm propped up on his knee, the muscle tone. She crossed her arms and raised her chin.

"What's that look for?"

"There's more to you and your past than academia."

He crossed his arms. When he did it, though, it didn't feel the same. When she crossed her arms, it served as a sort of barrier. When he did it, it seemed more like getting into a thinking position. She pictured him leaned back in his desk chair looking at his computer screen, arms crossed just like that.

She raised her eyebrows.

"Give me your theories," he said.

It annoyed her how much he was not annoying her. She was too curious and entertained to shut down the conversation like she normally would. She ticked off her observations on her fingers. "Someone tried to kill you."

"That could simply be related to my research."

"We'll get back to that shortly." She ticked off the next observation. "You keep a hidden thumb drive."

"There are several reasonable explanations for that."

"Is there a reasonable explanation for why you didn't give me a reasonable explanation when I first asked you about it? Instead you avoided the question."

"Touché."

She raised her third finger. "You're sitting here perfectly calm." Fourth finger. "You're trained in shooting." Fifth finger. "You found me when you had almost no information."

"That was simply having sharp perception."

"I'll give you that one." She kept five fingers up. "And you're not in the physical condition of someone who sits behind a desk day in and day out."

He tightened his crossed arms, and his muscles flexed. "Because I'm a nerd I have to be fat and lazy? Or maybe a skinny weakling?"

"You don't have to be either of those extremes, but it's not typical for an academic to be well-built. And I don't think it's out of vanity, either." If he were vain, he'd probably wear contacts, but then his thin-rimmed rectangular glasses enhanced the structure of his face, his strong jaw, straight nose, and even the shape of his eyes. He had that squint like male models, but it definitely wasn't intentional or fake—more like it was related to his perpetual keen awareness.

"So, you don't think I'm vain. I suppose that's a positive."

"You're too logical to be vain."

"Vanity doesn't serve a purpose," he agreed. "Another way we're not so different."

"And you presume to know this about me how?" She regretted asking the moment she said it.

"You'd at least let your hair down and wear tight shirts to show off your figure. I assume part of the reason you wear large shirts is to help hide your Glock, but I wonder if you ever use your figure to get your way. It can be very useful on some men."

She tilted her head. "But not on you."

His voice lowered slightly. "I don't get involved with people." Then he added, voice still quiet, "Another way we're not so different."

Quiet.

Mac walked over and plopped down with his shoulder leaned on her thigh. He gave her an excuse to look away from Lyndon. She stroked her hand slowly down his soft fur, and he rested his head against her. She was surprised he was being so relaxed with Lyndon here.

"He's your connection to your humanity."

She looked up at Lyndon's words. He was watching her pet Mac. Then he met her gaze, more intently. "You have a lot in your past. I posit you were some kind of elite military or probably more likely CIA black ops or similar. Then something happened to make you walk away from your life. You're running. He's the only relationship you let yourself have."

She looked away.

"I'm not asking you to confirm any of that," he said. "I know it's true."

Several seconds passed.

Finally, she looked over at him. "You seem to have me figured out. What's your story?"

SIX

LYNDON HESITATED, considering how much to say. He'd prefer to say nothing—no, that wasn't entirely accurate. He felt a strong impulse to keep talking to her, and just as strong an impulse to keep looking at her. This was his first opportunity to really look at her. He did his best to keep his gaze from wandering down to her figure, but he had the excuse of basic manners to look at her face. Her cheekbones were high but not in a harsh way, less like Angelina Jolie and more like Keira Knightly. Similar lips too—soft but not overly full, delicate. But her eyes, those were uniquely hers. As they'd been talking, another part of his brain had been trying to find the words to describe her eyes. They were large and dark, not really a chocolatey brown, darker than that. Shadowed. Her shockingly beautiful lashes seemed to pull you in, but then you stop in fear at the shadows. Stuck in kind of a limbo.

He realized she was waiting for him to talk, and he tried to figure out what to say. He hadn't felt distracted like this in years, not since that time he saw a girl from across the quad back at Johns Hopkins. He'd seen just her profile from a distance, partially obscured by her shining dark hair blowing in the breeze, but he'd stopped in his tracks and forgotten what he was doing. This time, the distraction frustrated him.

"The thumb drive," he finally said. "It's a combination of factors. I started being obsessively secure back while studying for my first doctorate."

"*First* doctorate?"

"I have three: microbiology, pathology, epidemiology. Plus a master's in cybersecurity."

"You are a nerd."

"I suppose."

"I interrupted. So, why the obsession with security?"

"A friend of my roommate stole a paper from my computer and turned it in as his own. That got him into medical school."

"You couldn't prove it was yours?"

"He said it was on my computer because I stole it from him. While working on my microbiology PhD, I earned my master's in cybersecurity so that wouldn't happen again."

"So, the computer they stole from your apartment . . ."

"The files are highly encrypted. It'll be very difficult to get anything off it."

"Having a secured backup wasn't the only reason for hiding the thumb drive. You'd have just said that up front."

"I have personal files on it." It wasn't anything she'd care about—scans of letters from his parents, pictures, even a video of his grandfather from his last Christmas—but he simply didn't share those things.

She paused, surely wanting to ask what kind of personal files, but then she moved on. "What's the book you took from your apartment? There can't have been something hidden in it. Whoever tossed the apartment would've found it."

"It's something my parents used to read to me." He'd thrown his bag with the book in her back seat when he'd jumped in her car. He had to remember to get it back before they parted ways.

"It didn't look like a kids' book."

"It's not. Our choices of family reading were unique."

"Can I ask what it is?" Her tone wasn't what he would call

sweet—*sweet* was not the right word for her in general—but there was a subdued kindness, something most people probably wouldn't catch.

"O. Henry short stories," he said. "Have you read O. Henry?"

"The classics weren't part of my particular education." Then she added, "But I like to read."

He felt a smile tweak the corner of his mouth. More evidence of how she fought to keep a grip on her humanity. He wouldn't say it to her, but he guessed she read things like comedies and romances, stories that reminded her the world wasn't so bad.

"I think you would like O. Henry, at least some of the short stories," he said.

"Because you know me so well."

"They're circular and ironic. I just have a feeling you'd appreciate them."

She tilted her head as she looked at him. "I think I know why you're not freaked out."

"I'm certainly concerned and feeling a bit lost."

"Good. Otherwise, I'd be worried about you," she said. "I think you're not actively freaking out because you intellectualize. You focus so much on the problem and possible solutions that your emotional state is reasonably under control."

"Reasonably." At least on the outside. Inside, his thoughts were buzzing—he was trying to understand the problem, think of the best way to take action, desperately trying not to look at her too much, and also trying to understand her. There was, admittedly, an underlying current of confusion and frustration. He sighed.

"I hear that," she said. "There's a little freaking out in there."

He ran a hand through his hair.

"What's your next move?" she asked.

He shook his head. "Not yet. I need to process more."

"Should I leave you alone?"

"No. Talking helps."

"We're not talking about anything related to your problem."

"That's what's helping."

"So, you're thinking through everything while having a completely unrelated conversation?"

He nodded.

She raised her eyebrows and smirked. He wasn't sure what that meant.

"Can I ask you one thing?" he said. "One thing you might actually answer?"

"You can try."

"Are you Native American?"

She hesitated. But then she answered, "On my mother's side. She was full-blooded Shoshoni."

"And your dad's white?"

She nodded. "My father says I look like my mother, but I got his skin tone. Mostly."

"But you tan easily when you're out in the sun a lot?"

"Yeah. That's been helpful in the past." She moved on. "What about you?"

"You mean my familial background? Just a white mutt, I suppose. I don't really know."

"Your family hasn't told you about your ancestors?"

He bent his knees and draped his arms across them. "Not much. I think I have some Irish in me."

"That's all you know?"

"My parents died when I was a kid. My grandfather raised me, but he died before I finished high school."

"Oh."

He rather liked how she didn't always follow social norms—no obligatory apology for the loss of his family.

They were quiet for a good minute. He looked at the blank wall across the room. Mac's purrs calmed into sleep.

Finally, she asked, "Any theories about what's going on?"

He continued looking at the wall. "I'm formulating possibilities, but I need more information."

"But you're going to get out of town, right?"

He turned his head to look at her. "I won't go back home, of course. But I'm going to figure out what's going on. For that, I need to stay in this area, at least for another day."

"I really don't think that's smart."

"I don't know enough about the situation to decide what action is smart at this point. I have to have more information."

"You can do that remotely."

"This task, I think, needs to be in person."

"What task?"

"An old professor."

"You think he has something to do with what's going on?"

"I have a hard time believing that. He has a lot of contacts and relationships with the scientific community, specifically medical research. Maybe he knows *something*."

"You say you don't think he has anything to do with it, but you feel you need to talk to him in person. I think you have your doubts."

He didn't respond.

"Well, I don't agree with it, but it's your life," she said. "You can stay here for tonight if you want. You look like you could use some more time to think."

"Are you sure you're all right with that?"

"There's no reasonable way to connect you to me or this apartment. They might eventually track down my plates, but I'll get them switched out."

He didn't ask how she could do that so easily. "I'll buy you dinner. We can have something delivered."

"No credit or debit cards."

Mac yawned and stretched his back legs. Then he got up and went over to his water bowl.

"I still have the cash on me from the storage facility auction. I'm fine on cash."

"You're being awful trusting telling a perfect stranger that."

"I may not know many facts about you, but you're trustworthy." She wouldn't have risked her life to help him just to get an opportunity to steal some cash.

She smirked.

"I shut off my phone last night, just to be safe. Would you mind placing an order for food?"

"Sure. What do you want?"

"I don't care. Order two of whatever you want."

She took a few minutes to find a place to order from. She obviously didn't know the area well—though she'd been able to give him directions back here. She was interesting. That was the only reason he felt so drawn to her. She was a puzzle to figure out, that was it.

He stood and walked over to the one window. He turned thoughts and theories around in his mind until it started to feel like a blender. He needed to take a run to clear his head. That probably wasn't the best idea, but he couldn't let his mind go on like this. He'd always had a hard time keeping his mind from getting too turbulent when he couldn't make logical sense of something. He felt the migraine coming on fast and pressed his palms to the sides of his head.

"Hey, are you okay?"

"I'm fine." His voice sounded tight.

"You don't look fine. Food will be here in half an hour or so."

He kept his palms pressed to his head and closed his eyes. "That's not the problem."

Her voice sounded closer, next to him. "Stress headache?"

"Kind of." Then he added, "It happens when I can't shut down my thoughts. It feels like overtaxing an engine." He opened his eyes, and she was right there. "Will you keep talking with me? It helps."

"Okay. What do you want to talk about?"

"It doesn't matter."

"Uh . . . does this happen a lot?"

"I've gotten better at taking countermeasures."

"What do you usually do?"

"Go for a run." He dropped his hands back to his sides, though his voice still sounded tight. "I haven't run for the past couple of days." And last night, he'd had the benefit of researching her; that had kept the pain mostly at bay.

"So, physical exertion helps, but obviously you shouldn't be running the streets right now. What else helps?"

"Sometimes blaring music."

She laughed a little. "Seriously? You deal with headaches by blasting music?"

"The migraine is just one of the effects. Intense music helps focus my thoughts. It's like putting a target in front of a gun. Instead of bullets ricocheting, they aim at the target."

"I don't have any music."

"Conversation has held it off so far today. Please just keep talking to me."

"You said migraines are just one of the effects. What else?"

"If I can't get my mind under control, the pain spreads, my muscles lock up. It's an unusual problem. Apparently, inherited."

"Your grandfather?"

"My father. My grandfather told me he had the same problems when he was younger. He helped my father learn how to handle it, and he taught me the methods my father used."

She lifted her chin. "That's why you know how to shoot. Let me guess, your grandfather taught you and your dad as a way to focus your mind on one thing and calm down the rest."

"Exactly. That's why I went ahead and shot some rounds when I came to find you."

"You look better now. Pain decreasing?"

"Better. Thank you."

She glanced around the empty room, empty but for that huge cat sitting there watching them. "I'm sorry I don't have someplace comfortable to offer you to relax."

"I don't need to relax. I just need to focus on one thing at a time." Out the window, he noticed a junky car pull up next to her Blazer. "Looks like the food is here." He reached in his pocket and pulled out a wad of money and peeled off a couple of bills.

A few minutes later, they were sitting on the kitchen floor with containers of Chinese food between them and Mac curled up against her leg.

"This has been a weird day," she said.

"I have a feeling you've seen your fair share of car chases and bullets flying."

She sighed. "Is it sad that those were the lesser of the weird things?"

He was shocked she admitted even that much. "What's the weirdest?"

"This." She motioned with her chopsticks at their meal on the floor and then to him.

"But not too bad?"

She poked around a container with her chopsticks. "I haven't had a real conversation in a long time. Years."

"Me either."

She looked up at him.

He hesitated as he looked at her eyes, at the lack of shadow for the first time. He admitted, "I've lost too many people. I decided a long time ago not to be close to anyone." She kept meeting his eyes, and warmth moved up his chest. He made his tone lighter. "We seem to have a similar tendency for bluntness where most people are more delicate. And we've let each other hold back where we feel the need to."

"I didn't aim a gun at you this time."

"Definite progress."

She laughed, the first real full laugh he'd heard from her. Her smile was bright and clear like the first rays of sunshine after a rainstorm. He realized he'd stopped eating and was just watching her. *Stop it, Lyndon. She's just beautiful. You see beautiful women every day.* But she was so much more, maybe because she didn't seem to have any idea of her effect.

He dropped his chopsticks into an empty container and then started putting the containers in one of the plastic bags in which they'd been delivered. He stood.

She stood as well. "Here, I'll take it out to the dumpster." She took the bag and walked out.

He expected Mac to follow, but he lay there on the floor looking up at him.

"I know, I know," he said to the cat. Then he ran his hands through his hair. *Maybe I should just leave.* If the situation was anything other than it was, he would've avoided her at all costs. She was stunning in an unintentional way, highly intelligent, intriguing—everything that was most attractive to him, which meant dangerous. But he didn't have any place else to go tonight. If he knew where Dr. Grant lived, he'd just go there now, but he didn't and had to wait for the morning to catch him at his office.

Kadance walked back inside and closed and locked the door. "I'm going with you tomorrow."

SEVEN

"WHY?" LYNDON ASKED.

"I think you should leave town immediately. I thought I'd talked you into it. I'll feel guilty if I let you roam around LA by yourself."

He opened his mouth to tell her he'd be fine, that he could handle himself, but then he stopped. He wasn't entirely convinced that bullet in the parking lot at his apartment hadn't been intended for her. The most obvious assumption was that it was intended for him and the aim wasn't superb, but he didn't make assumptions as a rule. He still had his 9 mm on him. He would feel better if she at least had backup.

Though he had no idea what would happen after tomorrow. Surely, they'd go their own ways. But maybe he could convince her to leave LA as well.

"All right," he said.

She walked past him and knelt on the floor to unzip her duffle. "You can use my blanket. I just washed it before driving to California. I don't have a pillow, though."

KADANCE LAY ON THE FLOOR several feet away from Lyndon. He'd refused to use her blanket. He lay on his back with his arms and ankles crossed, head resting on his bag that she'd gotten out of her car for him. She was surprised he was able to sleep without the comforts most people were used to.

She kept looking at him, analyzing.

His handgun lay on top of his book next to his head. That image seemed to sum him up rather well. She was certain no one else saw anything but the nerdy guy he presented to the world. But she'd seen enough to know he was a lot more than that.

And yet, she was letting him sleep a few feet away from her. With a gun lying next to him.

She looked up at the dark ceiling. *I'm finally losing my mind.*

Then she turned her head back to Lyndon.

The more she looked at him, the more she thought, the more she realized how dangerous he really was. She'd wager he was smarter than anyone understood, and he was certainly more physically skilled than anyone would guess. She'd underestimated him, and she was trained to look past the obvious. He was the kind of person you would never see coming. Very dangerous.

It took her a while to fall asleep, and when she did, her sleep was even lighter than usual.

IT WAS EARLY WHEN KADANCE WOKE. The apartment was dark but for the light from the streetlamp outside. Lyndon was still asleep, and Mac stretched against her side. She was again surprised at how Mac had decided to accept Lyndon's presence.

She sat up slowly and held Mac in her lap so she could see his face in the low light. She checked to make sure he looked all right, to make sure this change in behavior wasn't a sign of illness. But he seemed fine. He started purring at the attention she gave him.

Quietly, she got up and took her duffle into the bathroom with her. She was dying for a hot shower. Mac lay on the counter while she showered, dressed, and brushed her hair and teeth. It'd been several days since she'd felt properly clean.

When she came out, Lyndon was leaning against the kitchen counter. He looked over at her and paused. Then he went back to reading his book. "Good morning."

"Shower's all yours."

"Thank you." He set his book on the counter, next to his gun, grabbed his backpack, and disappeared into the bathroom. She wasn't sure whether to feel trusted that he left his gun or to yell at him for it.

A short while later, he came back out. His wet hair was falling over his forehead. He rubbed his square jaw. "Forgot to pack a razor."

"It's probably good for you to look different," she said. "Do you think it's too early to leave? When does this guy get to his office?"

Lyndon looked at his watch. "I'll buy us some breakfast, and by the time we're done, he should be there."

They each grabbed their bag, and Mac followed them out the door. She decided to keep her bag with her, just in case.

After a drive-thru breakfast eaten in her car, she followed his directions and drove toward UCLA. She found a place to park and followed him, while watching their surroundings, both for anything of concern and to memorize the area and location of her car. Since she didn't know how long they'd be, she let Mac come along. They walked a little distance and came up to a large brick building. Lyndon opened the door for both Kadance and Mac—he didn't even question why Mac was coming along or if he was allowed in the building.

"How do you plan to introduce me?" Kadance asked.

"I figured I'd just go with whatever he naturally assumes."

"What do you think that'll be? Girlfriend?"

"I haven't dated since before coming here for my final doctorate."

"Why?"

"He knows me well enough to know I don't date. He won't likely assume a romantic relationship."

"So, it's not that you haven't found someone you like enough to date or that you've been too busy and otherwise focused. You've *chosen* not to date."

"It's a reasonable guess that you've made that same choice."

"I have good reason."

"So do I."

She decided to let that go. If she didn't want him pushing her to explain her past, she couldn't push for his. "I go back to my previous question. What do you think he'll assume?"

"I'll just say you're a friend. A neighbor. I'll say my truck is in the shop, and you agreed to give me a ride."

"All right."

Lyndon stopped at a door and knocked. They waited a good minute.

"Is he not here?" Kadance asked.

Lyndon spoke extra loudly. "He is. He's just trying to ignore annoying students who don't adhere to office hours."

The door flung open, and there stood an average-looking man with graying hair. "I seem to remember you were one of those students once upon a time."

"Do you want me to apologize?" Lyndon asked.

"Why bother? You're not going to."

Lyndon laughed. "True."

Dr. Grant opened the door wider to let them in. "And who is this I have the pleasure of meeting?"

"Sarah," Kadance said with a smile. "Lyndon's truck is on the fritz, so I gave him a ride." She stood to the side of the room, and Mac sat next to her. Dr. Grant glanced at Mac. Kadance just kept smiling and looked at Lyndon.

Dr. Grant turned to Lyndon. "How many times have I told you to get a new car?"

"I like my truck."

"I think you like being chauffeured around by your lovely girlfriend."

Lyndon glanced over at Kadance. She stepped forward and took his hand. The physical contact sent a jolt through her, a quivering but not unpleasant sensation. It was even stronger than when he'd touched her arm at the shooting range. Unnerving.

Lyndon smiled a little at her. She saw the thanks in his eyes. She guessed the assumption of a girlfriend had thrown him off and he hadn't been sure how to react. She'd figured him out enough to guess his mind didn't compute as quickly with anything not wholly factual—his brain just didn't work that way. With facts, he was lightning speed—not so much with lies.

The corners of Dr. Grant's eyes crinkled with his smile. "I'm glad to see you're allowing yourself to have a life. Finally." He half sat on the edge of his desk and motioned for Lyndon and Kadance to have a seat in the chairs in front of the desk.

Lyndon didn't sit, so Kadance didn't either. But he did keep holding her hand.

Dr. Grant kept smiling. "Oh, do I have some stories to tell about this one." He nodded toward Lyndon.

Kadance lifted her brows. "Really? Do tell."

"Now, let's see." Dr. Grant pursed his lips. "What would be the most embarrassing?"

"What did I do in school that was embarrassing?" Lyndon asked.

"Not so much what you *did*."

"I may die of curiosity," Kadance said.

"How about the time—what was his name? Barrows? The time he put a rubber chicken in your cadaver?"

Lyndon rolled his eyes.

"What happened?" Kadance asked.

"Nothing," Dr. Grant said. "Lyndon removed it and continued with his work. The whole class just watched, expecting the great Dr. Vaile here to be outraged. Barrows sputtered, and everyone else burst out laughing. The room didn't calm down for a good five minutes."

"Let me guess," Kadance said. "The great Dr. Vaile continued with his work as if nothing had happened."

"You've got him pegged, my dear."

"Why would this Barrows do that to him anyway?"

Grant looked at Lyndon. "Do you want to tell her?"

"Barrows was juvenile. Likely still is."

Grant turned back to Kadance. "That's not entirely untrue. But he focused so much on Lyndon because he took the high score in every class. Every single one. Plus he was already a doctor when he came here, while everyone else was still busting tail to earn that title."

Kadance shifted closer to Lyndon's side and laid her hand on his arm. The contact sent another quivery jolt through her. Holding his hand was already threatening to overwhelm her—why was she instigating even more contact? "I was just telling him what a nerd he is."

"Three doctorates before the age of thirty," Dr. Grant said. "I didn't feel like I even knew what I was doing until thirty. Maybe even a few years after that." He laughed then pushed off from his desk. "Do either of you want something to drink? Coffee?"

"No, thank you." Kadance looked at Lyndon. She needed to let him take the lead on this visit, though it made her uncomfortable not to be in control.

"This isn't actually a social call," Lyndon said.

"Oh?" Dr. Grant walked around his large wooden desk and sat in his padded leather chair. Multiple framed degrees, certificates, and awards lined the wall behind him like a patchwork quilt. "I thought you'd slowed on your research. I was hoping you'd finally decided to have a life."

"I haven't slowed," Lyndon said.

"You haven't published anything in a while. About a year, right?"

"Just because I haven't published doesn't mean I've slowed."

Dr. Grant pulled his eyebrows together. "Have you come to hear my take on your last email? Unfortunately, I've been bogged down with exams. I haven't looked at it yet."

Kadance noted that Dr. Grant's desk was quite clean, no exams or papers waiting to be graded, nothing on it but a computer monitor on the corner and various acrylic etched awards across the front edge. Lyndon flicked a glance across the desk as well.

"No," Lyndon said. "That's not the area of my research I'm concerned about."

"Have you veered away from Ebola research?"

"On the contrary," Lyndon said. "Have you heard of any thefts recently in the research community?"

"Thefts?"

"Yes. Thefts."

"You mean . . . I'm sorry, I'm confused. Was something of yours stolen? Have you called the police?"

"Have you heard of anything?"

"I'm confused. Are you all right?"

Grant keeps throwing questions back at him, Kadance noted. He'd flipped the tone of the conversation abruptly.

Lyndon clenched his jaw.

Kadance tugged on Lyndon's arm, and he leaned closer so she could whisper in his ear. "He's lying about something."

Lyndon nodded. "I agree." He turned back to Dr. Grant. "What are you avoiding?"

"What do you mean? Lyndon, are you feeling all right?"

"It's quite obvious you're not in the middle of exams," Lyndon said. "Why would you lie about something so innocuous? And why are you being cagey? Has someone threatened you?"

"I have no idea what you're talking about."

Kadance dropped her hand from Lyndon's arm, ready to give him space, but he kept holding her other hand. She resisted the urge to put her hand back on his arm.

Lyndon's voice lowered. "I know you. This is not your standard behavior."

Grant smiled a little, like a parent might smile at a child saying silly things. "Understanding behavior has never been your strong suit."

"I'm also highly observant. I may not always understand the causes of behavior, but I recognize changes."

Dr. Grant said nothing.

"What's going on?" Lyndon pushed.

Kadance guessed Lyndon had lowered his voice to hide his anger, but she heard the dangerous strand threaded into his tone. Based on his expression, Dr. Grant did not hear it.

"This may be hard for you to hear, having been valedictorian at every one of your graduations," Dr. Grant said with that same indulgent tone. "But you're not perfect."

Kadance noticed the slightest flicker of Dr. Grant's eyes and the hint of emotion. "You're jealous," she said to Dr. Grant. "Of Lyndon."

Lyndon looked at her. She kept her focus on Grant, and Lyndon turned back to him as well.

"Is it because of his multiple doctorates?" she asked Dr. Grant. "Has he published more papers? Is he more respected in the medical community?"

Dr. Grant's expression started to slip, darker.

Lyndon just stared at him.

"Three doctorates," Dr. Grant said. "Do you realize how ridiculous that is? He had more credentials than I did when I was teaching him."

Lyndon continued to stare at Grant, but his expression shifted from shocked and confused to furious.

Kadance continued pushing Grant so Lyndon wouldn't have to. "He didn't think himself better than anyone. Why did that bother you?"

"He's always thought of himself as better," Grant said. "He

didn't even socialize. Still doesn't. No one is smart enough to keep up with him." Grant stood. "Well, there is at least *one* person capable of outsmarting you."

"What did you do?" Kadance asked. "Did you steal his research? Take his computer?"

"You mean did I break into his apartment? Of course not. I would never lower myself to that."

Kadance lifted her chin as she deciphered what Grant was not saying. "You didn't break into his apartment, but you did steal from him."

Grant crossed his arms.

"You stole something," Kadance said. "Then you gave it to someone. That's who broke into his apartment. That's who tried to kill him."

Grant dropped his arms. "Kill him?"

"What did you steal?" Kadance asked. "Who did you give it to?"

EIGHT

"WHAT DID YOU STEAL?" Kadance demanded again.

Lyndon finally spoke, voice low and dangerous. "How did you steal it? I showed you all my work. Everything but that."

Grant seemed to be slowly deflating. "There were some notes on your desk in a folder, hidden under other files. I took a picture."

Kadance expected Lyndon to move toward Dr. Grant, maybe even intimidate him physically. He was younger, taller, and certainly much stronger. But he stood there, still holding her hand.

"Why?" Lyndon asked. "I might have shared it with you had you simply asked."

Grant straightened. "Why? So you can show me how much smarter you are?"

"You don't get it, do you?" Kadance said. "He doesn't care."

"You really think that? If he doesn't care, why does he publish so much?"

"To share his findings," Kadance said. "To help everyone." She sighed. She knew this about Lyndon having spent only a short amount of time with him—how did Dr. Grant not know? "Who did you give it to?"

Grant crossed his arms.

"Who!" Kadance demanded.

Grant shifted back, and Lyndon looked at her.

"I . . . don't have a name," Grant stammered.

"How do you communicate?"

"A forum on medical research. Someone messaged me. All I have is a screen name."

"How did you get the picture of Lyndon's research to them?"

"I posted it, and—"

"You *posted* it? On a public forum?"

"Only for about twenty seconds so he could get a screen shot. Then I took it down."

Kadance worked to control her tone. "You say 'he.' Do you have any way to confirm it was a 'he'?"

Grant paused. "His screen name is MedGuy."

"Do you have any idea why this person wanted Lyndon's research? Did they specifically ask for him, or did they ask about Ebola research in general?"

"They . . . uh . . ."

"Can you bring up the forum posts so we can read the exchange?"

"It's been deleted."

Kadance glanced at Lyndon to make sure he was okay with her asking all the questions. He was still glaring at Dr. Grant and still holding her hand. Very odd. Odd behavior for him and odd that it wasn't annoying her. She decided to keep pushing forward so they could get out of there as quickly as possible. "Tell us what you do remember about the exchange," Kadance said to Dr. Grant.

"I don't really remember."

Kadance's voice lowered into a steely tone. "Try."

"I . . ." Dr. Grant dropped into his chair.

"This person flattered you," Kadance said. "Am I right?"

Grant glanced to the side.

Kadance smirked. "This person called you the foremost authority on the subject, or something to that effect, right?"

"I hold a chair on several—"

"That's a yes," Kadance said. "After that, how did they convince you to give them confidential research?"

Grant lifted his chin but didn't look at Lyndon. "If he's so concerned about others and so benevolent, why would he mind giving all his research away?"

"Because it's dangerous," Lyndon growled.

Kadance let her questions about the content of the research go for now and focused on getting everything she could out of Grant. "Answer my question," she said to Grant.

"Who are you to come in here and demand all this anyway?" Dr. Grant said to Kadance.

"I'm not the one who stole intellectual property, Dr. Grant. Right now, I'm serving as a buffer between Lyndon and you. You should be thankful you're talking to me, not him. You should be thankful he has enough self-control to stand there and let me do the talking."

"None of this has anything to do with you."

"You're absolutely right. You should still be thankful I'm here. Now answer my question."

Dr. Grant barely glanced at Lyndon and then back to her. His tone lost the edge of defiance. "He said he works for Doctors Without Borders in Africa and is looking for any help he possibly can to help fight the disease."

Lyndon tightened even more. She squeezed his hand to ask him to keep calm for a few more minutes. He squeezed back. Somewhere deep in the back of her mind, she memorized what this felt like, holding his hand. It would never happen again.

"Did they mention Lyndon specifically?" she asked.

"I . . . Yes, I think so."

"Did they refer to him as Lyndon or as Dr. Vaile?"

Grant paused. "Lyndon Vaile, I think."

"Did they say anything specific about him, other than about his research and his accomplishments in the medical field?"

"I think I . . . remember a conversation about disappointment he hasn't accomplished more."

Kadance realized . . . "You had a lot of conversations over time with this person, am I right?"

"I speak with a lot of colleagues."

"What else did you tell them about Lyndon? How much did they already know?"

"He said he'd read all Lyndon's research, but it wasn't enough. They can't effectively fight the disease."

Man, this person played Grant like a master. "Did they seem to know about Lyndon personally?"

"Just that I'm his teacher."

One of many teachers, one whom he thought he could trust. "What did you tell them about Lyndon?"

"Nothing important."

"What do you mean 'nothing important'?"

"I didn't give out his address, or anything. Whatever happened isn't my fault."

"What *exactly* did you tell them?" Kadance demanded. "Did you tell them he keeps his research at home? That he buys storage units for a living?"

"None of that is a big deal."

"Someone tried to kill him at a storage unit auction. Then someone ransacked his apartment and tried to kill him again."

Grant's eyes got wide, and the wrinkles in his forehead deepened.

Kadance looked at Lyndon, and her voice was quieter, softer. "I think that's about all he has that's useful. We should get out of here."

Lyndon nodded. Then he turned to walk out of Grant's office, still holding her hand. Kadance looked down to make sure Mac kept trotting along beside her. She loved that Mac never minded when she had to be aggressive; he saw another kinder side to her, a side she really wanted to believe was who she truly was.

They were out of the building before Lyndon let go of her hand. "I'm sorry."

"Are you all right?"

"No." He was silent the rest of the walk to the car, and his normal expression of bland intellectual curiosity had turned dark like storm clouds about to erupt.

Kadance watched their surroundings carefully. She didn't like Lyndon being out in the open like this, especially so close to home.

They got in her car, and she started the engine. "Are you ready to get out of town now?" she asked.

He didn't answer. She started driving and let him simmer for a few minutes.

Finally, he asked, "Will you drive around for a little bit?"

"Okay." She glanced over at him. He glared out the windshield, as if barely containing the urge to throw a fist through the glass. The change bothered her—not because he made her at all nervous, but because this wasn't him.

"Are you okay?" she asked.

"Yes."

"You're a horrible liar."

He took a controlled breath. "I know."

"You said talking is good for you, right? It helps you work things out."

He nodded.

She glanced over at him again and caught something more than the anger. "You're hurt. Let yourself feel that."

He looked over at her. "I'm enraged. He put people in danger. You could have easily been shot twice now."

"You're hurt too. I can see it. It's okay to be both."

He ran both hands through his hair.

"You're not used to so much emotion," she said.

"I've purposefully built my life on logic, not emotion."

"Because emotion is too hard."

He said nothing.

"But if you don't deal with it, it'll eat you alive."

He took a breath, slower. He let a few seconds pass. "This is my weakness—understanding people."

"You can't find the logic in why he would be so jealous and so willing to betray with almost no cajoling."

"He's the only person with whom I've shared any of my work."

"And he's probably the only person who understands how brilliant you are, and so the only one with cause to feel that level of jealousy."

He looked over at her. "You do have a scientific mind."

She laughed under her breath. "I just have more experience with people."

"The fact remains that we don't know if my theory is factual or foolhardy."

"Can I ask what that theory is? You give away all your other findings, right? What made you keep this one to yourself?"

"It's a hypothesis on its way to theory. Not ready to be shared." He paused. "And it could put people in danger. I can't see all the angles yet."

"How could a scientific hypothesis put anyone in danger?"

He hesitated.

"I walked into this on my own, remember? You don't need to protect me. I'm probably in the crosshairs already anyway. I should understand what we're talking about."

He sighed. He sounded not so much frustrated, more resigned. "I started looking into the origins more closely, hoping to find something helpful, some common bond to all the various viruses within the genus *Ebolavirus*."

"Did you find a common bond?"

"I think so."

"What is it?"

He paused. "I think Ebola is man-made."

NINE

"MAN-MADE?" KADANCE ASKED. "Why would someone do that? Is that even possible?"

"Yes, it's entirely possible, given the correct knowledge base and motivation. As to what would cause that motivation, I have no idea."

"But . . . most major diseases have been around a long time, right? How long has Ebola been around?"

"Since 1976. And we can pinpoint where it first manifested—near the Ebola River in the Congo."

"Could it have just been in nature but dormant, and only when people disturbed the wildlife did it infect humans?"

"Something to that effect is usually the consensus. But there are several points that keep bringing me back to my hypothesis: One. If it was naturally occurring, I think it's likely it would have been found in more than that one specific area. Two. If it was naturally occurring, it would have likely found its way into human populations long before 1976. Three. It was first found in primates, so some infer that humans simply didn't come into contact with these specific primates until 1976. But not all the strains are found in primates, so I hypothesize that it did not originally manifest in primates but that someone used them as test subjects for certain strains."

"So, you think someone made the original strain as well as all the others?"

"Perhaps one or two are mutations that occurred sporadically after the initial virus was released, but yes, I think most of the strains were designed. Someone experimenting, perfecting."

"But who?"

"Someone with a strong understanding of microbiology."

Kadance pulled off the road into a parking lot and stopped. "Based on everything that's happened, it sounds like your hypothesis is right."

"I can't make that assumption. It's the most logical leap, but what if I take action based on incorrect assumptions? It could make everything worse."

"That's why I say you should just leave town, disappear."

"And what if someone plans on spreading the disease? Using it as a weapon? I can't walk away and do nothing."

Kadance rested her head back on her seat.

"I'm not asking you for anything," Lyndon said. "You should leave town now, before you get any deeper into this."

She stared out the windshield at the beige stucco front of a bank for a few seconds.

He reached into the back seat, surely for his bag.

Kadance set her hand on his arm. "No. I'm not leaving you here in some random parking lot. You can't go back for your truck. I'll drive you where you need to go—just tell me where."

He paused. "I can't ask you to do that."

"You're not asking. It comes down to the same thing—you won't just disappear and let this drop for fear you could've helped others, and I won't leave when I can help you."

He looked at her.

She took her hand off his arm and put the car back in drive. That same quivery sensation had shot up her arm at their contact, and she wasn't sure how to react to it. "Where to?" She glanced at Mac in the back seat in the rearview mirror. He was sitting there with those big, round amber eyes looking right back at her. When Lyndon didn't answer, she added, "It's important to you to help if you possibly can. Then you should take whatever help you can get so you have the best chance of helping others."

He nodded.

"Where to?"

"I've been thinking about talking with an African Studies professor. I met him when I was at school at UCLA."

"Do you know where he is?"

"He retired. But I know where his neighborhood is. He mentioned it in a random conversation one time."

"How long ago was that?"

"Several years."

And he still remembered. She fought the urge to roll her eyes. "You don't think he's moved?"

"It's a family home. I don't think he'll leave until he's dead."

She pulled up to the street. "Give me directions."

He told her which way to go, and she drove.

"I'm impressed," he said.

"Impressed about what?"

"How you handled Dr. Grant."

"I was hoping you didn't mind that I kind of stepped in."

"I was at a loss once I realized he was hiding something. I appreciated your help."

"I think you just needed a few minutes to process that your friend wasn't really your friend."

"I think that's accurate."

"And understandable. You don't let yourself get close to people, and so being betrayed by one of the few people you did have some kind of relationship with hurt even worse."

"Anger is a more accurate word than hurt, I think."

"You're angry because you're hurt."

He looked over at her. Then he lowered his gaze and looked away.

She had the strangest urge to reach over and hold his hand. She ignored the urge. "So why infectious diseases anyway? Why did you choose that as your field of study?"

"I chose my fields of study specifically so I could better understand *Ebolavirus*."

"Is there some kind of personal connection there?"

He turned to look out the side window. "My parents died of Ebola. They were working for Doctors Without Borders in the Congo."

"That explains your dedication. Were you close to them?" Then she added, "You don't have to talk about this if you don't want to."

There was a long pause, so long she assumed it meant he did not want to talk about it. She was not going to push him.

"We were very close," he said.

She was quiet, letting him talk as much or as little as he wanted.

"I've always been like my mother—a little blunt sometimes, coming from a sense of hyper logic, not rudeness, which can make people uncomfortable, but also very reserved with anything of personal importance. She never thought she'd marry, until she met my dad. Her focus was research, but she joined Doctors Without Borders to be with him."

"What about your dad?"

The corner of Lyndon's mouth curved. "He was audacious. He had a miraculous ability to stop arguments, cause laughter, and make people love him."

"They sound like they balanced each other."

He nodded and left it at that. He was definitely like his mother.

A little while later, they pulled into an old neighborhood of California bungalows.

"Do you know which house?" Kadance asked.

"Drive slow. I'll recognize his car."

She paused at the next cross-street so he could look down the road and try to spot the car.

At the next street, he pointed to a 1950s Chevy, pale blue and white, in the driveway. "There."

She made the turn. "That's how you met—you both have a thing for 1950s Chevys, right?"

"He ran me down one day when he saw me getting into my truck."

She parked along the street, and they both got out of the car. She opened the back door, pulled Mac's bowl out of her bag, and dumped some of her bottled water into the bowl. She set the bowl carefully on the seat. "We'll be just a little bit, buddy." Then she rolled the window down, low enough for air and for him to get out if he needed to do his business.

"He probably won't mind if you bring him inside," Lyndon said.

"Mac will be okay." She stroked his head and down his back. He stood on his toes and arched his back, and then wagged his tail in that way of his, a quick wave back and forth.

Kadance and Lyndon walked up to the front door of the cute California bungalow. The tree in the front yard rustled in the breeze, and a wind chime somewhere tinkled.

Lyndon knocked. Then he turned to Kadance. "Are you sure Mac will be okay?"

"Trust me, he's fine." She glanced back at the car. He had his paws up on the door, watching them out the window. She could hear his meow from here.

Mac was fine, though maybe a little annoyed to be excluded, and everything in the neighborhood that she could see was fine. But for some reason, she felt hyperalert.

A woman walked by on the sidewalk, and her little dog yapped at Mac. Mac kept watching Kadance and Lyndon. Or maybe he was watching something about the house. She took another good look around. The curtains were closed, so she couldn't see inside. Only the one car was in the narrow driveway. She couldn't hear anything from inside the house.

Lyndon knocked again.

Finally, the door opened. An older man with dark skin and gray sprinkled into his short black hair stood in the doorway. "May I help you?"

Lyndon's eyebrows twitched together. "Professor Ibekwe. It's Lyndon Vaile."

Professor Ibekwe didn't answer, but the muscles in his neck looked tight.

Kadance scanned as much as she could see inside his house. The bookshelves and furniture in the front room looked tidy. She glanced up and down the street. Nothing appeared out of place. She set her hand on Lyndon's forearm, ready to yank him out of the way if needed.

Lyndon glanced at her and then back to Professor Ibekwe. "I hope you don't mind my showing up like this. I remembered where you mentioned your family home is, but I don't have a phone number for you now that you're retired. I wanted to see if I could have just a few minutes of your time."

Professor Ibekwe opened his mouth but paused. Then he said, "Of course. Your friend can wait on the porch and enjoy the breeze."

Kadance smiled. "I'd like a few minutes in the AC if you don't mind." A voice in the back of her mind didn't want Lyndon going in there. She didn't have a rational reason to ask him not to, but she certainly wasn't going to let him go in alone.

Professor Ibekwe smiled a tight smile and stepped back to allow them inside.

Kadance scanned every corner of the house that she could see—nothing but old, shiny wood floors running down a center hall, plaster walls painted a creamy color, and a mixture of antique and new furniture.

They followed the professor into the front room. He took a seat in an armchair in front of the wall of bookshelves, and she and Lyndon sat on a small sofa backed against the front window. Kadance stayed on the edge of her seat.

Lyndon glanced at her.

"What can I help you with?" Professor Ibekwe asked.

"I hear a hint of an accent," Kadance said. "May I ask where you're from originally?"

"My parents were born in Nigeria. I lived in Angola until I was ten years old and my father moved us here." He turned to Lyndon. "What can I help you with?"

"Do you know much about the peoples living along the Congo River?"

Professor Ibekwe hesitated. "Very little. My focus has always been northern Africa."

Lyndon's eyebrows twitched.

"You're from central Africa, right?" Kadance asked. If she remembered correctly, the Democratic Republic of the Congo was almost smack in the middle of the continent and bordered Angola. Plus, as an African Studies professor, surely he knew *something* about the area.

"It's been a very long time," Professor Ibekwe said.

"If I remember correctly, you've taken several trips back over the years," Lyndon said.

"Not for a while. There's so much turmoil and change in that area of the world, it's hard to keep up."

Finally, Kadance's unease forced her to her feet. "We should get going."

Lyndon stood as well. He asked Professor Ibekwe, "Is something wrong?"

Kadance took Lyndon's hand. "Let's go." She walked a few steps toward the center hall, and Lyndon followed. Then she paused at a sound coming from the dining room on the other side of the entryway.

TEN

"LEAVING SO SOON?"

Lyndon stood in front of Kadance as a man walked out of Professor Ibekwe's dining room. He itched to reach for the gun in his waistband, but the man already had a gun in his hand. Lyndon couldn't grab his before the man shot. He wouldn't risk it with Kadance here.

There was a creak in the old wood floors from down the center hall, and Lyndon peripherally saw another man walking toward them.

"Let him go," Professor Ibekwe said from behind them in the front sitting room. "They don't know anything."

The man in front of Lyndon answered. "You weren't much help figuring that out, now were you?"

Lyndon cataloged all the details he could to try to formulate a way to get out, or at least get Kadance out. The man in front of him wore a scruffy reddish-brown beard; a black leather jacket with several patches on it, which all appeared to be related to some kind of motorcycle club; and worn jeans. His gun appeared to be a simple Taurus 9 mm—inexpensive but still did the job. The man approaching from the side was a carbon copy except black hair and beard and a bigger gut.

"My fight isn't with you," Lyndon said to the apparent leader in front of him.

"No one said anything about a fight." His voice was scratchy, probably from years of cigarette smoking. "Did we, boys?"

Several voices affirmed. Lyndon noted the number of voices and the direction from which each voice came—six men, all from various directions and not all yet visible, surely all listening and watching from around corners.

"I meant," Lyndon said, "that you were hired. You're not the one behind all this."

The man's bushy eyebrows disappeared behind his bushy mane of hair. He nodded. "Very good." Then he cocked his head. "That's not gonna help you none, though."

"What would help us?"

"Answer my questions, and I'll let you be on your way."

Kadance squeezed his hand. He could just see peripherally that she was watching the man approaching slowly from down the hall as well as Professor Ibekwe. He took her squeeze to mean that they shouldn't trust what the man told him. He gently squeezed back in agreement.

"I'm not sure what you think I know," Lyndon said.

The man took a piece of paper out of a pocket inside his vest. "Write down exactly your theories, any evidence you have to back up your theories, and anything else of importance."

"What theories?"

The man shook the folds out of the paper and read something. "About Ebola."

"I've published everything I've found. Tell your benefactor to read the scientific journals."

The man's forearm rippled as he tightened his grip on his gun. "Stop playing games."

Kadance's words that he was a terrible liar came back to him. "I don't know what you're talking about."

The man aimed his gun at Lyndon's head. Lyndon stared back

at him. If the man shot Lyndon, that would likely give Kadance an opportunity to pull the Glock out of her waistband and maybe get out the door to her car.

The man lifted his chin, and then he shifted his weapon to aim at Kadance.

Lyndon tried to shift in front of her, but the man who'd slowly approached from down the hall grabbed him by the arm and pulled him away from her.

"We can't be blowing your valuable brains," the leader said. "But hers splattered all over the wall, I think, would add a nice accent to the place, don't you think?"

"Don't," Lyndon demanded.

Kadance stood there, not even tightened in fear, gaze calmly focused on the man in front of her.

"Let her go," Professor Ibekwe pleaded.

Some small part of Lyndon was thankful Professor Ibekwe obviously hadn't instigated this, but a larger part of him felt guilty that Ibekwe had been involved in this due to an old casual friendship with Lyndon. Maybe Dr. Grant had even reached out after they left earlier and let his contact know Lyndon was still in LA and talking with old professors.

Kadance barely glanced at Lyndon, and somehow, in that glance, he understood what she was about to do.

She exploded forward toward the leader, and Lyndon charged at the man in the hall.

He used his shoulder to tackle the man, and they slid down the hall across the smooth floors.

"No." Professor Ibekwe's protests and hurried footsteps followed him.

Straddling the black-haired man, Lyndon punched him in the face and knocked him out. He stood, ready to attack another of the mercenaries, but then Professor Ibekwe moved into his line of sight. He was being held in a choke with a gun pointed to his head.

The man holding him was dressed much the same as the others but younger with a beard not quite so scruffy.

"Don't hurt him," Lyndon said.

"That's entirely up to you."

Lyndon took a quick count of the men around him—the black-haired man on the floor knocked out, the younger one holding Ibekwe on his right, and a man with a handlebar mustache on his left doing the talking. He'd hoped more of them would focus on him, underestimate the beautiful woman, and leave her in just the hands of the leader.

"Are you ready to talk?" Handlebar Mustache asked.

"If you want me to talk, you have to let the professor go."

Professor Ibekwe's eyes were wide with fear. Though his gaze was on Lyndon, he didn't look like he was really seeing anything, surely too focused on the gun aimed at his head.

Lyndon added, "The professor is a gentle person. He's innocent and not involved in this. He's of no help to you."

"Why'd you come here if he's no help?"

Lyndon clenched his jaw. *All right, I can't lie. I have to come up with something else.* He used a calm, almost monotone voice. "Zaire Ebolavirus is more commonly known as Ebola virus or just Ebola, but what I'm researching is the genus *Ebolavirus*. There are several known species within that genus, most of which cause severe hemorrhagic fever. The Ebola virus genome is a single-stranded RNA, which is about 19,000 nucleotides long—"

The younger man holding Professor Ibekwe said, "What does all that have to do with anything?" He shook the barrel of his gun at Lyndon, as if to say, *Hurry it up.*

Lyndon surged forward, grabbed the gun in his left hand, and used his forearm to rake the man's elbow upward with enough force to make it pop out of its socket. He stripped the gun out of his hand. He aimed it at Handlebar Mustache on his left just as the man aimed a 9 mm at him.

The younger man he'd disarmed stumbled to the side, holding his elbow and cursing.

Lyndon shifted in front of the professor. "Out the back door," he ordered Ibekwe.

"Not if you want to live," Handlebar Mustache said.

"My brain is too valuable to lose," Lyndon said. "That's already been made clear."

The man sneered.

"It's either shoot through me or let the professor go." With his gaze on the mercenary, Lyndon tilted his head toward Ibekwe and muttered, "Go. Now."

Ibekwe stood frozen for a couple of seconds and then shifted back a step.

Handlebar Mustache aimed his gun lower, at Lyndon's thigh. "I don't have to shoot you in the head."

"And if you hit a major artery and I die of exsanguination? Will that satisfy your benefactor?"

Handlebar Mustache gripped his weapon tighter, and his forearm rippled.

Ibekwe's footsteps shuffled through the kitchen toward the back door.

Handlebar Mustache tried to get around Lyndon, but Lyndon shifted in his way, blocking the doorway to the kitchen. "I'll make you a deal. You let the professor and the woman go, and I'll give myself up."

"No one's going anywhere."

"Then I'm not talking."

Handlebar Mustache looked at his younger friend still cursing about his dislocated elbow. "Get him!"

Lyndon braced himself for an attack, but the younger man ran through the kitchen after Professor Ibekwe. Lyndon hurtled toward him and grabbed his collar.

But then Lyndon lost his grip and yanked to a stop himself. Handlebar Mustache had followed him and grabbed his shoulder.

He had Lyndon off-balance enough that he was able to strip the gun out of his hand and also take the gun out of his waistband.

Lyndon regained his balance and punched the younger man with the broken elbow in the face, and he stumbled back against the cabinets. He cursed and held his nose while blood streamed out between his fingers.

Lyndon barely glanced at the professor. "Go!" Before he could see what the professor did, Lyndon turned back to Handlebar Mustache, who was aiming his own gun at him and grinning.

Lyndon swung his hand around, wrapping his arm around Handlebar Mustache's gun hand, and drove an upset punch into his gut.

While the man doubled over, Lyndon took the second to look over his shoulder at the professor. Ibekwe was staring at him.

"Go!"

"Come with me."

The younger man at the cabinets pushed himself toward them. Rage festered on his face, and spittle ran down his chin.

Lyndon let go of Handlebar Mustache and shoved Professor Ibekwe out the door.

He heard Handlebar Mustache coming at him from behind. Instead of striking either of them, perhaps pulling one into the other's path, Lyndon slammed the door shut and stood against it.

A fist landed in his gut, and another snapped across his jaw. Lyndon held himself against the door, blocking it.

Footsteps pounded down the wooden stairs of the back porch.

Lyndon's sense of relief that Professor Ibekwe was safe was short-lived. *Where is Kadance?*

ELEVEN

KADANCE SLAMMED an elbow into the bearded man's nose. Then she skirted around the dining table, away from the footsteps approaching from behind. She rounded the table as two more men entered the room.

The bearded leader held his nose and cursed. Blood seeped out from between his fingers, and his voice was muffled by his hand. "Get her!"

There'd been six voices, she was sure. There were three here. *That means Lyndon is dealing with three.* Plus, she was sure he was doing all he could to protect the professor. Something deep inside her started to panic, a feeling she hadn't felt—hadn't been allowed to feel—since she was a small child. She stomped the feeling down and focused.

The men moved slowly around the table from both sides.

She left her Glock tucked behind her back. She made her expression twist in fear, something she'd perfected years ago. "Don't hurt me."

The man whose nose she'd broken had taken a cloth napkin from a drawer in the sideboard and had wiped most of the blood off his face, though there was still a lot in his beard. "No need to hurt anyone," he crooned.

The men approaching her from around the table paused.

"Just give me some information," the leader said. "And all this is over."

"I don't know," Kadance simpered—goodness, she hated that sound. "Lyndon's the scientist. I don't understand any of it."

"Just tell me some of the things he's said, even if you didn't understand it."

She guessed he was assuming the same thing Dr. Grant had, that she and Lyndon were dating.

"He said something last night about . . ." She scrunched up her face. "Bola?"

The man on her right rolled his eyes. *That's right, think I'm an idiot. Good job.*

"Who hired you?" she asked the leader.

"None of your concern."

"You don't know?"

"Tell me what he said about Ebola."

"Why are you taking orders from someone you don't know?"

"What did he say?"

"Do you know where they are? What they look like?"

He lowered his brows in a scowl.

"Do you even know if it's a man or woman?" she asked. She didn't trust Dr. Grant's assessment of gender.

"Grab her," he barked.

The men shifted forward.

Kadance listened carefully to the other sounds in the house. The lack of sounds. If Lyndon were still fighting, she'd be able to hear something. She knew with absolute certainty that he hadn't gotten out, hadn't left her. One likely cause for the quiet remained.

The men continued to move toward her.

She pulled the Glock from her waistband and fired at the man on her left. He stumbled back from the hit to his shoulder. The other man lurched forward and grabbed her right hand.

The leader laughed. "Need better aim."

She glanced at the man's shoulder, bare from his sleeveless shirt. The bullet had gone directly through the center of the tiger's eye on his tattoo. Inwardly, she smirked. On the outside, she created a distressed expression. She let the other man disarm her and pretended to be defeated.

"Where's Lyndon?" she asked.

"Let's go for a visit." The leader turned and led the way out of the dining room.

She allowed the other man to escort her down the hall with a big hand clamped around her upper arm. Apparently, they were going to leave the man she'd shot to fend for himself.

"So, you don't know who is behind all this?" Kadance asked the bushy back of the leader's head.

He continued walking.

"Why are you doing this person's bidding rather than come up with your own plans?"

Still no answer.

She looked over at the man escorting her. "Is he not smart enough?"

He pressed his lips together.

That's a yes.

In the kitchen, the man holding her arm took the sheathed knife at her hip and her phone, dropped her into a chair, tied her hands together behind the back of the chair, and then tied her to the chair at the waist. Lyndon was seated in the next chair. His lip was bloody, and he sat crooked. He was tied the same as she was. He still held his head high, with anger in his eyes. The professor was not in the room, and something told her Lyndon had gotten him out. Careful not to let any of the others see, she winked at him.

"Where's the other guy?" the leader demanded.

"He got away," a younger man, not so scruffy as the others, said. "Should I go after him?"

The leader hesitated while he looked around the room. One man had partially congealed blood in his beard and an elbow that was either broken or dislocated. A man with a thick black mane of hair was leaning against the kitchen cabinets wearing a groggy expression like he'd just woken, and his jaw was swelling. Kadance stifled a smirk—surely, they hadn't anticipated the nerdy scientist being such a good fighter. But then, neither had she. Sure, she'd seen he could shoot, but fight?

"No," the leader said. "I scared him to the edge of death. He'll hide in a corner somewhere rather than going to the cops." He faced Lyndon but addressed his men. "How much have you gotten out of him?"

Silence.

He turned away from Lyndon and looked around at his men. "Well?"

They glanced at each other and remained silent.

"Nothing?" the leader demanded. "Three of you handling one geek, and you got nothing?"

"He said something about genus and genome."

"And hemorrhagic," one of the others offered.

"What's any of that mean?" the leader said.

"Did the chick give you anything?" the younger man asked.

The leader turned to Lyndon. "Start talking. Now."

"What would you like to know?" Lyndon asked.

The leader grabbed Lyndon's shirt in his fist.

Lyndon stared him in the eye. "Can I help it if your men don't understand what I told them?"

The leader lifted his hand and back-fisted Lyndon across the face. Blood splattered from his mouth. Then the leader drove his fist into Lyndon's gut.

Kadance's body tightened with fury.

The leader lifted his fist, obviously about to punch Lyndon in the face. "Talk!"

"Go ahead and knock me out," Lyndon said. "That'll be helpful."

The leader sneered and turned away toward his men. "We need to move him."

"What do you want to do with the girl?"

"We could take her along. She'd be awful fun."

Lyndon shifted forward in his chair, and the muscles in his arms strained.

Kadance shook her head at him infinitesimally.

He stopped moving, but his chest and arms remained tight and strained.

"I think we should just dispose of her," one of the others said.

The leader glanced back at Kadance and Lyndon, apparently to make sure they were securely tied up, and then turned and led his men into the hall.

Kadance started working to dislocate her shoulder so she could get her arms up and over her head.

"We only have a week," one of the men in the hall said.

"We don't have a week."

"That's when the State of the Union is."

"We need to make sure the super-virus is released successfully." The leader sounded irritated. "And make sure it takes down the corrupt, illegitimate charade of a government."

"What about the vaccine?" one of the others asked.

"That guy in there is the only one in the country, maybe the world, who has the right knowledge."

Kadance listened but couldn't take the time to process what they were talking about. She only paused when the doggy flap on the lower part of the back door shifted. Mac popped his head through the opening.

"Good boy," Kadance whispered.

Mac walked into the kitchen and sat at her feet looking up at her.

She nodded toward the counter. "Up."

He looked over at the counter behind him. Then he turned and silently jumped up.

Lyndon whispered, "What're you doing?"

Kadance kept talking to Mac, making sure to keep his focus.

She just hoped he understood what she wanted when she wasn't able to make hand motions. She stared at the steak knife on the counter and made a sweeping motion with her head.

Mac looked at her and then at the knife. When he looked at her again, she made the same sweeping motion with her head. He turned back to the knife and lightly touched the handle with his paw.

"Good boy," she whispered.

He tapped it a few more times with his paw, and it clattered to the floor.

The younger man walked back into the kitchen and looked at Mac on the counter. Then he rolled his eyes and walked back out to the hall. Kadance heard him say, "Just a cat." Then the conversation about what to do with their captives continued.

"That's my good boy," she whispered to Mac. She carefully stood, leaned forward as much as she could so the chair wouldn't scrape the floor, and knelt. Then she managed to get to her side without making any noise. She could just barely reach her fingers to brush the floor.

"Scoot back about an inch more," Lyndon murmured.

She did as he said, and her fingertips grazed the knife handle. She used her legs to twist a bit, pivoting on the corner of the chair and smashing her right arm, so she could get her fingers around the knife handle. Finally, she gripped it and started sawing the serrated edge against the rope.

Lyndon glanced between the doorway to the hall and her progress with the knife.

"Almost," he said.

The rope snapped. She got back to her knees and cut the rope at her waist.

She silently stood, set the chair out of the way, and walked around behind Lyndon. As she cut his ropes, she whispered in his ear, "Out the back door."

He nodded and stood.

She walked over to grab Mac.

A loud curse came from the doorway to the hall. "They're loose," the younger man called over his shoulder and then drew a gun.

Kadance threw the knife in her hand, and it sunk into his chest. He crumpled to the floor and gasped for air.

Lyndon stared at the man dying in front of them.

"Get out," she demanded. "Take Mac."

Another man came through the doorway and almost fell over his friend.

Kadance grabbed all the knives out of the block on the counter. As the man reached for his gun, she hurled a knife at him. It wedged into his chest, more centered than the last man, and he stumbled back against the wall and then fell, dead.

"Get. Out!" she ordered Lyndon.

He snatched Mac off the counter and opened the back door.

Now, she was sure he'd escape and have no problem leaving her. He'd seen the side of her she'd been running from for a long time. She couldn't blame him for running away from her too. She was just thankful he'd grabbed Mac to get him out safely.

Then his footsteps stopped. "Let's go!"

She glanced back to see him waiting at the open door. Waiting for her.

"Shoot her!"

She turned back to see the leader and another man drawing their guns and aiming at her. One knife in each hand, she threw them at the men and ran for the door. As they made it outside, she heard the men drop to the floor.

They ran around the house to her car. Lyndon held Mac tightly to his chest. As they jumped in the car, Kadance watched the front door. She'd taken down four of the six. The one she'd shot in the shoulder was very possibly still out of commission, but that left one able-bodied man.

She shoved her key in the ignition, started the engine, and slammed on the gas.

A block away, she took a breath, but still watched the rearview mirror. The last man could follow them, or a neighbor could have called the police.

After several blocks and many turns, she let herself calm down.

"Are you all right?" Lyndon asked.

She couldn't look at him.

"Mac's fine," he said, and she realized he still had him on his lap and was stroking his soft fur.

She closed her eyes for a second. Then she finally spoke, while keeping her gaze on the road. "Thank you for making sure he got out safely."

"He saved our lives." He stroked Mac again. Then he lightly touched her shoulder. "Are you all right?"

She pulled away from his touch.

TWELVE

LYNDON TOOK HIS HAND AWAY from Kadance's shoulder. He set it on Mac's fluffy fur instead. Mac watched Kadance with those big amber eyes, as if analyzing her.

Kadance didn't look at either of them. But she didn't seem particularly upset. Her hands didn't shake, her expression didn't twist, and her breathing remained steady. But then he realized there was a change. Something in her eyes was flat. She had her barriers up, like when they'd first met.

He decided not to push her. That was always the last thing he wanted anyone to do to him, and yet it always seemed to be exactly what people wanted to do.

Instead, he turned his mind toward analyzing all he'd learned in a short period of time.

Super-virus, they'd said.

State of the Union.

Take down the United States government.

He was possibly the only one "with the right knowledge."

One week.

He absentmindedly stroked Mac and stared out the windshield, eyes unfocused. He shifted the different elements of the situation around in his mind like puzzle pieces, trying to make a coherent picture.

Several minutes passed.

He continued staring out the windshield. "They want to kill the entire House, the Senate, and the president. What's the motivation?"

Kadance glanced at him.

"Obviously to cripple the government," he said. "But what do they have to gain from it?"

Kadance continued driving. He finally focused on the road and realized they were on the freeway.

He turned to Kadance. "Did they say anything to you when we were separated?"

She finally looked at him, met his eyes. Then she turned back to the road. "Where do you want me to drop you?"

He drew his eyebrows together. Then he mentally shook his thoughts and tried to shift the puzzle out of the way and focus on her. "I'm sorry. You didn't want to be involved in this in the first place. You can leave me wherever you want."

She stared at him for a couple of seconds. "I just killed four men in front of you, and I shot another one who might die."

He looked back at her. Seeing that had admittedly shocked him, images that would stay in his mind the rest of his life, no matter how much he tried to rid himself of them. "You let them catch you," he said. "Didn't you?"

Her eyes widened slightly, and then she turned back to the road.

"I think this is the most genuine emotion I've ever seen from you," he said.

Silence.

She passed a big SUV and got back in the right lane.

Finally, she looked at him. "Aren't you horrified?"

"Of course."

"Then why are you still sitting there?"

"The vehicle is moving."

She glanced at him with creased brows, and then she laughed one weak laugh. It sounded like she wasn't sure whether to laugh or hit him. It wasn't the first time he'd caused that reaction.

"I'm right," he said. "Aren't I? You let them catch you."

She hesitated and then nodded once.

"Because you knew they'd bring you to me," he said.

"The inexperienced always corral their prisoners."

"You wanted to make sure I was all right, gauge the situation, and formulate a way to get us out. Both of us."

She nodded once.

"You could've gotten out yourself."

She clenched her jaw.

"But the thought didn't even occur to you," he said.

She didn't answer.

He lowered his voice. "I know what you did was hard on you. Much harder than you'll ever admit, even to yourself. But I want you to understand how I see it all. You were willing to sacrifice yourself to get me out. You barely know me, and you certainly don't owe me anything. And yet, you would've died to get me out." He stroked Mac's soft fur. "And you would've done the same thing for Mac."

She gave no reaction.

"That's how I see what just happened," he said. "And you know I'm not lying. Like you said, I'm a bad liar."

Quiet.

Her expression strained.

He turned his head to look out the side window, to allow her some small measure of privacy. He wanted to reach over to her, hold her, but he knew she didn't want that. She'd surely hit him if he tried. And holding her would be too much for him, too dangerous.

They drove for miles.

Though he didn't look, he was acutely aware of her, of each breath. He swore he could feel as her emotions calmed, or more accurately, as she got them under that harsh control of hers.

By the time she spoke again, they were out of the city on Route 40. "They were anti-government militia," she said. "They were hired anonymously. They had no idea who they were working for, not even a gender."

Lyndon nodded. "Obviously, it's someone with a medical science background, but that doesn't give us much to go on." Then he paused. "Is this us or me?"

"You mean am I ditching you?"

"You don't have to get involved."

"I am involved. I won't let what happened be for nothing. I'm seeing this through."

He felt relieved, which he hadn't anticipated. Typically, he preferred to work alone. "I assume the militia group was involved because they were told the government was going to get taken down."

"But was that the truth, or just something fed to them to get a desired behavior?"

"I think it was true. They weren't sophisticated but also not idiots. They wouldn't have gone to such lengths without some kind of confirmation of the plan. I can't possibly know what that confirmation was, but I think the best course of action is to assume there is a super-virus and the plan is to infect the House, Senate, and president, to kill all of them at once, and topple the government."

"It would have to be an almost immediate death. Or at least an immediate incapacitation."

"So there wouldn't be time to set up a secondary leadership."

She nodded.

"It would have to be the deadliest strain ever seen. And surely, they've made sure there is no cure, no effective treatment, and ideally, it would be highly contagious."

"Obviously, your theory that it was man-made is correct," she said. "And someone thinks you have the knowledge base to stop them. Perhaps they think you have some idea how to make a vaccine."

"My work doesn't focus on vaccine creation. I focus more on theory—patterns, histories, behaviors."

"Maybe you worry them because you've already hypothesized that they exist. No one else is even thinking that. You're so adept at those patterns and behaviors, you'll be able to recognize them."

"Recognize the mastermind, you mean."

"Understanding your enemy, knowing how they tick, is how you beat them. This person isn't even on anyone else's radar."

He lifted his chin. Knowing the disease was like knowing the person, and no one understood the disease better than he did.

He took a breath. "One week."

"One week."

"Is this even possible?"

"Wars have been fought and won in a week."

"One war—the Six-Day War between Israel and Egypt, Jordan, and Syria."

She smirked. "One war that you know of."

He liked that smirk. And not just because it made her dark eyes more alluring. If she was confident, she had good reason to be.

"We should fly," he said. "Get to DC as fast as possible."

"I can't fly."

"Why?"

"Multiple reasons. But I'll take you to an airport, and I'll get there as fast as I can." Then she added, "Maybe you shouldn't try flying either."

"Because of what happened at Professor Ibekwe's house."

She nodded. "He's gone to the police by now. If the police have a BOLO out for you, they'll pick you up and hold you for questioning, and we can't be sure they'll let you go. You shouldn't risk it."

"We'll take turns and drive through the night. We should be able to do it in about . . . forty hours or so."

"Less." She pressed harder on the gas pedal.

She drove for a while longer. She didn't even stop to check a map, as if she knew the major freeways across the entire country. He let his mind slip back into shifting around the puzzle pieces.

The sky grew darker.

"You should sleep for a while," he said. "I'll drive."

"You should know some things," she said. "You need to know—you deserve to know—who you're getting involved with. You've guessed some of my background, but you don't really have any idea who you're dealing with."

THIRTEEN

"YOU DON'T HAVE TO TELL ME ANYTHING," Lyndon said.

Kadance took a slow breath. "I have to." It wouldn't be fair to him to let him get entangled with her without understanding what he was getting into.

Lyndon quietly let her organize her thoughts.

"I was in the CIA, Special Activities Center."

"Covert operations," he said. "Black ops."

She nodded. Sometimes the fact that he seemed to know at least a little about everything made talking to him easier. She wasn't used to talking to people, and she liked that she didn't have to spell out every detail for him. "I specialized as a sniper."

"That's why you have that gun in your back seat and why you spotted the shooter at the storage facility."

"It's a McMillan TAC-50 sniper rifle. I've considered getting rid of it several times, but I feel unprepared without it."

"Unprepared for what?"

"I entered service just out of high school. I've completed a lot of missions." She looked over at him. "I've killed a lot of people."

He nodded.

She turned back to the road. "I was positioned in the Middle East for years. I was alone, entrenched in cultures so different from America. I speak fluent Farsi and Arabic, and with my coloring, I could blend in pretty well."

"They left you there a long time."

She closed her eyes for a second and nodded. She'd felt alone, had feared she'd been abandoned at times when she received no communication for months.

"It was hard on you," he said.

"I kept reminding myself of what I was there for—to protect not only our troops and our country but the innocent people trapped by evil regimes and terrorist groups. But some days were much harder than others. I could take action only when orders came in. There was so much I couldn't stop . . ."

"Tell me," he said.

She glanced at him.

"I think you'll feel better if you tell me the details," he said.

She wasn't so sure about that, but she'd started this and needed to follow through. "I spent years with certain villages. They'd give me a backstory and place me, and I had to blend in. The men who ran these villages believed in Sharia law, including *hudud*."

"I've heard of Sharia, but not *hudud*."

"It's the mandated punishments under Sharia law. They're extreme. *Hudud* is not enforced widespread, but some want it to be the unwavering standard. So many of these men used Sharia to terrorize. I saw things, and I knew of things going on, but I couldn't do anything, or else I could risk the larger plans in place."

"So you weren't just a sniper."

"It was my job to find intel, get it to my superiors, and when the order came to eliminate certain people, I knew the terrain and the patterns of the community to get it done quietly." Her handler had called her a "one-stop shop."

"Did anyone ever figure out it was you?"

She didn't answer.

He leaned forward to look at her more closely. "Someone did. And you had to eliminate them too."

"I did my job."

"But it was hard on you," he said. "More than you'll admit."

She was quiet. He was right—she still felt blood on her hands, of all the people she couldn't save, even of the evil terrorists she'd killed.

"I'm not going to sit here and tell you all of it was right. I honestly don't know."

For some reason, his blatant honesty was refreshing. It didn't make her feel better about what she'd done and seen, but it made her feel okay about not feeling okay. She'd always felt that she was wrong for feeling conflicted about some aspects of her service.

"But," he said, "I do know that you tried to protect the innocent. No matter what, that was the right thing to do."

She nodded. The problem was she was just scratching the surface of what she needed to tell him.

"A lot of the time," she said, "I didn't know who was in my sights. I had to trust that the intel was good and my superiors made good decisions when they gave me orders. Sometimes I imagined who my targets were leaving behind, but I tried to trust that I was making a difference."

He didn't respond, and she glanced over at him.

He was looking out the windshield at the darkening sky.

"I think you probably already guessed that part of my background," she said. "At least to some degree."

"Something like that."

"What I really need to tell you," she said, "is something entirely different."

She saw peripherally as he tilted his head.

"When I finally came home, I was so relieved," she said. "I'd never truly appreciated this country until I came home after ten years of living in communities where I barely had rights just because I'm female. I saw girls married off at the age of ten, women punished for the offense of having been brutally raped, child suicide bombers, and nonbelievers killed simply because they had a different faith. I became so entrenched in it that I could barely remember what it was like to live here, have rights, be equal.

"Then I went home. My first night home was hard. My family was so proud of my service, and they wanted to hear my stories, but I didn't want to relive them. I couldn't sleep. I couldn't concentrate. My dad said I just needed to get back into action. He's the one who'd trained me as a sniper. He and my uncle and all my cousins are accomplished. He got me out on the range on the ranch and raved about my skill. I'd always been good." Too good.

"Are you still dealing with PTSD?" he asked.

"I don't know. Probably."

She felt his gaze on her.

"This isn't the end of your story," he said.

"No," she admitted.

He reached over, took her hand, and squeezed it. His hand was warm, strong, but his grip gentle. Some emotion that she couldn't quite identify washed over her. She'd forced all emotion out of her life for so long, she could barely recognize it at all.

With their hands on the armrest between them, Mac scooted over to Lyndon's left thigh and rested his front paws and chin on their hands. Then he closed his eyes again. She was shocked at how relaxed Mac was being.

"Keep talking," Lyndon said gently.

"My family took me back out to the range every day. It was familiar, my childhood all over again, and I started sleeping better, eating more. I don't think I was happy really. I think I was letting the numbness of routine calm me. My father was pleased. He thought I was coming back to my old self, but my old self, the little girl who'd get up at dawn to try to beat her daddy at target practice, was gone." She sat up straighter in her seat. "I'd known that would happen when I went in the CIA. I'd made the decision that protecting my country was worth whatever it did to me."

He squeezed her hand.

"But that ten years isn't what cut away the last threads of who I was." She took a slow breath and looked over at Lyndon. "I became an assassin for hire."

FOURTEEN

KADANCE WAITED FOR LYNDON to pull away from her. But he kept his hand wrapped around hers.

She made herself keep talking. "My father told me about a mission he'd been given by his old superior in the Marines. They needed it to happen quietly. It needed to be off the record and untraceable, and so they'd called up my father, one of the best snipers the Marines has ever seen. The target was a recruiter for ISIS and also planning a large-scale attack on a university, with an estimation of thousands of deaths. But as he researched it, he wasn't sure if even he could pull it off. The shooter had to wait until just the right opportunity, which could take some time, so it would be better for someone close to college age, who could fit in, to do it. And the shot was going to be extremely tricky—the distance, the angle. That's when he asked me to do it. I was better than him. I was better than all of them."

"You completed it for him."

"Yes. He was so proud. He practically jumped up and down with excitement about the skill of the shot. The police didn't even consider it'd been a sniper. Off the record, untraceable. It was the same thing I'd done for the past ten years. Except it wasn't."

Lyndon tilted his head.

"The next morning, I woke and looked outside to see my father meeting with someone in the driveway. I couldn't see the person on the other side of a big truck, but I saw them hand my dad a black duffle bag. I met my father in the kitchen to see what was going on. I asked him who that was, what was in the bag, and he waved it off as nothing and asked me what I wanted for breakfast. He seemed really happy. I walked over to where he'd set the bag on a chair and opened it. It was full of bundles of cash."

Lyndon lifted his chin and cursed.

Kadance didn't risk looking over at him.

"He tricked you," Lyndon said. "The Marines hadn't asked him to do the job."

"No."

"Why'd he do that to you?"

"He didn't think he was doing anything to me." She sighed. "That's what I tell myself. I demanded he explain what'd happened, and as he finally talked, I realized he didn't see any moral problem with it. He'd been a sniper with the Marines for pay, so what was the problem continuing to get paid for his skill?"

"How can he think that?"

"I don't know."

"Does the rest of your family know what he did?"

She hesitated.

He lifted his chin in understanding. "You said they're all trained as snipers. That wasn't an isolated incident. Assassination is the family business."

"I didn't know," she said. "I realize now my upbringing was unique. My cousins and I were trained—survival skills, fighting, shooting, all of it. There were no Barbies and Legos—I didn't even know what those were until I was a teenager. My uncle and father were grooming us."

"When you say survival skills and fighting, you don't mean how to tie knots and basic self-defense."

"No, I mean left out in the woods alone and fight my cousins until one of us was knocked out." She continued, "My father would go out on assignments, but he always said they were for the Marines. Or maybe that's what he said a couple of times, and I assumed the rest. But I should've realized."

"Is this why you're on the run? Someone figured out you did that job?"

She appreciated that he was trying to be kind by not calling it what it was. Assassination. Murder. "No," she said.

"Your father didn't give over evidence in retaliation for your leaving?"

"He would never do that. He was too proud of it, and I have the feeling he didn't want to cross the client."

"You're running from your family then?"

"When he finally explained, he seemed to think it wasn't such a big deal. I lost it. I screamed and yelled. I'd never felt that kind of anger. I'd never thought I could feel like that toward my father."

His tone was gentle. "You keep referring to him as your father, but growing up, I suspect you called him Dad, or maybe even Daddy. He was your idol growing up, wasn't he?"

She nodded.

"You spent every moment you could out on the range with him, trying to master what he loved so he'd be proud of you. Am I right?"

She nodded but couldn't get any words out.

THOUGH SHE BLOCKED most emotion from her face, Lyndon was learning to read her—the slight twitch of her brows, the tightening of her lips, the way her eyes deadened. He knew there was nothing he could say to ease her pain, so he said nothing. That urge to hold her raged; he refused to let himself act on it. But he did slowly rub his thumb over the soft skin of her hand. It amazed him how she was hardened and deadly and yet still feminine and lovely.

After a minute or so of silence, he asked, "Are they trying to bring you into the family business?"

"He kept talking about how I'm so valuable. That it's selfish to squander my talents. In those few minutes, I realized my entire life wasn't what I thought it was. I thought my family was dedicated to the safety of the country, willing to sacrifice for others. But none of it was the truth. It was something I'd fabricated in my own head. I told him I was leaving. At first, he tried reasoning with me. Eventually, he called in my uncle and cousins, and I realized he'd force me to stay."

"But you got out."

When she hesitated to respond, he knew it'd been hard. She'd probably had to hurt some of her family. He didn't ask for details. "You think they'll try to force you back if they find you?"

"They're tracking me or trying to."

"They've caught up to you before?"

She nodded.

Again, he didn't ask her to relive the details.

She straightened her back but kept her focus out the windshield. "I'll understand if you don't want my help. I'm limited in what I can do. I have fake IDs, but they can't be put under too much scrutiny. I can't draw attention to myself. If I stay in one place too long, I risk being found." She paused. "And I'll understand if you're uncomfortable being around me."

He considered what she'd told him. She had a valid point, certainly. If her ID was flagged or if her family found her, the situation could get a lot more complicated than it already was. Finally, he said, "I don't think I can do this on my own. I think we'll need your skills to have any hope of being successful."

She glanced at him and then back to the road. "But are you uncomfortable with me?"

He brushed his thumb over her hand. "Do I seem uncomfortable?"

She looked at him, met his eyes, and he could start to see actual emotion. But he wasn't good at reading emotion. She turned back to the road.

Then she pulled her hand away from his. "I don't think we should risk complicating things any more than they already are."

He wanted to say he was just holding her hand, not asking her to sleep with him, but he held back the words. She was right. He wasn't sure what he'd been thinking. He shouldn't be holding her hand or making any kind of physical contact—no matter how attracted he was to her, *especially* because of how attracted he was. He'd resolved a long time ago not to have romantic relationships. Not after what happened to Angela.

FIFTEEN

"WHERE ARE WE?" Kadance woke when she felt the change in speed. She looked out the window from the passenger seat to see they were exiting the freeway.

"We need food," Lyndon said. "And I want to find a library."

"A library?"

"If the attack will happen at the State of the Union, we need to better understand the details. I know there is a designated survivor who would take over the presidency in the case of a major event, as outlined in the 1947 Presidential Succession Act, and since 9/11, at least one member of Congress has also been asked to serve as a designated survivor, but where are they taken? And what are the security and emergency procedures?"

"You think you'll find that in books?"

"I'm sure emergency procedures aren't fully outlined anywhere for the public to see. But there are computers at libraries."

"You're going to hack into government systems?"

"Won't be the first time."

"Are you serious?"

He looked over at her. "Why do people always seem to think I would never take any risks?" His tone sounded serious—he wanted an answer.

"I think people don't really understand you."

He didn't answer, but she could see on his face that didn't make sense to him.

"I think it's because you're different," she said.

He drew his eyebrows together. Then he made the turn onto the road off the exit ramp.

"You really don't see how different you are, do you?"

"What do you mean 'different'?"

She smiled a little. "Well . . . you're a genius, first of all. People are on edge around genius."

"I don't go around telling people about my doctorates or how many papers I've published or anything else."

"Yeah, exactly. They think you're some average, quiet, geeky guy, and then you pull out random information like it's normal to quote the 1947 Presidential Succession Act."

"I didn't quote it."

"You summarized it. And I bet you could quote it if you wanted to."

"I have an eidetic memory," he defended.

"What's an eidetic memory?"

"Photographic memory."

She rolled her eyes. "Of course you do. Add that to the fact that you can shoot and you can fight. People don't know what to think."

"Only the people who see me at the range know I can shoot, and you're one of a handful of people who know I can fight decently well."

She contained the urge to roll her eyes again. "Then there's . . ." She looked over at him.

"Then there's what?" He pulled into a gas station, stopped at a pump, and shifted into park.

"You're good-looking," she said. "People don't expect genius and gorgeous to go together."

He paused for a few seconds. Then he turned off the engine, got out of the car, and walked up to the store.

"Reason fifteen people don't understand you," she said as she watched him walk away. "Zero reaction to being called gorgeous." She laughed. Then she caught herself watching his masculine stride and how good he looked in jeans, and she made herself look away.

He came back a few minutes later, got the gas pump going, and handed her a breakfast sandwich and a bottle of water. "Is this all right?"

"Sure. Thanks."

He finished pumping and got in the car. "The clerk said there's a library about two miles away."

They both ate quickly while he drove, and they pulled into the library a few minutes later. She gave Mac some food and water in bowls on the back seat and left a window partially down. Inside, Lyndon stopped at the front desk to inquire about computer access, and she started browsing a couple of specific sections of books. Hopefully, he wouldn't take long—they needed to get back on the road.

After about ten minutes, she walked over to the computer section to find Lyndon typing intently. He didn't even use the mouse, just a steady stream of key input. He glanced at her but kept typing, not even a pause.

"Be ready to go as soon as I'm done," he said.

She stood behind him and bent over to see his screen. She ignored how nice he smelled, even after driving all night. "You're already in?" she whispered.

His keying slowed, and he scanned page after page of type. "Almost done."

"Are you speed reading all that?"

"I'm memorizing the pages. I'll read it later."

She stared at him. *And you wonder why people think you're different?* Though she knew he didn't share things like this about himself with almost anyone else.

She set the book in her hand down. She'd assumed she'd have a little more time to browse through it.

He glanced at the book and then looked back at the screen. "Why were you reading that?"

"To have some idea of what you're talking about."

"I can explain whatever you want to know. Some of the books out there don't get it all right."

"Are you still memorizing the type while talking to me?"

"Yes." He continued moving through page after page.

Are you serious?

"Done." He rebooted the computer and stood from the chair. "Let's go."

She stayed by his side out of the library and to the car.

"Will you drive?" he asked.

She took the key from him and got in the driver's seat. While she headed back down the road and turned onto the on ramp for the freeway, he stared at the dash, though he didn't look like he was seeing it.

"Are you reading it now?" she asked. "Everything you memorized?"

"Yes."

She quietly let him focus.

"The book on infectious diseases you were reading," he said. "Did you have any specific questions?"

"Are you done reading?"

"Not yet. Boring section."

"So, you want to answer my questions while you're still reading text that you memorized?"

He looked over at her. "This is why people don't understand me, isn't it?"

She burst out laughing, and he smiled as he watched her. She couldn't stop laughing for at least a mile.

After about two miles, he said, "Okay, done. Do you want me to answer your infectious disease questions or tell you what I read?"

"Do you realize how ridiculous what you just did is?"

"You mean hacking into classified government computer systems?"

"Let's set that little tidbit to the side for a minute. Do you have any idea how smart you are?"

"I think sometimes I don't interact with other people enough and I forget what's normal."

Her smile faded. "That I get."

"I think that's why I like talking to you." Then he went on, "I read the security plans for the State of the Union. I really need to study it more to find a possible weakness. I think I should draw it out."

"You memorized the layout of the House chamber, didn't you?"

"I'll draw everything out, and you can analyze it. You'll find security weaknesses much faster than I will."

"We should consider what this person is trying to accomplish. Do they just want chaos, or do they plan to take down the government? If they just want chaos or to make a statement, it won't have to be as clean a strike. If they want to be sure to kill everyone there, it'll need to be more precise."

"The question is, why would anyone want to cripple the government?"

"They could be like those anti-government militia. But then, if they were militia, they wouldn't have hired a different militia group."

"You have experience with foreign terrorists. Does this sound like anything you've seen or heard of?"

She shook her head. "It doesn't feel right." She looked over at his expectant expression, surely in anticipation of clarification. "Though they were starting to dabble in chemical warfare, I never saw any group with anything so advanced as a super-virus, though I've been out of the game several years. But I don't think this is a terrorist group from that region. I can't give you a logical reason. It's a gut thing."

His jaw tightened. She was starting to be able to read him—

she didn't think he was angry, but frustrated. She had a feeling he didn't have gut reactions. Every decision went through his head, never his gut or heart.

"Once we find the possible weak points," she said, "what do you plan to do to secure those weaknesses? I doubt we can get anyone important to listen. The FBI and Secret Service get so many tips a week it's ridiculous. Unless they have credible evidence of a possible breach, they aren't likely to make any changes to a detailed, well-considered plan."

"It is detailed. I don't immediately see any weaknesses, though I don't have a lot of experience with this kind of thing."

"But you do pay attention to minute elements."

His gaze changed, unfocused.

"What're you considering?" she asked.

"We're going to the wrong place. We shouldn't be headed to DC."

SIXTEEN

"WHAT DO YOU MEAN we're headed to the wrong place?" she asked. "Washington is where the State of the Union will be held."

He kept watching the road as he spoke. He'd been trying not to look at her, not since he'd made her laugh like that—really laugh. He hadn't been sure she was capable of laughing like that anymore, not with everything she'd been through. It had affected him far too much. "We should go to the CDC in Atlanta."

She paused, obviously considering. "You want to get them activated and ready. Make sure they have equipment and personnel in Washington."

"That, and I want to see what kind of protocol they have in place for an outbreak of this kind."

"You don't already know?"

The corner of his mouth quirked. She was right to guess he'd done extensive research on the subject, including information that wasn't exactly public. "I would like to know the finer details and see if I can help prepare them."

"Do you think you'll be able to get access and talk to the people you need to? You don't work for the CDC. Will they listen to you?"

"I know someone who works there, director level, I believe."

"A former classmate?"

"Yes."

"The jealous or arrogant type or a friend?"

"We'll see."

She paused for only a few more seconds. "Okay. When we get to Memphis, we should take I-22."

"Thank you."

"I'll trust you on this stuff, but you trust me when it's time to."

He nodded. And he realized with a shock how much he did trust her. He hadn't truly trusted anyone in years, not since his grandfather. For a moment, he worried his trust was rooted in his attraction to her, but he quickly put that worry aside. He'd never had trouble keeping his head straight around beautiful women. He decided his trust was due to her actions—she'd been both smart and selfless since they'd met. Yes, she'd pulled a gun on him shortly after saving his life, but now that he knew about her family, he understood she'd simply been trying to get him away from her for his own safety.

"You look pretty focused," she said. "Reading more memorized text?"

He glanced over at her. "Just thinking."

"Tell me if your brain goes into overdrive again and you need to talk to calm it down."

He hesitated. "I'm surprised I haven't had more issues during this drive."

"I thought you would. Maybe watching the scenery out the window helps?"

"I think we've been talking enough."

"I slept for a while."

"Sometimes I go several days without talking to anyone."

"I get that. My record is something like two months."

He fought the urge to take her hand to comfort her. She'd been clear she didn't want his contact, nor did she need his comfort. He turned his head to look out the window.

"Except Mac," she said. "Sometimes I talk to him like a person, like he understands me. I think I'll turn into that guy in the movie on a deserted island."

"Where he talks to the volleyball."

"Yeah."

"But Mac talks back." Lyndon turned and looked at Mac on the back seat. "Right?"

Mac barked a meow.

Lyndon turned to Kadance. "See?"

"He does like to talk." She looked in the rearview mirror. "Don't you, buddy?"

He answered with another meow.

"That's my boy."

"Are you sure he's not a dog?"

"Shh. You'll offend him."

She said it with such a perfectly straight face, Lyndon cracked a smile. But then he looked out the side window and tried to concentrate on the task at hand.

By the time they made it into Atlanta, it was evening. The CDC office was closed. It was frustrating to have to wait. They picked up some food and found a cheap motel. While they had a decent amount of cash, they weren't sure if they'd need a chunk of it for something more important, so they both agreed to share a room with double beds.

They walked from the car to the exterior entrance of their first-floor room, and Kadance locked the door behind them. They ate their meal quickly and quietly, and Mac crunched at some fresh food.

After Lyndon threw away his leftover food and the wrappers, he sat back down on his bed and ran his hands through his hair.

"You're frustrated to have to sit here tonight," she said.

"I'll be fine."

"You're getting a headache."

He wasn't sure how she knew that, but he didn't deny it. "It's all right."

"Did I mention you're a horrible liar?"

"Once or twice."

She tossed her empty food wrapper in the trash. "You've been too quiet the last few hours, thinking too much, and now having to sit here and wait all night is going to mess you up." She walked over and sat on the end of his bed. "We need you on all four cylinders tomorrow. Let's talk about something random for a while."

He sat back against the headboard with his arms rested on his bent knees.

"Just let me wash my hands first." She stood and walked into the bathroom.

A few minutes later, she came back out and sat back down on the end of his bed. She'd apparently decided to change her shirt as well, or maybe she'd worn the tank top under her usual big T-shirt. The tank top was fitted and cut lower than her T-shirt. Though it didn't show any cleavage, it did show her curves. Her incredibly perfect curves—tiny waist and flat stomach combined with a full bust and tight backside. He avoided looking at her for fear his gaze would linger inappropriately.

"What should we talk about?" she asked.

He made himself look at her out of respect, and he noticed something at her waist, a sheathed knife. "The militia didn't take that knife from you?"

"Had a spare in my bag."

He focused more on the black handle with holes down the middle to help distract himself from the rest of her. "That's not metal, is it?"

She unsheathed it. The entire thing was one continuous material, all black, even the blade. "Polycarbonate."

"Won't set off metal detectors."

"Always have it on me." She slid it back into the sheath without even looking, as easy as snapping her fingers.

He made the mistake of letting his gaze drift up over her waist and chest. He looked away. The combination of deadly and delicate affected him entirely too much.

"Your headache is worse?" she asked.

114

He knew he couldn't get a lie past her. "What do you want to talk about?"

"Do you want me to get you some aspirin?"

"No, thank you." He tried to think of something to talk about. Anything. "What do you think the CDC security will be like?"

She hesitated. "Probably a ton of electronic security—cameras and high-tech locks at minimum."

"Will cameras be a problem for you? Are CIA agents in a database like military?"

"I'm not. My records are sealed—only about three people know I existed as a part of the agency. Not even my family knows. They think I was an army sniper."

He lifted his brows. "You weren't supposed to tell me about your service."

"No."

"Why did you? You could've just warned me about your family coming after you. You didn't have to tell me about the CIA."

"I wanted you to know what you were getting into."

He was just realizing he still didn't fully understand what he was getting into with her. He lowered his voice. "I won't betray your trust."

"I know."

He met her gaze for a few seconds, and he saw trust there—surely not as much trust as he felt for her, but earning any amount from her must be unusual.

"Tell me what I need to know," she said. "About infectious disease. Specifically, Ebola."

"The initial symptoms are fever, headache, weakness, stomach pain, joint and muscle aches."

"That sounds like the flu. I thought Ebola was a lot worse."

"It feels like the flu at the beginning. That's part of the danger. People assume it's just the flu and don't seek treatment. That leads them to get much worse and also to infect other people."

"What're the later symptoms?"

"The virus kills cells, can even make them explode."

"It causes really bad bleeding, right?"

"Bleeding from the eyes, ears, gums, nose, internal organs, as well as internal bleeding, which looks like severe bruising, and skin rashes. I've seen cases where the skin turns completely black and boils form. And then the organs fail."

"How contagious is it?"

"It's spread by physical contact either with an infected person or some infected surface. Or through animal bites or insect stings."

"From an infected surface. So, direct contact isn't needed."

"No."

"That's scary," she said. "Can it be treated?"

"Yes, but the death rate is around seventy percent, but that's including developed nations. It's much higher in underdeveloped areas, more like ninety percent."

"If it's a super-virus, we're thinking the strengths will be amplified, as well as the contagious aspect."

"I would think so, yes. If I were to engineer a virus with maximum death toll in mind, I'd make the gestation shorter, so that there would be less time to determine an effective treatment, and the contagious aspect much more acute."

"Do you think it's possible to create a virus that can be contracted through air rather than physical touch?"

"That's one of my fears. It would be difficult, though. Based on my research, I think the next logical progression is transmission via water. It would be a more attainable goal than transmission via air. And more controllable."

"It's one of the few ways they could hope to infect that many people at once." Then she looked up and raised her brows. They both said at the same time, "Sprinkler system."

"Does the House chamber have a fire sprinkler system?" she asked.

"Yes. Someone would need access to the fire riser to contaminate the water."

"And if it were me, I'd find a way to seal the doors, at least for a minute or so. Make sure no one gets out before the water hits them."

"I agree."

She sighed and leaned back on her elbows, which just accentuated her curves that much more. He couldn't make it through the night like this.

He stood and stepped over Mac on his way over to the thermostat. "I'm warm. Do you mind?"

She shook her head.

He cranked the air down. He was warm, and he also hoped the cool air would chill her and she'd cover up with a blanket. Thankfully, within ten minutes, she grabbed the spare blanket off the closet shelf and wrapped it around herself as she sat cross-legged on the end of the bed.

"Tell me something," she said. "Something not many other people know."

He suspected she'd feel more at ease after sharing so much with him if he shared more of himself. Certain things, though, he wasn't ready to share with anyone. Certain things he didn't want her in particular to know. "I grew up with my grandpa," he said.

"After your parents died."

"Even before. When they were on one of their trips, I'd stay with him."

"What was he like?"

He smiled a little. "Ornery. He'd been in the navy when he was younger, and it was one of those things that stuck with him, part of his identity."

"He's the one who taught you how to shoot and fight."

"I wasn't the best student at first, better with books and equations, but he said it would help with the headaches. He was also determined to make me into a man."

"You don't have to be able to fight to be a man."

He laughed under his breath. "Grandpa said if I ever wanted a girl, I needed to learn to be tough."

"I have a feeling being tough was never hard for you," she said. "I don't see you as a whiny kid."

"Not whiny, just quiet. Too much of my mother in me and not enough of my father." He had no memories of crying as a child, except when his parents died—he hid in the attic and let himself mourn for a while, and his grandpa was kind enough to leave him alone until he was ready to come back down, which had taken over a day. "The first time he took me to the range was about a week after they died."

She smiled a little. "He knew how to handle his grandson."

Looking back, he did remember feeling different leaving the range, not less hurt, but like he could start to learn how to deal with it. He felt the corner of his mouth quirk. "He made me do things I didn't want to, but he did support my interests. He tried to show the same interest my parents had, though he didn't really get most of it. He was at every science fair, every math competition, every chess tournament."

"You *were* geeky," she said.

"I *am* geeky."

"You wear it well, though."

"Some would disagree." He adjusted his glasses. He didn't want to stop talking with her, which felt odd. He hadn't talked so much with someone since his grandpa died. "Where did you go to school?"

"Homeschooled."

"What was that like?"

She shrugged. "I don't really know if my education was like everyone else's or something completely different."

"How much math did you get to do? Geometry?"

"Through trig and calculus."

"Your father taught you that?"

"Yeah. Is that weird?"

"The average person can't do calculus, even if they took a course in college."

"I think he wanted me to learn as much math as I could."

"Why is that?"

"Calculating windage compensation, temperature changes, altitude effects, up/down compensation, exit pupil and low light observation, barrel's rate of twist, bullet length versus diameter, and Coriolis effect."

"Coriolis effect?" The movement of the Earth in relation to the bullet. "You can shoot that far?"

"I could shoot that far when I was fifteen," she admitted.

He leaned his head back against the wall and cursed. She had to be extraordinarily proficient in physics. "And you say I'm geeky," he said. "So, what about the rest of your education?"

She shrugged. "I guess I learned the basics."

"Did you ever play sports or learn an instrument?"

"We didn't do those things."

Something in her tone said so much. She had the interests that were dictated to her. No choices. And they'd kept her sheltered so she wouldn't realize there were other things out there.

He glanced over at Mac sprawled out on the floor, on his back with his paws splayed to the sides, dead asleep. "You weren't allowed pets when you were growing up, were you?"

"They were distractions." Then she looked down at Mac and smiled. She had a different look in her eyes when she watched Mac—that wall came down a bit.

Eventually, she went over to her bed and slid under the covers. He lay down as well. Both on their sides facing each other, they talked for a while longer. He wasn't sure who fell asleep first.

SHE WOKE BEFORE SUNRISE—she wanted to get moving early. But when she heard the shower running, she stayed in bed a few extra minutes to enjoy the rare opportunity to lie on a mattress. It'd been years. Mac snuggled closer to her side and purred, and she closed her eyes. Lyndon had left the lights off, so she had to focus on not falling back asleep.

The shower turned off, and a few minutes later, footsteps changed from tile to carpet. She slit her eyes open to see Lyndon walk in the room in jeans and nothing else.

She lay still and watched him.

SEVENTEEN

MAC JUMPED FROM KADANCE'S BED over to Lyndon's. Kadance watched while he stroked Mac. Something about this sculpted man being so gentle fascinated her. Perhaps because she'd never known a man like that. Then her gaze drifted . . .

She was sure he had no idea what he looked like to others, no idea what kind of reaction he caused. And maybe he didn't care. Maybe he just didn't work that way. Maybe he didn't feel desire or passion. Only logic.

"Have you ever been serious about anyone?" she asked.

He looked over at her, and then turned away, toward his bag on the floor. "Not really."

"You really need to stop trying to lie."

When he turned back to her, he took a breath. "There was someone when I was in school, but I cut it off."

She propped herself up on an elbow. She noticed a small and simple cross necklace shining against his skin. "You haven't been with anyone since?"

"No." He pulled on a T-shirt, covering the cross.

"Why not?"

His jaw was tight and kept flexing. "Please don't push this subject."

She paused. "All right."

He walked over to the window.

"Don't open the curtains." She pulled the covers back and sat up.

He peeked outside but left the curtains shut. "Are you still trying to protect me?"

"I'm being cautious."

"That's why you suggested sharing a room. So you could be here and make sure no one attacked. We're thousands of miles from anything familiar. I doubt anyone will find me in this random motel."

"It's habit." She walked into the bathroom.

She showered quickly, brushed her teeth, braided her hair, put on clean jeans and shirt, and sheathed her knife on her belt.

When she came back out, Lyndon was sitting on the edge of his bed with his head in his hands.

He looked up and stood. "Ready?" His eyes unfocused, as if he was dizzy, but then he quickly refocused.

"What's wrong?" she asked. "What has your mind spinning? Concerns about today?"

"No. I'm fine."

"I need to understand where your head is before we go anywhere."

"It's nothing to do with what we're doing today."

"But something has your mind in overdrive."

"Yes. But I'm fine."

"You're in pain." She looked at him more closely and could see the pain he was struggling to hide.

"I'm used to it. I'm fine."

She crossed her arms.

"It's not something I'm comfortable talking about," he said. "I'll be fine once I'm focused on the task at hand."

"Is it something that's going to stop you from focusing on the task at hand?"

"I can get past it. I always do." He added more quietly, "Please."

Something to do with that past relationship—she was sure that was it. She didn't want to discuss James any more than Lyndon wanted to discuss this. She understood. She just didn't like going to the CDC when his head wasn't completely in the game.

"Today hinges on me," he said. "You don't have a lot of control over the outcome. I understand how uncomfortable that makes you. But you have my word that I'm able to function through this." Then he added, "But I would really appreciate it if you talked with me some more. It helps."

"How often do you have these headaches? Does your work make it worse?"

He kept clenching his jaw, surely due to his struggle against the pain. "In my work, I can find logic and solutions. It's when my mind can't find answers that it goes around and around."

So, something about that past relationship was unresolved. "Can you talk to her? That old girlfriend. And come to terms with whatever happened?"

"Please," he said. "Please talk to me about something else."

She uncrossed her arms. "All right."

"Talking with you helps," he said.

She wanted to ask about the cross necklace he wore under his shirt. It seemed at odds with his nature—scientific, ultra-logical. But she decided that might be another complicated subject. "What's your plan for today? Should we buy you a suit so they take you more seriously?"

"I think being underdressed might work to my advantage."

"With your former classmate?"

He nodded.

"So, you think he'll be more likely to talk if he feels superior. You're going to goad him into showing off."

"That's my plan."

"Just don't lie. You really stink at lying."

The corner of his mouth twitched. "So I've been told." Then he added, "To be fair, I've never had to prove my deception skills against a human lie-detector before."

"You don't have any deception skills."

The corner of his mouth twitched even more. "But I can recite anything I've ever read or heard. That has to be worth something."

"Okay, recite the commencement speech at your second medical school graduation."

"Dr. Veda de Athia: I am honored to deliver this commencement speech for the Johns Hopkins University School of Medicine graduating class. When I graduated from this esteemed university way back in 1970, we thought we were cutting edge, but you have so many more advantages—"

"You can't be serious. You're making it up."

"I stink at lying, remember?"

"Okay, okay. Show off."

He picked up her car key off the dresser.

She snatched it out of his hand and turned for the door. She relaxed at seeing his grin.

She insisted on stopping for a quick breakfast to make sure his head was completely in the game. He seemed fine, so she drove toward the CDC.

She hated leaving Mac in the car so much, but she decided this wasn't the time to push the limits. Just getting onto the property took some creativity.

They walked into the lobby of the building Lyndon said they needed, and Kadance reminded herself to let Lyndon take the lead.

"Hello," he said to the receptionist. His usually bland, even stoic expression blossomed into a small but stunning smile.

The receptionist leaned closer with her elbows on her desk. "How may I help you?"

Kadance stayed back and just watched. She wondered if he never let this charming side show as a protection mechanism, so he didn't have to deal with relationships. Or maybe her first instinct was more correct—he had no idea what kind of effect he had on people, specifically women. Maybe it never occurred to him to care.

"An old friend of mine is a director," Lyndon said. "Dr. Spallings." He leaned his elbows on the counter, and his biceps flexed and stretched his T-shirt sleeves.

The receptionist's gaze flickered. "Yes, Dr. Spallings is a director."

"Would you mind telling him Dr. Lyndon Vaile is here and would like to see him for just a few minutes?"

She smiled. "Sure." She picked up her phone.

While she talked to what sounded like an assistant on the phone, Lyndon straightened and glanced over at Kadance.

"It'll be just a few minutes," the receptionist said.

"Thank you."

Lyndon stepped back from her desk and looked around the grand glass lobby. He didn't engage with Kadance, and she didn't engage with him, figuring she would appear to be an assistant or similar. She wasn't dressed professionally, but then neither was Lyndon. The receptionist kept glancing at him.

Several minutes passed.

At about ten minutes, Lyndon walked over to one of the small seating areas scattered about the huge lobby. Kadance followed.

After twenty minutes, Kadance was tempted to ask him if he should ask the receptionist to call again.

Thirty-one minutes had passed when a young man in a lab coat walked out into the lobby. "Lyndon Vaile?"

Lyndon stood. "Yes."

Kadance noted that, though Lyndon had used his title when introducing himself and the receptionist had also used the title on the phone, the man had dropped "Dr." off Lyndon's name.

"Follow me please." The man seemed very young, perhaps not even in need of a daily shave. He walked with his back rigidly straight and made no small talk, didn't even look back at them.

Kadance walked behind Lyndon. They went through enough security that she should relax, but she continued to note as much as she could about her surroundings. It was a habit she would surely never be able to break at this point.

They stopped at a small waiting area with just a few chairs and a TV on the wall.

"Wait here, please." Without waiting for a response, the young man walked away.

"That kid has something stuck up his butt," Kadance muttered.

"He's probably an intern." Lyndon sat in one of the chairs.

Kadance took the seat next to him. "You'd think he'd wait until he had his doctorate. He has his whole life ahead of him to act like a snot."

Lyndon shrugged. "It's not uncommon."

"Why don't you act like a snot?"

"Because my grandfather, not to mention my mother, would come back from the grave and beat me."

Kadance nodded. "Good reason." Then she added, "Do you think they'll make us wait some more?"

"Probably."

She stood. "Then I'm using the restroom."

"You know where one is?"

She looked down at him and raised an eyebrow. Did he really think she hadn't cataloged every single hall and door they'd passed?

"Right. Silly question."

She headed down the hall, back the direction they'd come.

LYNDON WATCHED KADANCE walk away but then forced his attention from her.

He tried to use the time to reanalyze everything he'd read about State of the Union security, while part of his mind vaguely listened to the television.

Then he noticed the channels start flipping. He glanced around —no one was within view or earshot. He lifted out of the chair to make sure he hadn't sat on a remote. Nothing.

"Come," someone on a commercial said. Then the channel flipped again to another commercial. "Find the best—" Flip. "Come to me." Flip. "—best experience of your life—" Flip. "Come find me—" Flip. "Our paths—" Flip. "Cross—" Flip. "—and will converge."

Lyndon stood and stared at the television.

Kadance walked back down the hall. She murmured, "Is something wrong?"

He kept staring at the television, ready to show her, but it'd stopped flipping channels and had settled on a news station.

"What happened?" she asked.

"The channels kept flipping." He paused. "I think a message was hidden in all the phrases."

"What're you talking about?"

"The channels kept flipping, and it pieced together bits of phrases."

"What'd it say?"

"Come find me. Our paths cross and will converge."

She lifted her brows in skepticism, but also looked around carefully. She turned back to him and spoke under her breath. "This is the CDC, probably one of the most secure buildings in the country. How could someone hack a TV here, and why would they want to?"

"It would take a lot of skill. Similar to creating a super-virus and releasing it at the State of the Union."

She didn't respond.

"But *why* is still the question." He sat back down.

"Lyndon Vaile?" A middle-aged, dark-skinned woman approached. She wore glasses and her black hair pulled back in a bun.

"DR. VAILE," KADANCE CORRECTED.

"Oh, I'm sorry. Dr. Spallings didn't mention your title. I'm Dr. Terry. Dr. Spallings asked me to come speak with you. He's tied up at the moment." She held a clipboard against her chest. While she didn't offer to shake hands, Kadance didn't think it was due to arrogance. If she had to guess, she'd say the woman was a bit of a germaphobe. She couldn't decide if that was humorous or inevitable.

"I have some information I'd like to share with him," Lyndon said. "It's of a highly sensitive manner."

"I'm a senior researcher. I can pass any pertinent information on to Dr. Spallings."

"I'm sure you're immensely qualified," Lyndon said. "But I'd prefer to speak with him."

"Okay. If you tell me what this is about, perhaps he'll be per-suaded to break away."

Lyndon took a breath. "I suspect an Ebola attack is being planned. I want to make sure the CDC is prepared."

"Unfortunately, we cannot share sensitive information with the general public, but I can assure you we are as prepared as possible for any eventuality."

"I fear you may not be prepared for this eventuality. I would simply like to tell him what I know so that he can take the steps he deems appropriate."

"What you know or what you suspect? Or what you speculate?"

"He knows enough about me to know I'm not a lunatic. And he can't possibly still be angry at me for beating him out for vale-dictorian at Harvard Medical."

She pressed her lips together, probably trying to look severe, but Kadance spied a hint of mirth in her eyes.

"Please wait here." She turned and walked away.

Lyndon crossed his arms.

"I don't think they're going to take us seriously," Kadance said.

"That crack about Harvard will get him out here."

"You think she'll tell him?"

"He'll make her repeat the conversation word for word. If there's one thing I can count on him for, it's thoroughness."

"And yet you still beat him for valedictorian. Was it close?"

"No." He glanced over at the TV. It was still on the same news station.

She wasn't sure whether or not to be worried about him. She'd heard genius was just a step away from crazy. If that was true, Lyndon had to be a mere nudge away.

Fifteen minutes later, Lyndon was still standing there with crossed arms. Kadance had sat down.

Finally, she heard shoes clacking from down the hall—fancy and new men's dress shoes. She stood as a man in his thirties wearing a lab coat and tailored slacks came around the corner.

Lyndon looked over at him.

"What's this nonsense you're telling my staff?" the man asked.

"I just need a few minutes of your time. I know you're busy," Lyndon said.

"You do realize what I'm doing here." The man gestured all around, as if he was in charge of the entire facility.

"I know your time is valuable."

Dr. Spallings crossed his arms over his chest. "So, what're you doing nowadays anyway? I heard you're not even working."

"I'm conducting independent research."

Dr. Spallings failed to squelch a smirk. "Independent, huh?"

"My research has been focused entirely on the history and origination, and through that, effective treatment and an eventual cure of *Ebolavirus*."

"And you're trying to tell me you're doing this independently? Do you have a lab? How do you pay for staff and equipment?"

"I certainly don't have the same benefits you've gained here at the CDC. But I—"

"I'm sorry, but I have time only for credible information."

Kadance could almost feel how hard Lyndon was trying to flatter him. That kind of thing just wasn't natural for him.

Lyndon glanced at Kadance, and she could see in his eyes what he was about to do.

EIGHTEEN

LYNDON TURNED BACK TO DR. SPALLINGS. "I realize you wanted to be valedictorian and that you would like to finally put me in my place. But this is far beyond concerns of ego."

"You think I have a problem with ego, when you're the one barging into the Centers for Disease Control and demanding the undivided attention of the principal deputy director?"

Kadance continued to stand there quietly. All she could think was, *Wow, can this guy not hear himself?*

"All I'm asking is that you put ego aside for a moment and listen to credible information from a fellow qualified doctor."

"Qualified? Where do you work again? I'm sorry—this is sounding more and more like a conspiracy theory. I always suspected you were a bit over the edge."

"I have reason to believe someone is planning an attack at the State of the Union address. It's an Ebola super-virus. I believe it'll be disseminated through the fire sprinkler system, or we currently think that's the most logical option."

For the first time, Dr. Spallings glanced past Lyndon to Kadance. He looked at her up and down. "This is the 'we' you're talking about?"

The last man who'd looked at her that way had very quickly

bled profusely from the nose, but she kept herself in check and stood there with her usual lack of expression.

Lyndon shifted to stand between her and Spallings. His back straightened in a protective stance. Kadance wanted to grin at his protectiveness, how unnecessary it was. And then her grin slipped when she realized no one had ever done something like that for her. She'd never needed nor wanted anyone to protect her, but having someone *want* to protect her was kind of nice.

Lyndon addressed Spallings. "Will you please ready the CDC as much as possible in preparation for such an attack and reach out to the director of the DC office?"

Spallings shifted to the side to look past Lyndon to her.

Lyndon shifted in the way again. "I realize she's a stunning woman, but contrary to popular belief, most women do not like to be stared at lecherously."

The word *stunning* replayed in Kadance's head.

"I don't need to stare at women."

So, they just fall at your feet, do they?

Kadance set a hand on Lyndon's back. "I think we've accomplished as much as we can."

Still facing Spallings, Lyndon answered, "I think you're right." Then he said to Spallings, "I ask simply that you serve the American people as you're supposed to and ready all resources at the CDC's disposal." He turned and motioned for Kadance to precede him back down the hall.

She started walking and glanced back at Lyndon trailing behind her.

He murmured, "I don't want him watching your backside as you walk away."

She kept going. Once they turned a corner, he moved to her side.

Back out at the car, he said, "I'm sorry."

"I'm not so easily offended or upset. I just wish he would've listened better." She opened the rear driver's side door to check on Mac. He was lying on the seat and purred like a lawn mower as she petted him. Then she got in the driver's seat, and Lyndon sat next to her.

"Maybe he'll still ready some resources, though," Kadance said.

"We can hope."

"You did the best you could." She put on her seat belt and started the engine.

"You're probably very well versed in dealing with that kind of thing," Lyndon said. "I'm sorry if I offended you."

"How could I be offended by someone trying to do the right thing?" she said. "While I don't need protection, he did need someone to point out to him that his behavior wasn't okay."

"And if you did it, he'd probably be bloody."

She nodded. "Probably."

"It's happened before?"

"A lady doesn't tell."

He grinned.

While she drove, the word *stunning* kept flashing across her mind. She kept wondering if he meant it, and then she reminded herself she didn't care—truthfully, she never had. Being considered pretty had never been helpful in the past, rather the opposite.

"Should I get on the freeway and head toward DC?" she asked.

"Are you hungry?"

She shrugged. She'd eaten more regular meals in the last few days than she ever had.

"Do you mind if we stop someplace for a little while? We should eat something decent, and I want to talk through everything with you. Obviously, we can't depend on anyone else to help, so we need to come up with some more structured plans."

"Probably a good idea." She drove until they came to a little Irish pub.

They parked and got out of the car, and this time, she brought Mac along. He trotted behind them. She was pleased to see his happy wagging tail.

They walked into a large darkened space with green walls and a massive bar made of dark-stained wood. Behind the bar were matching wood shelves full of liquor bottles.

A pretty woman with dark hair called from behind the bar, "Sit wherever ye like."

Kadance headed for a booth in the corner farthest from the bar. She motioned to Mac, and he jumped up into the booth. He sat on the bench and looked across the table, as if he were a person.

The server walked up to the table. "I'm sorry, but ye can't have a cat in here."

"He's my emotional support animal." Kadance leveled a steady gaze at the woman and waited for her to acquiesce.

The server pursed her lips. "What would ye loike to drink?"

They ordered, and she gave them some menus and walked away.

"I need to learn from you," Lyndon said.

"What? I didn't lie." She rubbed Mac's head, and he leaned into her hand. "You are my emotional support animal, aren't you?"

Mac meowed in response.

She turned back to Lyndon. "See?"

The server returned with their drinks. She glanced at Mac, who stared right back at her, but she didn't argue further.

"The next logical step," Lyndon said, "is to go to the FBI."

"Too bad we'll get some lackey who'll treat us like conspiracy theorists and might not even bother opening a file." If she thought it'd help, she would risk getting arrested to get him in to talk to someone higher up, someone who might listen, but she also didn't want to risk leaving him unprotected. "But, yes, we should at least give it a shot. Do you have any other contacts we could try? Any other old classmates or professors in important positions anywhere?"

"The only one I've kept in contact with was Dr. Grant. It was a fluke that I knew where Spallings worked. What about you? Any contacts from your previous position?"

She appreciated that he was careful what he said in public. "I've been disavowed."

He drew his eyebrows together. "Why?"

"My father 'leaked' information about me. He made sure the army got it, of course, but it also made it to the agency as well."

"How bad was it? Would they arrest you if they found you?"

"He didn't give them any actual evidence, of course, so they have nothing to arrest me for. It's more like they wiped me from existence."

"What did he leak? What could he leak that didn't implicate him and the rest of your family?"

"He said I'd married a Saudi man and had changed allegiances."

"And they believed it?"

"He made sure they could trace the information back to him, a trusted retired Marine and my father. Even though my record is perfect, they couldn't take the chance on trusting me further with the country's security."

He sighed, and she heard his frustration.

"This is why I like that your skills at lying are horrible." She looked down at the menu. She'd meant it to come out in a teasing tone, but it'd come out serious.

"Because you can trust I won't double-cross you," he said, lowering his voice, almost gentle, "or at least that you'd see it coming."

She didn't respond. That was exactly it. She hadn't trusted anyone in years, not since James, and that'd been disastrous. The experience had honed her ability to detect deception even more.

The server set their drinks down in front of them. "Ready to order?"

Kadance ordered whatever her gaze landed on first on the menu, and Lyndon ordered as well.

"It'll be roight up." The server took the menus and walked away.

Lyndon leaned his back against the booth and glanced over at the server, surely to make sure she was out of earshot. She wore a fitted shirt and skinny jeans and had the figure to pull it off nicely, and yet his gaze didn't linger on her, nor had he given her very pretty face any special notice when she was at their table. Maybe Kadance's first inclination to think he simply didn't feel attraction or passion was right.

He turned back to Kadance. "So, head to DC, meet with the FBI, and then investigate the layout and security of the House chamber as much as possible."

"Maybe try to befriend one of the guards."

He nodded, but then he sighed and knocked his glasses askew as he rubbed the bridge of his nose.

"Focus on one thing at a time," Kadance said. "Maybe that'll help."

He fixed his glasses and looked at her.

"Right, the guy who can memorize text at a glance and read it later in his head, all while explaining infectious diseases, doesn't focus on just one thing at a time."

"I wish I could sometimes."

"How in the world do you sleep, anyway?"

"Sometimes I don't."

Mac jumped down under the table and back up onto Lyndon's bench. He set his front paws on Lyndon's thigh and looked up at him.

Lyndon smiled down at him. "Of course. Petting a cat is the ultimate cure. How could I forget?"

Mac leaned into Lyndon's hand as he stroked him and purred.

"I literally can't remember the last time Mac let someone else pet him," Kadance said. She wondered if Mac sensed he was trustworthy, or if Lyndon was simply the only person Mac had had contact with for any length of time other than her.

"Are you Lyndon?" called the server from behind the bar. She had a phone in her hand.

Lyndon glanced at Kadance and then back to the server.

Kadance looked to the front door and then back at the kitchen entrance and a hallway that led to the restrooms and a back door. She'd spotted all the entrance points upon walking in and had watched them carefully. And she was positive no one had followed them at any point while they'd been in Atlanta.

"I should find out who it is," Lyndon said. "Maybe I can get some information."

"Be careful."

He stood and walked toward the bar.

She stood as well, parted the blinds on the nearest window and looked outside. The parking lot and road were empty. She motioned for Mac to follow and walked over to the front door, about ten feet back from the bar.

The server handed a cordless phone to Lyndon.

"Cancel our order please," Kadance said to the pretty woman.

The woman walked through the swinging door to the kitchen.

"Hello?" Lyndon said into the receiver.

NINETEEN

"HELLO?" Lyndon said again into the phone. He could feel Kadance watching him and everything around them intensely.

"It's probably an unusual feeling for you to be surprised." The voice was disguised with some kind of digital device. He couldn't even determine gender, let alone any subtleties.

"It is," Lyndon said. "But let's put an end to my surprise. Tell me who you are."

Laughter.

"That's all right," he said. "If you know me at all, you know I'll figure it out."

"Oh, I know you. I know you well enough to know I am one of few in the world who can stay one step ahead. I also know you should dump the unenlightened, primitive, brunette Barbie and get on the right path."

Lyndon realized this person had no idea who Kadance really was.

"I'm disappointed you're again letting a pretty face distract you," the voice said.

Alarm bells rang in Lyndon's head, but he focused on the most important information he needed to try to extract. "And on what path should I be?"

"The path that's been laid out for you. Stop allowing yourself to be distracted. You need to prove yourself to earn the right to survive the cleansing."

More alarm bells. "How long has this cleansing been forthcoming?"

"Long enough."

"And how do you know how to create an Ebola super-virus?"

"Very good. I'm impressed. How'd you figure that out?"

"You don't already know?"

"The mastermind of the great cleansing sees all."

"And you foresee I am the only one who can challenge your super-virus."

"You should be by my side for the new world, but don't forget who the mastermind is. You are running through the maze I constructed."

Unless I jump the walls. "That you constructed years ago."

The person made a small sound, like a smirk.

"If I'm to be by your side, why are you trying to kill me?"

"Kill you? You misunderstand. The shooter was aiming for your little brunette Barbie."

He clutched the phone so tightly his hand shook, but he managed to keep his voice calm. "So, why the call? To prove you're watching? To throw me off?"

"On the contrary. I have but one goal for you—focus. I'd thought you'd learned this lesson, but apparently, you need more help."

"Don't forget, I am a man. I have needs science does not satisfy." He needed to make sure this person remained blind to Kadance's value, did not realize the threat she presented.

"Now is not the time to let your base instincts lead you. Get rid of her. Now."

"A beautiful distraction can help my mind focus."

A sigh. "Fine." And then the call ended.

He set the phone down on the bar and turned to face Kadance. "Let me use the restroom before we get out of here."

Her expression was hard and focused. She didn't argue.

He headed down the hall, passed the men's room, and walked out the back door. He'd done what he could to shield her, but he had no right to keep her involved in this. He could not let her be hurt. Or worse.

He made sure the door closed silently, and he walked quickly around the side of the building. He'd have to find someplace to hide until she decided to leave.

At the sight of Mac sitting in the small space between the side of the building and the neighboring fence, he stopped. Mac meowed, an aggressive sound that was more like a bark.

He didn't want to hurt Mac, so he backed up. He'd have to jump the fence at the back of the property. He turned the corner and stopped short at Kadance leaned against the building with her arms crossed.

There was a long pause while they looked at each other. He saw no anger in her eyes, no menace. Just curiosity.

"The shooter at my apartment, he was aiming at you. This mastermind told me to get rid of you," Lyndon said. "I'm afraid for your safety."

"Sounded like you made me out to be nothing but a toy. Nice job, by the way."

"I can't keep putting you in danger."

"You're not putting me in danger."

"This isn't your fight. It never was."

"I took an oath to defend the country. I meant it. This is my fight, maybe more mine than yours."

He felt his jaw tighten.

"Neither of us can do this alone. I don't have your knowledge of science, and you don't know how a terrorist mind works."

Mac walked up to him and rubbed against his leg.

Lyndon looked down at his fluffy orange fur. "I thought he was going to try to attack me."

"He would have. And he would've stopped you too. At least

long enough for me to get to you." She squatted down and held her hand out, and Mac trotted over to get his back rubbed. She looked up at Lyndon. "Are you going to tell me what they said?"

Lyndon hesitated. He was becoming quite certain he wasn't going to keep her out of this. "Should we leave first?"

"Give me the gist of the conversation." She continued to pet Mac.

"I couldn't distinguish anything from their voice. They used a device to disguise it."

"Still try to remember the general cant of their speech and any words they liked to use. It might come in handy later."

He nodded. He'd already made sure to set every detail to memory. "They said they want me by their side and that I need to stay focused and earn the right to survive the cleansing."

"They used that word—cleansing?"

"Yes."

"What else?"

He went through the conversation from the beginning, word for word.

"I don't think they sent the sniper to help you *focus*," Kadance said. "That sniper was a professional. They would've killed you if I hadn't been there."

"I think it's all more complicated than they wanted to admit."

"Let's hear your theories," she said.

"Let's get out of here first."

"No one followed us here. I'm positive."

"Then how'd they know to call this random restaurant?"

"I think they followed us via cameras since we left the CDC. Security cameras, traffic cameras. There's a security camera at the gas station across the street that I bet picks up part of the restaurant's parking lot."

Lyndon glanced around at the fence and cinder block back wall of the building.

"No one can see us here. If we take back roads out of town,

they'll lose us." She picked up Mac and started toward the side of the building. "But you're right—we should get going. This is probably going to be a long conversation."

He stayed by her side.

She kept holding Mac and even set him in her lap behind the wheel. He wondered if she was wanting comfort for some reason. The thought struck him as bizarre.

She made several turns until they were on a little side road.

"How do you know where you're going?" he asked.

"I've been through Atlanta a few times."

"And that means you have every street memorized."

"Enough of them."

And the rest she was piecing together in her head. Impressive. Most people couldn't navigate the town they lived in without their phones.

"Let's hear your theories," she said.

"I think it's as we thought—my research started getting too close. Once they read what Dr. Grant leaked to them, they sent the sniper, then someone to toss my apartment, and when I still made it, they sent the anti-government militia group, figuring there was no way I'd get away from all of them."

"So, why change to this new tack? Trying to make you focus and survive the cleansing by their side?"

"I think all of this goes back a lot further than I thought."

"What do you mean?" She kept stroking Mac with one hand while she drove.

"Are you all right?"

She looked over at him. "What're you talking about?"

He glanced down at Mac in her lap. "He's comforting you."

Her hand stopped and rested on Mac's side. Mac looked up at her but stayed curled against her.

"It's not comfortable for either of us," he said. "But we should probably try to be open with each other. We need to understand where each other's head is."

She paused for several seconds. Finally, gaze still focused on the road, she said, "I didn't think you'd try running from me." Her tone was hard, but he saw something in her eyes, something . . . hurt.

"I just wanted to protect you. If you're hurt because you got involved in this—" He stopped and looked out the side window.

They drove for a good mile before she spoke again. "I'm not used to it," she said. "To someone trying to protect me."

Surely, her upbringing had been all about pushing her, building her strength. And then her time as an agent was the same. And now, running from her family, from what they wanted her to become.

"I know you don't need protecting," he said. "But that doesn't mean I'm not going to do everything in my power to try."

She glanced at him, just the flicker of her eyes, but for that brief instant, he saw actual emotion, though he couldn't decipher it.

"I'm sorry," he said.

She nodded once, barely a movement. And she slowly resumed stroking Mac's soft fur.

"What did you mean this goes back a lot further than you thought?" Her voice was back to the same clear tone as usual.

"I'm still working it all out. I prodded with a few careful questions. I think they knew my parents."

TWENTY

"YOUR PARENTS DIED in the Congo, right?" Kadance asked. "You said when you were a kid, so like twenty years ago?"

"After my grandfather died, I went through all the letters my dad had sent him. He talked about a lot of things, but he'd mentioned they'd met a scientist studying Ebola. He was excited because he thought this person might actually find a cure." Lyndon remembered that night when he found the letters. It'd been just after his grandfather had died. He'd had to move out of the house they lived in just a few days later. He'd stayed up for hours going through his grandfather's things, trying to convince himself not to keep every last possession. He'd sat on his grandfather's bed all night, reading the letters over and over, trying to pretend he still had a family. As he read about his parents' work, he'd decided what he wanted to do with his life—find a cure.

"What makes you think it's the same person?"

"The last letter my father had sent was scrawled and barely legible. He'd told my grandfather to move, someplace remote, and don't tell anyone where we went. He'd begged him to keep me safe from the cleansing. When I first read that, I thought my dad had been delirious with the disease. Doctors Without Borders confirmed my parents had died very shortly after that letter

143

was sent. But then this mastermind used that word in the same context."

"Are you sure it wasn't just—" She stopped and looked over at him. "I'm sorry. I shouldn't be doubting you. I doubted you about the TV flipping channels, but it's pretty obvious this person has the ability to manipulate technology at a high level. I trust your assessment." She turned back to the road.

He just looked at her for several seconds. Then he made himself go on. "My hypothesis is that my parents discovered this person wasn't looking for a cure but had actually created *Ebolavirus*. My mother was brilliant in the lab. If she'd gotten a look at just one specimen, I'm sure she'd have figured it out."

"Why would this person let your parents that close?"

"Again, just a hypothesis: this person recognized my parents' skills, especially my mother's, and tried to recruit them. When my parents refused, this person purposefully exposed them to the virus."

Kadance raised her chin. "Tried to recruit them like they're trying to recruit you now."

"The logic fits. It gives us something to work with."

"Based on all this information, what do you think is the next step?"

"I have a thought, but I want to be careful. We had almost no idea what to do next before that call. Was this mastermind planting ideas in my head to keep me running around their carefully constructed maze?"

"It was one word. You put all of that together based on one freaking word. No way did they plan on that. What's your idea of what to do next?"

"Doctors Without Borders. Their US office is in New York. I figured I'd call and see if I can find someone who was over there around the same time as my parents."

"Should I find a library so you can look up the number?"

"I know the number. I just need a phone."

144

"How do you know the number?"

"I called them once before."

She rolled her eyes. Then she asked, "Why'd you call them?"

"I thought about joining."

"Do you still think about it?"

"It would be fulfilling, but I can't stop my current work until it's finished." He owed it to his parents and to his grandfather.

She nodded.

After driving for a while, she pulled off at a tiny gas station in the middle of nowhere. It had an old pay phone attached to the worn wooden siding. While Kadance filled up the gas tank, Lyndon dialed.

He had to explain what he wanted to at least five different people.

In the little store, Kadance bought them each something to drink, including fresh water for Mac. She leaned against the wall next to the phone, and Mac noisily lapped water from his bowl.

Finally, Lyndon made it to someone who seemed to know what they were talking about and cared enough to go through the effort of sorting through files. The first several people had sounded like they didn't believe him when he'd said his parents were with the organization and he wanted to meet someone who'd known and worked with them.

"Ah, here we go," the woman on the phone said. "Congo."

"Were there any other doctors over there at the same time?"

"A few. Let's see . . ." Then she said, "But I can't give you personal information on them. I can reach out to them with your information. Would that work?"

"I'm going to be traveling for the next while. I'll be hard to get ahold of. Can you give me a name? I have my mother's old address book, though she didn't make notes about who anyone was—perhaps they'll be in there."

"Well . . . I suppose a name wouldn't hurt. I have a Dr. Frank Pearce and a Dr. Patricia Stone."

"Great. I'll look them up. Were those the only doctors in the area at the time?"

"There were a couple more, but they've since passed."

"Okay, thank you very much."

"Good luck."

He hung up the phone.

"Time to find a library with computers?" Kadance asked.

"Yes."

Kadance picked up Mac's bowl, and they headed to the car.

Shockingly, Kadance found a library within fifteen minutes. He was beyond impressed with her sense of direction and ability to read an area.

He looked up both of the names online. Dr. Patricia Stone didn't pop up in any searches, but Dr. Frank Pearce, assuming he'd found the right one, was living in Knoxville, Tennessee.

"At least it's north," Kadance said as they got back in the car. "Same direction as DC."

It was late in the evening by the time they made it to Knoxville. They decided to wait until morning, a reasonable hour, before showing up on the man's doorstep. They had a good chance of the man not talking to them, perfect strangers knocking on his door—let alone if they showed up at ten o'clock at night.

They found a cheap motel not far from the interstate, but the only room left had a single queen bed. Kadance insisted it was fine, and Lyndon didn't argue, though a part of him knew he should.

Mac followed Kadance into the room, and Lyndon closed and locked the door.

"I'll sleep on the floor," Lyndon said.

Kadance set her bag on the desk and looked down at the old shag carpet. "That is probably the most disgusting carpet I've ever seen. You're not sleeping on that."

"You really think I'm going to let *you* sleep on that?" Though he was sure she'd lived through conditions he could barely imagine.

"We'll share the bed. It's perfectly big enough, and we're grown adults." She turned and took her small toiletry bag out of her duffle.

She disappeared into the bathroom, and he heard as she started brushing her teeth.

He dropped his backpack on the floor and ran a hand through his hair. Mac jumped up on the bed, sat down, and looked at him. Lyndon wanted to snap, *What do you want me to do? I'm trying my best.*

Kadance came out of the bathroom. "All yours."

He grabbed his toothbrush and toothpaste out of his bag and went in to brush his teeth. When he came back out, Kadance had changed into her tank top and was brushing her hair. It shimmered like a black river down her back and over her chest. It reminded him of that time hiking in the woods at night and suddenly coming upon a stream. It was smooth and barely rippled along the bank. It reflected the black sky and glimmered with the light from the distant stars.

He forced his gaze away from her.

Mac was still watching him, but then he jumped from the end of the bed over to the dresser, found a spot behind the television, and curled up.

Lyndon glanced over at Kadance as she ran her fingers through her hair and shook it away from her face and off her shoulders. It brushed against the bare skin of her arms. It made Lyndon wonder what it would've been like to dip into that dark stream in the moonlight. With Kadance. Her dark eyes black in the lack of light, and shadows accentuating the perfect angles of her face. The water falling over her skin, making her clothes cling to her stunning figure . . .

He turned away and took a slow, deep breath.

He sat on the edge of the bed and kicked off his shoes and then socks. *I can do this.* He hadn't let himself be involved with a woman in many years. He'd had times when it was difficult, but it'd never felt this overwhelming.

The mattress shifted as she climbed into the bed.

The bed he had to share with her.

"Anything you want to talk about first?" she asked. "Or are you okay going to sleep?"

He turned his head partway, not enough that he had to look at her. "Sleep. In the morning, perhaps you'll help me plan out how to approach Dr. Pearce."

"Sure."

Rustling of sheets, likely as she lay down and got comfortable. "Looks like Mac found himself a spot."

Lyndon glanced over to where he lay. A little of his orange fur stuck out from under the flat-screen television sitting on the dresser. Otherwise, he was hidden. *Thanks for abandoning me.* He'd hoped Mac would snuggle up next to Kadance like he usually seemed to, preferably *between* him and Kadance. "He can't be comfortable over there. Want me to bring him over to you?" Lyndon twisted and looked at her and immediately wished he hadn't. She lay on her hip partially turned toward him, and the blankets were down at her waist. All he could focus on was how her thin tank top clung to her curves. *Please, Lord, give me strength.*

"He always sleeps wherever he wants. He'll come over if he wants more warmth."

He nodded, set his glasses on the nightstand, clicked off the lamp, and made himself lie down.

In the distance, he could hear cars on the freeway, and lights from a passing car on the road occasionally slipped through the crack in the curtains and flashed across the ceiling.

He couldn't get his breathing to calm. Warmth traveled through his body, and he struggled to contain what she made him feel.

But he only grew warmer.

She shifted, and the back of her hand rested on his arm. Her contact was like a live electrical wire. It shot energy through him.

His breathing increased. If she was paying any attention, she'd see his chest rising and falling rapidly. She would understand. And she'd be angry.

He closed his eyes and prayed for strength.

Then her hand shifted against his skin, only maybe half an inch, nothing at all. It was nothing to her, just the back of her hand, nothing even remotely intimate.

But it made passion race through him.

He pulled away from her and stood from the bed. He ran his hands through his hair and tried to calm himself down.

Her voice was just more than a whisper. "Another headache?"

He shook his head.

"Come talk to me." Her voice was soft. It sounded intimate, but he knew she didn't mean it that way—her tone was simply muted from sleep. The chemicals in his body were blazing out of control, making everything feel passionate.

"Lyndon?"

He couldn't figure out what to say. He couldn't think through his desire.

The sheets rustled, surely from her sitting up, and her voice was stronger. "Lyndon, are you all right?"

His body tightened as he ran his hands through his hair again. Finally, he made his voice work. "I'm fine."

"You're not fine."

Right, he had zero chance of lying to her. But he desperately didn't want to make her feel uncomfortable. The thought was unbearable.

Her light steps padded the carpet.

She stopped next to him and rested her gentle fingers on his arm. Through the fog of chemicals in his body, her touch felt sensuous.

He pulled away and faced her. "Please don't."

Her delicate brows pulled together. "Don't what?"

He couldn't think of a good lie, and he couldn't lie to her anyway.

A few seconds passed.

"I can't sleep next to you," he said.

"Why?"

"I'm attracted to you, Kadance."

Her brows pulled together even more.

KADANCE DIDN'T HAVE A RESPONSE. Men had come on to her before, but this was different. It was Lyndon. Sure, he'd held her hand before, but she'd been convinced it didn't really mean anything to him. More friendly than anything.

Finally, she said, "I don't understand."

"What do you mean you don't understand?"

"I just didn't think you worked that way."

His expression hardened. "What does that mean?"

"You're so scientific and logical, and you said you haven't dated anyone in years. I thought you just didn't feel that kind of passion."

"I know I'm different, but I am human, Kadance."

The anger in his voice and on his face hurt her much more than she was prepared for. "I'm sorry. I just—"

"Just what? Is this why you're relaxed around me—because you think I'm some kind of eunuch?"

She had no response. Why was she so relaxed around him? "You're my friend," she said. "That's why I'm relaxed around you." Friend—he *was* her friend. Her throat started to tighten. She'd never had a real friend before. She'd thought James was, but that'd been a lie. Lyndon didn't lie—he couldn't lie.

"If we're friends, why would you think I'm not capable of feeling?"

"Not feeling in general. I've seen your compassion—I've never known anyone as kind. I just didn't think you—"

"You don't see me as *male* is what you're trying to say."

"No." That was definitely *not* the case. She took a breath.

"You're unique, really special, and people don't always understand you. Including me, obviously."

He sighed.

"I didn't mean to offend you like that," she said. Vaguely, she realized how odd this conversation felt; she wasn't used to not being in control of every interaction, every situation.

"I want to be friends with you, Kadance. I just can't get too close." He sighed and closed his eyes. "And I don't want you to feel uncomfortable around me."

"Don't worry about me."

He opened his eyes, and his gaze seemed to burn into her. "I will always worry about you. I'm not those other people in your life. I care how you feel. I care that you're comfortable in my presence. I care about you."

Her voice came out as a whisper, almost choked. "You're not like anyone else in my life."

They watched each other for several seconds. She couldn't get herself to look away.

She had a sudden urge to wrap her arms around his waist and rest her head against his chest. She wanted him to hold her, pull her tightly against him.

She tried to shake the insane thought from her head but couldn't manage it.

He shifted toward her.

Then he turned, walked into the bathroom, and closed the door.

TWENTY-ONE

LYNDON SAT ON THE BATHROOM FLOOR with his back against the wall next to the tub for a while. He wasn't sure how long. He kept praying he hadn't ruined the best friendship he'd ever had. But then he'd remind himself being friends with her obviously wasn't an option, and he knew that once all this was over, she'd leave.

And it wasn't as if she saw him as a man anyway.

He sat there on the floor for a while, trying to rein in his frustration. She'd referred to him as gorgeous once. He hadn't known what to make of it at the time. It'd seemed flippant when she'd said it. Perhaps because she hadn't thought being called attractive would have any effect on a eunuch.

He rested his head back against the wall.

None of it matters, he kept telling himself. He was frustrated over nothing. She obviously didn't see him the way he saw her, she'd leave as soon as she could, and he'd decided a long time ago not to allow a relationship again.

But then he'd remember her silky hair flowing over the bare skin of her shoulder.

He eventually forced his frustration under control, but there was still something lingering, like an ache in his chest.

Finally, he decided the ache wasn't something he could control. It wasn't going to go away.

He made himself stand up and walk out into the main room.

She was asleep at the desk with her head rested on her folded arms. Her face was so beautiful. Nothing he'd ever seen or imagined could compare. There was something about her beauty he still couldn't quite comprehend, but somehow it didn't frustrate him, not anymore. He accepted she was simply beyond his mental capacity. There was a certain freedom in that.

Before considering if it was wise, he walked over, slipped one arm under her knees and the other around her back, and lifted her. He walked over to the bed. He was shocked she didn't immediately wake and go into attack mode. Instead, she rested her head against his chest.

He forced himself not to look at her or else he might lose his mind and kiss her. Then she'd definitely go into attack mode.

He carefully laid her down on the mattress with her head on the pillow. Then he gently pulled the blankets over her.

He stood there and looked at her for several seconds.

The ache in his chest splintered out, through his veins, until his entire being throbbed with it.

And he understood what the ache was.

Why, God? Why her?

He forced his gaze away from her, walked around the bed, took the other pillow, and lay down on the floor, as far from her as he could get in the small room. He tried to close his eyes and sleep, but he knew it was a lost cause.

Why did this have to happen? Hadn't he done well all these years? He'd stayed away from relationships, purposefully didn't interact with women if he could possibly help it. And then Kadance dropped into his life. Like a punishment. A punishment he knew he deserved. After what had happened to Angela, he knew he didn't deserve anything less.

Please, Lord, give me the strength to get through this. Please

*help me make sure Kadance doesn't get hurt. Please, God, I can't
live through that again. Not Kadance.*

He knew Kadance was different, so very different from Angela,
but that didn't stop the terror from strangling him. The same
thoughts kept circling his mind until pain spiked through his head.
He lay there and let the thoughts continue circling. He endured
the pain, accepted it.

He deserved it.

KADANCE WOKE, BOLTED UPRIGHT, and grabbed the handle
of her knife. How'd she get to the bed? Last she remembered,
she'd laid her head down on the desk. She looked around the
room. Lyndon was on the floor, no blanket, arms crossed over
his chest. His eyes were open, staring at the ceiling, but he didn't
seem really there. Maybe lost in thought, rereading something
he'd memorized?

Barely moving his head, he looked over at her. She could see
how tight his jaw was.

"You have another headache," she said.

He resumed staring at the ceiling.

Mac scooted backward out of his spot behind the TV, jumped
down, and went over to Lyndon. He stood with his front paws
on his chest.

Lyndon unfolded his arms and petted Mac's head, thumb gently rubbing up his nose like he liked. "Thanks, buddy," Lyndon
murmured. He kept his focus on Mac while he said to Kadance,
"You can shower first."

"If the hot water will help your head, you can shower first."

"It won't." He continued petting Mac.

She stood, grabbed what she needed out of her bag, and headed
for the bathroom.

After showering, dressing, and braiding her hair, she came back out to find Lyndon sitting in the desk chair staring at nothing. Mac was curled up on the bed. He looked up and meowed at her.

"I think he wants breakfast," Lyndon said without looking up. "But I didn't want to get in your bag for his food."

"Is your head better?"

"I'm reviewing everything I looked up about Dr. Pearce."

She walked over to her duffle on the desk, and he slid the chair back, away from her, gaze still unfocused. Mac started meowing loudly. She grabbed the ziplock bag of Mac's food, opened it, and set it on the bed in front of him. He sat up and started eating.

"I thought you couldn't find anything much about his work with Doctors Without Borders online," Kadance said. "Assuming he's the right Dr. Frank Pearce."

"I'm reviewing everything else, mostly social media posts."

"While still holding a conversation." She resumed her usual teasing with him, hoping to get their same comfort level back. Hoping they were still friends.

He lifted his gaze and focused on her. "I didn't mean to offend."

"You didn't. You heard and comprehended everything I said. Have you found anything useful?"

"I figured I could try talking to him about something he cares about to build rapport, so I'm cataloging anything about which I'm knowledgeable as well."

"So, everything, basically."

"I don't know the first thing about grandchildren or cooking greens."

She felt the corner of her mouth twitch. "I assume you want to get there later in the morning. A polite hour."

He nodded. "It's frustrating to have to wait."

"That's the worst part of any job." She sat on the end of the bed and stroked Mac while he crunched his food.

"I assume there's plenty of waiting involved in being a sniper."

"I've laid there for hours waiting for the right shot."

His gaze fell away from her, and he resumed staring at nothing.

She wanted to keep pretending last night hadn't happened, resume the friendship that'd grown between them. But the tension was still there.

"I'm sorry," she said.

He gave no reaction.

"Lyndon."

He didn't look at her. "Please just let it drop."

"I don't know why I thought that about you, that you don't feel passion. You're not the one who has trouble with emotion. I am." She hadn't let herself think about his admission that he was attracted to her. She didn't know what to do with that information.

Finally, he looked at her, but she didn't see the anger she'd expected. "You have every reason to have trouble with emotion." He stood and walked around the side of the bed, then turned and faced her. "I'm just asking that you're more cognizant of your actions."

"What actions?"

"Your tank top, your hair, trying to get me to share a bed. But then expecting me not to feel anything."

"I didn't . . ."

"It's fairly obvious you have no idea how beautiful you are. I just really need you to try to be aware of it."

She nodded.

He turned back toward the desk chair but then stopped. "I know you've had an unusual and difficult life, but haven't you noticed how men look at you?"

"I didn't know anyone but my family growing up, and then I went straight into the CIA. The areas where I was stationed were heavily dominated by extremists. Being attractive was a liability." A lot of those men thought it was their right to have a woman if they wanted her.

"How long have you been back in the States?"

"Long enough. I just, I don't have a lot of experience."

"I understand not having experience. I guess I don't understand how you can look in the mirror and not realize what you look like."

She wanted to throw that back at him—how he'd walked around yesterday morning without a shirt on. "I won't try to share a bed with you again." She made her tone as nonargumentative as she could. "I don't know what else I did."

He ran a hand through his hair, and she saw how tense his arm and chest muscles were. "I guess it was all innocent. Your shirt showed your figure so well, and with your hair down . . . I'm just extremely attracted to you. I'm sorry—it's nothing you did. It's something I have to deal with." His tone changed, less frustrated, more concerned. "I'm more worried about making you feel uncomfortable."

"I'm not uncomfortable around you." She considered asking him not to go shirtless again but decided against it. She felt like they'd reconciled, and she didn't want to risk messing that up. Her voice softened. "Thank you for your thoughtfulness."

A few seconds passed. Then he resumed his seat in the chair.

"It's interesting," she said. "Our conversations aren't at all normal. We tend to talk about things most people keep to themselves."

"I'm not good at normal conversations."

"I'm just better at faking than you are."

"I wish you could take the lead with Dr. Pearce."

"I think finding things in common to build a bond is a good idea. And just for the record, I don't want you to be better at being fake."

She was relieved the conversation had shifted. She wasn't sure how to deal with the admission of his attraction, how intensely he seemed to feel it. It didn't really matter, right? He was perfectly willing to put it aside. She knew he would never come on to her and certainly wouldn't try getting her into bed. So, why did she keep thinking about it? She didn't want to get involved with a man. She'd let her guard down once, and it'd almost gotten her killed. But she also knew—with perfect confidence—that Lyndon was not like James.

TWENTY-TWO

KADANCE PULLED TO A STOP at the curb in front of a large house with white siding and a huge porch that wrapped around the house. The street was crowded with houses of different styles but all of a similar quality. Some of them even had white picket fences.

"Would you be all right pretending to be my girlfriend again?" Lyndon asked.

"It'll make you seem more approachable and explain my presence. As long as you're all right with it."

"It's the smart thing to do." He opened the car door and stood.

She got out, lowered the driver's side rear window for Mac. It was cooler in Knoxville, cold enough that she was wearing her jacket, but she reminded herself Mac had a very thick coat of fur. She came around the car to Lyndon, and they headed up the front walk.

"We should hold hands," she murmured.

"No." Then he looked over at her. "It's not a good idea for me."

He'd held her hand before and had been fine.

Lyndon rang the doorbell.

Kadance glanced around, pretending to be interested in the neighborhood, the children riding bikes and giggling as they played in front yards, but was really cataloging and assessing each person, each car, each sound.

The door opened, and Kadance splashed a smile on her face.

"Can I help you?" The man was older with thick white hair and plenty of wrinkles, but he still had a strong frame, with just a little pudge at the waist.

"I'm sorry to bother you. My name is Lyndon Vaile. Are you the Dr. Frank Pearce who worked with Doctors Without Borders in the Congo?"

The man narrowed his eyes. "Who's asking?"

"I'm sorry to just show up like this. I believe you worked with my parents, Dr. Aurel Vaile and Dr. Lee Vaile."

The man lifted his white brows.

"Do you remember them?" In Lyndon's voice, she could hear the anticipation.

"What'd you say your name was?"

"Lyndon Vaile. Doctor." Lyndon took out his license and showed the man.

"Doctor? Followed in their footsteps, did you?"

"Yes, sir."

"Yeah, I remember Aurel and Lee. Hard to forget those two."

Lyndon smiled a little. "Like I said, I'm sorry to bother you. I wanted to meet someone who knew them, and I talked someone at Doctors Without Borders into giving me a couple of names. I hope you don't mind."

"What sent you on a journey like that?"

Kadance wrapped her hand around the crook of Lyndon's arm. She wanted to support him, help him know he was doing a good job.

Lyndon glanced over at her then back to Dr. Pearce. "I'm sorry—this is Sarah."

The man smiled at her. "Awful pretty name."

She smiled back. "Thanks. It gets the job done."

"Why don't we have a seat on the front porch here and chat a minute about those parents of yours."

"I would sincerely appreciate that," Lyndon said.

Kadance and Lyndon sat in a small wicker love seat, and after grabbing a jacket off a hook on the wall by the door, Dr. Pearce took a matching chair.

"You said you're a doctor?" Dr. Pearce asked.

"He has three doctorates." Kadance gloated like any girlfriend would.

"You sound like Lee and Aurel's son, all right. And you have your mom's eyes, that same gray-green. You must've been young when they passed."

"Yes, sir. Just eleven."

"And what made you come looking for someone who knew them?"

Lyndon glanced at Kadance. Surely, he didn't want to lie, but how could he tell the man the truth? He'd think he was a nut and throw him off his property.

Kadance answered Dr. Pearce, "We're getting married, and that got Lyndon to thinking about his family. He doesn't have anyone left." She slid her arm through his again and rubbed her other hand over his. "He wants to feel closer to them if he can. You know?"

"I'm sorry to hear you don't have anyone left," Dr. Pearce said. "Your grandfather has passed as well? They said he took you when they were out of the country—I assume you stayed with him after they died."

"Yes, sir," Lyndon said. "He was killed just before I finished high school."

Killed? She'd figured his death had been natural—a heart attack or stroke or some kind of illness. Maybe it was something like a car accident? But Lyndon still had his grandfather's truck. And it'd looked to be in great condition, no evidence of a life-ending crash.

"Well, I'm glad you found yourself a sweet young lady." Dr. Pearce smiled at them. "You look to be very much in love."

"Yes, sir."

Kadance looked at Lyndon. His gaze flickered to her and then back to Dr. Pearce.

"May I ask you what you remember about my parents?" Lyndon asked. "I know it's been a long time."

"Those two were difficult to forget. Your dad—you knew when he was in the room. He had that booming, jovial voice and presence. There were only a few times I saw him completely serious. Your mother, on the other hand, she downright scared some people."

"She wasn't good at being diplomatic."

"She was blunt as a hammer. But smart. That woman—she always knew what she was talking about. I never once saw her make an error."

"She was kind, though," Lyndon said. "It was just hard to see sometimes. People didn't understand her."

Kadance squeezed Lyndon's arm. He could be much like his mother.

Dr. Pearce sat back in his chair. "That woman would give her life for a stranger. And she almost did several times. After the elections, the civil unrest turned violent. Families ran to our camp for safety. I saw your mother stand in front of a gun to protect a young mother and her baby."

The look on Lyndon's face told Kadance how much he missed his parents, how much he'd loved them—maybe even idolized them. And maybe still did. And then his grandfather had been taken too.

A thought struck Kadance. If his father had asked Lyndon's grandfather to move to protect Lyndon because there was danger, perhaps Lyndon's grandfather's death hadn't been accidental. But it'd been years later—why would this mastermind come for him after so long? Maybe it was all unrelated.

"I think that selflessness is why my father fell in love with her," Lyndon said.

"They were an unusual couple, that's for sure," Dr. Pearce said.

"You'd think they'd have argued more than breathed. But not once did I see them utter a harsh word to each other."

"She enjoyed his personality. He did and said all the things she couldn't. And he saw every good thing about her that no one else did."

Like Lyndon saw the good in her, even after all she'd done. She held his hand tightly before she realized what she was doing. But she couldn't let go now in front of Dr. Pearce. She'd just have to apologize to Lyndon later.

"What about their work?" Lyndon asked. "I'm sure my mother found a way to conduct research along with her other duties. Did she collaborate with anyone? I'd like to meet anyone who worked with her."

Dr. Pearce pursed his lips. "Now that you say that, there was someone Aurel and Lee spent time with. She wasn't with our group. If I remember correctly, she was conducting independent research."

"Do you remember what kind?"

"Ebola, I believe. But I wouldn't recommend hunting her down."

"Why is that?"

"She seemed perfectly lovely at first. The hippy type who'd never outgrown her idealism. Tree hugger to the extreme. She'd yell at you for picking a flower by the roadside. She was eccentric, but then plenty of us were eccentric in our own ways. For goodness' sakes, we volunteered to go into war zones."

"Something happened to make you keep your distance from her?" Kadance asked.

"She came to our camp one night. Everyone else was out at one of the local villages. She was in rough shape—I quickly realized she'd had a very poorly performed abortion. I was able to stop the bleeding and kept her under observation for a while. We talked. I'd figured she'd gotten involved with someone she shouldn't have— some of the locals wouldn't have approved of an American white woman mixing with them—or maybe the pregnancy had been difficult, or the baby was unhealthy. But she said she just didn't believe in having children."

"What does that mean?" Lyndon asked. "She didn't *want* children?"

"No. She didn't *believe* in having children. She gave me this lecture about how people are killing the Earth, and humans don't have the right to live at the expense of another. That right there is when I decided to keep away from her."

"Wow," Kadance said. "Do you remember her name? We'll be sure to stay away from her while we're reaching out to any of his parents' friends."

"Oh, what was it?" Dr. Pearce mused. "I'm thinking something with a V, maybe." He shook his head. "No, it's lost."

"It was a long time ago," Kadance said.

"I'm thankful you remembered as much as you did about my parents," Lyndon said.

"Frank?" came a woman's voice from inside the house.

"Looks like I'm being paged." Dr. Pearce stood.

"Thank you for your time." Lyndon took his arm away from Kadance and reached to shake Dr. Pearce's hand.

They headed down the porch steps and to the car. Once they were down the street, Kadance said, "Too bad he didn't remember a name."

"I'm not sure how to search for someone with so little information."

"I have an idea, but we're going to have to look something up."

"What's your idea?"

"I remember hearing about this crazy movement one time. VPE, I think. Voluntary Population Extinction."

"What's that—some kind of group suicide pact?"

"More like a pact not to reproduce."

"It's an environmental group?"

"If I remember correctly, yes. Just like the crazy lady Dr. Pearce talked about. Did she maybe decide to take it a step further and *cleanse* the Earth of destructive human beings?"

Lyndon looked out the windshield, and his eyes glazed in thought.

"Off to find a library?" she asked.

His eyes remained glazed. "You know me well."

She smiled a little. "We should be fast. Libraries have cameras."

She found a library a little while later and stood with Lyndon while he zipped through screens of information as quickly as the internet speed would allow. It wasn't a mainstream movement, so she hoped he was able to find some decent information.

He stopped clicking through pages, and Kadance leaned down to look at the screen. "Is that a message?"

TWENTY-THREE

"THROUGH A FORUM I'M READING," Lyndon said.

Kadance shifted closer to read it: "That old man couldn't re-member to tie his shoes."

"Dr. Pearce?" Kadance whispered. She'd noticed a traffic cam-era not too far from his house. This mastermind must've been watching. Or maybe they had some kind of facial recognition software running through systems all over.

Lyndon typed, "He was wearing sandals."

Kadance smirked. And then glanced around the large space. She'd spotted a camera in the lobby, and there was one at the main desk, just behind them.

Another message popped up. "If he remembered a name—and that's a big if—it's not my real name."

Confirmation that hippy woman is the mastermind. Female, white, American, probably fifty to sixty years old.

Lyndon typed, "I'm dying of curiosity."

"I'm sure you are. One of your best traits is your curiosity. One of your worst traits is your failure to listen."

"Tell her I'm not going anywhere," Kadance whispered.

"No." Then Lyndon typed, "She doesn't slow me down, and she keeps me busy at night."

"You don't need to protect me," Kadance said.

His voice was quiet but hard. "Doesn't mean I'm not going to try." Then he typed, "Let's you and I stop playing games."

"Ah, but games are so fun. See you in DC."

He waited a few seconds. When no further messages came through, he cleared the cache, restarted the computer, and stood. "There's a club a couple of hours away. If we drive fast, we can try to get in on their meeting." He started toward the door, and she stayed with him.

She took the driver's seat, and while she drove, after giving her the address, he stared into space for a while, surely reviewing everything he'd researched.

"At least we have a general description now," she said.

His eyes continued to be unfocused. "We can start using the proper pronoun."

The corner of her mouth twitched. She didn't smile very much, never had, really, but he made her more than anyone she'd ever known. No one would likely guess he could be funny.

"And she confirmed DC," she said. "Though we should be careful of if or where she's trying to lead us."

"Agreed. We're probably nothing more than rats in a maze to her."

"Me, yes. But I think you're something more to her. Has she decided you're too fun to play with, or maybe it would be a waste to kill you?"

"I figure she's reaching out to me for one of two reasons: she's having fun playing, or she's decided I have information that might be useful."

"Or maybe both. Either way, she's definitely having fun playing. Or maybe she's testing you."

His eyes finally refocused, and he turned to her. "Perhaps she's so impressed I survived the attempts on my life that she decided I might be worth keeping around."

"Maybe."

"You're the only reason I survived."

"And we'll make sure you keep surviving." She turned back to the road.

She felt him looking at her and could almost feel what he was thinking—he wanted to keep her out of this, he wanted to protect her. He'd have to shoot her in the head before she'd back off.

He watched her for several more seconds and then went back to staring blankly at the dash.

LYNDON DIRECTED KADANCE to where the forum had said the VPE meeting was. She parked along the road. The place looked like a half-abandoned office building. The name of the old brick building wasn't legible because half the letters had fallen off.

"Will you leave Mac in the car?" he asked. "I don't know what kind of crowd this is going to be."

She turned and looked at Mac in the back seat. "Look at that, buddy. You've won him over. First time for everything, right?"

He meowed at her, as if answering.

"People don't usually like him?" Lyndon asked.

"More like he doesn't usually like people. He won't attack unless I tell him to, but you'd better not touch him."

Lyndon glanced back at Mac and remembered the cat's first reaction to him had been to growl. "So, I should be honored he lets me pet him?"

"Very."

They got out of the car and headed into the building. The stairs had grime tucked in the corners. In the upstairs hall, the chair rail was falling off in places, and the carpet felt sticky against Lyndon's shoes.

Lyndon stopped in front of 207. He didn't like coming here, not when the mastermind had found him on a forum and had surely figured out what he was researching. She could easily guess where they'd headed. But Kadance had agreed they should come anyway. "You should probably take the lead this time," Lyndon said. "Lying and misdirection will likely be necessary. I'll be the infatuated boyfriend following his girl like a puppy."

"I don't think you're the infatuated type, but we'll give it a shot." Kadance knocked on the door.

Not the infatuated type. He realized she was being funny, teasing him about his tendency toward science and logic, but the comment bothered him.

A young woman with long blonde hair opened the door.

"We're here for the meeting," Kadance said. "It's our first time. Is it open to new people?"

"Sure." Her long skirt swished as she stepped back and opened the door wider. "All Earth-lovers are welcome."

Kadance threw on a glowing smile. "Great. We're so excited. We heard about it on—" She turned to Lyndon. "What was the forum?" She turned back to the blonde and walked into the space. "Anyway, here we are. We're so excited."

Lyndon made himself smile. It didn't feel genuine, though, until he looked at Kadance. He'd just have to keep looking at her. It fit in with the infatuated boyfriend role he was playing, anyway.

"Have a seat wherever you like," the blonde said. "Josh will start in just a few minutes."

"Thanks." Kadance's voice was much more bubbly than normal.

The blonde walked away, and he and Kadance glanced around the room. Some crazy part of him hoped to find an older woman mingling with the small crowd, but they were mostly young, with a few middle-aged people wearing Birkenstocks and smelling of hemp.

Kadance headed toward a couple at the back by a folding table with an old coffeepot, and Lyndon followed obediently. As she talked with them, he got the impression they were a nice couple, very environmentally conscious, but not tipping over to the crazy end of the scale.

They, mostly Kadance, talked with a few other people. Nothing anyone said raised any flags.

"Have a seat please," the blonde called, and everyone shifted around each other in the small space to find a seat. Lyndon continued to play his role and followed Kadance. The man now standing at the front of the room eyed Kadance. Lyndon took a seat next to her, at the end of a row, near the door, and watched the man carefully.

The man—apparently Josh whom the blonde had mentioned—smoothed his hand down his short beard while he waited for the room to come to order and focus on him.

"We have some new faces, I see." Josh smiled, and his gaze landed for a few seconds on Kadance. "You're all here because you love the Earth."

Several people called out their affirmations or clapped.

"Maybe almost as much as me," Josh continued. "The question is how much do you love the Earth? Are you willing to give up all gas-powered transportation? Do you use only solar power or other clean energies? Are you willing to give up all meat consumption? I have made all of these commitments and more."

The room broke out in applause. Lyndon noticed it'd started with the blonde sitting in the front row.

"You seem excited," Josh said. "Good. But how strong is your commitment, really?"

He paused, and the room was quiet.

"How much do you love the Earth?" he continued. "Do you realize she is the only reason you're alive? You owe her everything. How much do you really appreciate her?"

He looked around the room. His gaze again drifted over Kadance.

Lyndon felt his back and chest tighten but did not allow himself to clench his jaw or his fist.

"Are you ready to treat her as she *should* be treated? Unsoiled and free of human pollutants?"

"Yes!" several people chimed.

"You're in the right place, then." Josh smiled. "I'm here to lead you down that path. I'm here to teach you how I have made the necessary commitments. Now, it's not easy. I can attest to that. It's difficult at times, especially when so many in society don't take the Earth seriously. They're selfish and hurtful to our mother. They deny the truth just so they can have what they want. And we have to live with these people, all while still holding ourselves to our virtuous ideals. If you don't think you can do that, if you don't think you're strong enough to take the steps that I've taken, I'll understand if you feel the need to leave."

He slowly looked around the room, making eye contact.

No one moved. *Of course no one is going to leave under that kind of pressure.*

"There are some secrets to making this choice an easier burden, ways to strengthen yourself against society's arrogance. And I will freely share these secrets. As you become ready."

Lyndon wanted to roll his eyes.

"The first thing you need to do," Josh continued, "is dedicate yourself to the VPE movement, to the commitment it demands. Voluntary population control. That's not too much to ask, is it? Simply choose not to add to Mother Earth's burden. Isn't that the least you can do to save your mother?"

The room broke out in applause. Kadance joined in, appearing to be enthusiastic, and Lyndon followed suit, though he was sure his enthusiasm was much less tangible. He let himself look at Kadance to help him hide his annoyance.

Josh stepped forward and started greeting people. Some of them hugged him and looked at him adoringly. The blonde moved around in the background, got him some water, answered questions, and took donations.

Lyndon caught Josh glancing over someone's shoulder at Kadance. Lyndon leaned close to her ear and murmured, "He has a thing for you."

She nodded once.

"It's up to you if you want to use that."

She kept her smile on her face. "My favorite thing. Being treated like a doll."

"You don't have to. We can leave right now."

"Walk with me but get distracted by something when the time is right."

"I'll follow your lead." And he'd also make sure no one touched her. Although he knew she could probably take out this whole room if she wanted to—and he had to admit that was a part of her attractiveness.

He followed her as she mingled through the small crowd. Lyndon peripherally watched Josh as he slowly moved closer. Lyndon slid to her other side, leaving Josh a clearer line of sight to her.

Lyndon moved a couple of feet away and talked with a group of three people—well, he tried to pretend to be interested and asked a few questions.

"Did you enjoy the talk?" Josh asked Kadance.

"Fascinating." Lyndon heard the smile in her voice. She was so good at faking that he started to wonder if she'd ever been fake with him, but then he remembered she'd always been blunt and never made an attempt to be charming.

"How did you hear about our group?"

"A friend of mine mentioned VPE once. James. When I heard about this meeting, I figured I should check it out."

Josh's eyebrow cocked at the name James. "You should come back again next time. Though your brother there didn't seem to be as enthusiastic."

Lyndon wanted to roll his eyes. He knew he'd allowed himself to look at her with much more freedom, to obviously appreciate her. He had not looked at her like a brother would.

"He's my boyfriend," Kadance said.

"Really? He just doesn't look like your type. Not nearly as strong as a lovely woman like you deserves."

Lyndon could almost feel Kadance's urge to punch Josh in the face. The image made him smile a little.

"So, what's the root of this movement?" Kadance asked.

"People who want to protect the Earth. You see, humans cause damage to the Earth in many ways. There's—"

Oh yeah, that guy's getting punched soon if he's not careful.

Kadance interrupted. "I mean who started the movement and why?"

"The true origination story is one of the secrets held for only the most worthy."

Of course it is.

The blonde walked up and said quietly to Josh, "You wanted to speak with Elizabeth before she left."

Josh glanced toward the back of the room. "Ah, yes." He turned back to Kadance. "Will you give me just a few minutes?"

"Sure."

"I'll be right back." He weaved his way through the crowd toward a young woman wearing her shiny brown hair in a bun at the base of her neck.

As he spoke to her, her brow furrowed, and she glanced past him toward the door.

Kadance started casually toward the back of the room, toward the table with coffee. A few seconds later, Lyndon broke off from the group he was with and joined two young men talking closer to the door. He could just hear Josh's conversation.

"I'd be happy to drive you and give you support," Josh said.

"I just don't think I can . . . ," the young woman said.

"I know you don't intend to be selfish," Josh said. "But that's exactly what it is. The Earth can't sustain more. She's past her limits."

Lyndon shifted and noticed the woman's protruding stomach. She had to be at least seven months pregnant. Heat rose up through his chest, a kind of anger he'd never felt before. His body tightened. It took everything in him to remain under control. He looked at Kadance, and she gave him the slightest shake of her head.

"We didn't mean to," the woman said. "I was on birth control. But Tom and I have talked about it and decided to keep her."

Josh sighed and then pressed his lips together. "Do you know what the biggest lie is we've been fed our whole lives?"

She shook her head.

"That all human life is innately valuable."

Lyndon shifted, but stopped when Kadance met his gaze. The only reason he stopped was because he trusted she would take care of this.

The woman's eyes glistened with tears.

"All you see is this little thing that vaguely resembles a baby. But it's really just a, well, kind of a parasite. You're seeing what it might maybe be someday, not what it really is right now, just a cluster of cells feeding off you."

Kadance glanced around at the emptying room. Lyndon nodded goodbye to the two men with whom he'd been talking. Only a few people plus the blonde, who was now cleaning up, remained.

The woman rested her hands on her stomach protectively. "She's my baby." Tears fell down her cheeks. "I just . . . can't . . ."

Josh shook his head. "I'm disappointed in you, Elizabeth. You're being selfish. It's disgusting, one of the most disgusting things I've ever seen in my life."

Kadance shoved Josh against the wall and held her knife to his throat. "Why don't you try torturing me for a while instead."

TWENTY-FOUR

FROZEN AGAINST THE WALL, Josh looked down with just his eyes to where the knife was starting to draw blood.

"Hey!" One of the two men left in the room barreled toward Kadance.

Lyndon stepped into his path and drove his fist into the man's nose. The man's back thumped against the floor, and he held his hands to his nose. Blood seeped out from between his fingers. "Back off," Lyndon growled.

The other man took a step toward him. Lyndon made eye contact, and the man stopped.

Lyndon stood in the way, protecting Kadance so she could focus on educating Josh.

"If you contact Elizabeth, if you even look at her again, I will come after you," Kadance said in a voice that was calm and level and yet laced with a threat more intense than the knife on Josh's throat.

Kadance's tone changed to become more businesslike. "Elizabeth, please leave and don't associate with this person again."

Lyndon heard Elizabeth's footsteps, and then she walked by him toward the door. She paused, looked back at Kadance, and whispered, "Thank you."

"Take good care of your daughter," Lyndon said.

Elizabeth set her hands on her stomach. "I will." She opened the door and bolted out. He heard her hurried footsteps down the hall.

"Now," Kadance said, "I'm not going to kill you. I've had enough of that in my life."

The one man still standing shifted toward the door and slid out.

"But I want you to remember this little lesson," Kadance continued. "Convincing mothers to kill their babies gives you some psychopathic high, a sense of power. Now, every time you think about that sense of power, I want you to remember this moment. Right now. This blade on your skin, mere seconds from severing major arteries and killing you. It's a pretty distinct feeling, right?"

Quiet.

"Right?"

Josh whimpered, "Yes."

"Good. Now take a moment to replace that sense of power with this feeling of powerlessness and terror. This is what you need to remember, this right here."

There was a sound of fabric shifting against the wall. Lyndon didn't turn to look but guessed Kadance had pushed the knife harder against his neck or perhaps shifted it up, making Josh stand on his toes.

"Are you feeling the terror adequately?"

Josh whined. "Yes, yes."

"Good." Kadance lowered her voice, a dangerous sound Lyndon hadn't imagined even her capable of. "If you do something like that again, I will find out." She paused. "And I will come back and kill you."

Quiet.

Kadance's voice resumed its calm tone. "Do you believe me?"

Josh barely got any sound out. "Yes."

"Excellent. Now that we've taken care of that bit of business, back to the reason we're here."

That same sound of fabric shifting against the wall. Lyndon

guessed she'd taken the knife away from his neck, and he slid back down from his toes.

"Let's hear that origin story of VPE," Kadance said.

"I . . . I don't know," Josh stammered. "I read a blog, and it spoke to me, so I started teaching it."

"What blog?"

"I don't know. It was taken down."

There was a tinging sound, probably Kadance tapping the tip of the blade against the table. "I realize you don't know me very well," Kadance said. "But I think we've had a moment today, don't you think? I think you understand exactly what will happen if you lie to me."

"She'll kill me."

"Think about this for a moment." The tinging sound again. "Who do you think is the most immediate threat?"

A pause.

She continued tapping the blade.

"It's VPE.extinction.com."

The man on the floor in front of Lyndon crawled toward the door. Once he was out, Lyndon locked the door. The only people in the room now were Kadance, Josh, the blonde, and him. He stood in front of the door and crossed his arms.

"What else can you tell me?" Kadance asked.

"She gives us direction on what to teach. It's in the mail. I don't know who she is."

"Let's see some of this mail."

"We have to burn it." Blood dripped down Josh's neck onto the collar of his T-shirt.

"You say 'we.' How many *teachers* are there?"

"I don't know. We get directions. That's it."

"How did she choose you?"

"There was a test on the website. An aptitude thing. She said I'm a perfect leader."

"How did you recognize the name James?"

"He came through here once. Said he was checking up on all the teachers. He didn't say anything else. He came to one meeting—that's all."

"How do you know she's female?"

Josh glanced at the blonde on the other side of the room. "Stacey figured it out. She said it was a couple of things she said. It's in her phrasing."

Kadance smiled at the blonde. "Very good. What exact phrases?"

The blonde's voice shook. "I don't remember all of them. There were only a couple."

"What do you remember?"

"In the last letter, she said something about her 'dear son.' That's a way a woman would phrase it."

Son?

"When was this, and what did she say about her 'dear son'?"

"A few days ago. She said he would be a leader."

"Be a leader of what?"

The blonde shook her head. "She didn't say. She's always really cryptic. I don't understand half of what she writes."

What Lyndon wouldn't do to get a copy of one of those letters.

"How does she sign the letters?"

"VPE."

"Thank you very much." Kadance tapped the knife against the table once more, and Josh flinched.

Kadance turned and sheathed her knife while walking toward Lyndon. Lyndon carefully watched the two, made sure they stayed put.

"Do you have any questions?" Kadance asked Lyndon.

"I think you covered it." Though he had some questions to ask her. He opened the door for her.

She started to step through but then paused and looked back at the blonde. She nodded toward Lyndon. "This is the kind of man you should be looking for. Someone who's strong enough not to have to be in control all the time."

The blonde looked at Lyndon. He didn't understand her expression, though he'd seen expressions like that on women's faces before. Kadance walked out, and he followed her.

They got in the car, and she started the engine.

"We should avoid libraries," Lyndon said. "Too many cameras."

"I have an idea." She reached back and grabbed a towel from the back seat and then opened the bottle of water in the console and dampened the towel. "But first, give me your hand."

He glanced down at his right knuckles, at the blood from the man he'd punched. He hesitated to let her touch him, but he didn't want to let on how difficult her touch was becoming for him. He set his hand on the armrest between them.

She held his hand and gently started wiping the dried blood off his skin. Though her skin wasn't as soft as some women's, her hands were still slender and lovely, graceful. Knowing how dangerous her hands could be made her gentleness feel all that much more special.

"You punched him just once, right?" she asked.

He just nodded.

"It was some punch. There's a lot of blood. All I heard was the smack of flesh and then his back hitting the floor." She smiled at him, an actual smile. "I'm impressed."

He didn't let himself respond.

She turned her gaze back down to his hand. "Thank you for having my back."

"I always will."

Her voice quieted. "I know."

They were quiet while she finished cleaning all the blood off his hand. It'd gotten into all the crevices of his battered knuckles. His grandfather had trained him on a canvas punching bag since he was little, and he'd kept up with it throughout his life.

Once she finished, she folded the towel and set it in the back seat next to Mac. She put the car in drive.

A short while later, she parked at a big box electronics store and took some cash out of her bag. "You should stay here. We need to keep your face off cameras as much as possible."

"She might be watching for you too."

"It's a lot less likely." She walked toward the store.

Lyndon waited. He didn't like her being alone with such an unpredictable opponent out there. But she came back only about ten minutes later with a bag in hand.

She got in, handed him the bag, and started driving. "I figured you'd know how to make it work."

He took a phone with a good-sized screen out of the bag. They had agreed to be as frugal as possible in case cash was needed at some point, but he agreed they had to have some kind of connection to the internet, and libraries were not safe.

"I bought prepaid talk and internet. No one should be able to trace it." She glanced over as he opened the box. "You can figure out how to set it up, right?"

He smirked and quickly began configuring the device.

"We should've gotten a second phone, something simple, so we can communicate if we separate," he said.

"I don't plan on leaving you alone."

He held back his frustration. He kept trying to think of ways to keep her safe, but she seemed bent on being the front line. He'd just have to find ways to protect her, even when she worked against it.

She kept driving north. Once he had the phone set up, he typed in the website address they'd gotten from Josh.

"What's it say?" She glanced over.

"There's basically a mission statement, a bunch of rules, and a test."

"Too much to ask for a bio of the leader?"

"If only people were so helpful. The letter V has come up a couple of times, though. I wonder if that is actually part of her name. Could be why she specifically said Dr. Pearce had never known her real name. He had actually known it, and she wanted to throw us off."

"What's the mission statement?"

"It's several thousand words. It basically comes down to we owe Mother Earth our lives, we're selfish creatures taking her life from her, all human life it not innately valuable, only sociopaths kill their mothers. Basically all of Josh's talking points but expounded upon ad nauseum."

"Does she explain her logic behind all human life not being innately valuable?"

"She touches on several points—the existence of sociopaths, murderers, sexual predators, child abusers, human traffickers. Then she makes a point that life doesn't really start until one chooses to do right, which I think is the most dangerous idea in this whole thing."

"When she says 'do right,' she really means live like she says and agree with her ideals?"

"Yes. So, she's basically saying anyone who disagrees with her is not human."

"And therefore not worthy of mercy. Not worthy of life at all."

"She then takes that point and moves on to say preborn children aren't sentient beings and therefore aren't valuable life."

"They're parasites like Josh said."

"Yes."

She gripped the steering wheel until her hands shook.

Lyndon wanted to touch her hand or her arm and try to soothe her, but he didn't trust himself to touch her. Being close to her was becoming more and more difficult. He was quiet while she controlled her anger.

"What about this son she talked about in her last letter?" Kadance asked.

"He's not mentioned. In fact, from this, I get the impression she doesn't have children."

"That would seem to fit her ideals better. Do you think it could be someone else, someone she's kind of adopted and molded?"

"I think that's a good possibility." He paused. "Who's James?"

Silence.

She gave zero reaction, kept her focus on the road, as if he hadn't said anything. But he knew her well enough to know that inscrutable expression was nothing more than a mask. He continued to look at her but didn't push her other than that.

TWENTY-FIVE

KADANCE NEVER THOUGHT she'd have to discuss James with another living person. It was hard enough living with the memories inside her own head, let alone verbalizing them. But she had to.

"You don't have to tell me anything personal," Lyndon said.

"It's all personal with James."

Lyndon quietly waited.

"He's how I heard about VPE," she finally said. "Though I didn't know the extent of the movement. He explained it as simply choosing not to have children to help reduce the population. I'd assumed that people who followed the movement and wanted families could simply adopt, which sounded honorable to me."

"But somewhere along the way you realized perhaps it wasn't as honorable as he'd described because you discovered he wasn't honorable either?"

If there was one thing she could count on Lyndon to do, it was read between the lines. "Yes."

He again quietly waited.

She sat straighter in her seat and tried to figure out how to start her explanation.

"Why don't we stop for a little while," he said.

"We need to get to DC."

"It'll take, what, five to six hours from here? It'll be too late to do anything or talk to anyone."

They were passing through a small town on a rural highway. There wasn't much—just a couple of abandoned buildings, a Dollar General, and a Subway. She pulled off into the empty parking lot of a building with boarded windows and crumbling brick facade. Gravel crunched under the tires as the car came to a stop.

"I need a walk." Kadance opened her door and stepped out. Then she opened the back door and let Mac jump down. She squatted in front of him and petted his soft fur. "Want to run around a little bit?" she asked him. "There's some grass over there."

He meowed.

"I swear he understands you," Lyndon said.

"He does." She locked the car, then picked Mac up and carried him to an overgrown grassy lot next to the gravel area. She set him down in the grass, and he sprinted off after a bird.

Lyndon followed her. "Looks like this used to be an orchard." He looked around at the trees, some dead, some overgrown.

"I bet it's still pretty in the spring."

There was a smile in his eyes before he looked away, toward Mac running around like a nut. She'd caught expressions like that in Lyndon's eyes before, but she wasn't entirely sure what they meant. Which was frustrating.

She ambled slowly around the lot, and Lyndon stayed by her side.

She took a deep breath. "I was in a relationship with James, but he wasn't who I thought he was."

"Your only relationship."

She glanced over at him and wanted to ask why he thought that, but then she admonished herself for caring. "We met not long after I left my family. He kept trying to strike up conversations with me."

"So, you weren't living like you are now—moving around, not following any patterns."

"Not yet. I thought using a fake ID and going someplace random that I didn't have any connection to would be enough. I liked this little farmer's market. I'd go once or twice a week. He was there sometimes and would try striking up a conversation. At first, I didn't even acknowledge him, but after a while . . . I was so lonely."

"You were alone in your service and then alone again back home." Then he added, "Is this before you found Mac?"

She nodded. "Finally, I gave in and started talking to him a little. He was considerate and sweet. He drew me in faster than I could imagine."

"But how did he do that? You're like a human lie detector."

"He didn't lie. Everything he told me about his family, his past, even his business was the truth."

"But he left out some details?"

"He was careful. I look back now, and I realize how careful, how precise. He even brought me home to meet his mother. Everything he'd said lined up. Eventually, he convinced me to move in with him. There was a part of me that wanted what everyone else has—a real home, family, security. I wanted to be normal."

"What made you realize something wasn't right?"

"I think moving in together was his failing."

"He couldn't be as precise about what he let you see, not with you right there all the time."

"The first time he lied was when I saw him end a call and I asked him who it was. He said it was a telemarketer. I knew him well enough that I caught the lie immediately. But I didn't want to suspect him of something wrong. I told myself it was innocent— maybe he was planning a special date or something. I noticed little details but kept telling myself I was being crazy, that I could trust him. But then he asked why I wouldn't consider seeing my family."

"How much had you told him about them?"

"Not much, but enough that he knew that topic was off-limits. At first, I tried to tell myself he was just concerned about me.

But then I started thinking—he put so much emphasis on family our whole relationship. He talked about his all the time, how great they were and how he valued those relationships. He talked about having children and how his mom would be so excited to be a grandma. All of it had sounded innocent, and quite frankly, lovely. But he didn't keep pictures of his family anywhere, not in his wallet or on the walls or even in his phone. Nothing. It was all a façade, an amazingly precise and planned façade."

She paused. They ambled through the abandoned orchard, and Mac ran through the overgrown grass charging at birds and even climbing one of the trees. She felt bad for having him cooped up all the time lately. Lyndon quietly walked with her and gave her space to think, to be ready to keep talking.

"Once I realized something was wrong," she said, "I started planning. I didn't want him to see me hustling people at the shooting range, so I'd stopped, which meant I didn't have much cash. I was so angry at myself for allowing myself to get into that situation. I started going to a range to raise cash, but I had to be careful. He called me a lot. I had thought it was sweet that he missed me, but now I see he was just keeping track of me. I couldn't very well answer the phone at a shooting range. It took almost a week to get enough money together and find someone to make me another fake ID. On the day I planned to leave, he didn't leave for the morning appointment I knew he had. I asked him didn't he need to go."

"Had he figured it out somehow?"

"I don't know if he just knew me so well that he noticed a difference, though I was sure I hadn't let on. Or maybe he caught wind through the guy who made my ID. But I think most likely it was some kind of tracker. He was a cybersecurity expert—he definitely had the expertise. I'd picked up my ID the day before, and he'd have had to do just a little research to figure out what I was doing at that location."

"He might be the one helping to track us through cameras and probably facial recognition."

"Now that I know he's involved, I agree." The thing still bugging her was, what was the likelihood someone she knew was somehow involved with this mastermind woman?

"What happened next?"

"I tried to pretend I needed to go out and get some groceries, but he wouldn't let me leave. It got ugly pretty fast."

"Was he *capable* of forcing you to stay? Not too many people would have a chance against you."

"He wasn't, no. But then my father showed up."

Lyndon stopped walking. "James was a plant? The whole time?"

Kadance looked out across the road and nodded.

"I'm so sorry, Kadance." His voice was so kind, she could almost believe he understood how hard it'd been. Devastating.

She turned her attention to Mac to distract herself. He bounded across the grass and through the trees, zigging and zagging. Every so often, a bird would flee out of the grass. Then he changed direction and came trotting toward her. He stood up on his back paws and reached up her leg with his front paws.

"Are you tired now?" she asked him.

He meowed.

She reached down and picked him up, and he wrapped his arms around her neck and laid his head on her shoulder.

Lyndon smiled. "He hugs you like a person." He moved closer and petted a hand down Mac's back. "He seems to know when you need a hug."

"He always has." She leaned her head against Mac. "He found me just after I escaped."

Lyndon continued slowly petting his hand down Mac's back. Mac purred in her ear.

"How did he find you?" Lyndon asked. "Did you have to fight your father?"

She sighed. "No. Thankfully. When my father walked in our townhouse, I pulled my knife from my belt, grabbed James in a choke from behind, and held the knife on him. Both of them—

they both seemed to think I would never hurt James. They were so arrogant about it. But I would have." She paused. "I've never felt that out of control."

"Of course you did."

Hearing him say that, knowing someone understood, was an odd feeling.

"But you didn't hurt him," Lyndon said.

"I wanted to. I'd never felt that before. I've killed a lot of people. They were evil. They hurt other people for pleasure. But I never *wanted* to kill anyone. I had a job to do, and I knew my job was to help protect innocent lives. But it was never enjoyable. It always hurt."

There was a softness in Lyndon's eyes, and then he looked out across the field dotted with trees. "How did you get away from them?"

"They both kept telling me I would never hurt James. He was too important. He was my first kiss, my first romance, first . . . everything. They seemed to know how much all of that had affected me."

"But they'd tricked you, manipulated you to the ultimate degree. I can't imagine the kind of rage that would produce. You've never had anyone, you finally let yourself feel something for someone, and then you find out not only were you betrayed, but it'd never been real in the first place."

"Not real for him."

Lyndon's voice quieted. "But real for you."

Her throat tightened, and she nodded.

Mac wrapped his arms around her neck more tightly.

"Did you hurt him?" Lyndon asked gently.

She took a slow breath and smoothed a hand down Mac's back. "I backed James up into the kitchen. I had him off-balance—he couldn't fight. I managed to open the back door. I plunged the knife into his thigh and ran. Thankfully, I'd plotted an escape already. I'd practiced. So I could run it even with . . ."

"Even with tears in your eyes."

She didn't answer.

"It's okay." His voice was soft. "You don't have to be Super-woman for everyone. I'm not James—I won't twist your emotions in some game."

Her voice barely made a sound. "I know." And she did know. She wasn't sure how it'd happened, how she'd allowed it to happen, but she trusted him. Panic started to rise—her fear that she'd allowed it to happen again. She'd decided never to trust anyone. Ever. She'd learned her lesson. But she'd been diligent with Lyndon. She hadn't let her loneliness win. She'd analyzed every single one of his actions. He actually was trustworthy.

The realization was surreal, like the world was all of a sudden a different color.

She made herself keep talking. "I was on foot, so I'd planned several hiding places just in case. I ended up stopping in an alley in a slummy area of town. I'd been running for a couple of hours, and I needed to rest for a while. I was confident I'd lost them. I climbed behind a dumpster and tried to sleep. But my mind wouldn't stop." She looked at Lyndon. "I think I understand how you feel, when your mind won't slow down, and your head just aches like an overexerted muscle. And that's when Mac found me. I heard a noise and stared at the end of my little nook behind the dumpster, and around the corner comes this huge orange cat. He stood there and just stared at me. It was the weirdest thing. I'd never been an animal person. Too much responsibility, too much commitment, too much everything. But I put my knife away, held my hand out, and called him over. He came straight to me. But then he started meowing. You know, that really demanding tone he has. It scared me—I was still in flee mode, still afraid to see my father's face peer around the corner. I grabbed up the big cat to try to quiet him, and he reached his paws around and hugged me. Just like this."

"I bet it felt nice."

She just nodded.

She kept talking to push her emotions away. "We stayed the night there. By morning, my urgency to flee had calmed and I could think more clearly, more calmly. I snuck out of the alley with Mac. He had a big abrasion on his back and several cigarette burns. I found a vet for him, used the little money I had. He healed, and he hasn't left me ever since."

Lyndon just smiled. "So, why did you name him Mac?"

"Multiple reasons. Mack truck, mac and cheese, Mac computers."

"So, big, orange, and smart."

"Exactly."

Lyndon's eyes turned soft again, and he looked away.

"What is it?" she asked. "You keep trying to hide your expression from me." She tried to sound more curious than demanding.

He paused for a couple of seconds.

TWENTY-SIX

THEN LYNDON FACED KADANCE. "You should be cold-blooded. You were literally raised to be a killer. Your soul should've died a long time ago. But here you are."

She had no idea how to respond.

He walked away and meandered back through the field toward the car.

She watched him walk, that masculine but understated stride, the way he held himself with confidence but not arrogance.

Mac lifted his head, looked at Lyndon, and meowed.

Kadance started toward the car as well.

They both got in the car, and Mac climbed over to Lyndon's lap. With a gentle hand, he pulled a couple of leaves out of Mac's fur, and then he rested his hand on Mac and rubbed his thumb over his soft orange coat. "Looks like he tired himself out," Lyndon said.

Kadance realized she was watching him and started the car.

"Back at the VPE meeting," Lyndon said, "I threw out the word *cleansing* while I was talking with different people to see if I'd get a reaction."

Kadance was sure he'd heard all of her conversations while holding his own conversations at the same time. "Any reaction?"

"None. I watched carefully. I honestly don't think any of them had any idea. Which makes sense seeing as how Josh doesn't appear to be in the loop either."

"I agree."

"Do you think James could be this 'son' she'd mentioned in her correspondence?"

"His real mom is still alive, as far as I know. And there is no way she's the person we're looking for."

"Maybe, like you said, this son is someone she's molded, not an actual son."

She appreciated that he trusted her assessment of James's mother. "That could be. Might seem a little weird if his mother is still alive."

"It does seem a little odd."

"But I don't think we should rule it out."

"Never rule out a hypothesis without doing the proper research."

"Yes, professor."

"Doctor, not professor." He adjusted his glasses just so.

The corner of her mouth tweaked into a slight smile.

He started to smile but then focused out the windshield. "Is there anything about James we can research—maybe look into a company he worked for, anyone he might have ever mentioned?"

"He was an independent consultant the whole time I knew him, and he never mentioned having done anything else. The only people he ever mentioned were family, surely all part of the plan to manipulate me. I met them all—I don't think there's any kind of lead there."

His brows pulled together. "What do you think the likelihood is—"

"That someone from my past is involved in what's happening now? Especially since you and I came together by pure chance?"

He nodded.

"I've been wondering the same thing myself. I suppose it could all be a weird coincidence." She shook her head. "But we should keep our eyes open. I'll keep thinking about anything we could research about James."

"Thank you." Then he added, "I'm sorry this is bringing up bad memories."

"Nothing you can do."

"I can listen if you want to talk."

They were quiet for a while. Still on Lyndon's lap, Mac laid his head down and fell asleep. Lyndon kept gently stroking his fur. A wild thought entered her head that she wanted to feel for herself how gentle Lyndon's hands were.

She blinked hard to try to shove the thought out of her head, but she couldn't quite get it out. She'd been close to only one man, and she'd vowed never to get close to anyone again, especially a man, and most certainly not physically. She'd started slipping down the slope of closeness with Lyndon—he knew so many of her secrets. But she would not allow it to develop past friendship.

No matter how lonely she was.

No matter how wild her thoughts got sometimes.

When Lyndon started talking, Kadance sat straighter in her seat and tried to concentrate on what he was saying, not what she was thinking. "James knows your past, right?" he asked. "So why doesn't this mastermind person seem to know anything about you? I know your family doesn't know you were CIA, but they thought you were an army sniper, right?"

She glanced over at Lyndon and then back to the windshield. "I assumed my family told him about my past, as much as they know, but maybe they didn't. James would've pushed for details before getting so involved, but maybe they lied to him."

"He knew you pretty well—would he have realized you weren't just some random beautiful woman?"

She ignored how his matter-of-fact statement of her beauty made her feel. "He's very smart. I didn't talk to him about my service, but he knew I had a past."

"And not something else, like a bad relationship or similar."

Then he added, "No, there's no way he'd have confused you for a fleeing battered woman."

"Are you saying I'm more like a batterer than a batteree?"

"I'm saying even an idiot would realize you'd likely rip off a man's testicles if he tried beating you."

"Why, sir, I think that's the nicest thing anyone's ever said to me."

He grinned.

She focused out the windshield.

They drove for hours. Eventually, he insisted on taking a turn driving so she could rest. She thought about refusing. It wasn't unusual for her to drive for fifteen hours straight. But she decided to let him be kind—he seemed to enjoy it.

When did I start caring about making him happy?

When they were parked on the side of the rural highway, Lyndon stood from the passenger seat and lifted Mac with him. Mac gave an annoyed meow. At the back of the car, Lyndon gently handed her Mac. Their hands brushed.

Mac yawned and laid his head on her shoulder.

In the passenger seat, she kept ahold of him, and he fell asleep within a few minutes after the steady hum of the car continued down the road.

"I stay on this road for how long?" Lyndon asked.

She explained the route she'd planned.

"Do you have the whole country memorized?"

"You're one to talk about memorizing."

"The major freeways I understand," he said. "But why do you know the rural routes as well?"

She hesitated to answer. The convincing lies that came so easily stopped at the tip of her tongue. She didn't like lying to him.

"How many times have they found you?" he asked.

"Enough."

"But how? You use fake IDs, you keep to yourself, you're virtually invisible." He glanced over at her then turned back to the road.

"You stop them. When you find out about a new assassination, you race there and stop them. Don't you?"

She looked out the side window. "You're dangerous to be around. Do you realize that?"

"You don't need to hide from me."

Several seconds of quiet.

He added, "I understand it's been necessary most of your life, but it's not necessary with me."

Barely a movement, she nodded.

"But it's second nature at this point."

She continued staring out the window into the darkness. "You already know more about me than anyone ever has."

He paused, and then his voice was quiet. "I'm honored."

They were quiet again.

The fields and trees flashed by. Eventually, she fell asleep.

It felt like a while later when the slowing of the car woke her. He was parking outside a large white church in a very small town. "How close are we to DC?" she asked.

"About an hour." He turned off the phone screen, a map program. "We should both try to get some decent sleep. Once we get into town, there's no hiding."

There would be cameras everywhere. "I don't see a hotel. We can just sleep in the car."

"It's a little cramped in here, at least for me. I was thinking we could stretch out on a couple of pews."

"In the church?"

"Small town like this, the church is probably unlocked all the time so the parishioners can visit with God whenever they need to."

She looked at him closer to try to determine if he was joking. It was too dark to see his face clearly. He stood from the car, and she followed. Mac shifted in her arms, and she put him down so he could stretch properly. She and Mac followed Lyndon into the church.

Inside was dark. She looked around, curious.

He turned, surely about to say something, and paused. "You've never been in a church, have you?"

"No."

He nodded once and turned toward the row of pews on the left. He sat down, leaned back, stretched out his legs, and ran his hands over his face.

She sat a few feet from him. "Eyes tired? Night driving can be hard."

"Mind tired." He dropped his hands into his lap. "I'm having difficulty getting it to slow down. It's becoming a constant problem."

"Want to talk a little?"

"You've got to be exhausted."

She shrugged.

"Right," he said. "You've probably gone days without sleep before."

"It was a contest when I was little—go longer than my cousins without sleep. Loser went a day without food."

"Sounds like child abuse."

She shrugged again. She didn't understand why she talked so easily with him, and it was getting worse. It had to be the loneliness finally getting to her.

"Did you ever lose the contest?" he asked.

"Once when I was five. I was the youngest, and I hadn't yet learned the tricks to staying awake."

"You never lost again?"

"I didn't want to see that look on my father's face again. Disappointment, embarrassment."

"I'm trying to wrap my mind around what your childhood was like."

"It was what it was. Yours was no picnic either."

"I had loss. That was hard because I loved them so much. I never lived in the same fear you did."

"I didn't live in fear. I got over that real fast."

He looked away from her toward the altar. Just visible through the darkness was a huge white cross on the wall, almost up to the peak of the rafters.

A few minutes passed. She kept waiting for him to stretch out across the pew.

He remained focused toward the altar, toward that big cross.

"Why do you keep staring at that thing?"

He looked at her but didn't answer.

"The cross," she said. "Is that what you keep looking at?"

"Yes."

"Why?"

His brows twitched. "Why does that bother you?"

"Why do you keep looking at it?"

"It's a reminder."

"Of what?"

His brows pulled together.

"I know what religion is," she said. "I get that some people are drawn to it. Maybe because it makes them feel like there's some kind of order to life or something. But why would *you* care about it?"

"What do you mean why would *I* care about it?"

"You're a scientist. You're educated. You're the most logic-driven person I've ever met."

"Exactly."

She stood and walked toward the center aisle.

"Why are you angry?" he asked.

She turned around. "Because I thought I understood you."

"I think you do."

She pointed at the cross.

"Have you ever studied it?" he asked.

"I know plenty about religion. I lived among terrorists who used it to justify bombings for ten years. Religion is just a way to control the masses."

"Would you sit with me for a few minutes? I'll explain why I think the way I do."

She stayed where she was.

"This isn't some attempt to convert you," he said. "If I explain my logic, you'll see you understand me just as well as you thought you did."

She sat down on the end of the pew. "Are you telling me you believe in God?"

"I thought about it for a long time, and that's the logical conclusion I came up with."

"What about science?"

"What about it?"

"It refutes the existence of God."

"Where?"

"The big bang theory."

"How does that refute God?"

"He didn't bring the universe into existence."

"We don't know for sure what brought the universe into existence, but the big bang theory is the most agreed upon. If that is how the universe began, why is it logical to assume God didn't put it into motion? To make an assumption that God does not exist and did not cause the big bang is unscientific. Plus, we have the law of cause and effect. Every effect must have a cause. The only thing that could possibly be the beginning of everything is an intelligent Being that has always been and therefore has no cause himself."

"There's no such thing as something that has always existed. Everything has a beginning."

"That's an assumption. Do you have any evidence it's impossible?"

"You just said the law of cause and effect means everything has to have a cause."

"If God is the one who created this orderly universe, including the law of cause and effect," he said, "it stands to reason he is the only thing that can exist outside of its laws."

"You don't have any evidence God exists, any more than anyone has proof he doesn't exist."

"That's why I've analyzed everything I could so carefully. Study just a few things about this universe, and you'll see how perfectly designed it is. The human eye, for example, is staggering in its precision. And there are millions of other examples. That's evidence for intelligent design. I can't prove it, but the hypothesis of his existence is much stronger than the assumption he does not exist. There's more logic on my side."

"Okay, you think it's possible God exists. But why are you looking at that cross like it can jump down off the wall and help you?"

"My thoughts on Jesus are a little different."

She smirked.

"I've studied all the evidence that shows he did actually exist, and the Bible appears to be accurate in its portrayal of his life. But none of that is what matters most."

"Are you throwing logic out the window now?"

"Before Jesus came, the world was pretty horrible. The Jews lived by the Ten Commandments, and don't get me wrong, those are immeasurably important. But Jesus is the one who brought the concepts of kindness, humility, compassion. He taught that we should love everyone—no matter their race, gender, wealth, social standing. His disciples spread his teachings, and people all over the world intuitively realized the value. The disciples were poor and didn't have authority to require people to follow those teachings. In fact, they were horribly persecuted, and most were eventually put to death. But the people chose to believe those teachings."

"Christians have done some horrible things in the name of their God."

"Humans are not perfect. Bad people will use whatever they can to get what they want. Throughout history, people have tried to steal the power of Christianity. It's a horrible sin, but it's the sin of those people. If someone stole your car and rammed it into a crowd of people, is that the car's fault? Is that your fault? No, it's the driver's fault."

Kadance stared straight ahead and didn't respond.

"For me, Jesus is more than logical. His teachings do make the world a better place—you can find empirical evidence for that. But even stronger than that, for me, is that his teachings reflect who I want to be. I probably fail more than I succeed, but I keep trying."

Quiet.

She watched as Mac walked around the church, smelled every surface, and investigated every crevice.

Her voice was quieter, no longer abrasive. "But why do you keep trying?"

Peripherally, she saw as he looked over at her. "The same reason you do."

She didn't understand. She didn't understand any of it.

But one thing she couldn't deny was that she trusted Lyndon's intelligence and honesty.

"I would never tell anyone they should believe anything simply because I said so," he said. "People should study for themselves. Read both theologians and atheists, read the history and the science, and then make your own logical conclusions."

She still kept her gaze straight ahead. "But why do you seem to take comfort in it?" It seemed like a lot more to him than research and hypothesizing.

"Because I've felt his presence."

She looked over at him.

He added, "I think you have too."

She stared at him.

He turned and stretched out across the pew.

I don't understand. Her entire life, she'd believed all religions were the same just with different wrapping, but he was right: she'd made assumptions; she'd believed anti-religion, and most specifically anti-Christian, propaganda; she hadn't really considered all sides.

She sat there on that pew and stared at that big cross on the wall for a long time.

TWENTY-SEVEN

LYNDON WOKE TO FAINT LIGHT starting to enter the church through the stained-glass windows. He sat up and realized Kadance was still seated in the same position. "Did you not sleep?"

She didn't answer.

Then, at the sound of the door opening, they both looked behind them. She set her hand on her knife at her hip.

A man entered, dressed in jeans, a sweater, and a work coat, and he stopped short at the sight of them.

Lyndon stood. "We're just leaving. We didn't have any place else to stay."

The man continued down the main aisle. "Much too cold to stay in your car last night."

The man passed, and Kadance took her hand off her knife, stood, and moved toward the aisle.

The man stopped and looked back, seemed to look at them more closely. "There's a shower downstairs. Not the fanciest, but if you want to use it, you're welcome."

"We need to get going," Kadance said.

Lyndon came up behind her and murmured in her ear so the man wouldn't hear. He was careful not to touch her, but he felt her body heat and could smell her natural sweet scent. "We'll be

200

meeting the FBI today. We should try to look as presentable as possible if we have any hope of being taken seriously."

She nodded, stepped away from him, and addressed the man. "Thank you, sir."

"It looks a little grungy, but it is clean."

She smiled. "A little grunge doesn't bother us."

"Stairs are just through there." He pointed to a hallway off the sanctuary. "Just holler if you have any trouble." He kept walking and disappeared through a door to the far left of the altar.

"I'll grab our bags." Lyndon slipped by her and out the door. After being so close to her, he needed the rush of cold air.

A few minutes later, they'd found the old bathroom in the basement. It was a small room off a larger room filled with rows of folding tables and metal folding chairs. Lyndon insisted Kadance shower first.

While he waited, he sat in one of the folding chairs. She hadn't spoken directly to him at all this morning. He wasn't sure if she was angry or pensive. Or maybe both.

Lyndon heard footsteps on the stairs and looked over as the man entered the room.

"Find everything all right?" the man asked.

"Yes, sir. Thank you again."

The man pulled a chair out and sat down next to Lyndon. "I'm Errol, by the way."

"You're the pastor here?"

"That I am." Errol leaned back in his chair. "Do you need something to eat?"

"Thank you, but no. We have some money. There was just no hotel around."

Errol nodded.

They sat for a moment in comfortable silence.

"She's important to you," Errol said.

Lyndon looked over at him. Errol's expression was kind. Something about him reminded Lyndon of his father.

Finally, Lyndon admitted, "She is." He turned away from Errol, looked straight ahead. "But she's not mine."

Lyndon felt Errol looking at him.

Errol nodded but said nothing more.

The bathroom door opened, and Kadance came out, fully dressed and hair already braided. Some part of him was disappointed not to get to see her hair, the way it flowed like a calm black river. But then he reminded himself it was for the best.

She glanced at him and then walked over and set her bag down several chairs away. Her expression didn't appear to be angry, but she was the master of controlling her expression.

He stood, picked up his bag, and headed into the bathroom. He had a wild thought that she might just leave him while he was in there.

KADANCE SAT in one of the folding metal chairs.

"I'm Errol," the man said. "The pastor here."

"I'm Sarah." Her alias came to her lips easily, even after using her real name with Lyndon these last several days. It struck her how much of a relief it'd been to be herself. Though she knew it wouldn't last. Even if she wanted to stay with him longer, have a real friendship, she couldn't do that to him. She was a hand grenade waiting to explode.

"You have a lot on your mind," Errol said.

She looked over at him and donned her sweetest smile. "Don't we all?"

He tilted his head. "Some more than others."

"If only we all had simple lives."

"Ah, but adversity is how we best learn. Blessed are those who have struggled."

"Not everyone learns from their struggles."

He nodded. "But at least they have the opportunity. No one can be forced to learn."

They were quiet for a couple of minutes. She listened to Lyndon's shower running and tried not to remember what he looked like with his shirt off. She forced the thought out of her head, and she picked up Mac, who'd followed them downstairs. Thankfully, he hadn't growled at the pastor.

"I can see you've struggled in your life, Sarah."

She looked over at him. She briefly considered if he was perhaps a plant, come to take information back to the mastermind, but she dismissed the idea. There was no way she could've tracked them here, and no alarm bells went off in her head when Errol spoke. He was just a nice older man, who was maybe a little lonely all alone in this church.

"No more than anyone else, I'd guess," she said.

"Oh, I don't think that's quite right." He smiled, and his blue eyes twinkled with kindness. "Have you learned from your struggles?"

She took a slow breath.

"Sounds complicated," he said.

"I didn't think so."

"But recently your view has changed?"

"Something like that." She really wasn't sure what to think right now.

"Sometimes a change of view is just what we need."

The shower turned off. Mac sat up on her lap and watched the bathroom door.

The pastor smiled at Mac. "Your cat misses his friend already."

She petted Mac's head then down his back, and his tail wagged. She worried he was getting too attached to Lyndon.

The bathroom door opened, and steam wafted toward them. Lyndon walked out, bag in one hand, shoes and shirt in the other. Nothing on but jeans. His lack of a shave the last few days accentuated his strong jaw.

He set his bag down on the table between her and Errol and dropped his shoes on the floor. While he leaned over the table looking through his bag, his stomach and arms flexed a bit. He'd mentioned once that he liked running. She could see it in his build—lean and muscular, thighs and backside that perfectly filled out jeans. And he probably ran shirtless—he was evenly tanned down to his waist.

He pulled a hand through his wet hair, then glanced over at her. She realized how closely she'd been looking at him and turned away. *What's wrong with me?*

He put on his shirt and then his glasses. Then he sat in a chair to put on his socks and shoes.

"Ready?" he asked her.

She stood and picked up her bag. She realized she hadn't spoken to him since last night. She wasn't sure what to say yet.

They thanked the pastor and were out in the car a few minutes later, with Kadance behind the wheel.

They drove in silence.

Finally, Lyndon broke the quiet. "Are you angry?" He didn't sound apologetic, just like he wanted to understand her emotional state.

She paused, thinking. Usually, her emotions were easy to manage—she didn't feel much. "I'm . . . No, I'm not angry."

"Are you all right?"

She liked how kind his voice was. She wondered if he realized he sounded a bit different when he spoke to her than with anyone else.

She answered with "I'm thinking."

He nodded and was quiet.

She thought about asking him not to go shirtless anymore. But she didn't.

She drove. As civilization thickened, so did her tension. Her gaze snagged on every camera.

Lyndon looked up directions on the phone and guided her. He also managed to hack the FBI to make sure he wasn't flagged in their system due to the incident at Dr. Ibekwe's house. Finally, they parked, made sure Mac was okay in the car, and walked toward the FBI headquarters, a large concrete building with windows that made it look like an oversized waffle—a waffle that would chip your teeth.

She spotted a man leaning against a pillar and shifted to Lyndon's other side, closer to the pillar. The man seemed to be watching peripherally.

They passed, and she kept watching out of the corner of her eye.

WHEN KADANCE SHIFTED to his other side, Lyndon looked more closely around them. She made no motion to indicate it, but he was sure she was watching the man behind the concrete column.

The man stepped out behind them.

She swung around and set her hand on her sheathed knife.

The man froze.

Surely, the man had assumed he'd take them off guard.

"What do you want?" she demanded in a quiet but deadly voice.

Lyndon moved to her side. He knew it probably annoyed her. He would let her handle this as she saw fit, but if that man attempted anything against her, Lyndon would drive his fist down the man's throat.

The man's focus flickered to her hand resting on her sheath. Then he smirked, showing missing and brown teeth. Splotchy facial hair grew from his papery skin. Lyndon noticed a little black dot on his coat.

"What d'you got there?" the man said. "Lipstick?"

"Take another step and find out," Kadance said.

"You ain't gonna do nothing here." He motioned toward the building.

"You think I can't make it look like self-defense? I can see the story in tomorrow's paper: Sweet young lady gets attacked by a junkie in our nation's capital. In a brave stance, she kills her attacker."

He smirked again. "You ain't no killer."

She shifted half a step closer, lowered her chin, and bore her gaze into him like a six-inch dagger through his eye.

The smirk melted off his face. Lyndon wasn't sure how he was still standing there, why he hadn't run away or at least lost continence.

Her voice barely made sound. "What do you want?"

He shifted his focus to Lyndon. "Him. I got a message."

Lyndon crossed his arms. "What is it?"

His gaze flickered to Kadance before returning to Lyndon. "Have fun in DC. Home of very strict weapon laws."

"That's it?" Lyndon's tone sounded bored.

The man didn't answer. Maybe he'd thought he was delivering a scarier message.

"Thank you for that highly astute observation," Lyndon said.

The man shifted back a step.

But then he lunged forward, knife in hand, toward Kadance.

Lyndon shifted to cut off the attack, but Kadance had already stepped forward and grabbed the man's right wrist in her left. She palm-struck him in the face, then reached over the top of his knife hand, gripped his hand, and twisted his arm, which caused his body to twist. Then she shoved him face first into the column.

Lyndon took the knife out of his hand for her.

"Thanks," she said.

"You're welcome."

"Have we learned a lesson?" she asked the man.

He couldn't speak clearly with his cheek smashed in the concrete of the column.

She released his hand, grabbed him by the jacket, and slammed his back against the concrete. His breath expelled. Lyndon could smell the sourness of it.

She ripped the black dot off his jacket. "Who gave this to you?"

"Some guy."

"Description," she demanded.

"I don't know. He was white, with brown hair. Said to take you down."

She shoved him away, and he almost fell to the sidewalk before catching himself. Lyndon moved so he was between the man and Kadance, and he kept the knife in an inverted grip, hidden behind his wrist but ready to strike.

She held up the tiny black camera she'd ripped off his jacket at her eye level. That deadly glare of hers focused on the tiny lens, and she growled, "Who do you think's been protecting him?"

She dropped it to the sidewalk and ground it into the concrete with her heel.

The junkie stumbled as he ran away.

"Why did you do that?" Lyndon asked her. He'd worked to keep her out of the crosshairs, and she'd just put herself smack in the middle of it.

She kept walking.

He dropped the knife in a trash can as they passed. There was only one rivet, and it was loose. He was surprised it hadn't fallen apart when he took it from the man.

He spoke under his breath, almost a growl. "I've been trying to parry the mastermind's attention, confuse her."

She stopped and faced him. "You've been trying to protect me. I don't need protection, or haven't you figured that out yet?"

"Do you think I don't understand how capable you are?"

She crossed her arms.

"That's it, isn't it? I know you're insanely capable of handling yourself, more than I will ever be." He shifted closer, just inches from her. "But there is nothing you can do that will make me stop trying to protect you."

"I don't need it."

"That fact isn't going to stop me."

"What happened to all your logic?"

"I don't care about logic. Not this time." He turned and continued walking around the corner.

She grabbed his arm and made him stop. "What aren't you telling me?" she demanded. "You're holding something back."

"Nothing," he said.

"Lyndon."

"Just let me have this one thing."

"I've shared more with you than anyone I've ever known. All for the sake of working together, building trust, so we can stop this crazy person. All I ask from you is honesty."

"I haven't been dishonest."

"You're hiding something."

"Something that won't matter to you. But to me . . ." He shook his head in frustration.

"I need to know where your head is."

He glanced up at a camera on the side of the building. "Not here." And he'd do his best to continue diverting her so he didn't have to talk about this. He started to turn.

She grabbed his hand. Her contact was getting more difficult with each day, almost torture at this point. "I'm not letting you go in there," she said, "until I understand what's going on."

"With this—" he waved toward the FBI building—"you know exactly what's going on. You have my word on that."

"Why're you fighting me so hard? What's wrong?"

He saw more than just frustration in her eyes, but concern. For him.

No one could break down his barriers like she could.

He glanced up at the camera, and then leaned closer to her, his lips at her ear, blocked from the camera's view. Her scent filled his head—more than just the simple scents of her soap and shampoo. She didn't wear flowery aromas. She didn't need them. Her natural scent was so much more, something just as sweet as perfume but uniquely her.

He paused, maybe to enjoy her closeness, maybe out of concern. Would she run from him?

He whispered, barely a sound, "I'm in love with you, Kadance."

He drew back.

He couldn't read her expression, had no idea if she was angry or annoyed. He turned and continued walking toward the door to the building.

They'd agreed he would go in alone and she would wait outside. He glanced back as he walked in the door, looked at her standing there, not sure if she would wait for him, if this was the last time he'd ever see her.

TWENTY-EIGHT

LYNDON HAD FIGURED this would be a waste of time. The agent across the desk had started taking notes, but now, he was just looking at Lyndon.

"So," the agent said, "someone you don't know, you think, is going to attack the State of the Union with a weapon that doesn't yet exist."

Lyndon tried yet again to explain his background, his research—tried again to clarify he wasn't some nut. But the agent's expression didn't change. Lyndon had wanted Kadance to help with this part—she was better with people.

And again, he tried to push her out of his head. The whole time in this building, he was mentally preparing for her to be gone when he walked back out. It was a very real possibility.

Another corner of his mind continued to pray she would be there.

He'd been alone a long time. He thought he'd grown used to it, even preferred it. No one to distract him from his work, to get on his case when he worked twenty-four hours straight, to complain that he could be making so much more money than he did. In a few short days, she shattered all of that.

But he kept trying to prepare himself. If she was gone, he knew it would hurt. He wouldn't allow himself to fathom how much it would hurt. But he had to keep going, stay focused.

Lyndon tried to pay attention to what the agent was saying, something about thanking him for the tip and they'd look into it.

Sure they would.

Lyndon stood and turned to leave. He noticed a man walk by. The same man had passed a few times. Perhaps his desk was close by.

Lyndon walked back through the building, toward the main door. He took a breath to prepare himself as he headed outside. On the sidewalk, he looked all around.

Kadance wasn't there.

KADANCE HAD JUST LOOKED AT HIM. What was he talking about? Before she could formulate a reaction, he walked away and into the FBI building.

She stepped back and stood next to a column, out of view of any cameras.

Leave.

That was her first instinct. Leave.

But why was that her first instinct? She had never been one to run away. She'd run from her family, but that was to make sure they didn't succeed in turning her into a killer. Again. And whenever she found out about another hit they were planning, she raced to stop them. She never hesitated. She'd never, not once, run away during her service. She didn't let fear control her.

Was that what she was feeling now? Fear?

Confusion—she hated confusion. Passionately.

Especially after last night's conversation in the church. She didn't want to handle more emotion. Her life wasn't usually so confusing. Life wasn't enjoyable most of the time, but she always knew what to do. Don't let people die if she could do anything about it. It wasn't complicated.

It was Lyndon. All of her confusion stemmed from Lyndon. Anger started to burn up her neck.

But just as quickly as the anger flared, it subsided. She wasn't angry at Lyndon. He was honest. That was something to be respected, not faulted.

The question was, could she stay with him?

She didn't want a relationship. But he wasn't trying to create one. She went back through all their interactions. He'd been trying to keep her at a distance for a while—he didn't want her to wear her hair down, to wear her tank top, and he didn't touch her, didn't flirt. Not that Lyndon was capable of flirting—it was too subtle and usually not entirely honest. She'd known he was attracted, but that was nothing. And maybe this was just as much a nothing. He obviously wasn't planning on acting on it, so what did it matter?

Why did she feel so confused?

She heard footsteps and looked up. Lyndon stopped at the sight of her.

"We should keep moving." She started walking back toward the car.

He hesitated, but then stayed by her side.

They didn't speak.

Back in the car, she pulled out of the parking space. "What did they say?" she asked.

"It was a waste, just like we thought it would be."

"We had to try. Maybe they'll be just a little more on alert."

He nodded.

They turned the next corner.

"I understand you don't want me like that," he said. "I'm not asking anything of you."

She wasn't sure how to respond.

"I thought this might upset you," he continued. "Even anger you. That's why I kept it to myself."

Finally, she spoke. "Is that the only reason you kept it to yourself?"

He paused. "All of this is difficult for me."

She didn't ask anything more.

Mac climbed from the back seat onto Lyndon's lap.

A few minutes later, Lyndon asked, "Where are we headed?"

"I haven't spent a ton of time in DC. I want to understand the layout better before we hatch any more drastic plans."

"And you have ideas for drastic plans," he said.

She nodded. "I'm sure you have some thoughts as well." And she was sure they would balance each other—his scientific skills and her tactical.

Lyndon leaned to look more closely at the side mirror.

"What is it?"

"We're being followed."

"I don't think so." She checked her mirrors again.

"Beige sedan just pulled into traffic two cars back."

"If they just pulled in, why do you think they're following us?"

"The driver is an agent I saw inside the FBI building. He walked by a few times while I spoke to another agent. I figured his desk was nearby and perhaps he didn't much care for sitting at it. But the probability he'd randomly be in traffic behind us is—"

"Remote," she finished. She continued to drive normally. "What else did you notice about him?"

"Light brown hair, standard cut, 5'11", about 180 pounds. Minor girth at the waist, but generally in decent physical condition. Shoulders slightly stooped, probably from sitting at a desk most of his workday. Standard black slacks, white dress shirt, blue-and-black striped tie. Rubber-soled dress shoes. Long but crooked nose, probably broken in youth. I'd guess Russian and English descent."

"And you saw him just in passing?"

"Yes."

"Did you get his birthday too?"

He looked over at her with drawn brows.

"You're a police sketch artist's dream."

He turned back to the side mirror. "And he's likely given blood recently."

"Are you psychic?"

"His sleeves were rolled up, and there was an almost-healed bruise on the inside of his elbow."

"Could be from drug use."

"He wouldn't have had his sleeves rolled up. There was only the one mark, and it was faint. I think it was from something medical and not chronic."

And he'd noticed all that about some random guy walking by, surely one of many, while he was talking to someone else, trying to get that someone to take him seriously, all while in a new environment that would've intimidated anyone else. She wondered what else he noticed, how much he saw about everyone and everything.

How much he saw about her.

She pushed that thought away and focused. "Do you think he's working for the mastermind?"

"That's my hypothesis."

"It's a disturbing thought that she's gotten to the FBI."

"I agree." Then he added, "Do you think you can lose him?"

"I'm not as familiar with the traffic patterns here as I'd like, but yes, I think I can lose him."

SHE TURNED at an ornate seven-story building with a Mexican café in the bottom floor.

The beige sedan followed.

Lyndon was quiet while she drove but watched their surroundings closely.

They passed a park on the right and a red-brick Romanesque building on the left. She drove with the flow of traffic, surely waiting for an opportunity to present itself, all while distancing them from their tail where she could.

At Columbus Circle, she turned off on a side street.

When they came to a rare parking space on the side of the road, she pulled in.

Lyndon waited for her next move.

The beige sedan sped down the street and flew right by. Tires screeched a few seconds later, but Kadance had already backed out and maneuvered the car into the other direction. Then she punched the gas. The beige sedan had no room to turn around.

After she put several turns and some distance between them, her demeanor relaxed back to normal. Though he noticed her checking the mirrors a few more times each minute than she usually did. She continued driving, learning the city.

They were quiet while she drove. He was glad she didn't bring up what he'd admitted earlier. He'd discussed it as much as he could tolerate for now. Maybe it would have been better for her to have simply left him there at the FBI building.

They passed the Verizon Center on 7th Street NW, and Lyndon glanced up at one of the large digital signs on the building.

The image flickered quickly, maybe a second, but he caught it all. Processed it.

Understood.

"What's wrong?" Kadance asked.

He paused. "The digital billboard flashed a message."

She glanced in the rearview mirror at the sign. "What'd it say?"

At least she believed him now. "It was a picture of a 1964 Chevy K10 truck with 'SDT' written across it."

"What could that mean?"

"The truck is the same one my grandfather drove."

"The one you still have."

He nodded.

"What could SDT mean?"

"Self-Determination Theory."

She glanced over at him, obviously not understanding.

"She's saying my grandfather's death was self-determined."

215

"Suicide?"

"No. He was shot in a hunting accident. I never questioned it. No one did. There wasn't even an investigation. The round was a standard caliber, and several hunters in the area were using it. It was the kind of area where hunting safety was taken seriously—there were rarely any accidents—but he was well into his seventies. I'd thought maybe his mind was finally starting to slow, or one of the hunters had been irresponsible and wouldn't admit to it, or it was just bad luck."

She touched the back of his hand with her fingertips, and his mind slowed down enough for him to focus on her. "She had him killed. The mastermind, she killed my grandfather."

"Why?"

Lyndon's head seared with pain. He pressed his palms to his temples and closed his eyes.

"Lyndon?"

He could barely comprehend her gentle voice. Pain overwhelmed him. His mind raced through so many thoughts he couldn't quite catch everything, couldn't make sense of *anything*. All he could understand was pain.

He faintly realized the car had stopped, but he couldn't open his eyes.

The car door next to him opened, and he registered Kadance's scent as she reached around him to unbuckle his seat belt.

Her hand on his arm, she guided him to standing. "Maybe some fresh air and movement will help," she murmured.

He tried opening his eyes. Everything around him was different, too much to try to comprehend. Usually, learning a new environment wasn't difficult. He cataloged everything within view and noted anything of consequence. But right now, even that was too much.

He collapsed to his knees, hands again at his temples and eyes closed.

She knelt in front of him. He could feel her nearness and smell her subtle scent.

"Lyndon," she whispered. "Look at me."

He managed to open his eyes. She was right there in front of him. He focused on her. That was easier. He knew every angle of her face, every expression. And he'd accepted he didn't have to understand her beauty intellectually. He didn't have to *think* about her.

"It's okay," she whispered.

He managed to force out. "Stay here." He couldn't stand to look at anything else, anything he'd have to think about.

"I'm right here." She touched her fingertips to his cheek.

All of his attention focused on the sensation. His head still seared with pain, but he could almost handle it.

"Stay," he murmured.

"Try to relax. We'll think through it together. Take your time."

His voice barely made sound as he said again, "Stay."

"I'm here." And then she pulled him closer. He would've done whatever she wanted. She pulled him into a hug, and he wrapped his arms around her and buried his face in her neck. Despite the chill in the air, she was warm. All he could feel was her arms around him, one hand in his hair, and the smoothness of her neck, the even beat of her pulse.

"It's okay," she whispered. "Just be in this moment. Just this, nothing else."

His pulse slowed to normal, and his breathing evened out.

He wasn't sure how much time passed.

He couldn't comprehend anything else around them, but he was aware of everything about her. Of how she made him feel. Strong and out of control. Peaceful and chaotic. The beautiful lines of her back under his hands, the scent of her hair, her warmth, what it would feel like to hold her more intimately.

He tried to force those thoughts out of his head, but they wouldn't go.

Gently, he tried to pull away, but she didn't let go of him completely. The hand that had been in his hair smoothed down to his neck, thumb brushing his jaw.

"Are you all right?" she asked.

No. No, this was too much. He couldn't handle being this close. He tried again to pull away.

She wouldn't let go. "Lyndon."

He made eye contact.

She smoothed her other hand through his hair.

Before he understood what he was doing, before he could stop himself, he was pulling her closer. She didn't fight him, didn't pull away.

He touched his lips to hers.

TWENTY-NINE

IT WAS SOFT. The kiss. The first kiss she'd had in so many years. She'd told herself she'd forgotten what it felt like, but that wasn't really true. She remembered. But this was nothing like what it was like with James. He'd been gentle, yes, and it'd been enjoyable. But this with Lyndon, this overwhelmed her.

She tilted her head, and he deepened the kiss.

Every sensation sent jolts through her. The slight tickle from his scruff, his strong hands, how one stayed on her back, gently holding on to her, and the other moved up to her hair, the side of her face. He touched her like she was porcelain.

She held on to him and kissed him back. Somewhere in her head, she knew she shouldn't, but she couldn't get that thought to surface enough to do anything about it.

He made her feel like she could be herself, whatever she was at that moment—forceful and demanding or soft and yielding. It didn't matter with him. He accepted her every facet. No one else had ever understood her, let alone accepted her.

He pulled away abruptly and sat back on his feet, away from her. "I'm sorry."

She almost reached for him again.

He slid back farther, sat on the concrete with his knees bent in front of him, and leaned against the base of a light pole. He ran his hands through his hair and closed his eyes.

She could almost feel how much pain he was in.

And she worried she'd only added to it, rather than comforting him like she'd wanted to.

Mac jumped down out of the still-open passenger door and meowed at her. People passing on the sidewalk stared. She'd made sure they were out of view of any cameras, but they shouldn't draw attention to themselves like this.

"We should go," she said.

Lyndon nodded but didn't move.

Maybe it would be easier if she moved away first. She stood and walked around to the driver's side. He sat in the passenger side a moment later. He waited for Mac to jump up before closing the door.

She resumed driving.

"You should talk," she said. "That'll help."

He stared at the dash and said nothing.

She waited a few more seconds, but he didn't talk.

She kept her voice gentle. "Talk to me."

"I don't know if it will help this time."

"You should try."

He closed his eyes, and his jaw clenched.

She hesitated to push him more. Was she the cause of his pain this time? She opened her mouth to say something but had no idea what to say.

Finally, he said, "I'm sorry."

She wanted to tell him not to be sorry. The idea of his regretting the kiss bothered her—a lot more than she could've imagined. But instead, she asked, "Why would she want to kill your grandfather? He obviously didn't know anything about Ebola. It was years after your parents died, right?"

He paused so long she thought he wasn't going to answer.

But then, again staring at the dash, he said, "I was seventeen when my grandfather died."

"Do you remember anything that might've drawn the mastermind's attention to him?"

"He'd been talking to me about either joining the military or maybe taking an electrician apprenticeship. Earn some money. So I wouldn't have to think about costs or worry so much about scholarships."

She wasn't putting together where he was going.

He looked at her. "The mastermind, she's told me to focus, get rid of distractions."

"She wanted you to go to college, not wait."

"That's the only thing I can think of. But why would she care? Why would she be paying attention in the first place?"

Things started to click together in her head. "Because you're brilliant. I bet she watched you and your grandfather at first to make sure he didn't know anything, that your parents hadn't told either of you anything. And she realized how advanced you are. She wants to recruit you."

"Then why did she try to kill me?"

"I'd assumed it was because you were getting too close to understanding her secrets, that she'd created Ebola. But I don't know why she switched from grooming, to targeting, to recruiting."

He resumed staring at the dash. She could see on his face he was still in pain, but he didn't close his eyes or press his hands to his temples.

They were quiet while she drove and he thought. She tried to think through things as well, but she had a hard time concentrating, which frustrated her. She'd never had a hard time concentrating before. Her thoughts kept returning to how he'd held her, what his kiss had felt like, gentle but passionate . . .

He finally spoke again. "I think there's more."

She glanced at him, waiting.

He paused, as if still sorting a thousand pieces and parts. "I'm trying to think of any times in my life when I haven't been perfectly focused."

"I doubt there are many."

"No. At least not since my grandfather died. I didn't have anyone, and I didn't let myself build connections with people."

"Because the connection always ends."

"Because people always leave." His gaze flickered but didn't quite make it to her. He focused on the dash again. "But there was an exception. I met her at Johns Hopkins. She was a nice girl, smart, ray-of-sunshine kind of person. My roommate said she kept coming around because she was flirting with me. I asked her out on a date. I had this wild idea that maybe I could have something like my parents had."

The attraction of opposites like his parents had had. But that kind of girl wasn't quite his opposite. He had more of his father in him than he seemed to realize. Kadance knew enough about people to know that those who draw others toward them, like his father had, are usually more than simply happy—they're kind and accepting; they help others see their own strengths. Like Lyndon. But he'd buried himself so thoroughly for so long that no one saw that part of him. Except her.

"You cared about her?" She'd intended for it to come out as a statement rather than a question.

"Not as much as I should have."

She waited for him to explain.

"We dated for a while," he said. "Several months. We had good conversations. She didn't always understand everything I talked about, but enough. And she didn't talk about silly things. She was a literature major. She thought deeply, just differently than me. I thought maybe that would help balance me."

She stopped herself from asking if they'd been intimate. She wasn't sure why that question came to mind at all. "Did she distract you?"

"She pulled me away from my books and studying, made me interact with the world. My GPA didn't suffer, but perhaps I could have had a few more insights in my papers. There were a couple of tests where I didn't earn my usual perfect score. But still the top grade."

"What happened?"

"Everything. All in one day. Something happened that made me realize I didn't feel strongly enough about her. I liked her, but I wasn't going to fall in love with her. She deserved better."

"What happened to make you realize that?" She immediately regretted the question, or at least part of her did.

"It was nothing. I saw some girl from a distance, across the quad. Just a beautiful figure and black hair blowing in the wind. Not unlike Angela, though this girl's skin was darker. I didn't even see her face. But my reaction to that girl made me face the fact that I didn't have a reaction to Angela like that. Never had. Angela was pretty. I liked her dark hair, how it contrasted with her skin tone, and she had a nice figure. But I saw her as more of a friend."

"So you broke up with her."

"I tried so hard to be kind, to convey that I thought too highly of her to keep her trapped with me. But I'm not good at that kind of thing. She cried. A lot. I didn't know how to help her. The next morning . . . I found out she'd killed herself. Shot herself in the head." He continued staring at the dash.

She tried to make her voice gentle. "But now you don't know if that's what really happened?"

"There wasn't much of an investigation. Everything pointed to suicide." Finally, he looked over at Kadance. "But I focused after that. I've never let myself consider another woman. I couldn't let that happen again."

He leaned forward and ran his hands through his hair. And now he'd let himself care for another woman.

She touched his arm. "It's not the same. I'm not going to commit suicide."

He sat straight and met Kadance's eyes. "The mastermind killed her. Because she was distracting me. Just like she thinks you're distracting me."

"We don't know that for sure. And it's not the same." She lifted her chin. "I'm very different from Angela."

He ran his hands over his face and focused on the dash. "She already admitted to trying to kill you once. Please, Kadance. Please let this go and walk away. If anything happens to you, I . . ."

There was absolutely no chance of her walking away. This mastermind woman would have to attack her from six directions with the most powerful forces on Earth to get her to stop protecting Lyndon. Instead of voicing her thoughts, she asked, "How did it happen? If we understand her tactics, it'll help us better understand her."

Lyndon paused but then finally took a breath. "They deemed that she'd shot herself in the head at her desk. She'd laid her head down as if to sleep. There was no sign of struggle. Her roommate said everything appeared to be in order."

"Maybe she *was* asleep and someone snuck in."

"She was a light sleeper. Her roommate used to jokingly complain about it." Then he added, "I did see a picture from the scene—"

"Why would you want to look at that?"

He shook his head. "I felt the need to see for myself. My guilt made me doubt what'd happened."

"I don't think it was your guilt. I think you knew something wasn't right."

"Maybe. I couldn't think as clearly as I'm used to."

"Did you notice something in the picture?"

"Her gun was close to her hand, but it also could've fallen out of her purse rather than out of her hand. She was never careful with her purse. She always just dumped it, and half the time some of the contents would fall out. And I thought she seemed off-balance. Like she'd shifted to the side somehow."

A thought overwhelmed Kadance's mind. Completely took her over. Lyndon said something, but she didn't hear.

She blinked.

No, it couldn't be.

No.

Please no.

"Kadance."

She finally heard him, wiped her face of all emotion, and looked over at him.

"Where'd you go?" he asked.

All she could comprehend was the sorrow on his face, how much it had all hurt him, how it made him block all people out of his life. His loneliness.

She heard his words from earlier echo through her mind, *I'm in love with you, Kadance.* He'd finally opened up to someone.

The completely wrong someone.

THIRTY

SOMETHING ABOUT KADANCE SEEMED OFF. But then Lyndon reminded himself of everything he'd thrown at her in the last twelve hours. God, love, a kiss. Of course she seemed off.

Perhaps all of it would be too much, and she'd leave. A part of him begged God to take her away from this, protect her, but another part clung to her. The memory of the kiss threatened to cloud his mind. It kept replaying in his head. Over and over. Automatically. Always there. He could barely think around it. How she'd felt in his arms, how she'd held him too, kissed him back. Why had she kissed him back? Because she felt bad for him? Because she felt responsible for his pain? Because she wanted to?

Regret overwhelmed him. He had to do better, had to hide how he felt. Surely, she didn't understand how deep it went for him. He knew this was it, just like how it'd been for his parents. There was no one else he would ever want. She was his forever.

But he couldn't let her see that.

He glanced in the side mirror again, as he'd become accustomed to doing. "Three cars back," he said.

"I see," Kadance said.

"If we lose him, he'll just find us again with the cameras all over this city."

"I have a different thought." She made deliberate turns—she'd apparently already memorized much of the city.

"It might be useful to talk to him."

"Exactly. And we'll use you as bait."

While she drove, they discussed.

Eventually, they found a place to park and got out of the car. Mac trotted alongside Kadance and looked around at all the people, the trees, and the field that stretched out ahead of them. Thankfully, the most recent snowfall had almost entirely melted.

At first, they walked quietly.

They browsed slowly by the Vietnam Veterans Memorial. Lyndon wanted to stop, read each name.

"Did your grandfather fight in this war?" Kadance asked.

"Yes. My father told me it changed him. He was different when he came home." A name caught his eye, and Lyndon brushed his fingers over it, one of the friends his grandfather had mentioned, one of the two times he'd ever shared anything about that experience. "He didn't talk much about it."

Kadance nodded.

"Probably for the same reasons you don't talk about your service."

"Probably."

A part of him wanted to ask her about it, but he'd learned not to ask his grandfather about Vietnam, and he figured the same reasons applied here. She had to talk about it in her own time. He wished he could be there for her when she was finally ready, but he knew she'd be long gone by then.

Kadance spoke under her breath, lips barely moving. "About two hundred yards, seven o'clock."

He continued his casual pace. "I see. Do you think he realizes we see him?"

She looked to the right across the field, to the trees, beyond which was the Lincoln Memorial Reflecting Pool. "I don't think so." She started walking across the field. "I'd like to play with him for a bit."

Get him nice and frustrated. He had a feeling Kadance was a master at that.

Mac meowed up at Kadance.

"Sorry, buddy. Not yet," she said.

"He wants to run around?"

"I don't want him out of my sight right now."

Probably wise.

Mac kept trotting along beside her. It fascinated Lyndon that the cat seemed to understand what she said. Maybe he understood her tone and body language.

They meandered through the trees, not a straight line. She pretended to look around at the limbs, as if fascinated by the different shapes, but Lyndon knew she was watching the FBI agent. He didn't try to keep an eye on the agent himself. He wouldn't be nearly as slick as her, and he trusted her to lead.

They walked around the west end of the reflecting pool, out in the open again. Lyndon couldn't help but look across the street to the Lincoln Memorial.

"So, were you named after Lyndon B. Johnson?" she asked.

"My father liked it because my mother's middle name is Lyn. He said I got his surname, and he wanted some part of my mother in my name as well. My mother agreed to it because she was a fan of Roger Lyndon." He looked over at her and added, "Mathematician."

A smile tweaked her lips but didn't make it to her eyes. "Of course."

He was starting to realize something more was wrong with her. Something had changed with her since their conversation about his grandfather's and Angela's deaths. But now wasn't the time to ask her.

She looked out across the reflecting pool.

"He's still there?" Lyndon murmured.

"Mm-hm."

"Where are we going?"

"I want to see the Martin Luther King Jr. Memorial," she said in what would sound to anyone else like a normal tone. "I think he's my favorite historical figure."

They kept going. They passed through the Korean War Memorial and then walked on the sidewalk along the road. At the next crosswalk, they crossed Independence Avenue. They walked through what looked like a crevasse in a huge boulder and then into an open concrete courtyard with a view out to the water. In the center of the courtyard was what looked like the missing piece of the boulder through which they'd just walked, and at the front, facing the water, a statue of Martin Luther King Jr. was carved into the boulder. On the side was etched, "Out of the mountain of despair, a stone of hope." More quotes were carved into the walls around the courtyard.

At the front of the monument, Kadance turned to look up at the statue. Lyndon did the same and caught a glimpse of the agent quickly veering off to his right, along the wall bordering the courtyard.

When a nearby tourist walked away, leaving them out of earshot of anyone else, Lyndon asked, "So, is the idea to make him doubt himself, that he has the wrong people?"

"Just trying to get into his head." Then she smiled at a woman walking past. "Excuse me. Would you mind taking our picture?"

"Sure." The woman reached for the phone Lyndon handed her.

With the statue in the background, Lyndon wrapped an arm around Kadance. She leaned into him and smiled brightly at the camera. He looked down at her beautiful face and forgot to look at the camera.

The woman handed the phone back. "Does that look all right?"

Lyndon looked at the photograph, first at Kadance's beauty and then at his own image boldly admiring her.

He took the phone out of Kadance's hand and said to the woman, "Perfect. Thank you so much."

The woman smiled and walked away.

Kadance looked up at Lyndon, and he thought for a moment she was going to say something about how he looked at her. Perhaps she was angry at him. "He's watching from behind that garden area."

There was a large island filled with cherry blossom trees and other landscaping to the side of the concrete courtyard.

He angled himself so that Kadance mostly blocked the agent's view of Lyndon. "Keep acting like tourists?"

"For a little longer. I always have really wanted to see this place. I hear it's amazing in the spring when all the trees are blooming." There were cherry blossom trees along the entire perimeter and in both of the landscape islands.

"I'm glad you get to see something you wanted to." He looked out toward the water. He guessed she didn't let herself do much of anything she wanted.

"Please don't," she murmured.

"Don't what?"

"Be so . . ." She looked away. "So freaking nice. All the time."

"I'm polite, but I'm certainly not nice all the time." In his regular life, he barely spoke to people. He rarely even smiled at people.

She turned and started walking toward the landscape island on the other side of the statue, opposite side of the courtyard from the agent. "You could be making insane amounts of money, have fancy houses and cars, anything you want, but instead, you devote all your time to research."

"That's being obsessive, not nice."

"That's being selfless."

His tone hardened. "I'm not selfless."

She smirked. "Being humble is part of being nice."

"I'm not being humble." He'd thought she understood. "God tells me to be kind, smile at people, make their day a little nicer, but I don't. I'm polite, and that's it. Sometimes not even that."

She stopped walking. "What do you mean God tells you?"

He took a couple more steps, but then stopped and turned. His gaze skimmed the area to make sure the agent wasn't in earshot.

"God *talks* to you?" She looked like she was concerned for his sanity.

"For me, it's probably different. I'm too much in my head. I don't really get gut feelings, but I notice things that other people don't—maybe specific numbers from my research show up in an address number, or I see the numerical equivalent of my name in a serial number." That was why he'd chosen that specific storage unit auction that day—the unit numbers being auctioned aligned with structural proteins encoded by the EBOV genome. "For you, you get feelings about things, right?"

"Yeah. That's instinct."

"You ever get a feeling that doesn't really make sense, not related to anything, not connected to your training, just a random feeling?"

She didn't answer.

"Maybe during your work overseas?" He moved closer and spoke more quietly so no one around would hear, but surely their expressions made them look like they were arguing. "When you were alone and relying on yourself only. No support team feeding you intelligence. Just you."

She was quiet, which told him she knew exactly what he was talking about.

"That was God," he said.

"That's a leap of logic."

He raised an eyebrow. "A random feeling not derived from any-thing in your environment or in your experience or training. Where else could it have *logically* come from? Thin air?"

She held eye contact but didn't respond.

"Based on everything you've been through, that you've survived, you've probably listened to those feelings. You felt a nudge to leave a place, not to trust a certain person, not to go out at a certain time—and you listened. Right?"

Her voice barely made sound. "Yes."

"Good. Keep listening." He turned and continued walking.

She stayed there.

He walked out of the courtyard and along the sidewalk border-ing Independence Avenue. Kadance didn't follow.

He paused at the crosswalk just before Kutz Bridge and looked to the left, toward the east-traveling traffic. The agent was there, several feet behind a woman walking down the sidewalk.

Lyndon crossed at the crosswalk and continued along the side-walk bordering the westbound lanes of Independence Avenue. He didn't glance behind him. He wanted the agent to think he had no idea he was there, that he was distracted from his argument with Kadance. Honestly, he was.

He made his way to the World War II Memorial. Up the steps, American and POW/MIA flags flanked the entrance, and the towering Washington Memorial stood guard behind him. There was a huge fountain surrounded by concrete, and the outer wall included fifty-six columns, each representing a 1945 state or ter-ritory. He'd read all about these monuments and various aspects of DC, but seeing them was something else entirely.

He wanted Kadance to see this, to enjoy it.

He meandered around the fountain, up the ramp, while read-ing each column, and he stopped in the Atlantic archway that overlooked the fountain. He stood there for a while enjoying the view of the monument. Or trying to.

And he hoped he was driving the agent nuts.

Finally, he turned and walked the back way out of the archway and out of the monument onto a path that nestled itself into trees. He listened carefully for footsteps to follow him. As he turned right toward more trees, he caught the sound of footsteps a few yards behind him.

He passed the turn that would take him between the reflecting pool and the back of the World War II Memorial and continued through the trees.

He didn't let himself look around in expectation.

Finally, no other people were around. The footsteps grew steadily closer.

When the footsteps sounded like they were just a few feet away, Lyndon spun around. "Hello. Agent . . . ? I didn't catch your name."

The man stopped dead. His unbuttoned trench flapped at his legs.

Kadance appeared like a specter from behind a tree. She walked behind the agent and picked his pocket before he could even turn to look at her. He glanced to the left and then twisted to the right as Kadance came around that side.

She had his wallet open. "Matthew Brown. Not a very imaginative name." She tossed his wallet back to him, and he fumbled catching it.

She continued walking around the man. "So, how can we help you, Agent Brown?"

THIRTY-ONE

MAC RUBBED AGAINST Lyndon's legs. He was ready to snatch him up if this went sideways.

"Do you know how to talk?" Kadance walked around the agent.

He twisted to look at her.

She stopped in front of him.

Finally, Agent Brown said, "I'm bringing you both in for questioning."

"I don't think so," she said.

"I'm an FBI ag—"

"You're not working for the FBI right now."

"Do you need to see my badge?"

"I didn't say you're *not* an FBI agent. I'm saying that's not who you're working for at this particular moment. If that were the case, you wouldn't be following an innocent, law-abiding citizen like Dr. Vaile."

He lifted his chin and straightened his back. "Who are you, anyway?"

"Haven't you heard? I'm Dr. Vaile's guardian angel."

He sneered.

"What?" she said. "You don't believe in guardian angels?"

He hesitated, but then his anger apparently got the better of him. "He doesn't deserve it. If such a thing existed."

"Whether or not they exist is another debate. But Dr. Vaile most certainly deserves an angel."

Lyndon didn't know what to make of her. He wanted to ask her where she was going with this, but he remained quiet and let her handle the agent—also ready to attack if the agent even considered laying a hand on her.

"I'm more of a fallen angel," she added. "But you get the point." She resumed slowly walking around him. "Why in the world would you think Dr. Vaile doesn't deserve a guardian?"

Brown had to twist around to look at her.

Lyndon kept waiting for him to lose patience, try to grab her, or pull his weapon.

As Kadance walked behind Agent Brown, the agent focused on Lyndon. Lyndon met his gaze straight on.

Kadance paused next to the agent.

Finally, the agent, still staring at Lyndon, murmured in a low and deadly voice, "I don't know why she hasn't eliminated you yet."

"She's tried," Kadance said. "And failed."

"If she wanted him dead, he'd be dead."

"So that begs the question," Kadance said. "Why do you think she's failed to kill him? Maybe she's not as smart as you think."

"She hasn't *failed*. She's given the order he's not to be eliminated."

"Must be more recent orders," Kadance said.

"Why is that?" Lyndon asked. "Why am I not to be eliminated?" Was it simply because she valued his intelligence?

Agent Brown pressed his lips together.

"He doesn't know," Kadance said. "He's a peon."

"Why are you following us?" Lyndon asked.

Agent Brown crossed his arms.

"Do you not know what's going on?" Lyndon asked.

Agent Brown shifted, but Kadance shifted as well. He stopped and looked at her. She had an intense look in her eyes that clearly showed what she was capable of. Agent Brown stayed put and refocused on Lyndon.

Sometimes Lyndon didn't understand why people got so touchy when he asked simple questions. "I would go ahead and answer my question if I were you."

"Maybe he's backup in case we avoid cameras," Kadance said. "I don't think he was supposed to make contact with us." She watched Agent Brown closely and smirked. "Thought so."

Lyndon quickly ran through the possibilities in his head. "Are you trying to make a name for yourself?" Lyndon asked Agent Brown.

Kadance, still watching Agent Brown closely, nodded and shifted her stance to face him more directly. "That's it. What, you thought your fantastic mastermind needed help?"

"She doesn't need anything."

"She must want something from me," Lyndon said. "Or else I wouldn't still be alive, correct?"

Agent Brown sneered.

"It's a rational question," Lyndon said. "Why're you so angry?"

Kadance glanced over at him with amusement in her eyes. She wiped the amusement away as she turned back to Agent Brown.

Lyndon asked, "Did she personally give you the vaccination shot, or did someone else?"

"What're you—"

"You have a faint bruise on your arm. She offered you a vaccination for the disease she's about to release. Did she give that to you?"

He lifted his chin.

"That's a no," Kadance said. "He's never even seen her."

Agent Brown sneered.

"I'm assuming she sent you the vaccine in the mail," Lyndon said. "Last question: Why did she give you the vaccine? What are you supposed to do in return?"

No answer.

"Okay. Let's play musical expressions." Lyndon glanced at Kadance, and she nodded infinitesimally.

"You're going to be stationed at Congress and are supposed to facilitate entry in some way."

Kadance, still closely watching Agent Brown, gave a slight shake of her head.

"Your role is to provide misinformation."

Kadance shook her head.

"You're to slow the response time once the attack happens and do whatever you can to fumble the coordination of efforts."

Kadance tilted her head the slightest degree, and then nodded.

Agent Brown's eyes widened slightly. He glanced at Kadance then quickly away. Then he turned and bolted.

Lyndon considered going after him but then decided against it.

"She's really good at propaganda," Kadance said.

He nodded. "I wonder how many more like him she has." Then he asked, "Do you think he'll try to keep following us?"

"He's pretty terrified at the moment. He's probably worried she's going to kill him for making contact with us and for leaking information."

"So, he might not even tell her what we've learned."

"Good possibility."

Mac meowed up at Kadance.

"Stay close to me," Kadance said to him and motioned toward the area directly around them.

Mac bounded off. Kadance watched him for a few seconds, surely to make sure he stayed close.

She turned back to Lyndon. "So, why doesn't she want you eliminated?"

"She obviously wanted me out of the picture pretty badly before. It had seemed fairly obvious that she wanted me dead because I had figured out her secret."

"And she hasn't simply stopped *trying* to kill you. She gave the order *not* to kill you."

"I'm not finding a rational line of thought that would fit the sequence of events."

She looked over at Mac, who had climbed halfway up a tree. "Me either."

"There must be some other variable."

She turned back to Lyndon. "But what?"

He sighed. "I don't know." He turned, walked a few feet away, and rubbed his temples.

KADANCE WATCHED LYNDON stand there thinking.

A few minutes passed.

She walked over and stood next to Lyndon. He was looking out over the grass and trees, but she knew he wasn't really registering any of it. She could almost see the thoughts and hypotheses flashing across his eyes, each thought analyzed and either thrown out or filed. He'd figure it all out, everything. She knew that with perfect certainty.

"I don't . . . ," she started, but stopped.

Lyndon looked at her. He'd paused his thoughts and was focused on her.

She let herself ask the question. "How could you feel so strongly?"

"You mean why do I love you."

She gave no response.

He hesitated but then leaned closer, just a few inches from her ear. "Because I see the light in you."

He walked away, toward Mac.

Mac ran around Lyndon, playing, and Lyndon chased him. Finally, Mac skidded to a stop and lay down. "That's it?" Lyndon asked. "That's all you have?"

Mac meowed up at him, and Lyndon smiled, though the smile strained a bit with pain.

"We should create a disturbance," Kadance said.

Lyndon looked over at her. "What kind of disturbance?"

She appreciated how he let her change the direction of their discussion. "At the Capitol," she said.

"Something big enough might delay or move the State of the Union."

"Exactly."

"There are too many cameras. I don't see how we can pull it off. She'll be tracking our every move." Then he said, "Unless we can find a way to break her connection or maybe turn off her facial recognition software."

"Can you hack in somehow?"

"I might. It depends on how sophisticated it is. But I'll need access."

She called Mac, and he jumped up and trotted over.

"We should get going." She headed in the direction where they'd parked. Lyndon stayed by her side.

"Where should we go?" she asked him.

"We should try a digital sign. She's obviously tapped in to at least some of them. There should be a computer connected to the sign somewhere. That'll give me an interface to work from."

"Where would the computer be?"

"Probably in a utility room close by. I assume it would be locked."

"I can take care of that."

He nodded. "I figured."

They moved quickly and were back in the car a few minutes later. Kadance drove, and Lyndon watched out the window.

Lyndon pointed to an indoor sports complex. High up on the building was a huge digital board, and below, just above the entrance, was another digital board, long but squat. There was parking along the road, so Kadance swooped into an open spot.

They walked inside. Based on all the signs and banners, this was where the Wizards basketball team played. They walked through the main hall, passing several shops and small restaurants. She looked for anything that might be a service or utility room. Non-public areas weren't as well marked, of course, so they tried a few rooms. Lyndon kept watch while she picked the locks.

After a few tries, they found the room Lyndon was looking for. She, Lyndon, and Mac squeezed inside the small space draped with wires and electrical equipment, and she closed the door. Lyndon stood at the terminal and started typing.

She liked watching him work. His expression was so intense.

"I think I have it." Lyndon's gaze stayed locked on the screen, and his fingers flew over the keyboard.

She was quiet and let him focus.

She looked over at Mac. He was staring at some wires. They were exactly the size that he liked to chew. She shook her head at him, and he curled up and lay down with his head rested on his paws. He looked depressed.

"I'm in," Lyndon said.

"That was fast." She moved to stand next to him so she could see the screen, though she had no idea what she was looking at. "Can you shut off facial recognition?"

"I think . . ." He continued typing. "I think I can track the source."

"Like where she is?"

"I doubt she's handling this part herself. But someone must be monitoring." He paused as he continued to type. "Someone in DC."

"It makes sense she'd want them nearby. Just in case."

He finally stopped typing. "I can't shut off facial recognition, and I can't sever her connection to anything but the signs in this complex. But I have an address."

"Do you think we can cut her off from there?"

"Definitely." He did a few more things on the computer, surely covering his tracks.

She listened at the door to make sure no one was around, and then they walked out into the hall, and around to the exit closest to the car.

Kadance got behind the wheel. "Where to?"

He typed the address into the cell phone's map program.

Kadance followed the directions, but with some variations. She tried to avoid cameras where possible. "They're likely going to see us coming," she said.

"I know. I'm hoping they're not prepared for us to find them and will either hunker down or just flee."

"What if there's a group of them? What if they're armed?" She didn't have a problem going in, but she knew she'd never get Lyndon to wait in the car. He'd be offended if she even asked.

"Whoever is working her technology side of things is extremely skilled. I think it's much more likely they don't have a plan for what to do if we find them. It's probably one person in some apartment surrounded by a lot of equipment."

"It was that difficult to hack in?"

"Just as difficult as government servers. If not more so."

And he'd done it within a few minutes. "I have an idea," she said. "Turn off the map program."

He did as she asked, and the annoying voice on the phone telling her she was going the wrong way shut up. She stayed on the main road and passed the street the phone had been yelling at her to take. Instead, she watched out the window, looking for an opportunity. A couple of blocks away, there was a huge brick church on the corner. And that little voice in the back of her mind that she'd listened to most of her life said to park.

She swooped into an open space. "We're going to throw them off," Kadance said.

Lyndon nodded and got out of the car when she did. Mac followed them as they went into the church. Luckily, no one seemed to be around.

"Help me find the back way out," Kadance said.

"I understand what you're doing," he said. "We'll have a shot at taking them off guard."

They found their way through the beautiful building and out to a back alley made of brick pavers.

"Look for cameras," Kadance said.

There were a few cameras on the backs of the houses and above garages. They were careful to stay out of their range. They walked along fence lines and around garage outbuildings. Toward the end of the alley, they hopped a fence and cut through a side yard between two houses. Another block over, they made it to the alley they needed.

Around a corner, they stopped and Kadance looked at the map program on the phone to figure out which of the apartments they needed without being able to see the street number on the fronts of the buildings.

She handed the phone back and led him to the correct building, while they continued to watch for cameras. They hopped a fence to avoid a camera angle, slid along the back wall, and up to the back door. Kadance picked the lock.

Once inside, they were in a small hallway. There was a door to an apartment in front of them, mailboxes on the wall, and stairs to the right, surely to upstairs apartments. Lyndon pointed to the mailboxes, to the only one not labeled with a name: 201.

Kadance headed up the stairs, and Lyndon and Mac followed.

There were two doors at the top of the stairs. From the door on the right, number 202, she could smell cookies baking. She listened at door 201 for any sound, anything that might tell her if someone was inside, how many, and where within the space. It was quiet. She continued to listen for another minute, and Lyndon patiently waited.

Finally, she heard a chair push against hardwood. She estimated the location of the sound within the space. She calculated the probable layout given the size and general design of the building.

She took her lockpicking tools out of her pocket and silently started working the lock. A few seconds later, it clicked.

Kadance took her knife out of its sheath and mouthed to Lyndon, *I'll go first.*

He didn't look particularly happy about it, but he didn't argue.

Then she looked at Mac and whispered, "Stay."

Mac sat, but he didn't look particularly happy either.

Kadance listened at the door for a few seconds until she heard footsteps. They sounded to be moving away from the door.

Silently, she turned the doorknob and then inched the door open. There was a hallway that ended at an open space at the front of the building. On either side of the hall were closed doors, likely bedroom and bathroom. She'd heard footsteps, but not a door, so the person inside was likely not in one of those rooms.

She silently but quickly moved toward the end of the hall. She felt Lyndon behind her but didn't hear his footsteps—impressive.

As she neared the end of the hall, she listened to determine where the person was, to the right or to the left. She shifted to the right side of the hall and inched to the end of the wall, where she could see into what was probably supposed to be a living room but was filled with computer equipment and a workstation set up on a large folding table.

She listened.

A cabinet door closed.

She turned the corner, with her knife held in front of her, and at the same time, Lyndon started toward the computer equipment. To the right, she saw a man standing at a kitchen island pouring a glass of Pepsi.

James.

THIRTY-TWO

JAMES DIDN'T EVEN LOOK UP. He dropped the Pepsi in his hand and ran around the island, the side farthest from Kadance, toward the computer equipment.

Lyndon was already there. James threw a fist, but Lyndon blocked and slammed a hook across James's jaw. James tried to tackle Lyndon. Lyndon stepped to the side and shoved James into the wall.

Kadance thought for sure he'd go down. James stumbled, caught himself against the wall. Then he turned and lunged at Lyndon again.

Fear for Lyndon overwhelmed her. Some part of her knew the fear was irrational, but that didn't matter. She started around the other side of the workstation.

But Lyndon had already grabbed James and hip-threw him. James smacked to the floor with a thud that reverberated through the floorboards. His breath expelled, and he paused long enough for Lyndon to straddle him and hold his hands to the floor.

"Stop," Lyndon commanded.

James glared up at him.

Kadance moved closer, and James glanced in her direction. Then he looked again and stared. "Kadance."

Lyndon looked up at her.

"This is James," she said.

"I thought we might come across him eventually. I just hoped we wouldn't."

She heard the sympathy deep in his tone.

Then he turned back to James, and his expression leveled into deadly. "Cut the feed."

James, still staring at Kadance, turned back to Lyndon. James struggled, but Lyndon kneed him in the ribs with surprising force given his position. James grunted in pain.

"Cut the feed," Lyndon growled.

James tried again to struggle.

Kadance kneeled by his head and held her knife to his throat. "I would do what he says."

James was still, perfectly. And he stared up at her. "Kadance." The way he said her name . . . almost like he was relieved to see her. "Kadance," he said again. "I can convince her to include you. She has vaccinations. I've been working on convincing her how important you could be. You could be the military leader in our new society."

"What're you talking about?"

"Then we can be together again," James said.

"What do you mean 'be together'? Are you insane?"

"I can convince her."

She glanced at Lyndon, at the way he was looking at her. The gentleness in his eyes. Several things made sense all at once. She felt so much hurt she wanted to curl into a ball and block out the world. All her mistakes. All the things she wanted, so desperately wanted, and could never have.

Then she looked back down at James, at his familiar face. All this time, she'd feared seeing him again, what her reaction would be. Would she be weak and let herself want him again, be with him? But she didn't want him, and she knew she never would again.

Not like the feelings she had for Lyndon.

The realization hurt worse than being shot. Part of her would gladly go back to Iran, Yemen, anywhere but here.

She strangled her emotions and threw them into the back of her mind. She'd always tried to treat her emotions like that, like trash to be tossed aside. Lyndon had shown her she didn't have to do that. He liked that she still cared. But now she cared too much. About something she could never have.

She focused on James, on her anger at him, on the situation. "Go ahead and convince her. Bring me to her. So I can slit her throat like I'm going to do to you." She pressed the knife harder against his skin, and blood trickled down his neck.

"Kadance, please." His voice was tight. "I love you."

Peripherally, she saw as Lyndon looked at her. She couldn't risk looking at him right now. She just had to believe that he would trust her.

"You love me?" she growled at James.

"Yes."

"Is that why you conspired against me? The whole thing was fake."

"No," he barely forced out.

She eased up on the knife a fraction of an inch.

"It wasn't fake," he said. "Not for me."

"It was a setup from the beginning. My father hired you to get close and turn me."

James said nothing.

"Admit it."

When he didn't respond, she pressed the knife.

He grimaced and made a sound of pain. She lifted the knife just enough to stop cutting his skin.

"Admit it," she demanded.

"It all changed," he said. "I fell in love with you."

She gripped the knife handle more tightly and tried to control the urge to slit his throat.

Lyndon's quiet voice burrowed through her anger. "I think he's telling the truth."

She gripped the knife so hard her hand started to shake.

"He saw the same thing," Lyndon said.

The same thing Lyndon sees. Her hand stopped shaking.

Lyndon looked down at James. "Why did you let her father come for her?"

James shifted his eyes over to Lyndon. "I don't know why she's so determined to bring you into the fold."

"Answer the question."

Kadance appreciated that Lyndon seemed to realize she needed answers and didn't mind using their limited time on this.

James shifted his gaze back to Kadance. "I can get her to vaccinate you. You'll rule over our entire new military."

"If you think she wants to rule anything," Lyndon said, "you don't know her at all."

James continued to focus on Kadance. "Please. I can save you."

"Answer the question," she said.

He paused. "He loves you, Kadance. Your father. He just wants the best for you."

"I almost feel bad for you," she said. And it was the truth. She realized James didn't understand, and that meant his betrayal didn't mean anything. He'd honestly thought he was doing the right thing. She was still angry at him, but pity muted it. A little.

Lyndon asked her, "Do you mind if I ask him something?"

She nodded toward James.

Lyndon looked down at James. "How is it you're connected to both Kadance's family and the attack that's about to happen?"

"It's a cleansing. We're saving the world."

"How are you connected to both?"

"It's none of your business. None of this is your business."

"Please answer the question."

No response.

A part of Kadance hoped he didn't answer. Lyndon wouldn't

put anything together yet, most likely, but she desperately wanted to keep him as far away from the realization as possible. She promised herself she would tell him eventually, but not yet, not when his focus was imperative to keeping him alive.

"If you have any hope of getting Kadance's affection, you'll need to give her answers."

James focused on her. Finally, he said, "She referred me."

"What do you mean?" Lyndon asked.

He continued speaking to Kadance, as if Lyndon didn't exist. "She'd hired your father for a job at some point, though he's never met her and doesn't know her name. I guess he realized she surrounds herself with talented people and asked her if she knew anyone who could help him with a project. She gave him my name. He had the plan, how to get you back, but he needed a man you didn't know who could handle the task. I met with him, he explained the problem and the plan, he showed me your picture, and I agreed."

James continued to stare at Kadance. "Please," he said. "I can save you."

"I don't need you to save me. We're here to turn off the feed."

"Please, Kadance."

She looked up at Lyndon. "We don't have a lot of time. I'm betting he has to check in with her regularly. Can you turn off the connection?"

"We should tie him up." Lyndon looked around the room.

Kadance was relieved he'd let go of his line of questions for James.

Lyndon's gaze stopped at a pile of spare cables on the workstation. Then he asked Kadance, "Will you hold him?"

"If he moves, he gets a slit throat." She stared down at James.

James stared back at her with the oddest mixture of emotion on his face—affection, fear, and attraction. It grossed her out, which wasn't easily done.

Lyndon let go of James, stood, and walked over to pick up several cables. Then he pulled the chair from the workstation out into the middle of the room.

Kadance stood and ordered James, "Get up."

James slowly pushed himself up to sitting and then off the ground. He walked over to the chair and sat. Kadance stood over James while Lyndon tied his hands to the arms of the chair and his feet to the legs. While Lyndon tied his waist to the back of the chair, Kadance sheathed her knife, walked over to the small table in the kitchen, and brought a chair over for Lyndon to use.

Lyndon finished with James and came over to the workstation. "Thank you," he said to Kadance, sat, and started typing.

"You really think that guy can hack my system?" James asked Kadance.

"Obviously, you haven't been paying very close attention. How do you think we found you?"

James scowled as he watched Lyndon break the password on the computer lock screen. "That was the easy part."

Lyndon kept typing as if he couldn't hear James, too focused, but she knew he was still fully aware of everything in their surroundings.

She gave Lyndon a few minutes to work, while James continued to tell her he could save her. She could see only the side of his face, but she caught Lyndon's slight smirk.

She moved over to Lyndon and leaned down so she could speak in his ear. "What's the smirk about?"

He continued typing. "He thinks you need to be saved."

She smiled a little. She knew she needed to move away from him, keep her distance, but instead, she murmured, "How's it going?"

"It's a little trickier than tracing the sign feed."

She rested her hand on his arm, his bicep, and whispered, "I'm not worried."

His hands paused for half a second before he continued working.

A loud meow, almost a bark, and scratching at the door.

"He finally got tired of being left out," Lyndon said.

She started toward the door. "Something's wrong."

Lyndon stood.

"Keep him quiet," she said over her shoulder.

Lyndon started toward James.

At the door, Kadance looked out the peephole. There was someone coming up the stairs. She cracked the door open, Mac scurried through, and she closed and locked the door. Mac stood next to her facing the door. She looked out the peephole again. It was a young man coming up the stairs, wearing a cheap jacket and jeans. As he made it to the top, she noticed he had a plastic bag in his hand. Food delivery? Though neither the bag, nor his clothes, had any logos or the name of a restaurant.

The young man knocked on the door.

She looked closely at him, at his posture, or lack thereof, and his expression, kind of bored and unfocused. She was confident he was just food delivery or something else innocuous, but she unsheathed her knife just in case.

She opened the door and smiled, while keeping her knife hidden behind the door.

"Oh, hi," he said. "Did Jim move?"

"He's just in the next room," she said. "I'm his girlfriend."

"Oh, cool. He mentioned his girl was coming to stay with him soon. Hope your trip was nice." He held out the bag.

She took the bag. "How much do I owe you?"

He told her the amount, and she took some cash out of her pocket with her left hand, right hand, holding the knife, still hidden behind the door.

"What else did he say about me?" she asked with a grin.

He smiled. "Just that he was excited to see you. I can see why." He took the cash and headed back down the stairs.

She closed and locked the door, sheathed her knife, and took the bag of food over to the kitchen counter.

She looked over at James. Lyndon was behind him holding a hand over his mouth. Lyndon let go and carefully took a wad of fabric out of James's mouth. It looked like a sock. Then she noticed James's one bare foot.

"Nice," she said to Lyndon.

"If I was really sadistic, I'd have used my own sock." He walked back over to the workstation.

James spit on the floor and cursed at Lyndon.

Lyndon gave no response.

She opened the bag of food. Chinese, of course—James's favorite. She sorted through the containers and found something that was easy to eat, not noodles or rice, but something that could easily be popped into the mouth.

She walked over and set it on the table next to Lyndon, along with a plastic fork. "You haven't eaten all day."

"I'm all right." He continued typing, gaze intensely focused on the screen.

Her voice was softer. "You should eat."

His hands paused, and he looked up at her.

She walked back over to the kitchen counter. Her hands shook while she took the other containers out of the bag. *You have to do better than this, Kadance.* She could not let him see what was going on inside her head.

Mac jumped up on the counter and rubbed against her arm.

She petted his back. "I'll get you some water, buddy." She found a plastic container in a cabinet, filled it from the tap, and set it on the counter.

She let herself glance over and saw Lyndon take a bite of food. *Good.* Then she turned back to Mac.

"Got it," Lyndon said.

"You're full of it!" James said.

Kadance moved closer to the workstation. "Can you shut down facial recognition?"

"I can shut it all down—I'll do it right before we leave. She might get some kind of alert when it goes down. And I found confirmation we're right about how the virus will be disseminated, both at the Capitol and where the designated survivors are staying, along with pictures of the men who are supposed to do it. Well, it's all in code, but I believe I understand it."

James cursed several more times, which told Kadance Lyndon had deciphered the code properly.

"Can you save what you found?" she asked Lyndon. "Should we take it to the FBI?"

"It's a complex code. And I don't think I made a great impression the first time—I think there's too good a chance they'd dismiss me again."

Or maybe hold him for questioning—not worth the risk. "Can you stop them from bringing the system back online?" Kadance asked Lyndon.

"I can disable this setup, but I can't be sure he wouldn't be able to find another computer. Based on what I've seen, he's the prepared type. I'd guess he has a backup system somewhere in the city."

She looked over at James. "What we really need to do is put James out of commission."

James stared at her.

THIRTY-THREE

"WHAT DO YOU WANT TO DO WITH HIM?" Lyndon asked Kadance.

She paused as she stared back at James. It was freeing that she could now look at him without that sense of betrayal and loss clouding her mind.

She turned back to Lyndon. "We'll leave him tied up. Looks like you did a good job—it'll hold. And we should tie the chair to something immobile so he can't shift around the room and cause a commotion."

"What if someone doesn't come for him?"

"I doubt anyone will. I get the feeling all the work goes one direction in this group—all effort goes toward the goal, not helping each other out of jams." She looked over at James, and she could see from how he tried to hide his expression that she was right. She turned back to Lyndon. "But I'll make an anonymous call after the State of the Union and get him rescued."

"What do you want to tie him to that's immobile? Kitchen island? There's a twenty-foot ethernet cable in that pile."

"Do you think it'll stay tight?"

"I'll use some zip ties to make sure the knot doesn't come undone." He walked over to James.

Together, they moved James and his chair over to the kitchen island, wrapped the wire around his waist and then around the island. The counter overhang would keep it from slipping up and off. Lyndon zip-tied that knot and all of the others as well.

"Kadance," James said. "Please." The blood on his neck had dripped down his skin and dried.

"How do we keep him quiet?" Lyndon asked. "The sock?"

"You've grown a dislike for him rather quickly, haven't you?"

"To be fair, I didn't like him before I met him."

James stared at Kadance. "You told *him* about us?"

She answered Lyndon's question. "The sock if we can't find something a little cleaner."

"Why would you tell *him*?" James demanded. "What did you tell him?"

Lyndon leaned down in front of James. "She told me everything."

James struggled against his bindings, but the chair didn't shift at all.

"Does that feel like a betrayal?" Lyndon asked. "Now you know how it feels." He walked away and started looking through cabinets.

"Who is this guy to you?" James demanded. He strained to turn enough to see her.

She stood at the other side of the island petting Mac.

"Are you sleeping with him?"

Kadance continued petting Mac. Mac stared at James and growled.

"Answer me," James demanded while twisting around, trying to look at her.

Mac growled louder and hissed.

"Mac has good instincts." Lyndon continued to look through cabinets.

She kept stroking her hand slowly down Mac's back. "He's my protective little man."

"You are sleeping with him, aren't you?" James said.

"You don't have any say in my life," Kadance said. "You don't have the right to manipulate anyone's life." She walked around and stood in front of him. "And we're going to make sure you don't hurt anyone else."

"You were happy with me."

"I was lonely."

He nodded toward Lyndon. "He's just a stand-in, a way to fill the void."

She leaned closer and murmured, "He's so much more than you."

She thought she saw Lyndon pause, but then he moved on to the next cabinet.

"This should work." Lyndon closed a drawer and then walked over with a couple of washcloths in his hand. They looked ratty. He lifted them to his nose. "I think they're clean."

She took them from Lyndon and stuffed them in James's mouth. He turned his head and tried to spit them out. She pressed his head back against the counter, probably a very uncomfortable angle for his neck. She pressed one hand down on his forehead to keep him still and stuffed the rags in his mouth with the other hand.

Lyndon connected a few zip ties and then wrapped them from James's mouth around the back of his neck. "That should hold him." He looked at Kadance. "Ready?"

She leaned close to James. "We'll get you rescued when we're done. If we remember. Until then, I hope you enjoy sitting in your own excrement." She picked Mac up off the counter and headed for the door.

Lyndon hit a few keys on the computer keyboard and followed her.

Before they walked out, Lyndon murmured, "You're sure you're all right leaving him like this?"

"He won't die."

"I meant does it bother you? You used to be close to him. If it upsets you, we can find another way."

"You're kinder to me than I deserve." She walked out the door.

LYNDON FOLLOWED KADANCE down the stairs. He had the feeling something had happened in there. Something had changed with Kadance. But he wasn't sure what. He'd started to worry perhaps she still had feelings for James. Now, he was fairly certain that wasn't it.

"Do you think she might have people watching the streets?" he asked as they walked outside.

"My gut tells me she keeps her group tight, small. Her little acolytes who follow her website don't know what's going on. She's chosen to keep only those who could offer a significant benefit. She's depending on James to be her eyes and ears. There's probably only a handful in on the plot. Too many and she risks exposure."

Her gut. He trusted her instincts, and where they came from.

They headed back toward the car. They kept mostly to the alleys again, but they didn't have to hide from cameras anymore. She didn't even ask if he was certain he'd killed the feed. That kind of trust seemed astonishing coming from her.

Something had definitely changed.

"He's been masking your identity," Lyndon said. "I looked through his communication with her. It's all in email—coded, but not difficult to understand if you have half a brain. He keeps calling you the 'unnamed female accompanying the target.'"

"She doesn't see the live feeds?"

"No. He sends her clips and explains everything else in text, maybe some in calls too. All the shots with you in them are of the back of your head. I think he actually was trying to get you inoculated and saved."

"I'd rather fight to the bitter end."

He readied himself for her annoyance. "I think we should keep your identity hidden."

She stopped.

Before she could say anything, he added, "We might be able to use it to our advantage. I wager that's part of why you were so successful in the CIA—no one saw you coming."

She continued walking but said nothing.

Instead of walking back through the church, she circled around the outside, and he followed. He figured she hadn't yelled at him yet because she was considering his point about strategy. He hoped, anyway.

"What are your thoughts for a disturbance at the Capitol building?" he asked.

"I think it should be specifically in the House chamber."

"I agree."

"I want to hear your ideas. You'll probably come up with something more appropriate."

"What do you mean 'more appropriate'?"

"My brand of disturbance has historically involved bloodshed."

He wished she hadn't had to live through that, and at the same time, he knew she'd saved many lives in the course of her service.

"What're your thoughts?" she asked.

"We need to show any gaps in security, and it should be something that grabs attention. If it ends up on the evening news, the State of the Union is more likely to be moved or postponed. Maybe even canceled."

"And my mind goes straight to sniping one of the stupider congresspeople while they sit there."

He paused his steps. "Maybe that's exactly what we should do."

"Are you serious?"

KADANCE WAITED FOR LYNDON on the sidewalk outside the Capitol building. He'd researched the layout pretty well on the phone, but they'd agreed they should also get eyes on as much as possible, so Lyndon had taken a tour. He walked down the steps toward her.

"That was interesting," he said as they headed down the sidewalk.

She looked over at him. She'd found herself taking any opportunity to look at him. She kept thinking back to the differences between him and James. Lyndon never asked anything of her. He'd hidden his feelings, simply because he believed that was what she wanted. No matter how much it hurt him.

She wasn't used to so many feelings. All of it was confusing.

"Something wrong?" he asked.

She blinked and looked away. "Lost in thought."

He paused while they passed someone on the sidewalk and then lowered his voice. "Are you sure you have the right kind of ammunition?"

"It'll work."

It was dark by the time they made it to the car hidden in a back parking lot several blocks from the Capitol. They'd decided to sleep here for the night. She sat in the driver's seat, and Lyndon took the passenger seat, though she offered that he could stretch out on the back seat. She wasn't sure it was wise for her to be so close to him in the dark.

She called Mac to sit on her lap. He curled up and rested his head on his paws.

They both tilted their seats back and sat there in the dark quietly. She couldn't sleep.

Finally, she said, "You should stay here tomorrow."

There was just enough light from a nearby pole that she could see as he looked over at her.

"I can do it all myself. There's no reason to risk both of us going to jail. If it doesn't work and I get arrested, you can still find a way to stop it."

He took his glasses off, set them on the dash, and sat back in his seat. "What would you say if I tried some line like that on you?"

"You already did—trying to keep my identity hidden."

"That has a strategic advantage. There's no upside to revealing your identity. But our plan for tomorrow is much more likely to succeed if we do it like we discussed."

"I'm perfectly able to do all of it myself."

"It would leave more time for the package to be discovered." He looked over at her. "Why're you pushing this all of a sudden?"

She turned her head to look out the side window and stroked Mac's fur.

Lyndon's voice was softer. "Something seems off with you. What's wrong?"

THIRTY-FOUR

LYNDON WATCHED KADANCE CAREFULLY.

"Nothing," she said.

"I can tell something is wrong."

She looked him dead in the eye. "Nothing's wrong. I'm working out our best strategy." She laid her head back and stared out the windshield.

Lyndon didn't keep pushing. Something was wrong with Kadance, but he knew there was no way to get her to talk to him. He had little to no influence over her, nothing like she had over him, and every time he thought about it, he felt like a little part of him chipped off and fell away. He feared the rest of his life would be like this. She would leave and forget about him, and he would keep thinking about her. Little parts of him would chip off every day, until there was nothing left.

He took a slow, quiet breath and looked out the side window.

Now was not the time to think about this. He had the rest of his life for that. Right now, he needed to focus on their plan. And hope whatever was wrong with Kadance didn't interfere with it.

ONCE THE SUN started to rise, Lyndon left to get something for them to eat. When he got back with croissants and orange juice, she was in the back seat loading her sniper rifle.

He waited for her to be done and set the gun down before handing her juice.

"Thank you." She sipped the juice.

"Everything ready?"

She nodded.

He handed her a bag with a couple of small croissants. She took one out of the bag and looked at it for a second before taking a bite.

"Have you never had a croissant before?" he asked.

"No." She took another bite.

He almost asked why not. It was a rather popular food to have never had one, but then he remembered where she'd lived for ten years and what her life had been like before and after her service. There were probably a lot of things she'd never experienced.

Though she didn't say anything, he could tell she liked it. This small thing made him feel just a little better—he wanted to bring happiness into her life, no matter how small and insignificant.

They had a little while to wait, and they spent it in silence. Other than Mac meowing for his breakfast.

Finally, it was time to leave. Lyndon walked off with his black generic backpack emptied except for the package they'd put together yesterday, and Kadance drove off with her sniper rifle in the back seat. She'd put it into what looked like a baseball bat case, though it was longer than a baseball bat. The case was a little worn and had a couple of White Sox and Cubs stickers on it.

At the Capitol building, Lyndon headed toward the service entrance they'd noticed yesterday. There were some renovations going on, and they'd seen the workers using this entrance. The workers had to go through a metal detector, but their bags weren't x-rayed. Tools were already onsite, so their bags were surely just lunch and maybe a fresh shirt.

While he went through security, he was careful to speak as little as possible, specifically so he wouldn't have to try to lie. He was sure no one else could detect lies as well as Kadance could, but he wasn't taking any chances.

After security, he followed another couple of workers down the hall, but when another hall branched off, he slipped down it. He followed the map of the building in his mind until he came to a tour group, and he assimilated into the back of the group.

A middle-aged woman looked at him. He smiled at her, and she turned back to the tour guide.

Once in the National Statuary Hall, he meandered toward the east side of the huge room. He looked up at the massive domed ceiling and then focused on the statues surrounding the perimeter of the room along with marble Corinthian columns.

The tour guide prattled on, and Lyndon watched for his opportunity.

When all backs were turned, he slipped through a doorway and turned right down a hall. Then he turned right again.

"Excuse me."

Lyndon turned to see a security guard headed toward him. Lyndon mentally reviewed the tips Kadance had given him.

The guard stopped in front of him. "Are you lost, sir?" His words were polite, but his expression and tone were hard.

Lyndon made his expression even more flustered. "I am. I'm so sorry. I didn't mean to go where I'm not supposed to. I have a pass to visit the House of Representatives." He handed the guard the pass Kadance had lifted for him from a tourist yesterday.

The guard inspected the pass, and then he stared at Lyndon for several seconds. Lyndon kept the flustered expression and fidgeted. Kadance had said this would help mask his lies.

The guard handed the pass back to Lyndon and led him down the hall.

Once inside the Hall of the House of Representatives, Lyndon breathed a little more easily. Of course, he couldn't walk around as he pleased, even though he had a pass and the House wasn't in session, but Lyndon managed to "forget" his backpack. The placement had to be precise. Thankfully, his sense of spatial reasoning was almost as good as Kadance's.

A short while later, he walked out of the building. He kept his pace casual but put as much distance as he could between him and the Capitol building. He'd see soon enough if the plan worked.

IT TOOK SOME DOING, but Kadance managed to make it through the building and up to the roof. At the corner of the roof, she could just see down the street to the side of the House wing of the Capitol building.

Careful to remain out of sight, she set up her McMillan TAC-50 sniper rifle and took out the second phone they'd bought yesterday.

Then she waited.

It was only a short while later that a text came through. "Done."

She put the rifle into place on the edge of the coping cap on the parapet wall, looked through the scope, and counted windows on the side of the Capitol building. There were no windows in the House chamber. Lyndon had offered to get the package into position in one of the perimeter rooms that did have windows, but Kadance felt it was important for this to happen in the House chamber itself. It made her job harder, but not impossible.

Lyndon had found detailed specifications for the building online, and they'd studied them together, along with specifications for the building she was on now. She'd calculated the exact angle and the exact distance. She lined up her shot on the window, the precise number of inches from the window frame. The blinds were open, so she could see no one was there, no one in harm's way. She could see through the doorway to the hall and the double doors opposite. She could just see the glass inlay in the doors but not the delicate mullions between the diamond-shaped glass panes. She couldn't quite see the package. The dark color of his backpack surely blended with the dark seats and the shadows in this area of the room. But she trusted it was there, in the exact spot they'd discussed. Though she'd never trusted anyone else to put her target in place for her, she didn't feel on edge, didn't question.

She calculated the effect of the current wind speed.

She calmed her breathing.

She wiped everything from her mind except the calculations. Just the numbers and the angles.

This was the part she liked best. The quiet and calm. Everything lined up exactly right.

She slowly squeezed the trigger.

The rifle fired, and she pulled back from the edge of the building.

She moved quickly but meticulously. Police would start swarming the buildings in the area, but they wouldn't come to this one, at least not yet. They wouldn't guess someone could make that shot from here. She had to use tracer ammunition in order to ignite the package, but she used a dim tracer round, which wasn't nearly as likely to have been seen on a bright day like this.

She left no evidence she'd been there, and a few minutes later she was in her car, her rifle on the back seat floor and Mac curled up on the passenger seat.

Sirens blared.

She drove in the opposite direction.

Keep driving, some part of her said. Leaving now would be easier, rather than having to face Lyndon before she left. But there were no guarantees this would work, and if it didn't, he wouldn't stop. She sighed. She couldn't leave until she was sure he was safe.

When she pulled up to the park they'd discussed, he was sitting on a bench. He walked over and took the seat next to her.

She stayed parked. "Did it hit the news yet?"

"Social media." He held up his phone to show her a video. Apparently, someone had caught it on tape and posted it, maybe a tourist.

Fireworks filled the House chamber with flashes of colored light and bangs.

"It worked," she said.

"You sound surprised." He tucked the phone back in his pocket.

"I wasn't totally sure it would, not so well, anyway." She put the car in gear.

"I knew you'd make the shot." He put on his seat belt.

"Now, just to wait and see if it has the desired effect." She pulled out of her parking space.

"Lunch?" he asked.

She wasn't in the mood to eat, but she didn't tell him no. He'd ask again what was wrong with her. She was tired of lying to him.

She drove out of the center of the city and found a little fast-food place.

She sat at a table near the door, with Mac on the chair next to her, and Lyndon went up and ordered. When he came over with a tray of food, they picked at it and continued to refresh news websites on their phones. It hit the news pretty quickly, and then they waited for news of plans for the State of the Union. Kadance started feeling antsy. The State of the Union was the next evening—they needed to find out what the plan was as soon as possible. If the Speaker of the House didn't move or cancel it, they needed to take even more drastic action, and that would take some time to set up.

They continued to sit at the fast-food place and watch their phones, and Kadance thought.

Finally, a couple of hours later, it was announced that the State of the Union would be held as planned.

Lyndon sighed and ran his hands through his hair.

Kadance stood. "I have a plan. Wait here while I make a call."

"What're you—"

"Trust me, okay?"

He stayed put and watched her walk out the door. At the front of the building, she stayed by the windows so he could see her and wouldn't think she was leaving. She didn't have the same kind of memory as Lyndon, but she still remembered this number.

A familiar male voice answered. "Hello?"

"I have a proposition."

He paused. "I'm listening."

"I need snipers. Several."

"For what?"

"How quickly can you get on a plane?"

"Depends."

"I'll give you what you want. With restrictions. If you help me with a job. But you have to guarantee you'll stick to my rules on this."

"And what exactly are the rules? And why would I want to follow them?"

She explained her plan, and he agreed.

She ended the call and motioned for Lyndon to come outside. He left the tray and came outside, Mac in tow. Then he followed her to the car.

"I need you to trust me," she said.

"I do trust you."

"You might not anymore once I explain what I've set up."

He waited.

"There's only one way to handle this now. We have to take drastic measures."

"What've you planned?"

"She'll send the man in dressed as a fire system technician most likely."

"I agree."

"But we don't know from which direction he'll approach. Plus, we have to handle the attacks on the designated survivors."

"What've you planned?"

"We need to take him out before he makes it into the building. Once he's inside, we don't have any chance of staying ahead of him or getting around security. We need to watch the outside, every possible entry point. We need snipers."

His jaw clenched. "You called in your family."

THIRTY-FIVE

"YES," SHE ADMITTED.

"You didn't think you should talk to me about it first?"

She hated seeing how angry he was. "I made sure they'll leave you alone."

"They'll take you, Kadance." As he looked at her, he lifted his chin. "You promised your father you'll go with them. That's how you got them to agree to do this."

"I explained everything, that it's in their best interest to stop this. And yes, I had to promise to go with them." She quickly added, "But I was clear that I will not become an assassin for them." She took a slow breath and looked at her lap.

A few seconds passed.

His voice was soft. "Kadance."

She looked over at him.

"Leave. Please. I'll meet them and explain what they need to do. I'll make sure the attack is stopped."

"They won't listen to you."

"Like you said, it's in their best interest. They haven't been inoculated. If she starts an epidemic, they'll be affected."

"No." She looked out the side window.

He took her hand gently in his.

She controlled her expression. She controlled the overwhelming urge to squeeze his hand, to pull him closer.

This was torture. Worse than all the beatings she'd taken.

"Kadance," he murmured. "Please talk to me. We've gained some trust, right? Please tell me what's going on with you."

She didn't respond.

"Please," he said. "Leave. Be safe." With his other hand, he reached over and softly stroked her cheek. "Please."

She pulled away from his touch and got out of the car. She started walking across the parking lot.

His footsteps followed her.

He took her hand, and she stopped. But she stayed faced away from him. He moved in front of her. She closed her eyes. "Please, Lyndon."

He rested his hand on her cheek.

She knew she needed to shove him away, but she couldn't. She should've left him, should've handled this on her own.

He moved closer. She could feel how near he was, not his heat or his scent, but something else altogether. There was something about his presence that both calmed her and brought her to life.

He wrapped his arms around her.

A tear escaped her lash line and slid down her cheek. She pressed her face into his chest to hide her tears, and he wrapped his arms more tightly around her.

I love him.

More tears came as she finally admitted it. She'd never felt like this, never said the words, never even thought them. Never.

He held her so perfectly. He wasn't controlling or forceful. He was just strong for her, as much or as little as she wanted. His hands in her hair and on her back, he held her. He gave no indication of letting go. She knew he'd hold her as long as she wanted, and she could feel how much he wanted to.

She could feel how much he loved her.

More tears came. She'd hurt him. She'd had no idea what

she was doing, but she should have. She should've figured it out sooner.

She wrapped her arms around him and held on. *Please don't let him find out. Please.* She would hurt him when she left, but she'd hurt him immeasurably more if he found out what she'd done, that the person he'd finally opened up to was not who he thought she was. The light he saw in her wasn't the sun; it was the fires of hell.

He whispered in her ear, "Let it out. I'm here."

She couldn't get herself to let go yet. This was a lie. She knew that. But it was a beautiful lie.

"I'm here for you," he whispered. "I love you. I'm here."

She pulled away. "Don't say that."

He looked like she'd slapped him and spit in his face. "I'm sorry."

"Don't be sorry." She turned away. "Don't anything."

"I shouldn't have said that." He controlled his voice, but she swore she could *feel* how hurt he was.

I'm so sorry. I'm so sorry. I'm so sorry.

"Give me a few minutes." She walked away.

He stayed.

She mentally berated herself. She was stronger than this. He deserved for her to be stronger than this. She could control, to an extent, how much she hurt him. And nothing was more important than that right now. Not even stopping the attack. Nothing.

She calmed her breathing and mentally built a wall, blocking out everything he made her feel. It was overwhelming. She had to block it out altogether.

A few minutes later, she walked back around the building. He was standing in the same place, not far from her car and Mac sitting on the front seat watching them. She walked past Lyndon and took the driver's seat. Lyndon followed and sat in the passenger seat.

They were silent.

They were silent for hours. She drove around the area surrounding the Capitol building, as close as she could get now that they had some of the surrounding areas blocked off after the firework incident, scouting all the entrances and the best locations to watch those entrances. She didn't look at him, tried to block his presence from her mind. She felt hardened inside. Dead.

LYNDON HAD NO IDEA WHAT TO DO. Something was wrong. Very wrong. And he didn't think it was related to her family. Whatever it was had started before they'd come across James, and it was growing steadily worse. And now she was completely cutting herself off from him.

Her silence felt like he was being stabbed in the chest.

He should've known better, should've tried harder to block out what he had started to feel when he first met her. When he passed her car at the storage place, he stared at Mac, but only to keep himself from staring at her. It wasn't just her beauty. There was something about her that spoke to him on a different level.

Like a part of him already knew her.

He squeezed his eyes shut and then opened them, trying to block out his thoughts.

Her phone buzzed with a text, and she read it. He figured it was from her father.

"When are they arriving?" he asked.

She didn't look at him, and her voice was cool, removed. "Tomorrow afternoon."

"Is that enough time?"

"I'll have everything planned. They'll just need to set up where I tell them to."

They were silent again. He had more questions, but he couldn't stand to hear her talk to him with that voice.

Mac kept switching from her lap to his and back again, as if trying to comfort them both. Lyndon made sure he stroked Mac whenever he came to him. Mac clearly felt something was wrong and was upset by it.

The rest of the day passed in silence. Kadance researched and wrote out the plan. She went through her ammunition and cleaned her gun. Lyndon tried to get her to eat, but she refused.

The feeling that she wanted nothing more than to be rid of him grew stronger and stronger with each passing hour. But he would not leave. He wasn't a sniper and couldn't be part of the plan, but he also wouldn't leave her. Not yet. When the danger was over, he'd let her go, wouldn't show how much it hurt. But right now, he would do whatever he could to protect her.

He would do everything in his power to try to stop her family from taking her.

He knew his chance of success was nil, but he had to try. That was what he spent the hours doing, trying to formulate a plan, all while ignoring the searing pain splintering through his head.

They stayed the night in the car again. He couldn't sleep. He wanted to take a walk, but some part of him knew she would drive away and leave him. So, he stayed.

IN THE MORNING, she still wouldn't eat. And neither would Mac. The poor thing had thrown up his dinner. Kadance managed to coax him into drinking some water. Lyndon watched her with Mac. Her kindness was still in there, but she showed it to Mac only, no longer to Lyndon.

It doesn't matter, he reminded himself. He'd always known he could never have her. His only focus was to try to protect her.

Finally, the hour drew near. She'd texted the plans to her father, and she headed out to set up at her assigned perch. Lyndon walked with her toward the building.

"You'll just be in the way." It was the first time she'd talked to him in almost twelve hours.

He didn't respond.

She continued walking. Mac trotted along beside her, and people passing them on the sidewalk looked at him. Surely, she'd brought him because she knew she wouldn't be going back to her car. She wouldn't have time to retrieve him.

Lyndon took her hand.

She stopped but didn't look at him and certainly didn't grip his hand.

"Please don't do this."

She paused, and he was sure she would continue ignoring him. But she said, "It's the only way."

"Everything is set," he said. "You can leave now."

"He's sending one of my cousins to babysit me. If I'm not in place, no one does anything."

"Don't they understand what's at stake? They haven't been inoculated. They'll die too."

"I don't think they believe me."

He let go of her hand. If he didn't understand the science, he might have a hard time believing as well.

She continued walking.

The building she'd assigned to herself had a line of sight to the entrance Lyndon had used when he smuggled in the fireworks, but it was several blocks away. It wasn't a government building, so the security wasn't difficult. They made their way up to the roof.

She walked across the roof to the farthest corner and started setting up. The parapet wall hid her from view from the street or any neighboring buildings.

Lyndon surveyed the area and tried to come up with some kind of plan that might have some possibility of success. There were several HVAC units scattered over the rooftop, which he could hide behind and perhaps take someone off guard. But he couldn't take down the cousin, at least not right away, or they wouldn't help stop the attack.

272

Kadance loaded her rifle. To his surprise, she said, "I've told them to try not to kill anyone."

He paused. "Because you don't want to be an assassin."

"I am whether I like it or not. But I won't do that again." She finished loading and used the bolt action to put one into the chamber.

"You're not an assassin, Kadance."

She stayed turned away, ignored him.

The door to the roof opened.

She turned to face Lyndon. "Don't talk to him. Don't even make eye contact. I told them you're just some scientist helping me. You're not important to them. You need to stay that way."

He felt his body tighten in frustration, in preparation. "I don't need you to shield me from them."

"Just do what I say. They won't think twice about killing you." Then her mask of deadness slipped. "Please, Lyndon." He couldn't quite identify the emotion on her face before she turned away.

A young man walked toward them. His boots clomped across the roof's tar and asphalt surface. He wore jeans and a military-style jacket zipped up. "Hey, cuz."

She didn't acknowledge him.

"Been a long time," he said.

"Not long enough," she said but still didn't look at him.

"You'll be happier when you come back home. You gotta be sick of living on the road."

Mac walked over and stood next to Kadance. He stared at her cousin, and the fur on his back stood up.

"What's that?" her cousin asked.

She didn't answer.

The cousin walked over and leaned casually against the HVAC unit closest to her.

Lyndon analyzed the young man. He had a strong build, though Lyndon was taller, and based on how he used his right hand to scratch his chin, Lyndon deduced he was right-hand dominant. Lyndon assumed the entire family was skilled at hand-to-hand as

273

well, not just shooting. Lyndon watched for any sign of weakness he could exploit.

Kadance set up at the corner of the parapet wall and watched through her scope. She was silent and still, and her cousin jabbered on occasionally. He didn't seem to care about her lack of responsiveness. He glanced over at Lyndon every so often but never addressed him.

Lyndon hunched a bit, kept fiddling with his glasses, and didn't make eye contact or speak—all in an attempt to appear as weak as possible, not a threat. While watching and analyzing everything the cousin did and said.

They waited for hours. They didn't know when the man would enter the building, so they'd set up well in advance.

The cousin sighed, apparently bored.

Kadance's posture changed slightly. Lyndon knew she'd spotted her target.

She pressed a button on her phone, and it rang on speakerphone.

"Yes" came a male voice.

"He's approaching the entrance closest to me."

"Taking the shot?"

"Surrounded by bystanders. Almost there."

Lyndon looked over the parapet, but it was much too far away to see without Kadance's high-powered scope. He watched her instead. She was perfectly still, controlling her breathing, focused. Her beauty juxtaposed sublimely with her intensity and perfect control.

"I see him. I can take it," the voice on the phone said, surely her father.

"No. I have him."

"I'm closer. I can take him."

"I have it. Just verify the hit and monitor the crowd."

"I'm getting a text from Redan. That FBI agent you warned us about is approaching from the west."

"Target his leg."

"He has a clear shot for a kill."

"No. The leg. He needs to be questioned."

"Copy."

A few seconds later, she said, "Clear." She took half a second and then squeezed the trigger and fired.

She pulled her rifle back from the edge of the parapet and said into the phone. "Verify."

"Your target is down. You hit his thigh. He dropped his bag."

"Redan's target?"

A pause. "Down."

"Alive?"

"Yes. How about the designated survivors?"

She looked at her phone and waited. Two texts dinged, one after the other, surely her other cousins reporting in. "We're clear," she said.

Her cousin hopped down from the HVAC unit he was sitting on. "Time to go."

Lyndon stood between him and Kadance. "She stays."

THIRTY-SIX

KADANCE'S COUSIN LOOKED at her around Lyndon. "What's this about?"

Lyndon could see in the cousin's face that he'd succeeded in making the cousin think he was weak.

"Lyndon." Kadance's voice was calm, not as gentle as she'd spoken to him in the past, but not so cold and dead.

Lyndon stayed where he was and stared down the cousin.

The cousin laughed.

Lyndon slammed a punch across the cousin's jaw. If he could take down the cousin before the rest of the family made it from their perches up here, maybe he could get Kadance out. If she cooperated, which felt like a big *if* right now.

The cousin stumbled to the side and looked at Lyndon in shock.

Lyndon took advantage of the cousin's lack of balance and swept his leg. The cousin fell to the rooftop with a thud. He scrambled to get up, but Lyndon kicked his ribs and the cousin fell back to the roof and cursed.

"She's not going with you," Lyndon growled and punched the cousin square in the face. His head thudded back down against the dark, grainy surface of the roof, and he stopped moving.

Lyndon stood and faced Kadance. "Let's go."

"Why did you do that?" He couldn't tell if she was angry or shocked.

"You know exactly why. Please, let's go."

She stared at him. "I can't."

"If you run now, you can get out before the rest make it here." He moved closer. "I'm not asking anything other than for you to stay safe. I know you don't want me. That's okay. But please run."

At the sound of footsteps on the concrete steps up to the roof access, Lyndon turned. Several men walked through the door onto the roof. They must've been prepared to get here quickly. He turned to face them and analyzed as quickly as he could. The man in the lead was likely her father. He had short dark hair, and Lyndon could see just a little of him in Kadance, something in the brow and jaw. He held a 9 mm Glock in his right hand. To his right, Lyndon's left, was a bulkier man but with similar features, perhaps his brother, Kadance's uncle. And behind them were five young men. Surely more cousins. No one else appeared to be armed, but they all held themselves as if prepared for a fight.

The cousin Lyndon had already taken down was lying on the ground behind an HVAC unit, not visible from the door.

"Just like the good old days," Kadance's father said as he approached.

Behind Lyndon, Kadance didn't respond.

Lyndon waited until they were just a few feet away. He shifted so he could come at her father at just the right angle, and then he lunged. He threw a fist, but it mostly glanced off his jaw. With the same fist, he landed a solid kidney shot, and her father stumbled.

Lyndon slammed an elbow at his temple and reached for the gun. He had his wrist and raked the gun back to break his grip.

But then someone grabbed him from behind.

"Lyndon, stop." It was Kadance's voice.

Lyndon didn't have a choice. Three of the cousins grabbed him.

Her father walked up to him while massaging his jaw. "Apparently, you're not the geek everyone seems to think you are."

"You're not taking her," Lyndon growled.

Her father raised his brows and then looked over at Kadance. "Got yourself a would-be bodyguard, huh? Adorable." He turned back to Lyndon. "Do you have any idea who you're dealing with?"

Lyndon struggled to get free. He managed to get an arm loose and swung a hammer fist at one of the men holding him. He made contact and heard a curse. Another set of hands grabbed him.

Her father raised a brow. "Not bad." Then he looked at Lyndon more carefully and smiled.

He glanced over at Kadance—Lyndon couldn't see her with her cousins in the way. Then her father turned back to Lyndon, still smiling. "You wouldn't be so excited to fight for her if you knew the whole story."

Lyndon struggled. "What story? That you've abused her all her life?"

"Abuse? Is that what you think? I've made her into what she is—the most skilled sniper in history. Do you have any idea what she just did? That shot was 3,500 meters away. No one else in the world could've pulled off that shot."

"That doesn't excuse what you've done to her."

Kadance walked over, into Lyndon's line of sight. She spoke to her father. "It's over. Let's go before they lock down the city."

Her father glanced at her and then back to Lyndon. "I think he needs an education first."

"No." Her voice was hard, a command.

Her father continued to look at Lyndon.

"He's just a scientist," Kadance said. "Of no importance. Not worth the effort."

Lyndon side-kicked the knee of the man to his right. The man fell and cursed. Lyndon used the same leg to throw a thrusting front kick at her father. His foot made contact with his hip, and her father fell back a couple of steps. Lyndon tried to break an arm free, but another young man grabbed him, in a better grip.

Her father stepped back up to Lyndon, in his face.

Lyndon stared back at him.

"I think you need to know the story."

"You're not taking her," Lyndon growled.

"What was her name? Angela, was it?"

Lyndon didn't respond. He didn't understand.

"Yeah," her father said. "Angela. That was it. Ever wonder how she really died?"

Kadance stepped forward. "No."

Mac growled.

"It was a hit," her father said. "One of the most beautiful I've ever seen. Perfect. But, you're probably thinking, there was no forced entry into her dorm room. You're correct. It was a sniper." He paused. "The most talented sniper in history."

Everything clicked together in Lyndon's head.

He looked at Kadance. She'd closed her eyes in defeat. Then she looked up at Lyndon, and for once, he was able to read an expression, the emotion behind it.

Regret.

The assassination her family had tricked her into doing—it was Angela. The mastermind had hired her family to do the job.

Her father stepped back with a smirk on his face. He started toward the door.

Kadance moved closer to Lyndon and barely murmured, "I'm sorry." She paused. "Please take care of Mac." She turned and followed her father.

Mac started after her, but she held her hand up and said, "Stay."

He stopped moving but stared after her.

Her father had handed his Glock off to one of the young men, and that man now held it to Lyndon's head, with his finger squeezing the trigger. Everyone else headed for the door. They disappeared down the stairs.

After a couple of minutes, the cousin with the gun stepped back, gun still aimed.

Out of the corner of his eye, Lyndon noticed Mac move closer to the young man. Then Mac lunged, dug his claws and teeth into the man's leg.

The young man cursed and tried to shake Mac off. Mac dug in deeper and growled.

Lyndon grabbed his wrist, holding the gun away from himself and Mac, and punched him in the face. Blood gushed from his nose.

"Release," Lyndon said to Mac, hoping he would understand.

Mac let go and backed up, and Lyndon raked the gun back out of the man's grip and then aimed it at him. He didn't want to shoot anyone, but he needed to make sure he wouldn't follow.

Lyndon kicked the man's leg, which started to buckle, and then Lyndon slammed the butt of the gun across his jaw. He landed with a thud on the roof, unconscious.

Lyndon ran to the door. "Mac, come," he called over his shoulder.

Mac sprinted forward and made it to the door before Lyndon.

While they rushed down the stairs, Lyndon tucked the gun into his waistband under his jacket. They ran out onto the sidewalk, and Lyndon looked up and down the road.

A large passenger van was driving away.

Lyndon bolted after it, and Mac followed.

"Kadance!" Lyndon roared.

He pushed himself as fast as he could go, but the van picked up speed. He prayed for a traffic light to turn red. Though he had no idea how he could possibly get her away from them if he did somehow manage to catch up. It didn't matter—he had to try.

"Kadance!"

The next light turned green, and the van sped up even more.

He realized it was pointless to try to catch them on foot. He turned and ran back toward where her car was parked. She'd given him the key that morning.

But they'd parked several blocks away.

Finally, he got in the driver's seat, and Mac jumped up, across his lap, and onto the passenger seat. Lyndon started the car, and the tires spun when he hit the gas. He headed back to where he'd last seen the van. There was no sign of them. He drove in the direction of the nearest airport, hoping he'd come across them.

Nothing.

He finally pulled off into a parking lot and punched the steering wheel.

KADANCE GLANCED OUT the back window of the van. Lyndon, along with Mac, was running after them. He yelled her name. It didn't make sense—didn't he understand what her father had told him?

Of course he did—she'd seen in his eyes when it all came clear. He was simply too kind to let her be taken without a fight. But he'd get over that soon enough.

She turned back around and did what she'd practiced her whole life—deadened her expression so much that the deadness started to seep into her skin, her brain, her chest.

She didn't let herself look back out the window again.

THIRTY-SEVEN

KADANCE HAD HANDED her phone to her father as they'd boarded the private plane one of his contacts had let him use. She'd known he'd take the phone anyway. She couldn't look up websites, but she was able to watch the news on the TV in her room to see that they'd succeeded in stopping the attack on the State of the Union. The bag the "fire system technician" had been carrying was described as having "unknown contents," which told her someone had recognized what the virus was, and it was being kept quiet so as not to cause panic. They also reported that an FBI agent had been arrested in connection with the incident, and both the FBI and Homeland Security were continuing to investigate. Kadance was thankful her actions hadn't been for nothing.

She sat at the desk in her old bedroom and watched the TV on the dresser. As soon as she'd been dumped in this room, she'd focused on the news, but her focus was harder to control the longer she sat here.

There was a knock on the door and it opened.

Her father walked in and set a plate in front of her. "Your favorite."

She could smell the pepperoni on the sandwich, but she wasn't hungry. She continued to stare at the little TV.

"We're headed to the range," he said. "You should come along."

"No, thank you." The range, as they called it, was simply a stretch of flat desert in the middle of the family land. They set up targets at various distances and tested themselves, tried to outdo each other.

"Come on," he said. "You love the range. You can destroy your cousins' best shots like you used to."

"No, thank you," she said again.

"You can't just sit here forever."

He kept the door locked from the outside. She didn't have a lot of choices but to sit here. She didn't respond.

"You're barely eating," he said. "At least get some fresh air."

She finally moved her gaze from the TV to him. "You're not going to wear me down." Her tone wasn't harsh, just kind of nothing.

"You love shooting. You always have. You shouldn't give up something you love so much."

"What you do is wrong. I won't be a part of it." She did love shooting, but not what they did with it.

"I'm just talking about the range."

"I understand exactly what you're talking about." She turned back to the TV, a commercial for a grocery store.

He turned to leave but paused at the door. "At least eat." He walked out and closed the door, and she heard the lock click.

She continued to stare at the TV and desperately tried not to think.

But so many things kept invading her mind.

How Lyndon had fought for her. How he'd charged after the van, even after he knew how she'd murdered Angela. She'd never seen kindness like that—not just kind on the surface, but when it was hard.

And Mac—she hadn't realized how much she would miss him. She'd never had a pet before, but then, he wasn't just a pet. He'd been her friend when she most needed one. That was part of why she'd left him with Lyndon. She could never make right what she'd done, but she could give Lyndon the best friend he could ever want. The other reason she'd left Mac was because she knew her father would use him against her if she'd tried to bring him. She didn't want to imagine what he might've done to him.

She tried to focus on the TV. One of the news hosts was interviewing someone in a suit. She couldn't pay enough attention to figure out who he was.

The backs of her eyes pricked.

Get it together, she told herself. She'd made her decisions knowing exactly the outcome, that her life was essentially over. And she didn't regret it. She'd done what Lyndon would've done. The right thing.

But she still hurt.

She'd never felt pain quite like this before. She'd learned to mentally step back from physical pain. This was different. She couldn't step back from it. The pain was so deep it felt like it was woven into her DNA. She tried to accept that it was just a part of who she was now.

Lyndon had changed her, and there was no going back. And she didn't want to go back. No matter how much this hurt, she was thankful. Thankful to have had Mac for as long as she did. Thankful she could give him a new home with Lyndon, a much better home than she could give him. Thankful to have met Lyndon, even to have fallen in love with him. She'd never known love before, and even though she felt like the pain might destroy her, she was thankful to have learned what love really was.

She sat at the desk for hours. She could hear the gunshots from the range in the distance. Eventually, she lay down on the bed, the same bed she'd slept in as a little girl, and drifted off.

LYNDON SPED THROUGH THE STREETS, parked at the curb, and ran up the steps, closely followed by Mac. This was the only place he could think to go. He hoped James was still here.

He walked in the door and stopped at the sight of the chair where they'd left James. Empty.

He looked around the kitchen and living room. The tables that'd served as the workstation were still there, and so were the monitors and a few other pieces of equipment. But the computer was gone.

Though he knew there was nothing worth finding, he started looking through every room and then every drawer and cabinet anyway. James was the only person he could think of who might know where Kadance's family lived, where they might have taken her. He needed to find some clue as to where he'd gone.

At the sound of scratching, he paused. For a second, his hope rose that maybe James wasn't gone. Maybe he was still here somewhere.

Then he realized the scratching had to be Mac.

He looked all around the apartment. No Mac.

A voice came from the hall. "Hello, little guy. Are you lost?"

Lyndon headed down the hall toward the door to the apartment, which he'd left open. There was an older woman standing in the open doorway of the apartment next door. She was smiling down at Mac. Mac must have scratched at her door. But why?

When Mac saw Lyndon, he rubbed against his legs and meowed. Lyndon felt like he understood exactly what Mac was doing.

He smiled at the older woman. "I'm so sorry." He leaned down and petted Mac. "I don't think I'm enough company for his big personality."

"He's an awful cute little man." She pulled her crocheted cardigan tighter around herself.

"I think that's the only time anyone has ever referred to him as little."

She chuckled. There was something he liked about the sound,

perhaps how he could hear her age in the laugh but also her vibrance, just like his grandfather.

"Are you friends with the young man living there?" She nodded toward James's apartment.

Lyndon went for honesty. It was what he was good at. "No. But I do need to find him."

"It has been awful quiet. He moved out?"

"Looks that way."

"Well, I won't say I'm upset. He blasted that darn music all hours. I couldn't sleep at all."

"I'm really sorry about that. It should be quiet now." Then Lyndon added, "Do you happen to know where he went?"

"You said you're not a friend?" She raised an eyebrow, and her forehead wrinkled in a well-practiced manner—she'd given that same look to many a person.

"No, ma'am."

"Then why are you wanting to find him?"

Lyndon took a breath and decided how much to tell her—the truth but not so much as to risk putting her in danger. "I think he might know where someone is. My friend. His ex-girlfriend."

"Ex, huh?"

"Yes, ma'am."

"I heard him talking to some delivery boy about his girlfriend coming to see him. Same girl?"

"Yes, ma'am."

"He seemed to think she'd be happy to see him. He sounded awful excited."

"He was certainly excited, but she did not want to see him. She'd run away from him. Now she's missing, and I'm worried."

"Why did she run away from him?"

Lyndon suspected she had some kind of information. Otherwise, she wouldn't be testing him like this, trying to determine if she should trust him. "He betrayed her and tried to hold her against her will."

"And who is she to you?"

"She's . . . she's my friend."

She raised her brow again, and her sharp gaze sliced into him. "She's more than your friend?"

"She's very important to me," he admitted. "She doesn't see me that way, but I would never ask for more than she wanted. I just want to make sure she's safe." He realized she could easily decide Lyndon was the crazy guy who wouldn't take no for an answer, rather than James.

Mac lifted up onto his hind legs and pawed at Lyndon's hand. Lyndon picked him up and cradled him.

"Is that your cat?" the woman asked.

"He's hers, actually. When she disappeared, he decided to stay with me."

"No collar or carrier."

"He's almost more like a dog. I don't think he's ever seen the inside of a carrier. And I don't think there are any leash laws for cats. If he is technically a cat."

She smiled. Then she reached out and petted Mac's head. Mac leaned into her hand and rubbed his face against her palm.

Is Mac purposefully flirting to get her to talk?

"That's a sweet boy." Then she turned her attention to Lyndon. "I believe you."

"I promise I only want to protect her."

Her wrinkles curved with her smile. "I think that's true."

"Do you have any idea where he might have gone?"

"We weren't friends, mind you. Not a bit."

"Anything might help."

"Well, he passed me in the hall once, and he said something about the smell of my baking reminding him of his mother's pecan pie and how much he missed Savannah. It was pecan tarts I was making, and I didn't give that boy not one of them."

"Savannah. That might be very helpful. Do you remember anything else? Did he mention his mother's name? I don't even know his surname, just that his first name is James."

"Griffin. That's his last name. Mailman gave me his mail once by mistake. As for his mom's name, I'm not sure. From the way he talked, though, she sounds like a real nice southern lady. Surely, she's ashamed of such a boy."

"Thank you," Lyndon said. "Thank you so much."

"I'm sorry I don't have more."

"You've been very gracious to give me what you can." Lyndon started down the stairs, Mac still in his arms.

A few minutes later, Lyndon sat in the driver's seat, took out his phone, and started digging. It was frustrating to work without a keyboard, but he moved as quickly as possible. He worked from the premise that Griffin was James's legal surname. Lyndon had gotten a good look at how James worked when he'd gone through his computer system. James was overly confident in his security—not unwarranted confidence, granted—so he probably wouldn't think using an alias would be necessary.

Lyndon broke several laws and hacked multiple systems. Once he found who he believed to be James's mother, he put the car in gear and punched the gas.

Mac clung to the seat but didn't meow in that angry way of his.

Lyndon drove through the night, didn't stop for anything but gas. He'd considered calling, but getting a mother to betray her son was better done in person than over the phone.

He expected Mac to fall asleep eventually, but he didn't. He kept switching positions and couldn't seem to relax like he normally did on a long car ride.

"It's all right," Lyndon said. "We'll find her."

Mac meowed.

Early morning, Lyndon came to a stop outside what he hoped was James's mother's house. The house was a little brick ranch in a cute but declining neighborhood. It was too early for a polite visit, but Lyndon got out of the car anyway.

The wind was increasing and clouds loomed, but rain had not yet started falling. According to the weather app on Lyndon's phone, a freak tropical storm was approaching Savannah from out in the Atlantic.

"Do you want to come?" Lyndon asked Mac. "You certainly were helpful last time." Lyndon had taken to talking to Mac like he understood perfectly, just like Kadance did. He thought he understood why she did that—to feel less alone, like she had a friend.

Mac jumped over to the driver's seat and then down onto the decaying asphalt. He followed Lyndon up the driveway and then onto the little covered porch with white-painted metal columns that had the common but outdated decorative *S* design. The place was small, humble, but tidy and clean. It reminded him of his grandfather's house.

Lyndon rang the doorbell.

THIRTY-EIGHT

THERE WAS A KNOCK AT THE DOOR. Kadance ignored it. She was trying to clean the cut her uncle's ring had slashed across her cheek when she'd refused to spar with them. Of course, there was no mirror in her room—nothing she could make into a weapon. She did as best as she could with water and an old T-shirt. The bleeding had finally stopped, at least.

Another knock. "Kadance, it's me."

She glared at the door. *What's James doing here?* She didn't answer.

A minute or so later, the door opened, and her father walked in. "You have a guest."

"No, thank you." She kept up the façade of politeness with her father. He liked that game, and it got her fewer beatings. When she was young, they'd had "sparring matches" often, but now that she refused to "spar," it was just beatings. She didn't want to show her family everything she'd learned in her service. She had a feeling she needed to hold on to that last bit of surprise she had left.

"Oh, come on. You've been cooped up an entire day. You need to socialize." Annoyance was starting to slip through his polite façade.

She knew when it was best not to push him too much. She dropped the old T-shirt onto the desk, stood, and followed him

290

out into the living room. The whole house was almost exactly the same as she remembered—the same paneled walls and wood floors, the beast of a brick fireplace at one end of the living space, the same antique dark-wood table at the other end. The couch was no longer the old soft goldenrod-colored thing, but a new brown leather sectional.

Ravelin, one of her Uncle Redan's sons, was in the kitchen with his wife. Kadance had only seen her in person once before. She'd hoped momentarily that she might be a kind face, but from the way she looked at her husband with adoration, it was clear she had no issues with the way things were done here.

Ravelin's wife didn't even look at Kadance.

Ravelin did look at her but didn't say anything, didn't even give an expression. She was tempted to mention his secret social media account. It was under an alias, but Kadance had found out about it years ago. He would post travel plans and occasionally other seemingly innocuous details—which she would piece together to find their next hit. But she decided to keep her mouth shut. If her father and uncle found out, she wasn't sure what they'd do to him.

Kadance followed past the kitchen that opened up to the living space toward the big couch. James stood with a big stupid grin on his face, and he straightened the sport coat he was wearing with his jeans. There had been a time when she'd appreciated how his shoulders filled out a nice jacket.

James took a step toward her. "What happened to your face?"

"Nothing," she said.

James looked to her father, and her father said, "She's just a little rusty. We're getting her back into the swing of things. She'll be her old self soon." He turned to Kadance and smiled. "Sit with James for a while. We'll give you some privacy."

Her father went out front, and Ravelin and his wife went out the back-patio door. Kadance knew they were standing guard at each door to make sure she didn't get out.

James waved toward the couch. "Sit."

She sat with a couple of feet between them.

"Do you feel better?" James asked. "Now that you're away from that guy."

She didn't respond. She didn't speak of Lyndon to anyone.

"Does that cut hurt? Can I help bandage it?"

"No, thank you."

She knew if Lyndon were here, he'd risk her anger and push until she gave him answers about the cut to make sure she was all right, but James moved on.

"Are you settling in?" James asked. "I bet you're happy to be back home."

"It's the same as I remember." Only now she saw things more clearly.

He smiled. He'd apparently taken her response as positive. Whatever. He slid a little closer. "I'm thinking I'll move out to this area. Lots of sunshine. We can use solar power for just about everything."

She didn't respond. Did he think she was going to play house with him again?

James glanced at both doors and spoke quietly. "I came to inoculate you. I have one dose."

She met his gaze. "We stopped the attack. The virus was confiscated."

"We have more. We're not so easily stopped."

Kadance slid to the edge of her seat. "What're you planning?"

He smiled a little at her. "Nothing you need to worry about. I'm here to make sure you're all right." He reached into his inside jacket pocket and took out a syringe.

"Tell me what you're planning."

"I'll tell you it's going a lot more smoothly now that that guy is out of the way. You did great ditching him. Man, he was difficult to get rid of."

She just looked at him. Could he really be this stupid? Then she realized . . . "It was you."

"What was me?"

"You put the hits out on Lyndon. The mastermind would've hired my family to do a sniper hit, but you didn't want it getting back to her that you'd set it up, so you used someone else, someone who wouldn't tell her. It was you—the sniper at the storage place, the mercenaries at Dr. Ibekwe's house, the image on the digital sign telling Lyndon how his grandfather died. You set it all up."

"Of course not." His expression was impassive, except the slightest hint of a smile in his eyes.

"You're jealous of Lyndon, aren't you? Because of the attention the mastermind gives him, and maybe later because of me too, because you saw me with him." Then she added, "You do realize the mercenaries almost killed me. They were trying to get information out of Lyndon and were threatening me to make him talk."

"Those mercenaries didn't know anything, just hired thugs. I told her not to use them."

She knew he was lying. "They knew about the virus, the attack, and where it would be."

His jaw tightened.

"You should've been more careful about controlling information. They must've figured out enough and decided Lyndon was the key to survival. You put me in danger."

"That guy put you in danger. If he'd have just—"

"If he'd have what? Just died in the first place?" Kadance's anger welled up in her chest like lava flowing. "Where is the next attack happening?"

"You don't need to worry about any of that. I'll make sure you're safe." He reached a hand out to her.

"What does it matter if you tell me? You know my family is not about to let me go anytime soon."

He paused, and he dropped his hand onto the couch cushion. "Please, just let me inoculate you. I just want to save you."

Her anger kept rising. She wasn't sure how much longer she could control it.

The screen door at the front of the house creaked. James stuffed the syringe back in his breast pocket.

Her father walked inside. "I was half worried I'd walk in on the two of you making out."

"I wouldn't be so disrespectful to you or to Kadance," James said.

Kadance lunged at James. She gripped his neck, but he managed to pull one hand off. She slammed an elbow across his jaw, and he fell sideways off the couch, smacked into the coffee table, and landed on the floor with a thud.

She threw herself at him, ready to beat him bloody, but her dad caught her from behind. He had an arm around her middle and flung her away from James. He was smart enough not to try to hold on to her but to keep her off-balance. She stumbled into the wall.

She caught her balance and glared at James. Her uncle and cousins had now come inside as well and were surrounding the scene. Her cousins were all armed with Berettas.

"Go," her father demanded.

She took a step toward James. The metal clank of several handgun slides being racked stopped her.

"Go," her father said again.

She continued to glare at James but backed up toward the hall that led to the bedrooms. She made herself walk into her room and close the door. There was no use getting herself beaten and injured, or worse, shot. Then, she wouldn't be any help to Lyndon.

The lock to her door clicked.

Her rage subsided and left her empty. She needed to escape, but she needed to know where Lyndon was, where the next attack was going to happen. He might already be on the trail.

And she was trapped.

She wanted to punch the wall, but she'd learned that lesson as a teenager. The walls were all poured concrete. She'd just end up breaking her hand as she had then.

But she couldn't just stand here.

She couldn't get her mind to work right. She wasn't used to all this *emotion*. She didn't know what to do with it, how to get it out of the way so she could think straight.

She crossed to the one window in the room and inspected it, for the hundredth time, for any weakness in the locking mechanism. Nothing. And if she broke the glass, her family would hear and stop her before she could get anywhere.

The door was reinforced. The lock was a dead bolt with no keyhole on the inside, nothing that could be picked, and the hinges were on the other side in the hall.

Think, Kadance.

She was going to have to be clever to get out of this one. But she couldn't get her thoughts and emotions to calm down enough. She tried pacing. She tried breathing exercises. All she kept thinking about was Lyndon, how she'd failed him.

Before she thought about what she was doing, she dropped to her knees. *I don't know if you're real, but Lyndon believes in you.* She paused to think of what to say, to consider if she was going nuts. *Please watch over him, keep him safe. And please, dear God, please help me find a way out of here.* She lowered her head and tried to control her breathing.

And then a sense of calm, like a warm blanket, fell over her.

And images came—Lyndon's smile when he joked with her, how he looked at her when he didn't think she noticed. The intensity in his eyes when he told her he loved her. She hadn't let herself dwell on those moments, but now they filled up the emptiness in her.

She remembered Lyndon talking about where gut feelings come from, and she knew . . . She knew God was trying to talk to her.

She needed to be calm and think straight, and he was helping her.

"Thank you," she whispered.

She took a breath, and her thoughts felt clearer.

And then she remembered . . . When she was ten, her father had dropped her off in the desert miles from home. It was a test to see if she could find her way. She wandered for hours, and as the sun set and coyotes howled in the distance, fear overwhelmed her, no matter how much she berated herself to be strong. But then there was a sudden blanket of calm, and the few memories she had of her mother had come to her, and she was able to think clearly again.

When she was very small, almost too young to remember, she'd cried for her mommy. She couldn't understand where she'd gone. Her father wouldn't come. He didn't comfort—he wanted her to be strong, not to need comfort. But she was too little to understand. And then she thought she felt someone holding her hand. She closed her eyes and squeezed this hand so hard her own hand shook. And finally, her tears had dried. She'd always told herself it hadn't been real, but now she knew—whether or not the hand holding hers was flesh and blood or not, it was the Presence that was real.

As she thought, she realized she'd felt the same Presence many times in her life, always when she most needed it. She'd just never paid attention. This was the only reason she'd survived so many times, the only reason she was still alive right now. But why would God do that for her, someone who'd done so much wrong and had never even considered believing in him?

The answer flashed across her mind—to do good, to protect others. He'd blessed her with skill so that she could use it.

And she would use it.

She started plotting her escape.

THIRTY-NINE

WHEN NO ONE CAME TO THE DOOR, Lyndon knocked on the battered screen door, and the sound reverberated so loudly that Mac turned his ears back. Lyndon glanced over at the driveway where an old but clean light blue Buick sedan sat. She had to be home.

He lifted his fist to knock again but paused at the sound of footsteps from inside the house. An older female voice called, "Whatever yur sellin', I don't need any."

"I'm not selling anything, ma'am," Lyndon called.

Nothing.

Lyndon knocked again and stood there for a minute longer.

He glanced down at Mac looking up at him with his wide expectant eyes. Then Lyndon glanced around the yard, thinking of what to do. Out of the corner of his eye, he noticed Mac's ears perk. He listened carefully and thought he heard a door closing. Maybe at the back of the house?

Lyndon stepped down off the porch and headed around the side of the house. At the back of the house was a raised back patio, and on the other side of that, against the back of the house, was a shed, rusty at the corners. The yard stretched out to a thinly wooded area, and a clothesline ran down the center.

An older woman, with gray hair up in curlers, came out of the shed. Her terrycloth robe brushed the long grass as she walked. She glanced over at Lyndon and stopped.

The wind gusted, and the clothes on the line started pulling out of their clothespins, scattering over the lawn.

The woman dropped the empty basket she'd had on her hip and ran after her clothes. Lyndon rushed to help, and so did Mac.

The woman glared over at Lyndon but continued gathering clothes. Many of the garments were light and flowy, so as the wind continued to gust, they blew farther and farther across the tall grass toward the woods.

Lyndon gathered all the clothes he could, balled against his chest. He walked back over to the woman, who'd retrieved her basket. "I think we got everything."

The woman snatched the bundle of fabric out of Lyndon's grasp, dumped it into the basket, and started rummaging. "It's not here."

"What's not here?"

She continued rummaging as if he wasn't there.

Then Mac came trotting back from the edge of the woods with what looked like a bright turquoise silk scarf in his mouth.

"There it is." She took the scarf from Mac and examined it. "Covered in cat spit. Now I gotta wash it again."

She grabbed her basket and started toward the back patio.

"Mrs. Griffin," Lyndon said. "I came to talk with you."

She didn't pause or look back. "Git off my property."

Lyndon followed. "Please, ma'am."

"Git."

The wind howled, and Mac crouched lower to the ground. Lyndon picked him up and held him to his chest. "It's all right, buddy."

The woman glanced back at Lyndon holding Mac but then stomped up the steps and into the house. The screen door snapped shut with a bang behind her.

Stinging rain began to fall, and Lyndon ran toward the patio to protect Mac. Unfortunately, there wasn't much of a roof overhang, so the patio didn't offer very good protection.

The rain let loose and pounded the ground.

Lyndon banged his knuckles on the screen door.

"I'm callin' the police," the woman yelled from inside.

"Please, ma'am. I need to talk to you. It's about James." He managed to keep the desperation out of his voice. If he couldn't get something out of this woman, some way to find Kadance, he was at a dead end.

She opened the door but not the screen door. "Who are you?"

"A friend of Kadance."

Recognition lit her eyes. "I'm still callin' the police."

"Because we helped you gather your clothes?"

"Because you're trespassing."

"I know you recognize the name Kadance. I know you've met her. James introduced you to her."

She crossed her arms.

"She's in trouble," Lyndon said.

"Jimmy's helping her. She's fine."

And now he had confirmation he had the right house and the right woman. "Why hasn't he brought her to visit in so long?"

She said nothing, but at least her scowl didn't deepen.

"Please," Lyndon said. "Can we come in out of the downpour?" He was holding Mac against the door and keeping him mostly dry, but Lyndon's back and side were getting drenched.

"Who are you? How d'you know my Jimmy?"

"I don't really know him that well, but I know Kadance. She's in trouble. I'm trying to help her."

"How in the world could coming to see *me* help *her*?"

"Please let me in, and I'll explain."

She continued to stare at him.

Lyndon adjusted his glasses and then adjusted Mac in his arms. "Do I look like a threat?"

She huffed and then pushed open the screen door.

Lyndon stepped in but stopped just inside the door, trying not to appear threatening in any way. He kept Mac in his arms mostly to help put the woman's mind at ease that he wasn't a threat.

"I'm sorry I'm dripping on your floor," he said. Luckily, the door opened into a kitchen with linoleum floors, not carpet.

The woman turned and walked around the kitchen table toward a hall. She returned with a big bath towel.

"Thank you, ma'am." Lyndon took the towel, set Mac on the floor, and dried him off. Mac lifted his head and purred.

"That's one big cat," the woman said.

Lyndon smiled. "Yes, ma'am."

"Why're you walkin' 'round with a cat of all things?" She motioned out the window. "And with a storm about to rage?"

"First, Mac here isn't one to be left behind. Second, I don't have time to worry about storms."

She paused. "Well, you can just be on yur way. You parked out front, I see. Off you go." She waved toward the front of the house.

Lyndon remained squatted down with Mac, still doing his best not to appear threatening, though he had the impression this woman was not the type to be easily victimized. Which just reminded him of Kadance. "I came to see you because I need your help, Mrs. Griffin." Then he added, "I guess I'm assuming your surname is the same as James's, but perhaps I'm incorrect . . ."

"I would never change my name after losin' my dear husband."

Lyndon smiled a little. "I'm happy to hear you had a good marriage. This world needs more good marriages."

"On that, I won't disagree."

Lyndon hoped she'd offer him a glass of water or a seat at the table, but she kept standing there looking down at him. She was going to be a tough one to crack. Again, just like Kadance. Every time he thought of Kadance, his chest tightened.

"I think I see why Kadance said she liked you," Lyndon said.

Mrs. Griffin didn't respond, but at least she wasn't threatening to call the police anymore.

"Would it be too much trouble," Lyndon asked, "for some water for Mac?"

"What kind of name is Mac for a cat?"

"Kadance said it's for Mac computers, mac and cheese, and Mack trucks. Smart, orange, and big."

"That's Kadance's cat?"

"Yes, ma'am."

"What're you doin' with him?"

"She was taken, and Mac was kind enough to stay with me."

"What d'you mean 'taken'?"

"Her family. They found out where she was, and they took her. That's why I'm here. I need to find out where she is so I can help her." *Please, God, let her have some kind of information that will help.*

"How on God's green earth would I have any idea where Kadance is?"

"Because I think James knows."

"My Jimmy would do not one thing to hurt a hair on that girl's head."

"I don't disagree that he cares for her." In his own warped way. Lyndon tried to phrase his words in a manner that might not be too offensive to James's mother. Hopefully. "But I think his concern has manifested in a way contrary to Kadance's preferences."

"Pretty quick with those shiny words of yurs. Like I said, Jimmy would never hurt dear Kadance."

Dear Kadance. She liked Kadance quite a bit, apparently. Good. That gave them something in common. Maybe he could use that to build some trust. He patted Mac's rump, more like one would a dog, stood, and folded the towel over the back of one of the kitchen chairs. "Mrs. Griffin, frankly, I'm better at being blunt, and I have a feeling that's what you prefer as well."

She lifted her chin.

"I'm in love with Kadance. She does not love me in return, but

I do believe she counts me as a friend, which includes a certain amount of trust, probably as much trust as she's willing to give."

"That girl is cautious, I'll certainly grant you that."

"She has very good reason to be. She was abused as a child, and she lived through hardships I can't even imagine while serving our country."

"I always figured she had a past. I never pried, though. Figured she'd open up in her own good time."

"I'm guessing she appreciated that."

"What does any of this have to do with my Jimmy?"

"I'm going to keep going with the bluntness. James is involved with a domestic terrorist. Have you seen the news—the incident at the Capitol building?"

Anger overtook her face like storm clouds. "Git out of my house."

Please let me play this right. "James wasn't there, but he is involved. He's a major player in the Voluntary Population Extinction movement, whose mandate has shifted away from 'voluntary.' They're trying to exterminate the population with a new deadly strain of Ebola as a way to preserve the Earth. Kadance and I theorize that they targeted the State of the Union to throw the government into chaos and make it more difficult to fight the outbreak."

Lightning flashed in her eyes just as the wind outside howled. "Git out of my house. Right now!"

"Did he give you a shot recently?"

She paused.

"He probably told you it was a flu shot or similar. But that's unusual for him, am I correct? He's a technology expert, not medical. Why would he be giving you a shot?"

"My Jimmy could never do such a thing. He's a good boy. And he loves Kadance. He's gonna marry her."

"Please think about something, Mrs. Griffin. Has he ever done or said anything at all that didn't seem to make sense?"

"That boy says all kinds of things I don't understand. Networks and subnets and all that other technical babble. Don't make him a terrorist."

"What about when he visited with Kadance. Did you hear him say anything to her that didn't seem to make sense?" Lyndon guessed it'd been a bit of a balancing act for James to keep Kadance in the dark all while dealing with his headstrong mother.

Mrs. Griffin went still.

"I've hit on something," Lyndon said. "Haven't I?"

She walked over to the sink under the window, took a bowl out of the drying rack, and filled it with water. She bent over and set it on the floor.

Lyndon said to Mac, "Go ahead, have some water."

Mac watched Mrs. Griffin cautiously but walked over and lapped at the water.

Mrs. Griffin watched him.

Then she turned and looked out the window to the storm.

Lyndon quietly let her think. The only sounds were the rain pounding the roof and Mac's noisy drinking.

Finally, Mrs. Griffin said, "He told her how he'd loved his childhood. He said how he appreciated how hard his father was on him and how he owed him so much."

"Was that not accurate?"

"His father was fair but tough. For good reason—Jimmy needed discipline when he was a boy." She paused, still looking out the window. "But Jimmy never appreciated the rules we set for him. I've always thought Jimmy was still angry at his father." Her voice had lost some of that hard edge.

"But you never let yourself dwell on it. You'd lost your husband, and you wanted to make sure your relationship with your son was good."

She gave no response.

"I truly believe James feels he's doing the right thing," Lyndon said. "In his mind, he's saving the Earth and managing to save Kadance at the same time. He risked the anger of the leader of the VPE by protecting Kadance's identity and trying to get her inoculated."

"He loves her."

"His actions show that he's doing the best he knows how for her."

She finally turned to look at him. "But you don't think what he's doin' is right."

"When it comes to Kadance, the only thing I care about is making sure she is free to make her own choices about her life. If she chose James over me, I would honor and respect her decision. But James isn't doing that. I think he wants to be with her so badly that he's not letting himself see that he's hurting her."

Mrs. Griffin sighed, and her shoulders sagged.

Lyndon moved slowly closer. "Do you have any idea where her family lives, where they might have taken her?"

"She never mentioned her family, and neither did Jimmy."

"Do you know anything about where James is, what he's doing, anything?"

"He's my only child," she said.

"Your and your husband's life goal was to raise a good man, right? Don't give up on that goal now."

"I don't want him hurt."

"The last thing I'm interested in is hurting anyone. I just want to make sure Kadance is free."

She paused for several seconds. "I think he . . . I think he might be helpin' to plan another attack."

Lyndon wanted to curse. "Where?"

"I don't know. He said something about destroying false medicine, something about Atlanta, the last I talked to him."

"The CDC. They're going to hit the CDC—that would significantly slow down the efforts to control the outbreak. Do you have any idea when?"

"I don't know." She shook her head. "But he told me to make sure I keep the house locked."

"You're not that far from Atlanta. Panic will definitely hit this area once people start getting sick." Then Lyndon said, "Did he ask you to go on a trip with him?"

"Yes," she said. "He wanted to take me out West on a vacation, but I told him I'd rather go in the spring. He seemed awful upset that I didn't wanna go right now."

"When did he want to leave?"

"He wanted me to take a flight today."

"I need to go. I need to stop it." He picked up Mac and headed for the front of the house.

Mrs. Griffin followed him. "You won't hurt Jimmy, will you?"

"I'll do everything possible not to. Thank you, Mrs. Griffin." Lyndon tucked Mac under his jacket to protect him as best he could and ran out into the pounding rain.

FORTY

"YOU SEEM IN A BETTER MOOD," Kadance's father said.

She kept her gaze on the book on the desk in front of her. "It's not a better mood." She paused. "It's acceptance of realities."

"That has always been one of your strengths."

"Acceptance of reality?" She looked up at him. "Sounds less like a strength and more like simple lack of insanity."

He smiled at her in that way she'd loved so much as a child. It was full of pride, and she used to think it was full of love as well. Maybe he did love her in his own way. "You didn't cry and scream as a little girl. You dealt with whatever was in front of you."

She nodded and turned back to the book.

"James is here to see you again," he said.

That was what she'd been hoping for. She had a couple of plans, but the one more likely to succeed hinged on James. Careful about her reaction, she flipped the next page in the book. "He never did take a hint."

"A man in love goes after what he wants, no matter what."

Even if the woman he wants doesn't want him in return? Isn't that stalking? But she said, "He has a funny way of showing love."

"Not all men are very good at these things. You have to be patient. You may not approve of every single thing he's ever done,
but he's shown very clearly that he loves you."

She sighed and looked up. "What does he want?"

"Just to spend some time with you. He said he's putting off
other pressing matters just to come see you. The least you can do
is go sit with him for a while."

She paused. Then she sighed again, flipped the book closed,
and stood.

"Try not to attack the poor boy again." There was a warning
in his voice but also a slight grin in his eyes.

"No promises."

"Just don't kill him. Too much mess to clean up." He turned
toward the door.

She followed him out to the living room. James was sitting in
the same spot on the sectional. He stood when he saw her.

She turned to the right toward the kitchen. Her father stayed
by her side.

"I just want something to drink." She opened the refrigerator
door.

Her father stood casually in front of the drawer with all the
utensils and knives.

She looked over at James. "Want something? Pepsi?"

He smiled. "My favorite."

"I know." She grabbed two bottles of Pepsi, closed the refrigerator, and walked past her father toward the dining table. She'd
wondered as a child how anyone had ever gotten the beast of a
table in through any of the doors. She sat in one of the chairs and
set the other bottle of Pepsi at the chair next to her, the head of
the table.

James walked over and sat down.

Her father stayed in the kitchen, leaned against the cabinets,
and looked at something on his phone. She tried to think of a way
to get him to leave.

"Are you feeling better?" James asked her.

She wanted to punch him in the face.

Instead, she unscrewed the cap off the bottle and took a sip.

"You look better," he said. "Get a decent night's sleep?"

She nodded. While she'd spent most of the night thinking things through, plotting, when she finally had gone to sleep, she'd slept better than she usually did.

"I have to leave tonight," he said. "I was hoping I'd get to see you again." He reached out and brushed his fingertips against the back of her hand.

The urge to punch him in the face rattled up her arm again, but she controlled it. She took another sip of Pepsi. "Where're you going?"

"Work stuff."

Her father's phone rang. He looked over at James and Kadance. Kadance guessed it was a call he didn't want to take in front of them, perhaps something about a job.

"We'll be all right," James said.

Her father met Kadance's eyes, a warning. She nodded once minutely. He walked past them out the front door.

James smiled at Kadance. "You seem better today."

"Acceptance of reality." She took a sip. She did actually want the sugar and caffeine. She hadn't been eating or sleeping properly. She needed any boost she could get for what she was about to try. She set the bottle on the table. "Where're you going?"

He kept smiling at her. "You don't need to worry about anything. It's all handled." He took the same syringe out of his inside jacket pocket. "Please."

She kept her demeanor calm, verging on kind. "You know I don't handle being kept in the dark well. If you want me to trust you, you need to tell me what's going on."

"You know the basics."

"Where?"

He paused as he looked at her. Then he reached out and tucked a stray hair behind her ear.

She managed not to hit him.

"Atlanta," he said.

"CDC." That made sense.

He smiled a little. "Sometimes I forget how smart you are."

That was something he *always* seemed to forget.

"When?" she asked.

"You don't need to worry about any of this."

She waited for an answer.

"I'm flying out tonight. Let's just say I'm cutting it close. I needed to make sure you're safe before I leave."

The front door started to open, and James slipped the syringe back into his pocket.

"You both look like you're enjoying this visit," her father said.

"Yes, sir," James said. "Thank you."

She looked over at her father. "I'd like to take a walk. I need some fresh air."

"Your cousins aren't home." Translation: he didn't feel he had enough people to control her in the open.

"There's nothing but barren land and a few cacti for miles." She wanted him to be convinced it would be pointless for her to run—there was nowhere to run to and nowhere to hide.

"I'd love some fresh air," James said.

Her father continued to look at her. Finally, he said, "Out back."

James stood and took Kadance's chair. They walked out the French doors by the kitchen onto the back patio. Sandy terrain stretched out in front of them. While the sun was warm, the air was no more than sixty degrees.

"Are you warm enough?" James asked.

"I'm fine." She glanced around, mostly using peripheral vision. Her uncle was nowhere in sight. Her father was watching out the kitchen window. She knew he was hoping she'd fall back under James's influence. That would make keeping her under control much easier. That was the only reason he was allowing them time alone—hoping she and James would bond.

She tucked her hand in the crook of James's elbow and led him off the concrete patio. James smiled and easily went with her. Some part of her wondered if James really did love her, in his own way. But that was the problem of her life, wasn't it? People who loved her in their own way. In a way that suited them, not her. Except Lyndon.

And it hit her why she'd allowed her family to take her. Some part of her was scared of Lyndon, of what she felt for him. She hadn't understood it. She understood better now—or was starting to.

She'd led James away from the patio toward the rock formations in the distance, and she slowly veered their path toward the right, slowly enough that her father, hopefully, wouldn't think she was purposefully getting out of his sight.

"We should probably head back," James said.

"I want to show you the mountains over here. Have you ever seen them from this vantage?"

His gaze softened as he looked down at her. "Show me."

She pulled him along a little more quickly. "See how the sun hits them?"

"Maybe we can get a place around here so you can always see them. Maybe build our own house."

She wanted to say, *Why don't we just move into my family's house, since you're obviously planning on letting them die in the outbreak?* But she kept her mouth shut.

"Here," he said quickly. "Let me give you the injection." He took his arm away from her and reached into his breast pocket.

She slammed a hook across his jaw.

He fell to the ground with a thud.

Part of her wanted to do more, cause him more pain, but right now, she just needed him knocked out and silent. And she needed to be fast.

She took his keys out of his pocket, and as silently as she could on the rocky terrain, she ran to the front corner of the house. Her family all parked in the garages to save the paint from the corrosive sun, so the silver Toyota parked at the front of the house had to be James's rental car.

She paused to examine the area, to listen.

Then she ran toward the car.

Her father walked out the front door, his M-40 rifle in his hands.

She stopped, fully expecting him to take aim at her, but he held it to his side.

"Where're you off to?" He was just a few feet from her.

She said nothing.

"Where's James? Beat him up again?"

"I didn't get to do it properly last time."

The corner of his mouth tweaked, somewhere between a smirk and a smile. "Where're you off to?" he asked again.

"Nothing you need to worry about."

"You're my daughter, Kadance. I always worry about you."

She was done playing his games. "You want to control me, use my abilities to suit your purposes. That's all you've ever wanted."

"How can you say something like that? I've fought for you your whole life. Admittedly, I wanted a son, but I quickly decided you were so much more. I fought your mother for custody because I loved you."

That was the first time he'd mentioned her mother since she was a child. She wanted to demand so many answers—what'd happened and where was she? Was she even alive? But she had another focus right now.

"We stopped the attack at the Capitol, but they're going to try again. I have to stop them. There's a syringe in James's pocket— take it and you'll be safe if I fail."

He paused, surely to digest the information.

"I'm the best option to stop it," she added.

"Give me the details, and we'll handle it."

For one wild second, she considered it. But she didn't trust them. And she assumed Lyndon was already working on stopping the CDC attack and would likely get in the way, and even if he didn't get hurt that way, he'd very possibly spot her father or cousins and go after them. No, there was too much risk to Lyndon.

"There's too much going on," she said. "I need to handle it."

"Well then, we're at an impasse." He shifted his grip of the M-40.

She moved toward him.

He lifted his chin, surely trying to figure her out. But she was different now—he couldn't possibly understand how different.

She continued walking.

He lifted the rifle. "I don't want to hurt you, Kadance. But I will if I have to."

"You'll have to kill me. And we both know you won't do that. I'm too valuable."

"I would never kill my only child."

"You'll have to if you want to stop me." She halted just in front of him, the barrel of the rifle pointed at her chest.

"Get back in the house," he demanded.

She shifted to the right and pushed the gun to the side with her left hand, and she landed an upset punch into her father's gut.

He coughed but then swung the gun at her head.

She blocked, though pain from the hard metal shot through her arm, and she fell sideways a step. He was so much bigger than she was and therefore more powerful. She'd obviously inherited her delicate frame from her mother. She was strong, but she'd never been able to put on a decent amount of weight.

He punched her in the chest, and she couldn't breathe.

He stood straight. "Get in the house."

She was bent over from trying to catch her breath, and as she stood, she hurled an uppercut at his chin. He managed to shift enough to get most of the power of the punch to glance off, and he grabbed her wrist.

She wanted to laugh at his error. The unwritten rule in sparring with her was never to try to hold on to her. The only chance her cousins had was to use their mass and power against her to keep her off-balance. She kicked out his knee, and as he stumbled and started to fall, she smashed her knuckles across his temple.

He landed in the dirt.

She knelt down. His eyes were closed. She needed to punch him again and make sure he was out, but she paused as she looked at his face, the man she'd spent her entire childhood trying to please. Losing parts of herself along the way.

Not anymore.

She punched him, and he didn't move.

She wrenched the rifle out of his grip and ran for the car.

She raced away from her father's land toward the freeway. With limited time, she needed to do everything exactly right.

Once inside the city limits, she found a shipping store and paid them to package and ship the rifle. Thankfully, her father had taken only weapons and her phone off her, not her ID and cash, surely his way of maintaining the illusion that she wasn't a prisoner.

Then she headed for the airport. She didn't have time to drive. She had to risk flying. She left the car at the drop-off area in front of the terminal and walked inside.

The woman at the counter issued her a ticket. But she knew this wasn't the hard part.

She headed toward security. Past a couple of TSA agents, she wound her way through the maze of ropes.

Then she waited.

Waiting was one thing she'd always been good at. She could lie there in the dirt, at the ready with her rifle, for hours. But this was harder. Lyndon's life was in danger. *Please stay with him, please stay with him, please stay with him.* She managed to remain calm and patient. At least on the outside.

Finally, she walked up to the TSA agent who was to inspect her boarding pass and ID. She handed him both.

He scanned the boarding pass and then looked at it and the ID carefully. Then he looked back and forth between her and her ID.

"My hair's longer," she said. Her braid was sitting on her shoulder. The picture on her ID was of a woman who looked very much like her but had shorter hair.

"It grows fast," he said.

"Blessing and a curse."

He looked at her ID one more time. And then he handed it back to her.

"Thanks." She walked past him, put her shoes and wallet in a bin, and waited in line at the scanner. That part was easy, and she was out of security in a few minutes and headed for the gate.

She had to wait twenty minutes for boarding to start and then for first class, anyone who needed additional time, or anyone traveling with young children to board the plane. She waited patiently in line with everyone else. If Mac were with her, he'd hate this part. He'd want to run around in the vast space of the terminal.

She walked down the jetway, smiled at the flight attendants as she passed, and found her seat.

Then she waited for everyone after her to board the plane, for everyone to get seated, and as the flight attendants closed the overhead bins and made sure everyone was buckled.

Finally, the plane pulled back from the gate.

All the while, barely noticing she was doing it, she prayed for Lyndon.

But before the plane made it to the runway, it stopped. Kadance looked out the window. Maybe they had to wait in line for the runway?

She caught a glimpse of flashing lights, and she could just see stairs being wheeled up to the plane. One of the flight attendants opened the door.

A man in a suit with cropped hair and a hard expression, followed by two TSA agents, walked down the aisle. He scanned the cabin, looking back and forth between the passengers and his phone.

He came to her and stopped.

She unbuckled her seat belt and stood.

"Come with me, please."

FORTY-ONE

LYNDON FELT LIKE HE WAS GOING NUTS.

He kept driving around the CDC campus. He wanted to go find Kadance, but stopping the attack was integral to saving her. If the disease was released, he'd be dead and most likely she would be as well. But he had no way to know when the attack would happen, and so he kept circling the campus, hoping no one called the police on the crazy guy hanging around the CDC.

He'd spent more than a day watching the perimeter, hoping he would spot whomever the mastermind sent in. But now he'd just spotted a car pulling into the complex with a license plate with the numbers 122514, the first three letters of his name and also his mother's middle name spelled numerically. And he knew it was time to go in.

When he'd come here with Kadance, they'd parked in a lot across the street and snuck onto the property. It was fenced, but not so hard to sneak into. At least Kadance had made it seem easy. He'd hacked the FBI again, and he'd found his ID was now flagged—wanted for questioning for the events at Professor Ibekwe's house—so he couldn't go through security and pose as a CDC museum visitor. As he spent a day driving around the perimeter, he decided the best access point was the fire station that was basically tucked into the

CDC property but still accessible from the main road. There were trees around the fire station parking lot, enough to hide him.

He parked at the back of the small fire station parking lot. He brought Mac with him out of concern the car might get towed—losing Mac would be the ultimate betrayal of Kadance's trust—and he snuck onto the CDC property.

Now where to go with this big orange cat? He crossed the street to the sidewalk at the back of one of the slightly curved twin buildings. He came to the end of that building and paused. Between the two curved buildings was a delivery area. There was a loading dock, multiple roll-up doors, and a few regular access doors, and the area was pretty well secluded from the rest of the campus. The mastermind had tried this same kind of back entry at the Capitol building. He guessed she'd try the same thing again. He considered walking around the rest of the campus and getting a better look. He'd gotten a decent look at the campus from his perimeter driving, plus his examination of the campus on Google Earth on his phone. This spot was both easily accessible and secluded.

He continued down the sidewalk until he found a tree he could casually lean against that would also hide him.

And he waited.

He worried Mac would get antsy and fussy, but he sat quietly on the ground next to Lyndon.

He waited some more.

After a while, he found a different spot to stand.

Morning turned into afternoon.

If today was the day, it would happen soon, when the CDC employees were all still at work.

Then he spotted a slow-moving car turning the corner. It was a nondescript gray sedan. Unmemorable. It turned and pulled to a stop next to the loading dock.

Lyndon started toward the car.

It sat there for about a minute while the driver fiddled with something on the passenger seat.

317

He was close now and squatted down at the back bumper.

He heard the car door open and close and then footsteps—fairly light sounding, probably female.

Just as the woman turned to walk around the back of the car, Lyndon stood.

She stopped short. "Lyndon."

He stared at her. "Dr. de Athia?"

"WE HAVE AN EYEWITNESS who saw you kill them, Miss Rogers."

Kadance continued to stare at the opposite wall of the interrogation room. She'd gathered that they'd caught one of the surviving mercenaries from Dr. Ibekwe's house. He'd given them a description of her, and she guessed they'd followed the path of destruction back to the storage facility where she'd used her Sarah Jeane Rogers alias to rent the unit.

The FBI agent sat down in the chair across from her. "I can wait here all night. I'm a very patient man."

Have you crouched in the dirt through a rainstorm for thirty-five hours waiting for a target, perfectly silent and still, focused? She could already see his frustration surfacing.

Finally, she said, "I'm waiting for my phone call." She'd weighed all her options, and she really had only one.

The agent got up and left the room. He closed the door a little too hard.

A few minutes later, a uniformed officer escorted her to a phone mounted to the cinderblock wall. She dialed from memory. It'd been a very long time since she'd dialed this number.

"Authentication," she said into the receiver.

"Go ahead," said a bland voice on the other end.

"Lima yankee november delta 12251441514." She just hoped someone might talk to her.

"Hold please."

There was a pause for about a minute. Kadance wasn't sure how long of a call she'd be allowed.

Another voice came on the phone, one she recognized—her old handler. "Recent bread-making?"

The code she and her handler had used for her missions. Her handler must've recognized her work in the Capitol building shooting. "Yes."

"Situation?"

"McCarran International Airport. FBI Agent Cornwallis."

"Understood." The line went dead.

The officer escorted her back to the interrogation room, she resumed her seat, and he cuffed her to the table.

Agent Cornwallis came back in. "Ready to talk now?"

"Just to say this is much bigger than you realize. I appreciate you're doing your job, but I'm protecting you by not talking."

He threw a file folder onto the table. "Is that so?"

She resumed staring at the opposite wall.

"Look at me," he demanded. His tone was harsh and might have made other people jump.

She continued to stare with a blank expression. She had no idea if her call had worked, if they'd continue to ignore a disavowed agent, or if they'd step in and control the situation due to the nature of what'd happened at the Capitol building.

Only a few minutes later, another agent in a suit walked into the interrogation room. He spoke quietly to Agent Cornwallis, but Kadance still heard. "Someone's here to take her."

"Who?" Cornwallis asked incredulously.

Another man walked into the room. He wasn't in a suit like the others but jeans, boots, and a black jacket. His skin was very dark, almost as dark as his short black hair.

The other agent turned to him. "I asked you to wait outside."

"You are to release her to me immediately."

Cornwallis cursed.

"Call your superior," the new man said. Kadance had never

seen him before, but she recognized his demeanor, his stance, his manner of speaking. Certain aspects were similar to her own.

Cornwallis took his phone out of his breast pocket and dialed. "Sir, someone is here to take—" He stopped and listened. "Sir, the jurisdiction on this case—" A longer pause. Cornwallis's voice was hard. "Yes, sir." He ended the call and put his phone back in his pocket.

He spoke to the other agent. "Take off the cuffs." He walked out of the room.

The other agent removed the handcuffs and stood to the side. The man in the black jacket walked out, and Kadance followed.

IT WAS DR. DE ATHIA. Lyndon was positive. She looked different these years later—gray hair, though still long and a little untamed, a peasant skirt, cardigan, and flowy scarf rather than the pantsuit. But it was definitely her. "You gave the commencement address at my graduation from Johns Hopkins," he said.

"Very good. I see you've finally freed yourself from that brunette Barbie. You're finally coming around."

She's the mastermind.

Peripherally, Lyndon eyed the cooler she had in her hand. It was fairly large and did not look to have a solid locking mechanism. He was concerned if he grabbed for the cooler or attacked her in any way, the virus could be exposed. "So, what's the plan?" he asked. "Plant the virus in the fire riser, cause the sprinkler system to go off, and move on to the next building? In the chaos, you might even get to all the buildings on the campus."

She paused. "I really only need to infect the scientists."

"The administrative staff will get infected eventually. They won't be helpful in stopping the progression of the virus."

"Exactly."

"Obviously, you've found a way to transmit the virus via water.

Impressive. How much more contagious is it than the already-known strains?"

"Brush your fingertip against a surface an infected person has touched, and within five hours, your whole body will be nothing but open sores and puss-filled blisters. If you make it that long."

He wasn't sure why she was standing here talking with him like this, but he was going to use the opportunity. "What's your plan to get it to spread outside the country? Do you have carriers set up to get on planes?"

"It'll spread too fast for anyone to stop it. I've run the numbers. It'll reach all major cities within a week. It's persistent. I need just this small amount to cleanse the Earth." She smiled a little.

"Has this been your plan all along, since the '70s, cleanse the Earth?"

"It wasn't until after my son was born that I realized my true calling. I needed to make the world better. For him."

"Where is your son?"

"Have you ever wondered about certain things? Your aptitude for science?"

"My mother was a scientist."

She smiled so brightly Lyndon wasn't sure what to think. He wished Kadance were here to help read her. "Exactly. A brilliant scientist."

"Yes." He didn't know where she was going with this.

"A woman who devoted her life to you. To making the world a better place for you."

A thousand thoughts rushed into Lyndon's mind all at once.

That was it.

Why she was so dead set on making him focus. In her mind, he was her legacy.

"You think I'm your son," he said.

FORTY-TWO

"I KNOW YOU'RE MY SON," Dr. de Athia said.

Lyndon wasn't sure what to do. His first instinct was to make her see logic, but he needed to be careful.

"I gave birth to you," she said. "I fought for your life in the jungle of the Congo."

She thinks I'm the child she aborted.

"But you were stolen from me," she said. "Aurel Vaile had recently had a miscarriage. Dr. Pearce tried to help her, but she couldn't deal with it and stole you. And then they sent you back to America, and Lee Vaile's father hid you away. I searched and searched for years. Then I finally found you, but it'd been too many years—you'd been brainwashed. So, I had to guide you from a distance." She'd lost most of that edge she usually had in her voice and was looking at him as if praying he understood and accepted her.

He had no idea what to do with that.

His phone dinged with a text, but he left it in his pocket.

Then he heard something. He'd heard something similar before, at the storage unit. The sound of a bullet hitting a wall. It'd hit behind him by a few feet. Apparently, it'd been quiet enough that Dr. de Athia didn't notice.

He knew exactly who it was. He had no idea how, but he knew. She was there to help, to back him up, and she'd rightly figured that her presence would just upset Dr. de Athia that much more. He took his phone out of his pocket and read the text: "Apartment building across the street. Signal if I should take her."

He texted back simply, "Wait." A plan formed in his head, but could he pull it off? "I need your help," he said to Dr. de Athia.

"I have an inoculation for you. We'll be together now. You'll carry on my legacy after I'm gone. You'll make sure the new world is done right."

"I need your protection."

"You're away from that woman and with me. Why would you need protection?"

"Someone has been trying to kill me." He had a theory forming about who had actually been behind that. Dr. de Athia seemed to be far too invested in the fantasy that he was her son—he didn't think she'd planned the attacks on him. "They're using that family of snipers. They're going to find me eventually. I need a way to get them to back off. Information on them."

"That won't matter soon enough."

"But what if they don't die from the disease right away? As I understand it, they live very remotely, so they'll be some of the last to be infected. I would feel better if I had information on them."

She paused to consider. "I have a recording of Bastion Tolle accepting a job and explaining exactly how he'd get it done."

"Does he mention who actually carries it out?"

"I assume he did it. He's very clear that he's accepting the job." She took her phone out of a pocket in her cardigan.

She emailed the recording to an address he'd set up on his cell phone.

Now how to get this phone into the right hands? He glanced down at Mac standing patiently beside him. He turned back to Dr. de Athia. "Can I borrow your scarf? I think he's cold."

She smiled. "You've always been kind to animals. They're a part of Mother Earth."

He took the scarf from her, wrapped it around Mac's middle while slipping the phone into the folds, and tied it to him. "Thank you."

"We should get moving." She shifted toward the building.

"Wait," he said. "We need to talk."

She paused. "We don't have long."

"When is my birthday?"

Her forehead wrinkled. "May fifth."

He guessed that was the day she had the abortion, because it certainly wasn't his birthday. "How old am I?"

"Lyndon, what're you talking about?"

He scrambled for something that was technically not a lie. "I feel confused about where my life is going. I just want to feel like I have a firm grasp on *something*."

"I have to remember how overwhelming all of this must be. You're twenty-five. I've been counting the years, celebrating your birthday by myself."

"Did you know I have three doctorates?"

"I know. I couldn't be prouder. You even followed in my footsteps at Johns Hopkins. I like to think some part of you was trying to find me there."

"It took so long to finish school."

"With a little nudging, you stayed on track."

He'd allowed himself to push his grandfather's and Angela's deaths out of his mind, and now rage threatened to take over. But he focused past it. "I moved faster than most, but it still took over ten years."

"It was a good thing you started right after high school."

"Yes. At eighteen." He paused to see if it would hit her—the problem with her math. He'd been eleven when his parents died, which based on his estimations, was probably a few months after her abortion.

She just looked at him, as if waiting for him to be ready to go. Then she stared at him—at his thirty-six-year-old face.

Then she whispered, "You're my son. They took you from me."

He kept his voice gentle. "I look like my mother. I have her hazel eyes." He could hear sirens now—he prayed that didn't send her hurtling over the edge. He assumed either Kadance or perhaps the workers he could see in the windows of the nearest building had called the police.

Dr. de Athia stared at him with her pale blue eyes. "No . . ."

"You care about life," he said, "don't you?"

She just kept staring at him.

"Obviously, you care about life." He kept a close eye on the cooler in her hand. "Or else the abortion you had wouldn't have been so devastating to you."

"No . . ."

"I'm asking you to continue to care about life. Please. Please put the cooler down."

Her eyes were wide. Then she looked down at the cooler, as if surprised to see it in her hand.

"There are better ways to help the Earth. Please put the cooler down."

She set it down and then backed up a step.

Sirens pierced the air, and police cars came at them from both directions.

Lyndon held his hands up. He looked down at Mac. "Go. Find Kadance."

Mac looked up at him and then around at the loud noises and flashing lights.

"GO," Lyndon said.

Mac ran.

Officers approached from all directions, weapons drawn.

"You're my son," Dr. de Athia whispered.

Lyndon held eye contact with her, willing her to stand there and not struggle.

She stared at him. "Lyndon," she begged.

An officer approached her from the side.

"No!" she screamed. "You're my son!"

Two officers grabbed her. She kept screaming.

Another officer approached the cooler on the ground.

"Be careful," Lyndon said, still with his hands up. "Don't open that. It's dangerous."

Someone took his hands, wrenched them behind him, and put handcuffs on him.

It's over. He didn't let himself look at the tall apartment building across the street until an officer turned him to escort him to a car. He caught a flash of silky black hair at the rooftop. Kadance's hair. And he remembered something . . .

He was sure he'd never see her again, but he was thankful she was safe.

He was shoved into the back of a police cruiser and didn't let himself look over at the rooftop. It was over. All of it.

FORTY-THREE

THE INTERROGATION LASTED FOR HOURS. He told the agents everything—his research; the attempts on his life; Dr. Ibekwe's house, though he made it sound like the mercenaries killed each other; the fireworks at the Capitol; James and his ties to Dr. de Athia. Everything except for Kadance. He made it seem as though he'd been alone through it all, which meant he had to fudge some things. He was surprised when he seemed to pull it off.

And then they took him to a cell, a dank little hole of cinderblocks and bars. One of the agents told him he was being held under the Patriot Act. He didn't bother asking further questions.

He sat on the cot in the corner and leaned back against the cold wall.

His mind went to Kadance, to his relief that she'd managed to get free of her family. Of course she had. And he was confident Mac had found her and Kadance had found the recording on the phone.

She was free.

He pulled his feet up on the cot and rested his elbows on his knees. He was exhausted but couldn't bring himself to lie down. He tried to grasp the fact that he'd probably never see freedom again, but it wouldn't quite compute. Perhaps he simply didn't care enough at the moment. Not that he wanted to spend the rest of his life incarcerated. He supposed it had to do with the fact that he wasn't giving up much of a life. Once he settled into a permanent prison, he'd probably be able to continue some kind of research, though they might make him choose a different subject. He'd bury himself in it just like he always had. He took a deep breath and sighed.

Days passed.

They took blood from him once. He suspected they were confirming his assertion that he was not Veda de Athia's son, as she was surely still claiming.

Various agents questioned him several more times. They tried to trip him up, but he had his story straight. He acted nervous when appropriate, and when he recited events, he varied the minor details he provided to mimic the imperfect memory of the average nervous person. If he was too perfect in the details, they'd suspect it was all a rehearsed lie. He surprised himself more each time he was questioned.

As he lay on his cot one night, he realized why he'd suddenly found the ability to pull off lying. It was because he was protecting Kadance. Nothing was more important. Though if she were here, she'd surely see through him just as easily as she always had. The thought made him smile a little.

The outer door clanged open, and then an agent appeared at his cell. "You're out of here, Vaile."

Lyndon lifted his head. "What?"

"You're out of here. You're being released." He unlocked the cell door.

Lyndon stood. He wanted to ask why or how, but he kept his mouth shut. They hadn't charged him with anything, but he'd assumed they'd eventually decide to charge him with something. Just setting off fireworks at Congress was surely enough to get him some good hard time.

He followed the agent out. They gave him back his things and showed him out of the building.

Just like that.

He looked back at the building, still wondering what in the world was going on. Then he turned and started walking.

But then he stopped.

Kadance was standing there on the sidewalk, with Mac sitting by her feet. Shadows obscured her expression.

"HOW'D YOU DO IT?" Kadance asked.

He looked a little disheveled. "Are you all right?"

She wanted to smile at that, at the first thing out of his mouth being to ask if she was okay, even with everything he now knew about her and everything he'd just been through. But she kept her expression impassive.

Without waiting for her to answer, he moved closer, and his voice hardened. "They beat you." She still had bruises and some abrasions from her family on her face, though they were now mostly healed. She'd hoped he wouldn't notice in the dim light.

"How'd you do it?" she asked again.

He glanced back at the building. "They're not the lie detectors you are."

"You didn't implicate me at all."

"How do you know?" But then he lifted his chin. "You called your contacts. CIA."

"I didn't think they'd do anything to help, but I got in touch with my old handler, and once I told her what was going on, she pulled a lot of strings." She was still surprised. She added, "I'm sorry it took so long."

"You didn't have to do it."

"You set me free. How could I leave you to rot?"

They were quiet.

Mac walked over and rubbed against Lyndon's leg.

"Good boy," Lyndon said.

"They caught James," Kadance said. "I suspect you helped with that somehow. They confiscated the last of the virus."

"Good."

More quiet.

Finally, Kadance said, "I'm sorry. For Angela."

He paused. "They tricked you."

That wasn't an excuse—she'd never forgive herself for it. But she left it at that. She'd just needed to say the words to him, even knowing they wouldn't fix anything, wouldn't redeem her in his eyes. He still knew she was a murderer. It was worse than what he'd seen her do to the mercenaries at Dr. Ibekwe's house. That'd been self-defense. Angela had been an innocent.

"Thank you for everything." He started down the sidewalk.

She turned the opposite direction, toward where she'd parked her car.

Each step hurt.

But she didn't deserve him, and now he understood that. It was better this way.

She paused and looked back at his retreating figure. She wanted to memorize him.

But then she kept going.

"Kadance."

She turned.

He hesitated but then walked toward her. He stopped a few feet away and just looked at her.

Silence.

"I told you why I broke up with Angela."

"You didn't feel strongly enough."

"And the reason I figured that out was because of the girl across the quad."

She nodded.

"She had hair like a flowing black river. It blew in the wind and showed her neck and profile, her golden skin." He paused. "Why didn't you wear a braid that day?"

She couldn't respond.

"I still think about that memory. All the time. I think that's the real reason I haven't ever been with anyone else. Some part of me was always thinking of that girl," he said. "It was you."

Quiet.

"It broke," she said. Then she added, "My hairband."

There was a slight smile in his eyes. "I probably wouldn't have noticed from so far away if your hair hadn't caught the wind. And your skin was darker because you'd just returned from the Middle East, or perhaps because you'd been out on the range with your family every day since returning."

She had no idea what to say.

"I just want you to know—" He paused. "I will always be there for you. I respect your wishes, but I will always feel the same. If you ever need anything, I'll always be there. Anything."

A tear fell down her cheek.

He moved a step closer and murmured, "Kadance?"

Another tear fell. She couldn't think clearly.

"What's wrong?" he asked.

"I . . . You know what I've done. How could you still . . . ?"

His tone was muted. "I see the light in you."

She covered her mouth with her hand. She didn't know how to deal with so much emotion. It strangled her.

He wrapped his arms around her and held her to his chest.

She breathed.

That was all she could do—just breathe.

He was warm, and his heart was a steady and quiet thud. He caressed his fingertips lightly over her hair. She felt calm and safe. And not just safe from physical harm, but from all the other things that'd hurt her all her life, all the things so much worse than physical harm. All the things she'd always believed she'd have to live through.

Several minutes passed. Her tears stopped, and her breathing evened out.

"Are you all right?" he murmured.

She curled into his chest and held herself to him.

She heard as his heart beat a little harder.

"Thank you," she whispered.

He gently lifted her chin, and she looked up at him. The way he looked at her made her feel like her armor had been ripped away from her. And for once, that didn't scare her.

He brushed his thumb over her cheekbone.

Her lips parted.

He pulled her more tightly against him.

"Are you sure?" she whispered.

He rested his hand on her cheek with his fingers curled into her hair, and he slowly leaned closer.

His lips touched hers lightly, barely a feathery touch.

She couldn't breathe.

And then he kissed her again, lips slightly parted.

Time seemed to stop. She had no idea how long they stood there on the sidewalk. All she knew was she didn't want this moment to end. His touch was soft. She could sense how much he wanted her, but she also knew that if she gave the slightest indication she wanted out of his grip, he'd immediately release her.

She wrapped her arms around his neck and lifted onto her toes.

He finally deepened the kiss.

And everything changed, everything her life had been. The vastness overwhelmed her. She could think about the future, a future with Lyndon. She could make plans and be excited about things to come. She wasn't sure what she even wanted. She was just excited to have the freedom to consider it.

The one thing she did know was this, right here, how this felt, this was what she would always want. She clung to him more tightly.

They stopped, both breathing heavily.

She noticed people in passing cars were staring.

He touched her face with his fingertips. "I didn't think," he said, "that I'd ever get to touch you."

"I didn't think you'd ever want to, not anymore."

There was a smile in his eyes as he brushed his fingers through her hair. Then he reached around her for her braid, took the hairband off the end, and unraveled her hair. The smile tweaked his lips.

Mac meowed.

His smile broadened as he looked down at Mac. "Are you feeling left out?"

Mac stood on his hind legs and pawed Lyndon's leg. Lyndon picked him up and included him in a hug with Kadance.

Kadance rested her head on Lyndon's chest.

"Thank you," she whispered. "For saving me."

"Are you talking to me or Mac?"

She laughed. "Both."

KEEP READING FOR A SNEAK PEEK

at Melissa Koslin's Next Breathtaking Romantic Suspense

SHE RAN.

She'd finally orchestrated an opportunity, and she'd run.

Twigs snapped under her bare feet. She hardly felt the pain. It was the sound that rattled through her. *They'll hear. They'll find me.*

She somehow ran faster.

Branches reached out and scraped at her skin.

She slipped on some wet leaves but managed to stay on her feet.

She couldn't breathe, but she kept going.

To her left, she could hear cars. It didn't sound like a freeway, but maybe a rural highway. Should she try to hitchhike? But the thought of getting into a car with another stranger was too much. She needed to get as far away as quickly as she could, but she wasn't getting into a car with someone. Logically, she knew the likelihood of finding someone as bad as those she was running from was remote, but logic wasn't forefront for her. Right now she was in flee mode. Survival.

Darkness started to fall like a shroud.

Go deeper into the woods and stay there tonight? She thought about rest, that she needed to stop and sleep at some point, but she couldn't get her legs to stop running. She'd run miles already. She'd probably collapse before finding enough control to get herself to stop.

Lights in the distance.

Flee mode subsided slightly. Her survival instincts screamed at her to stay away from all people, but she knew she couldn't very well stay out here in the woods the rest of her life, however long that ended up being. If she was back home, she'd have a fighting chance, but she didn't know this area, what kinds of animals were native, which plants were edible. As she slowed her pace, she realized how cold it was.

She approached the edge of the woods and peered around a tree to the source of lights—a truck stop. There were so many gas pumps she couldn't count them. There were big semitrucks with their rumbling engines that made her nerves feel like lit matches. They sounded just like the truck she'd been thrown into back home, the one that'd taken her over the border to this country. That was actually better than what she'd been living through the last several days. On the truck, there had been many women. They'd had each other for warmth, for comfort.

She hid behind the tree. Since when had that nightmare on the truck morphed into a positive memory? They'd lost a few of the women—a couple of them just didn't wake up, and one had had a heart attack, she was fairly certain. But she was almost thankful they'd been taken early. It was a better fate.

The chill seeped into her bones, and she wrapped her arms around herself.

She looked over at the truck stop—warmth, a restroom where she could wash. She dearly wished she had some money. She hadn't eaten in two days. And she couldn't steal; her parents had raised her to be honorable, even when it was difficult, especially when it was difficult. But maybe she could find some food in a garbage can.

Carefully, she analyzed the area, identified all entrances and exits, watched the people. They looked so different here. But they didn't appear to be particularly threatening.

She stood straight, took a breath, and pulled her fingers through her long black hair. Hopefully, her appearance didn't draw too much attention. As she walked across the grass, she tried to wipe the dirt off her feet. All while watching every person, every vehicle.

She moved quickly across the asphalt and into the store. It was huge. There were cases and cases of cold drinks, shelves of food, even two different fast-food restaurants. She made herself ignore the bottles of water so close and headed straight for the ladies' restroom. Mercifully, it was empty. She turned on a faucet, washed her hands, and drank. She filled her cupped hands over and over. Then she washed her face, her hands, her arms. She glanced at the door and decided to risk washing her lower half as well. She lifted her short dress and rapidly washed. Maybe she could blend in, disappear, if she was clean enough. She was drying off her feet with rough paper towels when the door opened. She watched the middle-aged woman peripherally but didn't make eye contact.

The woman said something that she didn't understand.

She looked up. The woman was staring at her, at the bruises on her arms and legs.

She stood, walked into a stall, and locked it.

The woman paused but then used the restroom, washed her hands, and left.

She stood there in the stall and stared at a sticker on the back of the door, written in both English and Spanish. "Human trafficking. Do you need help?"

MERIC PARKED AND GOT OUT OF HIS CAR. He glanced down at the other entrance before walking inside the store. As he passed the counter, he overheard a middle-aged woman telling the cashier, "I asked her if she was okay, but she just locked herself in a stall. She looked pretty battered."

Meric turned and headed for the hall that led to the restrooms. He stopped outside the ladies' room.

SHE WAITED LONG ENOUGH that the woman should be gone, walked out of the stall, ignoring her image in the mirror, and headed for the door.

She peeked into the hall before slipping out the door.

A strong hand grabbed her arm.

Rage roared through her. She yanked at her arm, but before she could hit him or scream, he demanded, "Be quiet." It took her a second to realize he'd said it in Spanish, not English. He lowered his voice, not calming, just quiet. "They're outside."

"Who are you? Let me go." She was sure he wasn't with the men who'd been holding her. He was far too well-dressed and polished. She struggled to free her arm.

"I'm not going to hurt you," he said. "They have both entrances covered. You need to call the police."

"I can take care of myself. Let me go."

"This country is different. The police will help."

"No they won't." She yanked at her arm again, but he was so strong and she was weak from lack of food, almost no sleep, and all the running.

He held both of her arms and shifted closer. "Stop and think rationally. I know what you've been through, but you need to slow down and think. You have to accept help."

She stopped struggling but glared up at him. He was tall with broad shoulders and strong hands, but she refused to feel intimidated. "You have no idea what I've been through."

"They kidnapped you—out of Mexico, based on your accent. They've abused you and plan to sell you. Am I getting it right?"

"How do you know that? Who are you?"

"Someone who pays attention and who happened to stop for a bottle of water at exactly the right time and place," he said. "If you don't call the police, I will. But you're going to have to tell them your story."

For some reason, tears pricked the backs of her eyes. She hadn't cried at all since they'd taken her—cursed and screamed and fought, but not cried. Why did the tears want to come now?

As he looked at her, his expression changed—just something in his eyes. There was a coldness to him that covered him like a sheet of ice, but in his eyes, there was something else. Fury, but also pain.

"Stay here," he said.

Then he walked away. Without pausing, he told the cashier something as he walked by. One of the words sounded like *policia*. Was he telling the cashier to call the police?

She shifted to the end of the hall and watched out the window.

He grabbed a man standing by the door, slammed him up against the glass with his face toward her, and looked at her. She realized he was waiting for her to confirm it was one of the men who'd been keeping her prisoner. It was the shorter one with receding blond hair, though he was only maybe late twenties. He called himself Carl.

As she looked at Carl, rage flamed up in her chest.

The polished man seemed to understand her expression. He turned Carl around, even as Carl struggled, and punched him square in the face. Blood splattered against the window, and Carl crumpled to the ground.

Then the polished man burst with speed she wouldn't have guessed a man in such fine clothes capable of and caught another man who'd been running away from the other entrance to the store. He caught him halfway across the parking lot, put him in a headlock from behind, and dragged him back to the window.

She walked out from the hall to get a better look. She recognized Josh's face, the face that tormented her nightmares. She made eye contact with the polished man and nodded.

He released the headlock, threw Josh against the glass, and punched him just as hard as he had Carl. Josh slumped to the ground.

The man walked back inside. "Is that all of them?"

She barely got the word out. "*Sí.*"

He turned to the cashier and said something. She heard the word that sounded like *policia* again.

The cashier stammered a response.

The man grumbled "useless" under his breath in Spanish. Then he took a cell phone out of his inside jacket pocket and dialed three numbers.

As she stood there, she realized the entire store had stopped and was staring at both her and the man who'd just knocked out two young, able-bodied men.

He had a short conversation on the phone, hung up, and went back outside to stand over his victims.

She was too shocked to move. Was she really free?

She couldn't stand to be stared at any longer and went outside.

"You shouldn't leave," the polished man said.

There were just as many people staring out here, but it didn't feel so bad. Maybe because there was one person here who understood her language. "I don't know . . ."

"I understand you don't know what to think yet. That's a reasonable reaction. But you need to stay here and tell the police what happened."

She realized she'd placed herself with the polished man blocking her view of Josh. Just the thought of looking at him made her want to run.

"If you don't tell the police, they'll be released and will be free to do the same thing to someone else."

A thought struck her. "And they'll arrest you for assaulting them."

"Probably." He didn't seem terribly concerned about that.

But she was. "I'm staying."

"That's brave of you." He said it matter-of-factly, obviously not intending to give a compliment, simply stating a truth. He glanced over at Carl, who was still unconscious like Josh.

"Who are you?" she asked. "What's your name?"

"Meric."

A couple of women standing by a parked car whispered to each other.

He glanced at the women and back to her. "May I ask your name?"

She hesitated. "Liliana."

He glanced down at Josh and then back to her. There was that something in his eyes again. "Thank you for letting me help you."

"You didn't exactly get permission."

She thought the corner of his mouth twitched just slightly.

The sound of sirens made her jump. A few seconds later, two police cars pulled into the lot.

"I'll stay," Meric said. "You won't be alone."

She'd almost forgotten what it felt like to feel comforted. Everything was suddenly alien.

Meric motioned to the police officers, and they both walked over to him. "What's the situation?" one of them asked.

"Español?" Meric asked.

They both nodded.

"I'm Meric Toledan"—both the officers' expressions flickered with recognition—"and this is Liliana. She was being trafficked by these two men." Meric nodded toward Josh and Carl.

"Is that correct, miss?" one officer asked with a heavy American English accent. It was a little hard to understand him.

The other officer checked on Josh and Carl, surely making certain they were just knocked out.

"Yes, sir." She glanced at Meric and then back to the officer. "The cartel took me from my home in Mexico and brought me and about twenty other women across the border in a truck. Then these two men paid them and took me. They said something about a buyer. I think they're middlemen."

"Do you know where the other women are?"

Her shoulders slumped. "No, sir. I've been with these two men for several days. I have no idea where the other women were taken. I don't know why they separated me."

The other officer, after talking into his radio, came back over.

"Because you brought a higher price," Meric said.

Her brows twitched together.

"Exceptional beauty brings a higher price."

"And how are you involved, Mr. Toledan?" one of the officers asked. The way the officer addressed him sounded like he knew who Meric was, and did she catch a hint of suspicion?

She spoke up. "He saved me. He saw what was happening, and he saved me."

The officer addressed Meric. "How did you know what was happening? Do you know these men? Are you involved?"

Liliana's voice hardened. "He's not involved with them. He risked his own safety to help me."

"Thank you, miss," the officer said and then turned back to Meric. "How did you know what was happening?"

Meric's tone and manner continued to be unemotional. "I overheard a woman telling the cashier about a woman in the restroom looking scared and battered. I'd already noticed the men standing at both entrances. I waited for Liliana to come out, and that confirmed my suspicions."

The clerk had come outside. "That's right, Officer. This man parked and came inside well after the other two men arrived. He didn't interact with them, not until after he'd spoken to her." She indicated Liliana. "I can pull the security camera footage for you."

"Please do. Thank you." The officer seemed mostly appeased.

The officers asked Liliana several more questions. Inside, she was upset. Now that she didn't need her rage to fuel her and help her survive, she was on the verge of breaking down. While they questioned her, two more officers arrived and an ambulance. The EMTs checked on Josh and Carl, while the officers watched over them.

She answered another question, and her voice shook.

Meric shifted closer and murmured, "You're safe now."

She nodded once, barely a movement.

He hesitated, and then he turned to the officers. "What's going to happen to her? Where will she go?"

"She's undocumented, so we'll have to call ICE. She'll likely be kept here while the courts work out what happens with these two." He indicated Josh and Carl, who were now being loaded onto gurneys. "After that, I assume she'll go back home."

"I can't go back." It popped out of her mouth before she could stop it.

"You don't want to go back to Mexico?" Meric asked.

"I can't . . . My parents and my sister are gone. If I go back, they'll just take me again." She kept looking at Meric, and more of her story spilled from her lips. "They tried to take me once before, but my father fought them off. The next time, they came prepared." She had no idea why she'd been targeted, but she'd seen far too much—there was no way the cartel would let her live.

"They killed your family," Meric said.

She nodded. And finally, a tear escaped and fell down her cheek.

Meric turned to the officers. "She needs asylum."

"She can certainly request it." Then he added in an apologetic tone, "But asylum is usually for those who fear persecution from their government, typically due to race, religion, or political opinion or activism. In this case, the government of Mexico isn't trying to harm her. They should technically be the ones to protect her." The officer turned to Liliana. "I'm very sorry."

Meric looked at Liliana. She felt like his gaze was boring into her. Men had always looked at her, but with him, it felt different. She should be scared of him—he was cold and distant, and she had the impression he was used to being in command. But she wasn't scared of him. Maybe she wasn't thinking clearly. Maybe she was too overwhelmed.

Meric asked the officers, "May I speak to her for a moment?"

"We need to question the witnesses. Stay here." The officers headed in different directions and began taking statements from people in the parking lot and inside the store.

Meric took off his suit jacket and wrapped it around Liliana's shoulders. "You must be cold."

The jacket held his warmth, and the scent was slightly musky—not cologne, just clean body chemistry. The fabric was thick and soft, nicer than she'd ever felt in her life.

"Do you think you can trust me?" he asked her.

She didn't know how to respond to that.

"If you get sent back to Mexico," he said, "do you have any other family? Any place you can go that would be safe?"

She felt uncomfortable telling him all this. She had the feeling he was trying to do something to help her even more. He'd done enough. "They're dead." She paused to control her voice. "I don't have any money. They took the little my parents had."

"The cartels are powerful in Mexico. You think they'll still target you."

"I don't know what will happen when I'm not delivered to the buyer." She paused. "I . . . There's a leader near where we lived. He . . . he tried to buy me from my father. When that didn't work . . ."

"They're not going to let you go," he said. "You're valuable, you've angered and embarrassed them, and you've seen too much." He looked at her in that intense way of his. "You can't go back."

"I think I have to."

"There's a way I can keep you here. But you'd have to trust me."

She waited.

"You'd have to marry me."

Acknowledgments

Thank you to Mike Nappa, yet again.

Thank you to Vicki Crumpton and Revell for giving me a shot.

Thank you to Sergeant Mike Fay, former Marine sniper, for the technical expertise.

Melissa Koslin is a fourth-degree black belt in and certified instructor of Songahm Taekwondo. In her day job as a commercial property manager, she secretly notes personal quirks and funny situations, ready to tweak them into colorful additions for her books. She and Corey, her husband of twenty years, live in Florida, where they do their best not to melt in the sun.

MEET
MELISSA

Find Melissa online at
MelissaKoslin.com
and on social media at

| melissa_koslin | MelissaKoslin | MelissaKoslin |